HEAVEN SENT

I0602086

BOOK TWO
HELLBOUND

JL ROTHSTEIN

Cover design by Jeff Brown

Printed in the United States of America

DEDICATION

To my husband Alan, your partnership in this publication journey has been such a gift. Though 2020 was a year we will never forget for many horrible and humbling reasons. Working on launching the Heaven Sent Series together was a bright spot that I will be forever grateful for.

ACKNOWLEDGMENTS

Thank you to Beth Dorward, my Editor and Mentor. I could not get this far without your attention to detail and your desire to help authors reach their full potential.

Thank you to Jeff Brown who designed the book covers for both Book One & Two of this series. I appreciate your artistic interpretations of the book series and for pushing me to think beyond the cover.

As always, special thanks to my family & circle of friends. Your unwavering support and patience cannot be measured, it means the world to me.

"A woman is like a tea bag – you never know how strong she is until she gets into hot water."

Eleanor Roosevelt

CHAPTER ONE

Deb walked through the sliding glass doors and onto the large deck that ran the length of Harry's cottage. She took a deep breath and inhaled the salt air. The calming sound of waves rocking against the shoreline on the small private beach below felt like Heaven on Earth. The ocean was still visible with the moonglow fading and the sun yet to make an entrance.

She finally convinced her sisters to take a short trip to Cape Cod. It was mid-September; kids were back in school and the tourists had all but evacuated the island. This was their third morning here and without an alarm clock—something Deb was fundamentally opposed to unless absolutely needed—she had timed getting up before the sunrise perfectly yet again. It was still dark when she had quietly crept through the house to gather a few things and make her way downstairs to make tea.

I could live here, Deb thought as she pushed loose strands of her brown hair behind her ear. *Stay and never return to the battle against Hell.*

Despite the hour, it was warmer than she expected. Hooking a small canvas bag that held all her beach-going essentials onto the back of a chair, Deb placed the cup of tea on an end table she had taken care to wipe free of dew.

She draped a towel over one of the many Adirondack chairs lazily facing the ocean and climbed onto one. During the day, the chairs provided a virtual carnival of color across the salt-battered natural gray shingled house. She sat on a navy blue chair, but there were green, yellow, and orange ones too. The outdoor cushions were slightly wet this early in the morning, but the sun would soon rise and dry everything.

Heat wave is still going. Deb smiled as her bright blue eyes scanned the beach. *More swimming for me this morning.*

Her entire body unknotted as the sound of the ocean coaxed her into serenity. The sea air mixed with the scent of large pitch pines dotting the property. The trees seemed to whisper as the bay breeze swung through them in greeting. The large willow tree, closest to the deck, had a massive trunk with thick rambling roots that jutted up through the crushed seashell path leading to the outdoor shower.

The ocean air drifted up. Leaves were swishing and Deb smelled the beach roses growing wild along the embankment. It was as if nature's perfume was wafting up to greet her. As the sun burst free of the ocean, the sky was stained a beautiful orange streaked with pink. The round yellow ball seemingly sailed skyward, and Deb felt the heat rise with it.

What an amazing way to start the day, she mused. *A world away from beating back Hell and fighting demons with*

2

their ravenous appetite to destroy humanity.

Deb's mind drifted back over the past few months. Battles against Hell were not unusual for them, but the past few months were something else entirely: Gen murdering a demon, Michael and Harry nearly enveloped in Hell Fire and then taken away, Kelly's near-death experience, if that was even a thing for a Guardian. All leading to a confrontation with the Four Horsemen. It's no wonder Deb needed a vacation of sorts. Vacation implied they were off duty, something they never were. If a charge needed them or their marks went off, they would meet the challenge.

If there was a silver lining, Deb thought, *it was Gabriel and Jared's return.* Though it was short lived, it did give her sisters hope.

Deb sighed, feeling her mind entangling her in more memories from the past few weeks. *I need to know what happened to you Marcus. Where are you? Why can't I find you as I have in the past? You said you were laying low, but you didn't say for how long.*

Deb sat contemplating long enough for the sun's rays to reach her. The beach beckoned her. She made her way around the side of the house where a small clothesline held her bathing suit from the day before. Dampness lingered, not that it mattered; she would be fully immersed in the ocean soon enough.

She used the small downstairs bathroom to change, struggling a bit to maneuver the damp suit onto her body, the coolness of it making her quiver. Deb placed her mug in the sink, a message to her sisters she was down on the beach already. That was assuming they woke before she returned from what was quickly becoming her favorite ritual.

She was not in human form, even though the private beach was secluded. There was comfort knowing there were no people around to see her footprints in the sand or witness the ripples her body would make as she swam.

Hiding her beach bag by the bottom of the steps that lead down from the house she made her way across the cool morning sand to the edge of the water. The foam that rolled forward was cold despite the warm air, but she didn't care. She dove in and began swimming. Her lungs expanded as she inhaled deeply and fell into a rhythm. The exercise of controlling her breathing as she plunged her head in and out of the water calmed her. Her body's muscle memory responded to the movement. She cleared her mind and let her body adapt to the feel of the sea. It was therapy really, swinging her arms over her head and kicking as she glided athletically through the water. Occasionally, an unpleasant thought or scene from one of their more recent battles would fight its way through: an image of Michael being dragged away, the bloodied scorched earth left in his wake. She pushed the images from her mind. She needed to stay present, in the moment, so she could appreciate the warmth of the sun on her back and the coolness of the bay as it refreshed her.

Deb swam out for about 100 meters, then turned left and began swimming back and forth along the bay. After she worked all the tension from her muscles, she slowed her pace. In mid-stroke she glimpsed the image of two people standing on the shoreline. Their appearance startled her, and she abruptly pulled her arms under the surface and slowed her feet to a gentle paddle below the water. Instinctively, she let her body sink with her chin dipping just beneath the surface while her shoulders became fully submerged. She looked left, then right, but no one was there.

What was that?

Peering along the sandy beach, even beyond the rocky boarder, she saw nothing—no person, no animal, nothing. She stayed still, seemingly floating in a standing position. An image flashed in her mind's eye and for a moment her heartbeat increased with the realization she had been here before.

I know it's not impossible for me to have been here before, but I cannot remember a time when I was. My powers allow me to sense a demon's presence and I feel nothing. I'm confident there are no demons here. It must have been an optical illusion, trick of the eye brought on by swirling memories. Gen and Kell are inside the house. It's just me alone on the beach and I'm going to enjoy it.

The wind picked up and the bay water rippled across the surface in response. Goosebumps rode along the part of her arms above the surface. Nausea rolled through her while her heart thumped wildly.

My body is trying to tell me something.

Never one to ignore signs, she stayed as covered as possible and made her way slowly toward the beach. Her kicks became frog like, and she slowly pushed her arms forward under the water. When her toes grazed the sandy bottom, she paused and took a closer look around before standing up. Her breathing was labored. She walked briskly from the edge back toward the staircase. Grabbing the towel from her beach bag she spun around with a strong sense something was behind her.

She stared out at the ocean and examined the small rocky area that lay just beyond the beach. She saw nothing. Dizziness rode through Deb in big waves, like she was trapped in a small boat in the middle of a storm.

Before she could jog up the stairs to the house a memory of her on a beach running and laughing with a man flashed before her. The same vision she had the night the Horsemen took Schlosser and left Earth—the night she sought out Marcus on a beach near their home in Boston.

Why am I remembering this now? I tried for weeks to make sense of this and couldn't.

The memory manifested into a life-size vision playing out several yards across the sand from her. Instead of walking away, she walked toward it, as if it were real. She left the safety of the staircase and her sisters. She was no more than ten feet away from the picturesque scene when the couple playfully ran back to the water's edge. Deb slowly wandered to the water but kept her distance from the vision. The coldness of the ocean washed over her toes and she stopped.

This is crazy, it's not like I'm walking up to an actual couple. It's just my imagination relaying this memory to me. But if this is my memory, why can't I remember it?

The sunlight in the vision seemed to get brighter. Deb moved her hand up to shield her eyes against the strong rays. The man turned and looked right at her. She gasped and stumbled back in disbelief.

No, it can't be. This can't be right. I never went anywhere with him!

The vision continued to play itself out. Her breathing became strained, and her chest heaved and tightened, but she couldn't turn away. The couple in the vision embraced, kissing passionately. The vision faded as the edges of it began to shrink, but not before she caught sight of what lay in the water just beyond the happy couple. It was the salt rocks, the same ones that lay before her now. The memory was from this very beach.

Her head spun with questions. Nausea bowled her over. She crouched down, one hand on her chest, one hand on the sand. She looked up seeing the image fade, but closed her eyes trying to prolong it. She needed to know more.

Pain coursed through her skull, lurching her onto her knees. Her hands grasped the sides of her head. She moaned as the rolling nausea forced the tea out of her system. She looked up to see the vision return in a distorted state. The outline of the image was in a grayish black smoke as if it were some sort of magic trick about to disappear.

What's happening?

Deb struggled to keep a coherent thought as images bombarded her, none of them making sense. The pressure in her head increased. Then thick fluid oozed down her face staining the sand red. Blood was seeping from both her nose and ears, and she couldn't speak. She crawled along the shoreline, heading away from the vision and back toward the cottage, leaving a bloody trail in the wet sand.

Kelly, Gen, something's on the beach. Help me! Something's wrong!

The ocean lapped onto her body from her left. Her right hand scrunched into the wet sand. She struggled as fatigue settled in and her movements slowed.

The sound of broken glass drew her eyes toward the cottage. Gen was on the deck, her mane of unruly blonde curls billowing in the wind. Her favorite new yellow coffee mug lay shattered in pieces at her feet. She was yelling, but Deb couldn't hear the words. Gen teleported from the deck.

Kelly arrived in front of Deb. Her sister's jet black hair swept up on top of her head in a haphazard bun. She wore sweat shorts and a T-shirt three sizes too big for her. Kelly peered side to side around the beach as she brandished a knife in her left hand.

"Where is it?" Kelly barked. "I can't see anything in this blinding light."

"Deb," Gen gasped as she arrived leaning down over Deb's collapsed form. "What's happened?" Gen grabbed Deb's arm and pulled her to her feet.

"I don't know." Deb was unnerved at her own slurred speech. "Something's wrong, do you see it?"

"What do you mean?" Kelly demanded. "Do we see what? What's here Deb?"

"She's bleeding!" Gen yelled. "We need to get her inside."

Kelly took Deb's other arm and they teleported to the living room. Deb was gingerly dropped onto the warm sofa. Her sisters placed their hands in the air just above Deb attempting to heal her. Their power coursed through her. A male voice startled her. Her brother Michael was hovering above her.

"What's going on?" Michael asked with authority. Stepping around his sisters he bent down and lightly gripped Deb's shoulder. Lowering his voice, he locked eyes with Deb and spoke calmly. "You need to slow your breathing, you're panicking. Remember, push the fear down, breathe through the pain. Nice slow breaths in and hold it, then breathe out to bring your heart rate back to normal."

Despite seeing concern reflected in Michael's light brown eyes she found comfort in his gentle touch and soft tone.

Maybe some things with Michael have changed for the better after our last battle together, thought Deb.

She listened to her brother's voice as he worked to focus her mind. Every time she thought she was making progress, the memory from the beach would reappear and send a new wave of pain through her skull.

Deb's mind cleared enough to blurt out, "I need Greg." Gen and Kelly dropped their arms, and Michael snapped his hand from her shoulder. She couldn't tell if he was hurt or just surprised.

Greg appeared behind Gen, his shoulder length untamed black hair looking messy and unkempt as usual. "What is it Deb?"

"A memory," she moaned through another shock wave of pain. "It's looping, it won't stop."

Greg stepped forward and knelt on the floor next to Deb. Lifting her arm, his calloused hand enveloped hers. "I'm going to come in now, try and relax and lower your shield, it's coming on and off and taking energy away from you."

That's why no one came when I called out, Deb realized through muddled thoughts. *I must have reflexively projected my shield and then lost control when the pain came.*

Deb closed her eyes concentrating on letting her shield down, not even aware she had been intermittently projecting it. Greg entered her mind, his presence mimicked real life as if he were suddenly standing next to her, toes in the sand, reliving the memory with her on the beach.

"Alright Deb." Greg's hand closed tightly around hers. "I'm going to pull the memory forward. Once it's in front of you, and no longer looping, you must decide what to do with it, understand?"

Deb grunted in response and the image stopped looping. As it gained clarity it got larger. The couple in the memory faced away from her, but she didn't need to see the woman's face, for Deb knew she was the woman in the vision. She recognized her old seashell beach coverup. Deb's mousey brown hair in the memory was long and wavy, falling past her shoulders. What she wanted to see was the face of the man she was holding hands with. Deb needed to see it again; she had to be sure.

As the male in the vision began to turn toward Deb, the outline of a scar in the shape of a shark's tail peeked out from underneath his shirt. She had her answer.

Deb used her shield to push Greg out of her head. Her brother released her hand. Upon opening her eyes, all eight of Deb's siblings were standing over her.

"Are you alright?" Frankie asked, his deep brown eyes reflecting concern.

"Yes," Deb answered. "I'm sorry, I don't know what just happened."

"It was a memory core that got stuck," Greg contemplated as he rubbed the thick stubble he nearly always had soon after shaving. "I think I've only seen it once before. It's extremely rare."

"A memory core, what's that?" Deb asked.

"We bury memories all the time, it's normal. It's how our minds can process all that we've seen and done," Greg told her.

"Can it be wrong?" Deb allowed herself a glimmer of hope.

"No." Greg shook his head slightly. "In our world nothing is definitive, but you might say the core is the truest part of the memory, the heart of it. It's the one part that is embedded in our soul. It's the one or two images our mind records and it can't be altered or manipulated."

The room was surprisingly quiet. Deb was imagining Gen warning their brothers telepathically to be gentle and not launch into some sort of interrogation.

"Do you want to tell us about the memory?" Michael asked, his raised eyebrows indicating he knew the answer already.

"There's nothing to tell," Deb said curtly, as she flipped her legs off the sofa and sat up. "I saw myself, but I don't know who the other person was."

Deb locked eyes with Greg as if to send him a silent plea. She couldn't send Greg a telepathic message this close to the others without them hearing it also. She had to hope the darting stare into his dark blue eyes was enough to keep him from telling everyone who was in the vision with her. Dried blood had crusted under her nose and in her ears. Deb looked pale and a mess.

"We know who it was, Deb," Michael said stone-faced. "Frankie was projecting while Greg was inside."

11

Heat rose in Deb's face. "Well then, I guess there's nothing to tell." Anger floated to the surface; a once rare feeling had become all too familiar these past few weeks for Deb.

Of course, Frankie was projecting my memories to everyone, Deb thought begrudgingly. *I know he was probably just concerned and thought projecting was helpful and efficient, but there's never any privacy in this family.* A wave of agitation washed over her.

"You guys can go," Gen announced. "You can see she's physically fine and she obviously doesn't want to talk about it."

"We'll head out," Michael said, as he nodded to the others who one by one left the house. "We can circle back when we all return to training in two days." Without waiting for a reply Michael gave a nod to his sisters and left the three of them alone.

"Deb, are you feeling up for some tea?" Gen asked.

"Maybe some mint tea, my stomach is still off from getting sick."

"There better be snacks to go with that tea," Kelly huffed and walked toward the kitchen.

"Wait." Deb's sisters stopped and turned to face her. "You saw who it was?"

Kelly and Gen nodded in acknowledgement.

"Yeah," Kelly sighed. "We all saw, like Michael said."

"Did you see the beach?" Deb paused but didn't wait for an answer. "Did you notice it was *this* beach?"

"I thought you said you'd never been here before." Kelly's forehead creased.

Deb nodded. "I've never been here before and certainly not with Dmitri."

CHAPTER TWO

Deb sat at the kitchen table in their Boston home waiting for her sisters to wake. The sun had not yet made an appearance. They had come back from their unusual stay at Harry's cottage the same day as the memory core incident. Even though she was back in her own bed, she wasn't getting much sleep. The only solace was she had no nightmares since returning. Deb had assumed she would be plagued by disturbing dreams after what happened on the beach. The possibility that she had been on that beach in the past in some sort of passionate rendezvous with Dmitri was puzzling. It's not that she found him unattractive, she just never thought of him in that way.

Dmitri was handsome but in a rough kind of way. He was burly and stood well over six feet tall. With broad shoulders and massive muscles Dmitri towered over Deb, but she never felt small around him. Deb remembered his shoulder length dark brown hair and thick beard and wondered if he still let it get overgrown and untamed. He was witty and smart, and his deep brown eyes seemed to sparkle when he told wild tales from his experience tracking down the Lost and Fallen. Try as she might, Deb could not remember a moment of passion between them, not on that beach, not anywhere.

How could that be? She quietly pleaded. *The memory showed how close and comfortable we were. That was clearly not a first kiss.*

She went back through the images in her mind for the thousandth time but couldn't remember being with him that way. Months ago, Gen and Kelly told her they thought she had been in a relationship with Dmitri. They relayed some story about her coming home one night and telling them she had kissed him. Deb dismissed the idea right away, telling them there had never been anything more than a friendship between them.

Obviously based on the memory core, I was wrong. I wonder what other memories I'm unable to recall. Are there pieces of my past lost, never to be recovered?

Water rushed through the pipes alerting Deb that someone was using the bathroom upstairs.

Over the past couple of days, Deb had mulled over speaking to her sisters. She was anxious, restless even. She couldn't find Marcus. She had visited all the spots she had previously encountered him. These were places she used to be able to simply think of him and he would appear, like down by the river in Boston. She was running out of ideas of where else to look for him.

She couldn't bring herself to try on the ring he left for her without him present.

I wish he didn't leave a ring for me to deal with on my own. Any other piece of jewelry and I would already be wearing it. If the ring binds, and Marcus really is from Hell as Kelly and Gen believe, what does that say about me? What does that mean for a future with him? Could a Guardian really be bound to a demonic entity?

Deb tried to tell herself Gen and Kelly would be supportive, they would be there for her, she could trust them with the note Marcus left her. Yet, she still hadn't told them about it.

She was starting to feel claustrophobic, as if for the first time in her two hundred and thirty-four years, she didn't belong with her family anymore. Just acknowledging the thought unsettled her greatly. Though she didn't always live with one of her siblings, she rarely, if ever, lived far away. For forty years she'd been living with her sisters, they'd lived on the east coast, the west coast, even a short stint in Europe. After Gabriel disappeared both she and Kelly moved in with Gen. At first, it was to be supportive. Then it was out of fear Gen was driving herself mad searching for answers about what happened to Gabriel. Later living together just felt right, comfortable, fun even.

Who else would I have Margarita Mondays with? Deb smiled. *Late night trips to Jake's for cheeseburgers. Countless conversations about this war between Heaven and Hell, never once worrying about who would go into battle with me. Kelly entertaining me with funny tales about the "O'Mara Men" as she affectionately referred to our brothers. The three of them showing up for Michael's training routines hungover. Walks through floral gardens with Gen talking about anything and everything.*

Living with her sisters these last forty years had been memorable to say the least. Sure, there had been heartaches, injuries, and mysteries, but more fun than she believed a Guardian hoped for in their crazy world.

I'm going to miss it, miss them. A small tear escaped and trickled down her cheek. *Now, I just need to tell them I'm leaving and hope they understand.*

Hearing footsteps padding gently toward the kitchen, Deb quickly blotted her face.

"Deb, you're up early. You sleep okay?" Gen asked.

"I'm fine, not a lot of sleep, but enough."

Gen's face crinkled with concern. "Still working through what happened at Harry's cottage?"

"I think I'll be sorting through what happened for quite a while," Deb replied. "I wanted to talk to you and Kelly about something. What are the chances she's going to wake anytime soon?"

"Good, since we have training today at Michael's." Gen pulled a frying pan out of a lower cabinet and placed it on the stove.

Ugh, I forgot Michael had training this morning. Deb sighed. *I am not up for that.*

"That's a heavy sigh." Gen rummaged through the fridge. She retrieved what she had been after and turned toward Deb. "You aren't usually the one resistant to training."

"I know, it's just the whole vacation thing being interrupted the way it was, has me a little off. Plus, training usually means dragging Kelly out of bed, we'll have no time to chat before we head over there."

Gen smiled. "That's true for most mornings, but I have a secret weapon today. I managed to make it out to the grocery store yesterday afternoon and I bought this."

Gen picked up the package she retrieved from the fridge and held it up for Deb to read.

"Bacon," Deb chuckled. "Good choice!"

"Yup, a few slabs of this and she'll be down in no time."

Deb stayed at the kitchen table as Gen busied herself with cooking. The kettle was refilled and placed on the stove. The bacon was just starting to fry and the first scent of it wafted over to Deb.

Shouldn't be long now, Deb mused.

Deb grabbed the remote and turned the TV on to play music. That wouldn't help wake Kelly, but it may help settle Deb's nerves a bit.

Gen pulled the bacon from the pan and placed it on a plate covered in paper towels. As if on cue, footsteps were heard on the second floor.

"Looks like it worked."

Gen laughed. "Of course, it did!"

Kelly came into the kitchen wearing a long blue bathrobe with mismatched yellow and pink fuzzy socks. Her long black hair was pulled on top of her head in a messy bun. Her cheeks were still flush from sleep.

"So, we're making bacon in the middle of the night now," Kelly said dryly, as she made her way to the espresso machine.

"It's nearly six thirty and you know it drives Michael crazy when we're late." Gen smirked.

"Is the sun up?" Kelly shot back but didn't wait for a reply. "Then why am I?"

"You love bacon, and you love your brother so it's a win–win," Deb teased.

"Waking up before the sun should never be considered a win," Kelly told them. "But yes of course I love my brother and I don't even mind training but for the love of chips and cheeseburgers can we do it at a respectable time?"

"Like when?" Gen asked.

"I don't know!" Kelly said in mock exaggeration, hands waving for effect. "Noon? I mean seriously, would it kill Michael to start later?"

"I think it might actually," Gen answered sarcastically.

"Very funny," Deb said. "I believe he has training at this hour to reduce the potential for anything we destroy to be seen or heard."

"Why are you always so understanding?" Kelly huffed at Deb before taking pieces of bacon from the plate and sauntering over to sit at the table.

"I guess I'm just born that way." Deb smirked at Kelly. "Not to change the subject, but I want to talk to you two about something."

Gen had finished cooking the bacon and brought it over to the table along with a cup of espresso. She placed both in front of Kelly.

"You're the best Gen," Kelly said, before devouring another piece of bacon.

Once Gen was seated, Deb decided the best course of action was to just get it out there. "I want to move out of the house."

"Where are we going?" Kelly asked obviously not understanding Deb's intention.

Deb looked at Gen, who seemed to stiffen at the

question. Looking down at the table Deb searched for words that didn't feel accusatory.

"I think she means she wants to move out," Gen said. "Alone."

"What?!" Kelly exclaimed. "Why? What's wrong?"

Deb shook her head. "It's not you guys."

"Are you seriously using breakup language with us right now?" Kelly blurted.

"Deb, please just a take a beat and think this through," Gen pleaded. "I know things have been hard, and the short trip to the beach house didn't go as planned but—"

"No, it's not that. Please, just listen," Deb appealed to them. "I feel very disconnected right now and what happened at the beach is just making it worse. I want some time and space for myself, and I can't get that living here with the two of you. I have loved so much of our time here, and who knows maybe we'll do this again in the future, but for now I need this."

Kelly and Gen just stared at her in shocked bewilderment. It was as if Deb was speaking to them in a foreign language they had yet to comprehend.

"I don't know what to say," Gen said, looking a little teary eyed.

"I say go for it," Kelly remarked. "I mean I'll miss you, and you better make more than the occasional visit, but if it's what you want, what you say you need, then do it."

"This just all feels so sudden, Deb," Gen told her. "Are you sure? I mean why not try talking it out with us. You know you can tell us anything. We have proven our bond is our strength. Moving out, it's just—"

"I know, Gen." Deb tried to keep the moment positive. "You know I will never be far away and if you ever need me, I'll be there for all of you."

"I just don't understand," Gen's tone turned defensive. "What did we do? Does this have to do with Marcus?"

"To be honest some of it does, yes," Deb answered. "It's not all him, though I do need to find him."

"How exactly are you going to do that more effectively without us?" Gen crossed her arms over her chest, the direction of the conversation clearly changing.

"Gen, if she wants to move out, then we should support her." Kelly looked between her sisters. "It's not going to be easy on any of us, but at some point, we won't all live together."

"Yes, but why now? I mean after everything we all just went through, now she's choosing to leave. Something's not right. What aren't you telling us, Deb?"

Frustrated, Deb stood up preparing to leave. "I don't owe anyone anything."

Gen's face fell and her arms dropped to her sides. "I didn't mean it like that."

"No?!" Deb glared across the table. "What did you mean then?"

"Hold on." Kelly put her hands in the air as if to quell the rising tension. "There is no need to fight about this."

"She's clearly defensive for a reason." Gen let the accusation hang in the air.

Deb bit the inside of her lip ready to deliver an ugly

retort. Suddenly she winced and was aware that something was coming, another being closing in on the house, someone powerful.

Her sisters were alarmed at the change in Deb's body language.

"Something's coming," Deb warned.

Gen looked around while Kelly beelined to a cabinet in the corner where she kept a stash of weapons.

"What is it?" Gen asked.

"I don't know," Deb responded. "It's on the street, powerful, and getting closer."

Kelly yelled out to her brothers: "Bros, get your butts over here."

Gen strode over to Kelly at the weapons cabinet, and took the spear her sister held out to her plus another to toss to Deb. "They aren't coming. I can't hear any of our brothers. Whatever's coming is cloaking."

"Of course, it is," Kelly said sarcastically. "But I actually have the stupid cell phone charged." She picked up the device on the counter and began tapping away when the doorbell rang. "Did it just ring our doorbell?"

"Well, that's a new one," Gen announced.

"I can't believe I'm asking this." Kelly sighed. "Do we answer it?"

"I'm going to go open the door," Deb said. "I have a weapon and you two will be right here."

Deb walked down the hallway feeling her sister's penetrating eyes following her. She opened the door wide, so her sisters had a view of their visitor. On the other side of the door stood a male figure staring back.

"Good morning," he said a little too cheerfully.

The visitor was dressed in a white three-piece suit, with matching white shirt and shoes. He stood a good foot taller than Deb, his blue eyes stealing a glance down the hallway toward her sisters still in the kitchen.

"Who are you?" Deb asked.

His tanned face burst into a smile revealing a set of stunningly white teeth. The suit was fitted to hug every inch of his thin frame and his short blonde hair was slicked back with some sort of oily product.

"I'm Peter," he said, as if that alone were enough to explain his arrival.

"What do you want, Pete?" Kelly yelled from the kitchen. "You have about thirty seconds before we slam the door in your face."

Peter's smile thinned, nearly forming a sneer. "I'm here with the Verdict. I assumed I would receive a more professional response."

Deb was stunned. *The Verdict,* she said telepathically. *We need the entire family. I hope that text went through to our brothers, Kell.*

CHAPTER THREE

*D*on't panic, we don't know what he is yet, Gen told her sisters.

"Well, let's get on with it then, Pete," Kelly yelled toward the front door.

The figure seemed to bristle at Kelly's request. "My name is Peter."

Deb stepped aside and held her hand out to direct the unexpected guest inside. Peter nodded to Deb and walked past her down the hallway toward Gen and Kelly.

Verdicts come from Arch Angels, don't they? Deb asked her sisters, as she followed Peter down the hallway toward the kitchen.

Yes, Kelly answered. *Yes, they do.*

Any chance you've seen this Arch Angel before Kell? Gen asked.

"Apologies, I see I've interrupted some sort of meal ritual," Peter said, as he fidgeted with the cuff of one of his sleeves.

"So, Pete is it?" Kelly said in an unfriendly tone attempting to get under his skin. "Why are you here alone?"

"I'm sorry, have I offended you in some way?" Peter asked, clearly annoyed by Kelly's question.

"No," Kelly replied. "But that suit certainly does."

Peter looked down at his suit and then back at Kelly. "You don't like white?"

"You look like a television version of an Angel," Kelly retorted as things devolved quickly.

"Enough," Gen said. "If you're an Arch Angel here with the Verdict, then our entire family needs to hear it. So, drop your cloak and let us call our brothers."

Peter seemed to contemplate the request. A chill filled the room. *Why would he have a problem with dropping the cloak?*

"Is that a problem, Pete?" Kelly said, her voice inviting a confrontation.

A glow formed between Peter and Gen. Greg arrived first.

Peter straightened. "No. There's no problem."

"How did you find this house?" Greg asked. "Why are you cloaking?"

"I'm sure you have lots of questions, please let's get to the rendering of the Verdict so we can get them all answered."

As her brothers arrived, Michael nodded for Deb to join them on the opposite side of the room. She had lingered slightly behind Peter hoping to get a better sense of what kind of being he was, suspicious he wasn't an Angel, of any kind. There was obviously something not right about his being here, but there was something else. Deb could sense a disconnect, like the entity was projecting something or impersonating.

That's it, Deb told her siblings telepathically. *He's mimicking. Whatever he's attempting to project, it's not original to his kind.*

More reason for you to get to this side of the room Deb, Frankie argued as his eyes darted toward his side of the room.

Deb walked around the table and stood at the far end next to Tom.

"We're not asking again," Michael told Peter. "Get to it or get out."

Peter nodded in agreement. "Yes, very well then. The Verdict is in and I am obviously here to read it to you. I was told where you reside so that I could deliver the sentence in person."

The sentence, Tom said to them. *That's unusual phrasing, implies a negative outcome which is not normally how these things are presented.*

You've witnessed the presentation of a Verdict before, Tom? Kelly asked.

Yes. Just a few, but it was more a negotiation and the Angel assigned to that Guardian team had given them advance warning and was present for the meeting.

Peter looked between them and continued before anyone could argue the merits of his assumption. "Now, I know how hard this will be for you to hear."

"Well, it wouldn't be hard if you had followed protocol," Deb lamented. "You should have given our Angel advanced warning you were coming and with what terms you wished to negotiate."

Peter seemed caught off guard by Deb's remark.

"Yes, well time was of the essence."

"So, what terms are we negotiating, Pete?" Kelly continued goading. Peter's shoulders tensed. Wiping a finger across his brow he seemed to be attempting to calm himself every time Kelly called him Pete. He clearly didn't like it.

"You can certainly appeal, but the Verdict has been rendered," Peter said through gritted teeth, clearly out of patience.

"Both Heaven and Hell have agreed to terms with no investigation?" Tom asked.

"The investigation is concluded, it's why I'm here," Peter answered.

"An investigation by whom?" Michael asked. "What Sentinel investigated without talking to all the parties involved?"

Hearing the word Sentinel, Deb inhaled sharply. Marcus is a Sentinel, a police officer of sorts. He is a neutral negotiator in the war between Heaven and Hell, and he has a good reputation for thoroughness. Could he be involved with this case? Is that why he hasn't been around? Deb's attention came back to the present when Kelly's tone snapped her mind free from worry.

"You're no Angel, Pete," Kelly almost sang the words. "In fact, we're all standing here wondering what rock in Hell you crawled out from underneath."

Peter inhaled deeply and seemed to stand taller as the accusation settled across the room. "I understand how upsetting it must be to be found guilty of breaking the rules of the Accord."

Let him tell us whatever he came here to say, Michael

27

warned.

I Agree, Dan added. *If nothing else, maybe he'll give something away in the rendering.*

"Yes, it is upsetting," Greg told Peter. "Why don't you read it to us now?"

"Agreed!" Peter said emphatically, as he pulled out a small notecard from his inside jacket pocket. "The O'Mara family has been formerly charged and subsequently found guilty of crimes against the Accord. Both Heaven and Hell have agreed to the following terms: Schlosser will be properly punished by those in Hell. The charge who benefited from Genevieve's interference will receive a painless death."

Genevieve gasped. *This cannot be true,* she silently yelled to her siblings. *Heaven would never agree to let Hell murder an innocent person!*

Hold it together, Gen, Xavier remarked. *He doesn't appear to be done.*

No, Kelly quipped. *He appears to just be getting started and enjoying every minute of discomfort if you ask me.*

"Now," Peter continued, "given that Genevieve crossed the line to protect her human charge, it seems reasonable there be repercussions."

Peter looked up from the notecard, possibly sensing the mounting anger being directed at him. "In addition to Becky, Sophia and Gerry were meant to die in horrendous fashion."

"And Heaven is allowing Hell to complete that task?" Kelly began pacing at the back of the room. She had shed the comfy bathrobe and pulled her hair into a ponytail.

Deb noticed most of her brothers had inched closer to Peter. A fight was coming.

"You are Guardians, are you not?!" Peter announced rhetorically. "You know there are consequences for your actions. You can't go around killing demons unprovoked." Peter's eyes settled on Gen.

"Maybe we should change that rule," Kelly snickered. "I'd like to kill one unprovoked right now."

"Shut your mouth Guardian!" Peter retorted, "or I'll shut it for you!" Peter seemed to slither closer to them.

Kelly moved forward but Dan held her back. *We don't know what he is Kell.*

"Hell has demanded to be made whole." Peter stared Kelly down, to her sister's credit she didn't flinch.

"How does the appeal work, Peter?" Tom asked cool and calm, attempting to refocus the room.

Peter turned his attention toward Tom. "You go to the Sentinel that worked the case and request one."

"Who worked the case?" Deb asked, knowing the answer before it came.

"Marcus." Peter smiled at Deb. "You know Marcus, don't you, Ms. O'Mara?"

Panic rose within Deb. She was in disbelief. Her hands started to tremble, and her mouth went dry. *No, it can't be,* she told herself. *That can't be right. Marcus wouldn't investigate without telling me. He wouldn't have helped Hell against us.*

"Find Marcus and you'll be able to submit an appeal," Peter reiterated.

"And if we can't catch up with Marcus?" Tom asked.

"Well, that would be unfortunate," Peter replied. "Only the Sentinel assigned to the case can process an appeal."

The room seemed stunned into silence. *What have they done?* Deb queried telepathically to her siblings. *Hell must have done something to Marcus. Did you hear the insincerity in Peter's voice? We have to find him. I know he needs our help!*

Try and stay calm, Michael told Deb.

We don't know how much of this is true, Frankie said, attempting to console Deb.

Deb's heart thundered in her chest. Panic welled up, and she grew impatient.

Peter seemed to sense Deb's mood shift. "You don't look well," he told her. "I sense anger rising inside you, like a tidal wave about to overwhelm the senses."

Deb's shield exploded projecting outward. She wrapped it around her siblings surprised at the amount of space she was able to cover. Peter took several steps back in shocked surprise.

Deb, what is it? Frankie asked, concern echoing in his voice.

Talk to us, Michael ordered. *Tell us what's happening right now.*

Your face is flush, you're beginning to sweat, Gen added.

You need to breathe through it, remember? Michael tried to focus Deb.

I know he's evil, Deb told them. *I know he's not who he says he is. I know he did something to Marcus.*

"I think you should go now," Xavier told Peter, one

eyebrow arched sharply. "As you can see no one here believes nor trusts you."

"How dare you speak to me that way?!" Peter's voice turned malevolent. "You will pay for what these three have done."

Deb's siblings quickly shifted into high alert. Her shield was still up, but she didn't know how long she could keep it around them.

"You think you're special, don't you?" Peter practically spit the question at them. "You think you can get away with crossing and double-crossing Hell! That you decide who lives and who dies!" Peter's face reddened and he shook his head violently. "Well, you aren't the arbiters of this world. As for you," Peter pivoted and pointed his finger at Deb. "You can't protect anything from me—not your charges, not your siblings, definitely not Marcus!"

Deb inhaled sharply. There was no quelling the burning energy soaring to the surface to escape.

"Get Out!" Deb took a step forward, but it was like an out of body experience. "Get Out," she yelled at Peter again.

Peter laughed at Deb's demands. It was a sinister laugh that invited confrontation.

Panic turned to rage. Deb raised her arm out in front of her and took a deep breath. When she released the energy at Peter she screamed, "I said, get out!"

Peter stumbled backward slamming his shoulder against the doorway.

Frankie get to Deb, Michael ordered. *Use your power to augment Deb's. Let's see what she's able to do.*

Deb never turned away from Peter. Her left arm in

the air, Frankie grasped her right hand.

What now? Kelly asked.

Breathe through the sensation Deb, it's the only way you'll learn to control it. Let it come. Michael continued to direct Deb telepathically. *When you feel it mix with Frankie's power direct it and then release it, just like letting go of a baseball.*

Frankie's power flow through Deb like a wave. She realized the sweat was coming from her attempts to push the energy back down, she was fighting herself. Michael was telling her to breathe in and release, she had never done that before. She had no idea what would happen.

Peter regained his footing and turned back toward her.

"You bitch, you think—" Peter was interrupted in mid-sentence.

"I said get out!" Deb shouted. "Now. Get. Out!" Deb's power collided with Frankie's. It was like gasoline on a fire. It took hold in seconds and surged upward to the surface.

She focused on Peter. The world turned to slow motion. Deb could feel her shield forming into a weapon, as if the air could take shape into some sort of battering ram. Her ears were ringing, and her vision narrowed in on the object of her rage. She seemed able to direct the energy outward through her raised hand aiming it right for Peter's chest.

Peter's face contorted upon impact of the invisible blow. The air sounded like thunder rolling through the house. The force picked Peter up off his feet and sent him hurtling violently down the hallway. His smirk was obliterated, his eyes betraying shock. Slamming off walls and rolling wildly toward the front of the house, Peter's body smashed through the front door. Glass exploded and splintered wood ricocheted through the enclosed space. Peter landed with a hard thud on the sidewalk at the bottom of their front steps.

CHAPTER FOUR

"Nice shot, Deb!" Kelly howled.

Deb collapsed into one of the chairs at the table. "I feel like I just ran a marathon."

Gen was stunned. *Well, that certainly sent a message,* she thought. *But now Deb looks wiped.*

"Rest, up," Kelly said, as she made her way out of the kitchen. "We got this."

Gen went to the fridge, retrieved a bottle of water, and slid it across the table to Deb. Her siblings were exchanging unpleasantries with Peter outside.

Peter's yelling seemed to reverberate through the house. "How dare you? You are nothing! I will crush you for what you've done here today!"

"Calm down, Pete," Kelly needled. "It's just a minor incident. Deb was upset, you were the one who said how understanding you were of our situation."

"You have no idea what I can unleash," Peter bellowed. "You will pay, and so will your charges."

With all the drama of a Shakespearian play, Peter rose to his feet, dusted the dirt off his no longer pristine white suit, and then leered up at the house. He gave one final warning through clenched teeth. "You will most definitely pay." Then he disappeared from the street as Gen's siblings made their way back to the kitchen.

"Remember, you're going to be exhausted now, Deb," Greg told her. "It's been some time since you've developed a new power. You know how it is when you're first learning to use and control the surges of new power: it's like a battle is raging inside of you."

Frankie sat down at the table. "Yeah, when you first push the boundaries of your power, your body resists. It's as if it's protecting itself, wanting to pull back to some sort of safety within. That push and pull will exhaust you."

Fatigue settled into Deb's eyes. She looked like she hadn't slept in days and now Gen wondered if perhaps she hadn't.

"Do you want to go lay down Deb?" Gen asked. "Maybe take a power nap?"

"No. There's no time. We know he's going after our charges. We should go check on them, right now!"

Deb gingerly got up from the table.

She looks like she's going to pass out, Gen thought.

All eyes were on Deb. Clearly their sister was light-headed. She struggled to stand, and after a few seconds, slumped back into the chair.

"You are in no shape to go out," Kelly commented as she sat down and proceeded to finish off the bacon.

"I need to check on Sophia," Deb pleaded. "And we need to find Marcus."

"Yes," Tom agreed, "we need to check on your charges, but I think one of us should also find Harry."

"Harry?" Deb asked. "Do you think he knows who Peter is?"

"Only one way to find out," Michael told them. "I'll go get him.

Michael teleported out of the kitchen.

"Don't worry, Deb," Frankie said. "If your charges were in danger all of your marks would be going off. Once we talk to Harry, I'll go check on Sophia for you."

"No one should go alone," Tom told them.

"I'll go with Frankie," Dan added.

As the soft glow of Michael's aura surrounded her, Gen sensed the presence of Heaven even before Harry arrived.

"Well," Harry announced. "This looks somber." He removed his old fishing hat and tucked it into his back pocket. His bald head was shiny and glistened with sweat. His beady blue eyes narrowed in on Deb as he swiped the perspiration from his forehead.

"We just had a rather unpleasant visit," Gen began. "Someone named Peter. He rang the doorbell, announced he was here to read the Verdict."

Harry scrunched his eyebrows forming a deep crease across his forehead. "That's impossible."

"Really," Kelly bellowed. "You're using the word impossible in this house!"

"What I mean to say is there isn't going to be a Verdict," Harry clarified. "Quite simply, there is no case."

"No one has lodged a complaint you mean?" Tom asked.

"Correct," Harry answered. "You can't have a Verdict if there was no case opened, no investigation."

"No investigation," Deb repeated. "Are you sure? Peter said that Marcus was the Sentinel assigned to the case."

"He did say that," Frankie agreed. "He said if we wanted to appeal, we had to do it through the Sentinel who investigated the case."

Harry seemed to ponder these revelations before responding. "Has Marcus been here since the battle? Has he inquired as to what happened?"

All eyes fell on Deb. "No. I haven't seen him in weeks, and I've been looking."

Uneasiness fell across the room. *She's been looking,* Gen thought. *Not a surprise, but what else has she been doing without us?*

"If Harry believes there's no case, then there's no case," Michael said. "It would have been highly unlikely Marcus would be assigned to our case even if there had been one."

"I agree," Harry added. "Marcus was involved in many aspects of what happened, not to mention his closeness to the parties involved."

Kelly chortled. "You sound like an attorney, Harry."

"I just mean, a Sentinel assigned to any case would have to be impartial. But it doesn't matter because no case has been brought forth against you, of any kind."

"That you know of," Gen added. "You were involved too Harry, are you sure the powers that be would tell you if there were such an investigation going on?"

"No," Harry answered swiftly. "But I know lots of players, on both sides, and I would have found out if there were a case, believe me."

"Alright, so the better question is why did he even mention Marcus?" Tom argued. "Peter, whoever he is, has inside knowledge of what transpired. Who else would have that kind of knowledge?"

"Well, there are a lot of rumors out there," Dan remarked. "I don't think it's a secret the O'Maras got into a heated fight with Hell.

"That's not exactly breaking news," Xavier said sarcastically.

"True," Frankie added. "But Peter knew about their charges and he knew about this house in Boston. He knew this was where he would find our sisters."

"That is troubling," Harry stated. "What else did he say?"

"He said our charges were meant to die," Gen told him. "That they would die painlessly now for my crime against the Accord."

"Then he wasn't from Heaven!" Harry said emphatically.

"Yeah," Kelly said snidely. "We figured that part out already."

"We obviously need to find Peter," Deb told them. "But first we should go check on our charges."

Michael took charge. "Tom and I will go talk to the other Guardian groups nearby. If Peter was pretending to be from Heaven and faking an investigation, maybe he paid them a visit also."

"Frankie and I told Deb we'd check on Sophia for her," Dan said. "Then she can get some rest."

"Are you not feeling well?" Harry asked.

Kelly boasted, "We forgot to tell you the best part. Deb used her powers to throw Peter out of the house, literally. It was incredible!"

"What?" Harry stared at Deb in disbelief.

"Kelly can tell you all about it," Michael offered. "When you go with her to check on Gerry."

"I'll stay with Deb," Greg volunteered. "I can explain more about what's going on with her powers and the aftereffects of it."

"Fine," Michael responded. "And while you're here, get the front door replaced."

"Xav, are you with me to check on Becky?" Gen asked. Before Xavier could answer her mark burned. The light burst through the crown of thorns encircling her left wrist.

"Let's move, Gen!" Xavier rushed to grab Gen's right hand. "Looks like Peter's making good on his threat."

***

Gen directed her and Xavier to the master bedroom of Becky and Ron's house. This was a new home for her charges; they moved from the East Coast to California about four months after their encounter with Schlosser. Ron believed the accident and Becky's pregnancy were a wakeup call. He quit the hospital and they moved to the West Coast to be closer to Becky's parents. Gen had only been here a few times since the move.

"Why did you direct us here?" Xavier asked. "There are no demons here."

"The mark dictates where I go," Gen replied. "Isn't

39

that what happens when your mark goes off?"

"It used to. Michael trained us to be able to divert to where the threat is, so we arrive where needed. In this case, that's obviously the baby's room."

The baby's door was ajar, but Gen heard and detected nothing. She whispered, "Now that you say it, I don't feel the baby. His room's up the hall on the left."

"Exactly," Xavier responded. "That's where we needed to land."

At this short distance, Gen's brother chose to move quickly up the hallway instead of teleporting into the baby's room. Brandishing a weapon in each hand, he disappeared into the room. Xavier was all business.

Gen quickly caught up to him where he had stopped short in the doorway at the sight of two demons hovering over the baby's crib. The female appeared to be holding the baby in place, while the male had his arm raised in mid-air. Gen looked down at the crib and her heart sank. The child wasn't breathing, his normal reddish cheeks taking on a pale blueish hue.

Xavier grabbed the female demon's shoulder and threw her down to the floor, sending her spiraling away from the crib. The female demon cowered in the corner no doubt intimidated at their sudden arrival.

Gen paused a second before deciding her next move. *She could heal the baby, but would that be considered interference?* She silently second-guessed herself.

Xav, Gen told her brother without speaking. *The baby's father is an emergency room doctor. I'm going to wake him up.*

Is there time for that? Xavier questioned. *The poor kid*

is blue.

You just chase these two away, Gen told her brother. *And, whatever you do, don't kill them unprovoked.*

Gen moved swiftly back to the master bedroom. Becky and Ron were still sleeping soundly, the demonic interference completely cloaked from human senses. Becky was partially under the covers, while Ron was wrapped up like it was winter. Their ceiling fan circled slowly above them humming along.

How should I wake them? Gen pondered.

Gen moved her hands out in front of her letting them hover over Becky's head causing the woman to stir, but not wake.

Gen reconsidered. *Maybe I should just go heal the baby.*

A thud came from the other room and she knew Xavier had expelled both demons from the house. The sound would have been undetectable to Becky and Ron.

Hurry Gen, this kid has no time left, Xavier urged. *Whatever you're going to do, do it now.*

In a moment of panic, Gen leaned down and whispered in Becky's ear.

"Check the baby!" Gen said with urgency, then clapped loudly, allowing the humans to hear.

Becky bolted upright fighting to get to the lamp on the nightstand.

"Ron!" Becky urged groggily. "The baby."

Ron shot up and ran down the hallway not waiting for further explanation.

Gen followed Ron into the baby's room and he flipped the light switch on. Xavier was off to the side of the crib but not visible to humans. Ron sprinted to the crib.

41

Gen stepped inside the room and moved off to the side knowing Becky would be hot on her heels.

"It was the right call, Gen," Xavier said out loud, with no worries of being heard by human ears.

"Becky, call 911!" Ron urgently announced. "He's not breathing. I'm going to give him CPR, but go, call them now!"

Becky turned and ran back down the hallway to make the call.

"I hope so," Gen answered.

"I would have backed you up on healing him," Xavier told her. "Afterall, his injuries are the direct result of demonic interference."

The baby coughed and Ron turned the baby over on his side. Reddish brown liquid oozed from the infants trembling lips.

"What is that?" Xavier asked.

"Some sort of Hellish elixir I'm sure," Gen responded.

"That's it, buddy," Ron cooed softly. "You got this, now hold on for me little one."

Sirens rang in the background and Gen knew they could leave. Her and Xavier had been updating their siblings telepathically in bits and pieces during the encounter. According to Dan and Frankie there were no demons at Sophia's house. Kelly and Harry had yet to find Gerry, but Kelly's mark was not going off, at least not yet.

The baby began to cry more boisterously, and Becky ran back inside the room. Gen sensed her relief and her trauma; the need to keep calm for the baby's sake was nearing the end. The well of emotion inside Becky was boiling just below the surface.

Becky removed the child's soiled clothing and gently wiped him down. Carefully, she changed his diaper and wrapped him in a clean dry swaddling blanket. She pulled him into her arms comforting him as best she could before the dam broke and tears streamed downed Becky's face.

"He's going to be okay, Beck," Ron said. "I'm going to go let the paramedics in and tell them what I know."

"Should I just bring him down Ron?" Becky asked urgently.

"No, give me a minute with them," Ron replied. "He's been moved enough and he's calmer now. They can come up to you. The worst is over Beck, he's breathing, and his coloring is already returning."

Becky simply nodded as Ron left to head downstairs.

"I can sense some permanent damage," Xavier looked at Gen. "I'm heading back. Do what you do best and take care of that baby." A glow enveloped her brother and took him from the house.

The front door of the house opened, and words were exchanged as Ron explained the situation. A few moments later, trampling footsteps came up the stairs as the emergency personnel got closer.

Stepping toward Becky, Gen raised her left hand over the child. Her mark no longer aglow as the threat from Hell had passed. Closing her eyes, Gen used her powers to heal the damage Xavier had sensed.

"Please be okay," Becky whispered. "Please God, let him be okay."

The room became a cacophony of noise as EMT personnel entered and took the baby from Becky's arms to examine him.

Becky's short plea to Heaven rippled like adrenaline through Gen's body. "He's going to be okay Becky, you all are."

The wave of Heavenly warmth rushed over Becky. Becky sensed the baby would be okay, even though she wouldn't have been able to hear Gen's assurances.

Becky nodded. "Thank you."

One of the EMTs patted Becky on the arm. "Of course! This is what we do, we're going to take good care of your baby."

CHAPTER FIVE

After speaking with Greg at some length about what was possibly going on with her powers, Deb grabbed an apple and went to her room to recuperate.

She was resting, but very much awake as she tuned in to the updates from Gen and Xavier. There were demons at Becky's house that her siblings had to chase off.

Frightening, Deb thought. *This is crazy. Why is Hell still coming for our charges if there's no Verdict? Maybe Harry's wrong.*

The thought chilled Deb. Feeling anxious she got up and began pacing in her bedroom. She wanted to get out of the house. Although she was feeling much better, she knew she wasn't strong enough for any sort of confrontation. That would take an actual meal and sound uninterrupted sleep.

"Maybe Kelly would be up for a trip to Jake's later," Deb said softly to herself. "Any opportunity to run into Marcus—it could happen, I found him there once before."

As she waited for another update from Frankie and Dan at Sophia's house, Kelly told them Gerry wasn't at home or at the firehouse. She and Harry were moving on to the shipyard. Kelly's mark still wasn't going off, so that was good news.

Just as Deb was about to give up and head over to the tea shop down the street, she sensed Xavier arriving. She knew he would find Greg, who was still at the house not wanting to leave Deb alone. The two brothers would share updates. Believing full recovery was going to have to wait until she was able to get some real sleep, Deb decided to go back downstairs. She grabbed the ring Marcus had left her from its hiding spot in a sock drawer.

I have no idea why I'm hiding this, Deb thought. *I'm being ridiculous and just need to deal with this.*

Deb looked at the simple gold band resting in her palm.

How can such a small thing cause this much anxiety? she thought.

Folding her fingers over the ring she held it firmly in her left hand as she made her way down the hall. She focused on Marcus, remembering times when she would simply think of him and then suddenly run into him or know where he was at that exact moment. In the past, she found him down by the river multiple times using that technique. The most embarrassing of which was when Frankie witnessed her and Marcus kiss.

That kiss, Deb sighed. *So romantic, yet somehow all wrong at the same time. I remember when one look from those penetrating eyes would make me swoon.* Deb spun deeper into the past and thoughts of Marcus. *Everything about you seems dark: your hair, your charcoal-colored eyes, even the clothes you wear, always black. Am I attracted to your darkness?*

Deb shook her head slightly trying to pull herself back to the present. *It doesn't matter, our connection must be broken or blocked. You know where I am Marcus, if you were able, I know you would come for me.*

Kelly interrupted Deb's thoughts with telepathic updates. Deb had neared the bathroom door when a soft glow formed in front of her. It wasn't her siblings, and it wasn't Marcus.

***

Kelly arrived at the shipyard having no idea where to start looking.

"What's the name of his boat?" Harry asked as he pulled the fishing hat out of his back pocket and placed it back on his small round head.

"I have no idea."

"That's a unique name for a boat," Harry replied with a wink.

Kelly looked around at the old shipyard; it was long and wide, a plot of land that had been a working commercial shipyard up until the early twenty-first century. Now the land was divided into a marina, private boat shipyard, and a repository for Navy equipment. The old weathered wooden railing was too short to pass today's building codes. The overcrowded city was separated from the shipyard by a thin strip of ocean. The small strip of bay water was churning and streaked with a slight greenish-gray color today.

Storm out at sea, Kelly thought.

The breeze was light, and it carried the smell of salt

air mixed with fuel and engine smog. There was a flurry of activity toward the guard shack and the front buildings, but less as you got further along the row of boats set atop large blocks. Not all were being worked on; some were covered and ready for off-season storage.

They stood at the edge of the dock. The deeper ocean water that lay beyond was dark blue, nearly black in color. The gentle lapping of the water as it continually splashed against the wooden pylons was one of Deb's favorite sounds.

"Which sibling are you worried about?" Harry asked.

"How do you know how to do that?"

"Just a feeling. Not very different from when you sense a charge is in need I imagine."

"I'm worried about Deb. She told us this morning she wants to move out of the house."

"Well, it does belong to Gen and Gabriel. Perhaps you could find a place with more privacy, something that suits all of you."

"Yeah. Well, I would if Gen and I were invited, but we're not. She wants to move out, alone."

Harry's eyebrows rose in surprise. "Really?"

"Yeah, weird isn't it?" Kelly looked at him more intently. "You wouldn't happen to know what caused this sudden desire for alone time, would you?"

"Me? Why would I know something about Deborah that you and Genevieve do not?"

"Because you asked," Kelly quipped.

"Well," he smiled quickly, "if I did know something, and I don't, it most definitely would have come from asking Deborah about it. You could all learn to do that from time to time."

Kelly sighed and shook her head. "She stayed with you back when Gabriel was here. She didn't give you any indication of—" Kelly didn't know how to finish the question.

"She told me she was worried about Marcus," Harry interrupted Kelly's thoughts. "I assume you already knew that though."

Kelly nodded. Just then Gerry came out from between two boats, took one look at her, and stopped short. "I found Gerry," she announced to Harry.

Harry looked behind him. Gerry dropped the metal toolbox he was carrying and stared between the two of them.

"He's able to see us even though we are not in human view," Harry spoke softly. His body language was relaxed and open, attempting not to frighten Gerry.

"It really freaks me out, Harry."

"I agree." He commented as Gerry approached them. "This is rather disconcerting."

"What do you people want?" Gerry asked. The middle-aged man's dark skin shimmered in the sunlight. His gray T-shirt marred by small circles of sweat. "Why are you following me?"

"I assume you can also hear us, Gerry?" Kelly asked.

"Yes, I can hear you. I'm not deaf. Now what in the devil's world is going on?"

"The Devil's world?" Kelly repeated. "Interesting way to greet an Angel and a Guardian."

"Careful now, Kelly." Harry put his hands up slowly. "No need to overwhelm."

Gerry took a closer look at Harry. "Do I know you?"

"Well now, normally I would say that's impossible," Kelly remarked, drawing Gerry's attention back toward her. "But since Harry hangs out from time to time at Jake's with Father Donovan it's actually possible you do know him."

"Gerry," Harry said. "Before we get too far along in this conversation, is there a place a little less crowded where we can talk more freely?"

"Why?" Gerry shot back. "I'm not going anywhere until you start talking. Starting with you." Gerry pointed at Kelly. "Why and how were you in my hospital room?"

Kelly could sense people approaching ahead. "Well this just got a whole lot more complicated." Kelly peeked over her shoulder. Two men were approaching. One older, wearing a bright red baseball cap, the other younger carrying a large bag in each hand. She gave a warning. "Gerry, please believe me, you are the only one who can see us."

"Yeah right." He shook his head. Before he could continue, his brow creased as he saw the facial expressions of the men approaching.

"Are you alright, man?" The older man in the red hat asked. "Who you talking to?"

"You might want to tell them you're okay, Gerry," Kelly told him.

Gerry looked away from Kelly and back at the two men who were now moving closer. "Yeah, yeah, I'm fine, Chuck." Gerry swiped some perspiration that had formed on his forehead. "Maybe a little too much sun, you know?"

Kelly influenced Chuck and the young man to stop moving forward.

"Sun's pretty strong today," Chuck replied. "Make sure you take it easy and stay hydrated, you're still recovering after all."

"Will do," Gerry replied with a slight wave in their direction. "Thanks."

When the men had turned away, Harry tried to refocus the conversation. "About that place to talk."

Gerry looked at Harry with frightful eyes. "I'm going crazy."

"No," Kelly answered emphatically. "We really are here to help you."

"My boat is at the end." Gerry pointed past Kelly to the end of the pier. "They covered it and placed it down there a few months back when I was hospitalized. That heart attack damn near killed me. Today's my first day back to feeling somewhat normal. I was going to wash down my boat and put her back in the water. With this weather, it might be my last chance for the season."

"Let's take a walk to the end, shall we? I can sense there are no humans there." Harry held his arm up gesturing for Gerry to go first. which he did.

"No humans," Gerry mumbled.

Kelly updated her siblings telepathically. *Found Gerry at the boat yard. We are heading to a more private spot to speak with him. Harry witnessed how Gerry can see and hear us. I will update you again when we are done speaking with him. So far, no demons. As Deb would say, "at least not yet."* Gerry glanced over his shoulder at Kelly. A perplexed look crossed his face as she made air quotes and realized her lips hadn't moved.

***

Deb smiled at Kelly's reference, but it was short-lived. She was in the midst of yet another encounter with an uninvited guest to their home. This one was teleporting straight to her location. Deb would have called her brothers up from the first floor, but she knew whoever was arriving was not a threat. She sensed the Heavenly influence before the outline of the entity took shape.

As the blueish glow evaporated, Leo and Lucas stood before her in the second-floor hallway. The angels' stepped back and appeared stunned. They were as surprised to have arrived on the second floor as she was to see them there.

"Hi," Leo blurted out. "I didn't realize we would be brought to your exact location."

The twins mirrored each other in almost every way. Their brown hair was trimmed short, and they were clean shaven. The angels were about five foot nine and lean, each wore a suit, but their footwear is where they varied. Lucas always wore leather dress shoes, while Leo wore sneakers.

Leo's always ready to make a hasty getaway, Deb mused.

"We needed to speak with you," Leo continued. "We weren't sure if your brother would relay the message."

Lucas, as usual, projected a much calmer demeanor. "What Leo is trying to say is we felt it best to speak with you directly, Deborah."

"How did you find me?" Deb asked. "Did Marcus send you? Where is he?"

The twin Angels exchanged a worried glance between them.

"What is it?" she asked. "What's happened?"

Before either could answer, Frankie and Dan arrived in the house. Deb had projected her shield once she identified her visitors were Leo and Lucas, wanting to speak with them privately. However, if Frankie realized he couldn't feel her in the house, he'd surely come looking for her. He was the brother inclined to be over-protective.

No use in hiding this, Deb thought.

Dropping her shield Deb spoke to her brothers. "I have some company up here."

Before she had a chance to explain further, her brothers Frankie, Dan, Greg, and Xavier surrounded Leo and Lucas.

"What's going on here?" Greg asked sarcastically. "Is your address in some sort of supernatural Google search?"

"Very funny," Deb quipped.

"We just told you two we would let Deb know you wanted to speak to her." Dan was clearly irritated.

"Where did you run into them?" Greg asked.

"We just came from Sophia's house," Frankie answered. "We ran into them there."

"Look, give them some space," Deb said, pushing her brothers back on her way toward the twins.

"We don't have time for this," Leo squealed. "Marcus is in danger, he's missing. And this family needs to help him!"

Deb sensed the rising tension knowing her brothers wouldn't take kindly to Leo's order.

"Okay, everyone downstairs to the kitchen," Deb ordered. "I can feel Gen coming back and I'm sure one of you has already called Michael so there isn't enough room in this tiny hallway for this conversation."

"Michael," Leo said in a reverent tone. "He scares me."

"He scares a lot of entities," Greg remarked. "Let's go you two. Kitchen's this way."

While the others made their way to the kitchen, Frankie stayed behind. He faced Deb. "I would ask how you're feeling, but I feel like that's all I do lately."

Deb missed time with her brother, things between them used to be so easy and carefree. Now things seemed strained.

"I've been better. I know we haven't really had time to catch up or hang out like we used to."

"Yeah, that would be nice. Seems like just when things calm down, they crank back up again."

"I miss our Thursday pizza night. There are a lot of episodes of *The Bachelor* on DVR downstairs," she chuckled.

"I'm sure there are," Frankie laughed, his brown eyes flickering with amusement. "Probably almost as many wrestling shows as I have recorded."

"One for one." Deb held up her forefinger. "That's the deal."

"I know, I remember our deal, Deb."

Deb sighed. She'd much rather go order takeout and relax with her brother, but that wasn't an option, not now.

"Let's get down there before our brothers grill the twins too much," Deb told him.

Frankie nodded with a hint of a frown. They made their way to the kitchen as Gen returned.

"Well, this is a surprise," Gen noted. Lucas sat at their kitchen table and Leo paced in front of the china cabinet stocked with weapons.

"Is everyone here that you wanted, Deb?" Lucas asked. "I'd like to begin."

"Please do," Michael announced. Leo yelped, jumping at the sound of Michael's authoritative voice.

Deb stifled a laugh; Xavier did not.

Leo stopped pacing and moved closer to Lucas. Leo kept his eyes glued to Michael.

"We're Marcus' nephews," Lucas announced. "When we were human, and I realize not every Heavenly entity has a human past, Marcus died before Leo and I were born. Our mother spoke of him often. They were very close. The longer story I will leave until there's more time."

"Why were you at Sophia's house?" Tom asked. "Who is she to you?"

Leo stopped biting his nails long enough to answer. "Our baby sister."

Deb groaned in frustration. "We know this already."

"Not true, Deb," Tom scolded her. "Not everything you tell Gen and Kelly makes it to us."

Deb frowned, but Leo continued, ignoring the uncomfortable exchange. "Marcus is missing, and no one is looking for him."

"What makes you think he's missing?" Tom asked.

"He could be on assignment or in charge of an investigation."

"We can't tell you that." Leo shot back and began pacing again.

"Can't or won't?" Michael questioned.

Lucas replied, "Won't," as Leo simultaneously bellowed, "Can't!"

"Look, we need your help," Lucas told them. "Marcus helped you and your family when you needed him. He risked everything to go past the line between night and day to get Kelly into that purity pool, not to mention Deb."

"What about Deb?" Frankie asked.

"Well, they're in love," Leo told them breathlessly. "I presume you knew that."

The walls were collapsing down around Deb. Before she could say anything to stop the swelling tide of tension in the room, Leo burst the dam open.

"That's why he had us give her that note with our grandmother's wedding ring in it." Leo stopped when the room became uncomfortably muted.

Deb knew by the silence in the room her siblings were shellshocked.

"What?!" Gen snapped the room out of their stupor. "Marcus gave you a ring?" Gen asked, sounding more like an accusation than a question. "That's what you're keeping from us? That's why you want to move out, to work through that?"

Anger bubbled inside Deb. "I don't owe you anything." Deb turned toward Leo and Lucas. "I'll help you find Marcus, and I'll start right now. I'm done asking my siblings for help on something they clearly don't feel is urgent."

Deb pushed past her siblings and used her powers to teleport Leo, Lucas, and herself from the house. She didn't care that her siblings were yelling for her to stay and explain. She would take Leo and Lucas someplace they could speak freely and away from judgement.

You had your chance, Deb thought angrily. *Now I'm going to find him with or without your help.*

CHAPTER SIX

"What is it?" Harry asked.

Kelly stayed focused on Gerry as he reached his boat and climbed aboard. He dropped the toolbox he had gone back to retrieve and tossed a couple of rags across one of the seats on the deck.

"Leo and Lucas just showed up at our house," Kelly told Harry. "This day is just getting stranger and stranger."

Before Harry could respond, Gerry was climbing back down to the dock to rejoin them. "Who are Leo and Lucas?" he asked Kelly.

"Not important. So, you can see us, and by now you know no one else can."

"Mmm hmm." Gerry stroked the sides of his unshaven face. "That does appear to be the case."

"I know how strange this is," Kelly told him. "We are a little taken aback by it also."

"Who are you to each other?" Gerry asked as he pointed back and forth between them.

"I think we're getting ahead of ourselves," Harry answered. "We need to be straight with you on who we are, but first I want to ask how you're doing?"

"Oh, I'm fine, just fine. For someone who is seeing ghosts."

"Ghosts!" Kelly blurted a little louder than she intended. "Oh, no. I didn't even think of that, but now that you say it—"

Harry interrupted. "We aren't ghosts, Gerry. Kelly and I are not actually related, but we are members of a family of sorts."

"True." Kelly smiled broadly revealing her pride at the comment.

"What kind of family are you?" Gerry asked. "When people use the term *of sorts*, I find it's usually a fancy way of saying not at all."

"Well, I am an Angel of the Guard," Harry said plainly.

"*An Angel of the Guard*," Gerry repeated in a sing-song manner, as if he were speaking to a person that was a little crazy. "And what or who are you guarding?"

"Technically, me," Kelly answered. "But, I mean, I'm really the muscle, you know what I mean?"

"No, I actually don't know what you mean," Gerry snapped, clearly frustrated. "And you are what exactly? Are you also an Angel?"

"No!" Kelly answered emphatically. "Thank goodness for that, no offense Harry."

"Offense completely taken," Harry remarked sarcastically.

"I'm a Guardian," Kelly replied ignoring Harry's wisecrack. "He's the Angel assigned to me and my siblings. He watches over us, gives guidance, etcetera."

"Etcetera," Gerry replied. "As if I would know what follows that?"

He's right to be aggravated, Kelly thought. *I would be too.*

"Look Gerry," Kelly mustered as much sincerity as she could. "I'm being curt to speed things up. I'm worried you're in danger."

"I think I am too!" Gerry remarked sarcastically. "My own damn mind is cracking up."

"I promise that is not happening," Kelly said calmly. "I'm going to tell you what I can about this world that Harry and I are from, but it's going to be short and to the point, alright?"

Kelly held her breath waiting for Gerry to acknowledge. *Where to begin?* she thought. *I've never had to explain this before.*

Gerry nodded. "Alright, tell me about your world."

Harry looked at Kelly and nodded. "You got this."

"Heaven and Hell have been warring over the souls of all humanity for thousands of years," Kelly began. "Millenia ago, a deal was struck, ending the infernal battle here on Earth. Both sides agreed to end the bloody violence—a peace treaty if you will. We call it the Accord. It's a much longer story, but the summary version is that both sides abide by a non-invasive means of winning over a human soul."

Gerry cleared his throat. "And by what means is that? What do you all consider non-invasive?"

"We use influence," Kelly answered. "But, because Hell can't exactly be trusted, Heaven sent us to Earth." Kelly paused to give Gerry a moment to catch up.

"Us?" Gerry repeated. "Heaven sent Guardians, that's what you told me you were."

"Exactly!" Kelly was excited Gerry seemed to understand and continued. "In Heaven there are several different types of Angels. There are lower-level Angels that bestow gifts of grace and serenity. There are Angels like Harry who are assigned to Guardian clans or families, like mine. Then there are Arch Angels, warriors who ready themselves for—" Kelly looked at Harry.

"What are the warriors readying themselves for exactly?" Gerry asked.

"For whatever might come, Gerry," Harry answered. "The point is, Kelly is not an Angel, she's a Guardian sent by Heaven to live here on Earth, among humanity. To protect it from anything Hell might do against the Accord."

Kelly sighed with relief. *Harry totally saved me from talking about the apocalypse. That would have been a bit much for lesson one.*

"We don't know why you can see or hear us, Gerry," Harry told him. "And we really want to talk to you about that, answer questions, alleviate any anxieties."

"But?" Gerry looked at Harry. "Sounds like there's a but coming."

"Gerry," Harry started, then took a moment. "I would like to call someone here, an expert if you will in this sort of arena?"

"An expert?" Gerry asked. "You're going to call someone else, because you two, a supposed Angel and his muscle, aren't enough?"

"Gerry, believe me, we know how this sounds,"

Kelly told him. "We would not be having this conversation if we didn't have to, but you shouldn't be able to see us. It's not normal."

"It ain't exactly normal for me either. I'm standing here in front of my boat talking to an Angel and a Guardian." Gerry waved his hand between Harry and Kelly. "And I'm not crazy? I think what I am is damn lucky there are no cameras down this side of the boatyard."

"We understand," Harry reassured. "I know this is difficult. Given the unusualness of the situation I would really like to call my friend. Are you alright with that?"

"And who is your friend, Superman?" Gerry scoffed.

"He's an Arch Angel. His name is Jacob," Harry answered seriously.

"Oh, an Arch Angel." Gerry looked at Harry. "The boss of the man in the fishing hat. I mean you look like you should be climbing on one of these boats and heading out to sea with me."

"I wish I were, believe me," Harry chuckled. "But Jacob is a colleague, a trusted ally, and we could really use his help."

"This is crazy," Gerry huffed, and began pacing back and forth in front of his boat. "I'm having a ridiculous conversation with two people no one else can see. I have definitely lost it."

"I'm going to call my friend now, Gerry." Harry tried to brace Gerry for what would come next.

As Gerry made the turn to come back toward them, a bright glowing light manifested in a large circle. Gerry thrust his hand up in front of his face to shield his eyes from the light. As the light faded, a male figure stood in front of them. Jacob was tall, over six feet with broad shoulders. He wore a white T-shirt and his deep brown skin shimmered in the bright sun. His loose-fitting cargo pants were of a blue fatigue color.

Jacob's dark brown eyes peered between all of them, then settled on Harry.

"A most unusual human, Harry." Jacob had a husky voice and when he smiled, he revealed a set of pristine white teeth. His muscles rippled from head to toe, a perfect specimen of Angelic creation.

"It's good to see you Jacob, thank you for coming," Harry said. "As you can see, we need some assistance understanding why Gerry is able to see and communicate with us."

Gerry's mouth hung open for a long moment before speaking. "Where—"

"I came from above," Jacob answered the question before Gerry could finish it. "I can feel you are coming around to the idea this is all very real, Gerry and that you are not crazy, nor hallucinating. That's good, very good, because this is real."

"Why me?" Gerry managed to get the question out before Jacob continued.

"There's always time for contemplation later," Jacob told him. "For now, I need to understand where Ms. O'Mara found you."

"About six months ago my mark went off," Kelly began as she adjusted the strap of the weapon's bag that hung across her chest. "I found Gerry in his house, no demons, but he was clearly in distress. I swayed him to get up and look for aspirin. He was going to just ignore the pain he was experiencing and try and take a nap."

"Yes," Jacob interrupted. "I can see his path now, it's still a little fuzzy, but I think you did more than sway Ms. O'Mara."

"I got him the aspirin, if that's what you mean," Kelly said flatly.

"Kelly O'Mara," Harry scolded. "Was that wise?"

"What do you mean?" Kelly shrugged her shoulders. "My mark went off. I was obviously called to help."

"You went and got the aspirin, placing it in his path?" Jacob asked.

"We can debate the merits of that choice later." Harry's tone rang of disappointment.

"I don't see how these little details are relevant," Kelly started but Gerry interrupted.

"I knew there was no aspirin in the house," Gerry told them. "It always bothered me where that bottle came from. I knew it wasn't my wife's. She's been dead more than five years now, too long to still have anything in the house from her. It wasn't my daughter's. I asked her at the hospital; she told me she never takes aspirin, so it was you."

"We need to speed this up Jacob," Kelly snapped. "We are worried something else wants to have a conversation with Gerry, if you catch my drift."

"Someone else did." Jacob turned his eyes to Kelly. "Death, and you shortchanged him."

"Oh no," Harry muttered.

"I'm sorry, did you just say Death, as in, The Death? The Angel of Death, The Grim Reaper." Gerry was panicking, the words tumbling out in a steady stream.

"Okay, good to know Jacob," Kelly retorted. "Time to go now, thanks for making this situation worse, we've got it from here."

Before Jacob had time to answer her, Kelly's mark went off. Like a beacon it lit up the back corner of her left shoulder.

"What in Heaven's name is that?" Gerry asked as he once again had to bring his hand up to shield his eyes from the brightness of a Heavenly glow.

"Incoming!" Kelly yelled as she pulled out a small punching dagger from the bag she had draped over her body.

"What is that?" Gerry asked her. "What are you going to do with that thing?"

Jacob thrust his arms behind him to release the curved sword that was strapped to his back. Kelly stood in front of Harry and Gerry, waiting for Jacob to unsheathe his weapon.

"Jacob, move a little faster please," Kelly pleaded. "I cannot communicate with my family. Assume the area is being cloaked."

Kelly motioned for Gerry and Harry to move away from the edge of the water. "Let's make our way out of this end and toward where people are."

Kelly tossed the bag she was carrying over to Harry. He caught it mid-air and opened it. "What am I looking for Kelly?"

"My cell phone is in there. Dan is speed dial number one."

Harry nodded and dug into the bag as the three of

them started for the guard shack. Kelly sensed Jacob wasn't following. Just as she was about to turn back, a howl bellowed from behind her. She swung around. A figure stood behind Jacob. It took her a second to register it was Peter. He had changed out of his all-white suit and now wore a long red trench coat over black pants and combat boots. His hair was still slicked back but his eyes were as red as the deepest claret wine. He had shoved a saber right through Jacob's body, the blade protruding out of the Arch Angel's chest. Blood doused the ground and flowed freely from the open puncture. Peter kept Jacob upright as if he weighed nothing at all. He thrust the blade to its hilt inflicting maximum damage and ensuring Jacob's demise.

"No!" Kelly yelled as she ran straight for Peter. Just as she got to their position, Peter vanished in a smoky haze. Reaching Jacob, Kelly bent down and grabbed his hand to comfort him. "I'm so sorry, Jacob."

Jacob used his last breath to warn her. "He's not finished. His anger is his weapon."

Kelly turned her attention back toward Harry who was standing in front of Gerry in a protective stance. The look in Gerry's eyes was one of pure terror.

"Look out!" Harry screamed as he pointed past Kelly.

Assuming Peter had materialized behind her, she spun around swinging her dagger hard, but no one was there. The momentum caused her to lose her balance and she fell awkwardly to the ground. Bouncing back to a standing position she spun back only to be hit in the face with a large metal object. The force was so strong it sent her stumbling backward several feet. As she shook off the blow, Peter was on top of her. He lifted her off the ground and threw her several yards beyond the pier railing. Kelly's body flailed wildly through the air as she fell toward the ocean. She hit the cold water with stinging force and sunk several feet before twitching her legs rapidly to stop from sinking further. Kelly struggled to make sense of the speed and power Peter possessed.

Upper-level Demon? Kelly's muddled mind questioned. *No idea what he is, but Peter is not of this world. He's not an earth-bound species, not with that kind of strength.*

Kelly thrust her arms upward to swim for the surface. Somewhere in the confrontation she lost her dagger, and her bag was still with Harry.

I have no weapon.

Bursting from the water she sputtered and struggled to catch her breath. She immediately tasted her own blood coming from a large gash she could feel swelling on her forehead. The salt water stung her open wound, and she used her hands to swipe the blood and ocean water from her eyes. She was so far out from the deck she was able to take in the scene in its totality. Peter and Harry were wrestling. Peter punched Harry square in his chest, the blow was so powerful it sent her Angel several yards across the boatyard, like he weighed nothing. Harry's head slammed against another boat and he tumbled to the ground.

Gerry swung wildly at Peter's head, but the demon easily side-stepped the attempt.

I need to get out of here. I need to help Gerry. Kelly silently pleaded for her body to respond.

Kelly couldn't seem to clear her mind long enough

to focus. She needed to coax her body to sync with her mind. She couldn't teleport and she still couldn't hear her siblings. She lurched forward in an awkward swim to a nearby metal ladder that ran up the side of the dock. She pulled herself up, one painful movement after another. She crested the top in time to see Peter stab Gerry in the heart and slice downward essentially ripping her charge open. Gerry was dead before his body collapsed onto the pier.

"NO!" Kelly yelled in desperation as she fumbled her way over the top of the railing, her knees smacking down hard on the wooden planks.

Peter walked back to the lifeless body of Jacob. Yanking up the dead Arch Angel's arm he taunted Kelly. "You can't win Guardian," Peter mocked. "I'm invincible." He took his sabre and with one swift movement he cut off Jacob's left hand at the wrist. "I told you they'd pay."

Kelly's anger propelled her to her feet. She stumbled forward into a wild run toward Peter. "I'll rip you apart with my bare hands demon!"

Peter laughed. "Stay angry!" He inhaled deeply. "It makes me strong."

Just as she reached his position, he vanished. She could once again hear her siblings as they were yelling for Deb to return.

"The Boatyard now!" Kelly screamed to her family. "He killed Gerry!"

Kelly bent forward feeling nauseous and fighting the desire to throw up. The small steady stream of blood that dripped down her face would have been scary if she didn't feel her siblings arriving alongside her.

"What happened?" Michael barked as he leaned

down to lend Harry a hand getting to his feet.

"Peter cloaked and attacked," Kelly muttered.

"Let's get her out of here, Gen," Dan ordered as he grabbed Kelly and went to teleport back to the house.

"No, wait," Kelly huffed. "We need to call Antonio."

"Why?" Tom asked.

"Jacob." Kelly pointed at the slumped, bloody form on the ground. "He's an Arch Angel. Harry called him here. Peter murdered him and cut off his hand."

"Oh my." Gen couldn't finish, her words failing to capture her sentiment.

"Peter just broke the Accord," Tom said in shocked surprise.

"Frankie," Michael ordered. "Go with Gen and get Kelly back to the house to heal her. Gen will need a boost since Deb is gone and must have her shield up."

"We should take Harry," Gen said. "He's hurt also."

"I'll help him." Frankie walked over to the Angel who was leaning against a boat for strength. "Dan's got Kelly, let's get moving."

"Wait," Harry told them. "Where's Gerry?"

"Harry, I'm sorry. He's right there." Kelly pointed at Gerry's lifeless form on the ground. "He's dead, Peter killed him too. It was horrific, he took a sword and nearly ripped him in two."

"I know, I witnessed it," Harry answered. "Where is he?"

Everyone scanned the boatyard. Kelly suddenly understood Harry was referring to Gerry's soul.

"Do you see the line?" Harry asked. "Because I

don't see one of Death's Sages."

"Death's Sages," Kelly shook her head. "What a ridiculously fancy term for a grim reaper."

Her siblings fanned out, some walking several rows up and around the varying boats sitting on the drydock.

"I don't see anything," Tom announced. "No line, no light of any kind. Obviously, we can't see Reapers, but with no light, it seems Death did not come for Gerry."

Kelly looked up and spotted Gerry sitting on his boat. With his back to the grisly scene Gerry opted to face the ocean instead. "There." Kelly pointed. "He's up there."

Xavier was closest, with his athletic five-foot nine frame he easily hopped up onto the boat and approached Gerry. "You'll need to come with us."

"Why?" Gerry asked him.

"We need to leave, do you understand?" Xavier asked.

"No," Gerry replied simply.

Xavier spoke to his siblings telepathically: *I've seen this before in violent deaths, Gerry's confused, in shock. Give me a minute with him.*

Xavier sat next to Gerry and stared out at the ocean.

"It's beautiful here Gerry," Xavier told him. "I can see why you spent so much time here, working on your boat."

"Yeah," Gerry sighed. "It was my happy place, but now—" Gerry stole a glance behind him, seeing his slumped human body in a pool of his own blood caused him to turn back quickly toward the ocean. "Why did this happen? What's going to happen now? My poor daughter she'll have to live with the agony of me dying out here like this, a victim of violence, it's not right."

"Gerry," Xavier's hazel eyes fell empathically on Gerry. "Your children will think you died of the heart attack you were meant to die of months ago. Humans will not see the condition your body's in now. The violence you experienced, the assault was against your soul Gerry, not your body."

Xavier let a moment of silence pass before he continued. "I'm sorry Gerry, we can talk more, but we need to leave. It's not safe here now."

"It's not safe anywhere, is it?" Gerry said rhetorically.

"Death isn't coming for him." Harry realized and told the group, "He's out of sync with his ending. We need to make this right and get him where he needs to be."

"Xavier," Tom yelled. "We should move, a person in Gerry's situation is a target. We need to get him somewhere safe."

"Well, that isn't our house," Kelly mumbled.

"We can take him to Harry's beach house," Xavier replied.

"Good, get him out of here," Tom answered.

"What about Jacob?" Kelly asked Harry. "We can't leave him here."

"No, we mustn't leave him here alone," Harry answered. "Greg, please take Jacob and go with Xavier to the cottage."

Dan pulled Kelly back to the house she shared with her sisters in Boston. Kelly immediately collapsed into a chair at the kitchen table. Gen and Frankie used their powers to partially heal her. Her wound was sealed and with clarity came a pounding headache. Gen, even with Frankie boosting her powers, couldn't heal Kelly's wounds. For that, they needed Deb.

"Where's Deb?" Kelly murmured as she gingerly got up and labored her way to the cabinet to rummage for aspirin.

Aspirin, Kelly thought. *Just what I wasn't supposed to give Gerry.*

"She went with Leo and Lucas to look for Marcus," Gen answered.

Kelly shot Gen a hard glance over her shoulder.

Understanding the look, Gen raised her hand and added. "It's a long story."

Kelly nodded and knocked back the aspirin with a swig of whiskey to dull the pain.

All our stories are long. Just another day in the O'Mara household.

CHAPTER SEVEN

"Should we really be here?" Kelly asked.

"No," Gen huffed. "We should head to the safe house with the others, but I wanted to give you a chance to grab some clothes, maybe dry off."

"Are these all the weapons you have?" Dan didn't turn toward them. His broad shoulders blocked the view of him rummaging through the china cabinet. He had already torn through the closets in Kelly's office, and until that moment Gen had not realized what he was looking for.

"You're joking, right?" Gen asked.

Having finished ransacking the entire cabinet, Dan turned to face them. He scratched his thick beard. "What?"

"There is literally a stockpile in the basement," Gen told him. "You know Kelly's ready for war at any moment."

"War seems to break out at any moment around here," Kelly deadpanned. "I would normally happily run downstairs and give you the grand tour Dan, but I really need a quick shower. Help yourself, nothing's locked up."

Dan made his way down the hall toward the

basement door.

Chairs were pulled out and scattered around the kitchen. The whiteboard Dan had used several weeks ago had been wiped clean. The boxes of case files and old texts they were using for reference material were gone too.

Kelly had eventually returned to using her office after the battle with Sonoran, but it was practically empty now. After Tom had returned all the books to the Vatican, he stashed case files in the basement of an old church, but not St. Ann's. Even though the O'Mara family trusted Father Donovan, the church grounds were compromised after the battle with the Gutter Demons there. They asked Father Donovan to suggest another church for Tom to use. One the Priest trusted to house what he believed were case files from the Archdiocese.

This morning, after Peter was unceremoniously ousted from the house, several of Gen's brothers removed more material and personal effects from the house. They took pictures including family photos of them that Deb had framed and arranged throughout the house. Kelly's office was large with beautiful dark wood floors, light gray walls, eight-foot ceilings, and crown molding everywhere. It even had two large windows, original to the house, that let in an abundance of natural light. It was a gem, but somehow Gen missed how it used to look.

It used to feel lived in. It seems like our time here is ending, Gabe. Gen sighed. *I can't let that happen, not yet. I was hoping I might still be here when you came back to me.*

Though Gen knew her husband wouldn't hear her words, the wedding ring she wore around her finger sent him the sentiment. In return, comfort reverberated back to her. It was as if Gabriel were telling her the house wasn't what was important. She knew her husband would tell her this if he were standing in front of her.

Xavier arrived down the hallway and peeked around the corner.

"Dan found her stash." Xavier smiled his signature crooked grin.

"He called for backup?" Gen asked with a snicker.

Xavier's hazel eyes seem to sparkle with an extra splash of green. His boyish grin always reminded Gen of a child attempting to hide a big secret. "He called for a cleanup crew."

Tom and Michael arrived at that moment. They made their way to Dan in the basement, while Xavier stopped to check on Gen.

"Thanks for the heads up," Gen told him.

"You know I always have your back," he answered. "We better be quick. Kelly will be down any minute to kick our butts for hauling away her treasure."

Gen smiled. "I'll try and reason with her."

"Good luck with that." Xavier laughed as he wandered toward her.

Gen had missed her brother's laugh and the camaraderie they shared.

Pursuing the truth about Gabe made me push everyone away, Gen thought. *Even Xavier. I need to make that right.*

"Hope you find enough snacks and booze to placate her." Xavier placed a hand on Gen's shoulder and gave it an affectionate squeeze before turning back toward the basement door.

Xavier disappeared into the basement, his wavy

brown hair the last thing Gen saw before he jogged down the steps. She went back to the kitchen and began opening cabinets.

The water to the shower upstairs turned off. Gen debated teleporting to Jake's, but even with those powers it wouldn't be fast enough to get there and back before Kelly came downstairs. The only thing she found was an unopened jar of popcorn kernels. She grabbed a heavy bottom pot and quickly turned on the stove. When she opened the cabinet for the coconut oil, she saw a small bottle of popcorn seasoning.

"Caramel toffee topping will most definitely work to lessen the blow." Gen smiled.

With the oil hot, Gen dumped two test kernels in and covered the pan. When the two kernels popped, Kelly's footsteps padded down the stairs. Pouring in the remaining kernels, Gen removed the pot from the heat and waited a minute while the kernels primed without making the oil overly hot.

"What's wrong?" Kelly asked as she breezed into the kitchen.

"Nothing," Gen answered as she moved the pan back onto the lit flame of the gas stovetop. "Thought you might be hungry."

Kelly put one hand on her waist and squared off with Gen. "One, you're a terrible liar. Two, you don't like making popcorn, not even sure you like eating it."

"I do too. But I don't like the smell of microwave popcorn, that's totally different."

"Three," Kelly continued without missing a beat. "I can feel them in the basement."

"I'm sorry," Gen said. "I'm guessing they're moving your collection somewhere for safe keeping."

Kelly sighed. "I assumed it was coming the minute Dan headed downstairs. I will really miss living here, especially with all the room in the basement for me to hide my stash."

The popcorn began popping rapidly filling the room with the scent of hot oil. Gen walked to the microwave with a small glass bowl of butter she intended to melt for the popcorn.

"You're unusually calm," Gen told her. "I was expecting a revolt. I'm pretty sure they are too." Gen pointed at the door as her brother's footsteps ascending the stairs echoed into the kitchen.

"That was by far the greatest collection of medieval weaponry I've seen in one place ever," Xavier pronounced with enthusiasm.

"But," Kelly said, as a pause settled over the room.

"You probably shouldn't have had it here," Michael told her with a lot less scorn in his voice than normal.

"We moved it for safe keeping," Tom announced. "We'll bring it back when you settle into a less visited house."

"Well, Deb wanted to move out anyway," Kelly huffed. "We might as well all move out."

"No!" Gen blurted without turning to face them. "I'm not ready to give up on this house. We'll figure something else out."

The room fell silent, and Gen continued to focus on the popcorn. Pulling a giant white bowl out of the cabinet she dumped the popcorn into it. She drizzled the melted butter over the popcorn and swirled the popcorn to spread it evenly. Gen set the bowl and the bottle of topping in front of Kelly who was seated at the island.

"I know you told us before, but it's strange Deb wants to move out suddenly." Dan broke the silence, his voice steady and calm as he slid onto the stool next to Kelly. He picked up the caramel topping and shook it over the popcorn.

"Where is Deb?" Xavier asked as he retrieved several cans of soda from the fridge sliding them across the island to Kelly and Dan.

"Deb hasn't returned yet," Gen answered noticing Tom's eyebrow arch in response.

"You're worried," Tom said, as his sky-blue eyes met Gen's.

"We should go looking for her," Michael commanded as his shoulders tensed.

"Not yet," Gen answered. "If it comes to that, Kelly and I will go first."

"Kelly's not exactly in game shape," Michael commented.

"Speak for yourself," Kelly muttered with a mouth full of popcorn. "Just because I'm not kicking your ass for stealing my loot, doesn't mean I'm not ready."

To their surprise, Michael relaxed and his lips curved into a smile that seemed to reach his deep brown eyes. "Alright fine, just remember—"

Before Michael could finish, they all replied, "Don't go alone."

"Good to know the message has gotten through," Michael told them. "I'm heading back to the safe house.

Don't hang here too long, this house is compromised, and we have no idea who else knows about this place."

Tom left with Michael while Xavier and Dan stayed behind.

"Who's getting the booze?" Xavier asked.

"Depends," Kelly told him. "How many weapons did you leave me?"

Xavier laughed. "Michael told us to take them all."

Kelly's face fell, but before she could speak Dan added, "But, it was just a suggestion. We didn't take your favorites."

"No?!" Kelly's voice lilted in hope.

"Michael must not have noticed them," Dan told her.

"Yeah," Xavier added, "hard for him to notice weapons Dan stashed in the ceiling tiles.

Kelly tossed more popcorn into her mouth as the curves of a mischievous smile formed, and her eyes sparked in delight.

***

Deb huffed as she had reached her sixth dead end. She could feel the hopes of Leo and Lucas waning behind her. She didn't need to look at them, she knew they were disappointed. The park they were standing in was quiet, just a few people mulling around. If it were earlier in the day, it would be a bustle of activity. Parents bring their children here to play on the swings and get ice cream cones at the small shack at the back of the property. The day was bright with sunshine, but in the late afternoon Deb assumed the smaller crowd was due to the approaching dinner hour. Even with a dwindling crowd the three of them were sure to stay out of human view. Deb wasn't taking any chances.

How could Leo and Lucas not be disappointed? Deb thought. *I'm the one Marcus said to go to. They are expecting I can find him.*

"Looks like he's not here either," Lucas stated.

"Obviously," Leo blurted. "This is getting us nowhere. What are we doing jumping from place to place?"

"I'm sorry," Deb answered. "I had hoped with you two with me, we could tap into his connection to you, that we would have found him or at least clues to his whereabouts by now."

"Well, we're sorry too," Lucas told her. "I think it was probably a little much to expect you could do what we've been unsuccessful at these last couple of weeks."

"No," Deb quickly told them. "You were right to come to me. We just need to keep at it, keep looking."

The two brothers shared a glance and Deb knew they doubted her.

"I know you mean well," Lucas started then stopped.

"You don't know where he is or how to reach him," Leo scoffed. Lucas glared at his brother, clearly disappointed with his tone. "What?!" Leo shrugged his shoulders feigning innocence. "It's true, she doesn't know any more than we do."

"He's right," Deb said. "I don't know where he is or how to find him. Even before you came to me at the house, I had been out looking for him. I have been roaming from place to place trying to find clues as to his whereabouts, but it's like he's disappeared."

"I assume none of your siblings have tracking powers?" Lucas shook his head before the answer came.

"I'm afraid not." Deb replied.

"Do you know a Collector who will work with us?" Leo asked sardonically.

"Actually—" Deb paused feeling foolish for not having thought of it before. "That's a really good idea, Leo."

"What is?" Lucas asked. "Having a Collector look for Marcus?"

"That's actually a terrifying idea," Leo admitted.

As usual, Lucas interceded to keep things productive and on task. "You know a Collector, Deb?"

"A long time ago, I knew one of the best." Deb was unable to stop the image of Dmitri from springing forward. Her and Dmitri flirtatiously running along the beach was now a repeating thought she couldn't seem to shutoff.

Dmitri was one of the best Collectors back in the day, Deb thought, her mind spinning forty years into the past. *He rarely failed to keep his charges from Falling. He even spent time guiding the Lost.* Each time Deb thought of Dmitri, more memories became vivid, yet none of them were romantic.

"And?" Leo demanded. "Do you not know him anymore?"

"He's away," Deb muttered as she found it hard to concentrate with the receding picture of her wrapped up in Dmitri's arms still visible in her mind.

"Well," Leo deadpanned. "That's really helpful."

"Leo!" Lucas scolded. "Stop it! You're not helping."

Leo huffed. "Fine, whatever." The anxious half of the angel twins sauntered away from where she and Lucas stood.

"I understand his frustration," Deb told Lucas. "I was a little cryptic there, I wasn't trying to be. I'm just distracted."

"It doesn't look like you've slept much," Lucas told her. "We haven't either."

"I know," Deb told him. "But getting a Collector to help us is actually a good idea. Even though the person I was thinking of is not available I might know where to find other colleagues of his that could help us."

"Okay," Lucas told her. "How do we do that? I mean Collectors aren't usually for hire so to speak. I'm worried that if they do find Marcus, they might, you know—"

Keep him, Deb thought. *The Collectors must remove the Fallen from Earth, so they don't end up under the influence of Hell. Dmitri would go above and beyond to keep his charges from Falling, but not all Collectors were so patient. Leo was right, having a Collector look for Marcus was indeed a terrifying thought.*

"You have to trust me," Deb pleaded. "Unfortunately, I'm afraid I have to do this alone." Her eyes pleaded with Lucas for agreement. The last thing she wanted was to upset him further.

Leo had wandered back over and stood next to his brother. Arms crossed he seemed intent on silence.

"Alright," Lucas answered. "You promise you'll call us once you know something, anything about where Marcus is or what happened to him?"

"I will contact you as soon as I have something to share," Deb told them. "I promise."

The two Angels exchanged a look then nodded their agreement. Without another word Leo left the park.

"We do trust you, Deb," Lucas told her. "We wouldn't have come to you if we didn't. Please find him. The not knowing, it's—"

"I know." Deb's simple acknowledgement seemed to placate Lucas. His angelic orb enveloped him and then he was gone.

CHAPTER EIGHT

Gerry's soul paced on the small beach beyond Harry's cottage while Kelly stood on the deck that ran the length of the back of the house. It was quite a view of the ocean. She had left this house only days before, after Deb's mind got caught in a memory loop.

Nearly broke her, Kelly thought. *I can't imagine discovering something in a memory core that had been buried in my mind.*

All her siblings were inside the cottage except Deb. She had yet to return, and her shield was cloaking her movements. Kelly's brothers' voices rose and fell as they discussed what to do next. Harry had left the cottage about twenty minutes before to speak with Antonio in private. No doubt Harry would want time with him alone before bringing him to the cottage.

Poor Antonio, Kelly thought. *There's no amount of preparedness you can do to be ready for this kind of news. The loss of his brethren, his mentor and friend, it will be devastating.*

Jacob wasn't just a colleague to him. Antonio would say he was a brother. A confidant and respected member of the Arch Angel hierarchy. He had served in his capacity for hundreds of years, now his body lay in one of the front bedrooms. Genevieve and Xavier washed Jacob's body, with the blood now gone they covered him reverently with clean sheets. Xavier used white bandages around his severed wrist to shroud his missing hand.

Genevieve cut white hydrangeas and wild roses from the surrounding bushes and placed them across the lifeless Arch Angel's chest. Harry had anointed Jacob's forehead with Holy Oil and wrapped a long strand of old wooden rosary beads around his waistline.

Outside, Kelly's eyes never left the beach. She was worried about Gerry. Everything he had been through in the last few months was traumatic enough, but now he'd been murdered by an upper-level demon and Death didn't come for him.

That's enough to make anyone restless, Kelly thought.

Gerry stopped pacing and looked up at the sky and then back toward Kelly.

What is it, Gerry? Kelly thought *What are you anticipating?*

Kelly wondered if Gerry could sense Harry and Antonio arriving back at the cottage.

That would be pretty amazing if Gerry could feel them coming when we can't, Kelly mused. *Who or what are you, Gerry?*

Just as Kelly was about to teleport down onto the beach to inquire further, Genevieve came out onto the deck to join her.

"Everything alright out here?" Gen asked.

"I think so," Kelly answered. "Gerry was pacing,

but then stopped and peered up at the sky, then over toward me."

Gen looked at Gerry who was once again looking up at the sky.

"You think he feels Harry returning with Antonio?" Gen asked.

"That's what I was just wondering. It would be more evidence that Gerry is special. More reason to keep him close, figure out why he's not moving on."

The wind picked up and the seagulls that had been bathing themselves on the salt rocks shot into the air and started squawking. The trees swayed and the leaves rattled against one another in an almost musical response.

"I think something is most definitely coming." Kelly spoke loud enough for her brothers still inside the house to hear.

One by one, her brothers appeared on the long deck. Walking to the railing they all peered down at the beach. Gerry looked up at the house once more. Kelly assumed he sensed all of them staring down at him. Gerry stared upward as the sky darkened and rumbled. Squirrels scurried further into the woodland area nearby, as more birds flew up and away from the beach.

"Antonio must not be coming alone," Tom announced.

"We're sure it's Antonio and not Peter, right?" Xavier asked.

Before anyone could answer, the sound of flapping grew louder as dark objects in the sky descended toward them. A sea of swirling red obliterated the sun.

"Oh my," Kelly said in a near whisper, as

goosebumps rode along her arms. "I've never seen so many."

"I've never seen their wings out," Xavier confessed.

"It's majestic and imposing," Gen said in awe.

Arch Angels swooshed down from above and hovered in the air above the beach, their brilliant wings the color of the deepest red wine flapping up and down to keep them afloat.

Kelly was mesmerized. There had to be at least thirty. They were beautiful and striking, male and female Arch Angels lined up with military precision in the sky, adorned in full regalia. The females in lilac and white colored robes that seem to dance in the wind created by their vivid wings. Each female held a sword in one hand and a lit lantern in the other. Symbols of escorting Jacob through the darkened journey from death to the fullness of light in Heaven. The males wore dark purple cloaks, with golden helmets and large shields that hung across one arm. In the other hand they held oversized palm branches that swayed in the breeze. It was a massive gathering designed to show respect and fraternal kinship.

This is God's Army, Kelly thought. *They're here to bring Jacob home, another loss in this infernal war.*

Kelly was brought out of her reverie at the sight of Gerry taking the stairs back up to the cottage two at a time. His pace betraying his fear at the enormity of the procession in the sky.

"He's frightened," Tom said

"I don't blame him," Kelly answered as she scooted around her brothers and over toward the top of the stairs.

"What in the name of sweet Jesus is happening?"

Gerry said panting, his breathing labored.

"It's alright Gerry," Kelly said, as he neared her position. "Don't be afraid, they're just here to collect Jacob."

Gerry reached the top and spun around to see Antonio land on the deck beside Harry who was just teleporting back to the house.

"Antonio." Kelly's eyes watered as she looked upon her friend's broken expression. His normal pleasant demeanor clouded in sorrow. His eyes rimmed red and raw as though he had cried a thousand tears already.

"Where is he?" Antonio asked. "Where's our fallen brother?"

"He's in the front bedroom," Michael answered. "I'll take you to him."

Antonio walked toward Kelly. His shoulders sunk as if he were being pulled to the ground by an invisible force. He took Kelly's outstretched hand and squeezed it. "I'm so sorry Antonio."

There's nothing we can say to him to make this easier. Kelly knew all words were insufficient now.

He nodded in response as his wings curled inward, shrunk, and disappeared into his back. "I appreciate you all watching over him until we could come."

Kelly choked back the desire to cry. Antonio followed Michael into the house.

A few moments later, Antonio carried the limp body of Jacob from the house. Two Arch Angels flew to the railing and covered the lifeless body with a purple cloak that mimicked their own, except across the top was the white outline of a dove in flight. Antonio handed Jacob's limp body over to one of them. The Arch Angel folded his wings around Jacob while the other Arch Angel began to sing. The song was in a language Kelly could not understand, but it was beautiful. The two ascended skyward reverently. The other Arch Angels waited for them to pass before joining behind them in a virtual parade to the Heavens.

"Angels?" Gerry questioned openly as he stared up into the sky.

"Yes," Harry responded. "Arch Angels."

Gerry looked at Harry and then back toward the sky. "Their wings—"

"Beautiful aren't they," Harry said. "They came to retrieve one of their own in a ceremonial way, out of respect."

"Yes, they are miraculous, but why are their wings that color and not white?" Gerry asked.

"Because our power comes from the Lamb of God," Antonio answered. "Our very essence is the lifeblood that pumps through those wings."

There was a moment of silence before Antonio spoke again. He peered at Kelly. "Harry summarized what happened. But I need to hear it from you my friend. Tell me what happened, Kelly?"

Kelly's heart nearly broke as she looked at Antonio, his brow furrowed with concern. "It happened so fast."

"Who did this to my brother?" Antonio asked.

"A demon who told us his name is Peter," Michael answered. "He showed up at the house my sisters share and announced he was there with the rendering of the Verdict."

"Nonsense!" Antonio snapped the response, his

voice echoing with anger. "There is no case, therefore, no Verdict. How did he know about it?"

"He didn't elaborate," Michael told him. "He left in a huff after making several threats to all three of our sisters' charges."

"Jacob wasn't the only victim today," Harry added. "Gerry, he was Kelly's charge, he was also murdered by the demon."

Antonio looked at Gerry finally piecing together who he was. "Death did not come for you?"

Gerry stood staring at Antonio, clearly unsure how to respond.

"No," Kelly finally answered. "Jacob was called because we were hoping he could help us understand why Gerry could see and speak with Harry and me when he was human."

Antonio's gaze flew back toward Gerry, and he peered more closely at her charge. "What is he?"

Gerry raised his hands in the air. "Just a man. I mean, I was just a man."

"Did Jacob have a theory?" Antonio asked.

"If he did, he didn't have the chance to tell us," Kelly told her friend.

Antonio turned back toward Kelly. "I want to be kept informed of the investigation. We will obviously conduct one ourselves, but please let me know right away if you figure out who this Peter is." Antonio raised his finger in the air. "He must be brought to justice!"

"Of course!" Kelly raised her palms face up. "You'll be the first to know—"

Michael interrupted her. "Why the left hand,

Antonio? What would Peter want with Jacob's left hand."

Antonio whipped his head around toward Michael and took two steps toward him. "What are you talking about?"

Kelly knew a lesser being would have taken a step back. To Michael's credit he took a small step forward. "Peter cut off Jacob's left hand at the wrist and took it with him, why?"

Antonio's face crumbled, his head jerking backward. He was horrified at the thought of Jacob's body being mutilated. His eyes darted to the ground and his head shook slightly as if unwilling to believe Michael.

Kelly's heart ached. Her friend seemed unable to comprehend what Michael was telling him. She took a step forward, but Antonio put his hand out in front of him as if to keep all at bay.

"I have to go." Antonio stepped away from Michael and his wings burst free from his back spreading wide up and into the air.

"Antonio, wait!" Kelly yelled. "Don't leave like this, we need to talk, and you could use our help."

He bent his right knee forward preparing to leap into the air. Michael quickly stepped between them and grabbed the Arch Angel's left forearm elevating it into the air where all of them could see.

The two Heavenly beings locked eyes. The world seemed to stand still as Kelly's breath caught in her throat. Xavier and Frankie changed positions lining up next to Michael.

What are you doing Michael? Kelly pleaded to her brother telepathically. *Leave him be, can't you see the pain he's in?*

"What can Peter do with this?" Michael asked as the thick gold band around Antonio's left ring finger gleamed in the sunlight.

There would be no answer. Antonio yanked his arm away and swept himself up into the air soaring skyward, never turning back.

CHAPTER NINE

Deb stood underneath the darkened doorway of a closed corner shop in Beckinshire, England. In its heyday Beckinshire was a bustling manufacturing town located seventy kilometers northeast of London. The boarded-up windows indicated the neighborhood had seen better days. The incessant rain dampened the small space she was occupying making it feel colder.

When she first arrived in the town about an hour previous, the sun had already set. Heavy cloud cover quickly rolled in and brought with it a typical England rainstorm. The rain had kept people's eyes downward as they scurried over the cobblestone streets. Deb had taken many a turn before she found what she was looking for. Stopping inside this small enclosure gave her a good view to evaluate things.

The only cars on the street in front of her appeared to be undriveable. Glass littered the ground from broken car windows; one vehicle was missing both front tires. Everything about the town seemed covered in a thick haze of dust, like an old vase left upon a shelf uncared for and forgotten for far too long. The breeze carried with it an unpleasant aroma blending fuel, curry, and urine.

Petrol they call it here, Deb thought as she grimaced. *I wish the smell were stronger; compared to the other two it would be preferable.*

Of the six visible lampposts only three were lit. The one closest to the building Deb was surveying flickered every few minutes, like a dying heartbeat about to be extinguished.

Just like the soul of this town.

She wasn't in human view and she was still projecting her shield, something she knew she'd have to drop if she wanted to get past the defensive shield around the run-down warehouse across the street.

The three-story structure was one of two, it's twin to the left was in better shape, but neither appeared operational. A fifteen-foot alley separated the two gray stone buildings. The opening was visible from the street, but not its activities. Any light from the moon or stars was blocked by thick clouds that fed the rain.

She peered at the warehouse to her right. Even the graffiti covering part of the front was worn and faded. The words were a mishmash of shapes as new paint had been sprayed over old to create a mosaic the sun had dulled over time. Wooden boards hung haphazardly over what used to be windows. No lights appeared to be on inside and what she presumed to be the entrance was not on the street side. The only door was at the far end of the long building, requiring an individual to walk down the unlit alley to access it.

Like walking into the belly of the beast, Deb thought.

The gravel lot behind the buildings had been

reclaimed by nature. It was now a nest of overgrown weeds, toppled barrels, and littered debris. Makeshift firepits and garbage dotted the landscape like castaway streamers from a party long ago.

An old sign lay broken and bent in a heap in front of the building; time had eroded most of the letters. Deb pieced together it had once been known as The Last Refuge.

Doesn't exactly give me the warm and fuzzies, Deb thought. *It's not like I'm going to call Kelly to accompany me. Her and Gen are probably mad I haven't returned home, best to wait until my emotions aren't in the way of a logical argument for what I am doing.*

Deb shifted her position and rubbed the back of her neck trying to stretch out the kinks. She had been standing there a good thirty minutes, but no one had entered or exited the building.

I feel tired right down to my bones. A yawn escaped her lips.

She was feeling the aftershock of her encounter with Peter, but she knew leaving now was just an excuse not to go inside. This was supposed to be neutral territory for Heaven and Hell. A rare place to cross the divide with no questions asked. A space to negotiate or trade for services.

It doesn't look like Switzerland, Deb thought dryly.

There was no reason for those from Heaven to frequent a place like this; most would consider it beneath them. Coming here looking for a Collector was a longshot.

The entities inside, Deb bemoaned, *are probably from Hell. I'm more likely to walk out with a demon who can track, than to find a Collector from Heaven.*

Shaking her head slightly as if she could scatter her

anxiety away, she stood taller, took a deep breath, and coughed.

Oh man the smell here is rancid.

Straightening, Deb tried to bolster herself. "I got this," she whispered. "I'm going to walk in and find a Collector to help me find Marcus. Easy."

Taking a few steps forward out onto the street, Deb hesitated at the sound of hastening footsteps. Looking right, a female approached. Before she had the chance to sway the person to turn back the figure veered right and stepped off the sidewalk heading in the direction of the warehouse and adjacent alley.

The female was young. She appeared to be a teenager wearing navy blue leggings, a bright yellow sweatshirt and worn-out sneakers. The teen picked up her pace and her long black air swung in response.

What is she doing? Deb thought.

The girl had come close enough to Deb for her to sense she wasn't human.

What are you? Deb mused. *Probably not someone that should be entering that building alone. If I'm hesitating, you probably should too.*

The young female made it through the alley unimpeded and banged loudly on the wooden plank covering the opening. A door swung open, but Deb couldn't see who was on the other side. After a brief exchange of words, the girl stepped inside, and the door slammed shut behind her.

Well, that was unexpected. I thought she would be turned away. Maybe this place has changed. Perhaps they are less discerning who they allow in. It has been a long time since I've been here.

Deb couldn't remember exactly when she was here last, but she knew it was decades, not years. Hence why it took her time to locate it again. The boarded-up door swung back open with force. The door ricocheted against the stone exterior and snapped back toward those exiting. The young female was unceremoniously being hauled outside by her arm. Even at this distance Deb could sense the male was demonic. He shoved the teen up against the neighboring building's facade. Deb couldn't hear the conversation, but she could tell by the tone it was anything but pleasant.

The female held her hands up in front of her face and yelled out.

"Leave me alone, demon."

The female attempted to shove her attacker, but he towered over her by at least a foot and probably a hundred pounds or more.

The male snickered and goosebumps rose along her arms.

"Your kind isn't welcome here," the demon yelled in her face.

The female kneed the brute between the legs and took off running toward the street. The male took only a few strides to catch up to her. Grabbing her, he pulled her up off her feet. Closer to the street, Deb could clearly see the female's face. The male had a large chunk of her hair. Tears escaped her eyes as they filled with terror.

She's over her head, Deb thought.

Briskly, Deb walked across the street and dropped her shield in front of them as the girl hung nearly frozen in the air.

"Why don't you pick on someone your own size, demon." Deb's voice was calm, determined.

The Demon swung his large bulky arm to the left and the female tumbled out of his grasp rolling to a violent stop to Deb's right.

"What do you want?" he asked. "She with you? You should tell your friend that not all of us from Hell have the same anatomy."

"I'll be sure to explain your inadequate manhood to her later," Deb quipped.

He didn't retort, he just lunged. His broad shoulders and bulging neck were indications he trained often. The girl scrambled to her feet.

"Look out," the teen warned.

Deb adeptly slid out of the way, unsheathing the dagger she had stashed in the inside of her raincoat. Before he could recover Deb swung the blade down across his chest. His shirt tore open. The black patchiness of his skin revealed what he was, a vampire.

Deb hadn't encountered a vampire for many decades. In her memory, they were fiercely trained soldiers making up Hell's First Army. Unlike how the humans portrayed them, vampires didn't have fangs or fear sunlight. They more resembled the Spartan army from the 5th Century BC. They did, however, consume human blood to maintain their strength and vitality. At least they did until the Amendment to the Heaven/Hell Accord was enacted.

The old scars of battle had healed on this vampire, but without consuming the essence found in human blood they were burnt and marred. Deb swung again and managed to break open the skin under the most mutilated of his scars.

He growled and stepped back using his hand to stem the bleeding.

"You're going to pay for that," he sneered.

"I doubt it," a female voice echoed from behind the vampire. "You guys need better lines."

Deb pushed down the wave of relief welling up. Kelly had arrived further down in the alley. She was wearing all black; Deb had to squint to make out her sister's profile. Kelly held a knife in each hand, a clear indication she came prepared for a fight.

Glancing back at Kelly, the vampire snickered. "Well, aren't you a pretty young thing."

Kelly sucker punched the vampire in the face and then used her left shoulder to knock him into the wall.

Turning to her right Deb spotted Gen standing behind her.

"What's going on here, Deb?" Gen asked.

"A little misunderstanding between these two, that's all," Deb answered as she turned back toward the vampire.

"Someone else is coming," the teenager announced.

The metal door creaked at the end of the alleyway and Deb stole a glance in that direction.

"I take it there's a problem here," the newly arrived male declared as he proceeded to head in their direction.

Kelly turned her back on the wounded vampire to face the entity coming toward them.

"You should go back to whatever cell you just

crawled out of," Kelly warned.

The newly arriving male wore a suit and held his hands up in front of him as if to surrender.

"No need for those, Guardian," he said to Kelly.

Deb was confused, the male seemed to be attempting to quell the situation. He was as hulking as the vampire, but there were no scars, in fact his face was almost too pretty for a demon. He wore his black hair cropped and he was clean shaven.

"Garrick, go back inside and finish your drink," he ordered of the vampire.

"She started it," Garrick stated as he pointed at Deb. "I'm going to finish it."

"There is no fighting on the grounds!" he scowled at the vampire. "You know the arrangement. Now, go back inside or they won't be the only ones asked to leave."

With a grunt, Garrick walked toward the door. He scoffed at Kelly on his way by and she sneered back.

"What are you, the vampire whisperer?" Kelly remarked to the newly arrived male figure.

"No, I'm Ray and I'm simply trying to enforce the rules and regulations. If you don't know them, then you probably shouldn't—"

"I thought this place was neutral," Deb interrupted.

"It is," the male answered as he lowered his hands and shrugged slightly. "Mostly."

Deb chuckled sarcastically. "Good to know."

"I'm afraid you'll all need to leave now." He nodded toward the street. "If you visit again, it's expected you'll be less, shall we say, aggressive."

The demon turned and walked toward the door,

following Garrick back inside.

"You're Guardians?" The teenager asked from behind her. "Why did they just leave? What do you mean by neutral?"

"I would like to know all those things and more," Kelly said, shooting a quick glance at Deb. "Let's start by making our way back toward the street. I assume this place has cameras since Ray knew to come out and rescue the vampire."

Deb followed Gen and the teen out onto the street where they turned left and walked a half block up. The teen's shiny black hair was wet from the rain and hung straight to the middle of her back. When she stopped walking and turned back, Deb noticed her long black eye lashes and olive skin. She was naturally beautiful, even in casual clothes and an unmade face.

Deb asked the teen a series of questions. "What were you doing in there? Aggressive, what did he mean by that? Did you go inside to start a fight?"

Before the teen could answer Gen interrupted. "Maybe we could start with who she is?" The teen's big brown eyes swung in Gen's direction. "What's your name?"

"Why do I have to answer all the questions first. I didn't ask for your help." The teen looked back at Deb. "I went into the club looking for a friend."

"That was foolish and dangerous," Deb commented.

"Yes, Mom," the girl remarked sarcastically. "But, like you, I didn't have a lot of options."

"What do you mean, like me?" Deb asked.

"You're here, aren't you?" The teen deadpanned.

Kelly chuckled. "Good one."

Deb smiled and her shoulders relaxed a bit. "I guess I am. I'm Deb and these are my sisters, Kelly and Gen."

"My name's Gardenia." The girl eyed Deb cautiously. "Thank you, you know for stepping in. I didn't know he was a vampire until I saw the black scars on his chest. It was only recently that I came to learn that vampires were real. Do they have fangs and drink human blood?"

"They don't have fangs," Kelly answered. "When they want your blood, they just slice you open. They're soldiers, or at least they were until the Accord Amendment. Now, they don't really have a purpose and human blood is toxic to them."

Deb noticed Gardenia's sweatshirt was torn and grew concerned. "Are you alright Gardenia? Did he hurt you?"

The girl's eyebrows furrowed as she looked down at the torn front pocket of her sweatshirt. "This was already torn."

"Do you want to tell me what happened in there?" Deb asked.

"It doesn't matter anymore, I found what I was looking for," Gardenia responded.

"And what was that?" Gen asked.

"A Guardian," Gardenia replied. "Any chance your last name is O'Mara, and you make your home in Boston?"

"Seriously?!" Kelly squealed.

Deb was taken aback, she had never seen Gardenia before, at least not that she could remember.

Is this another thing I've forgotten? Deb agonized. *How*

many are there? How many more lost memories do I have?

"I'm guessing by the reaction that's a yes," Gardenia told her.

"Yes," Deb mustered. "I'm sorry, I don't remember you. Have we met?"

"No, but we have a mutual friend," Gardenia told her. "And he told me if anything ever happened to him, that I should find you. Actually, he told me there was a good chance you might find me. It appears he was right."

"Who?" Deb asked sensing the answer before it came.

"Marcus," Gardenia responded. "I think he's missing."

"Oh boy," Kelly muttered.

Deb stepped forward and guided Gardenia further away from her sisters for a private moment with the teen. Thankfully, they didn't object, though Deb couldn't miss the scowl on Gen's face.

"How do you know Marcus?" Deb asked.

"He helps me sometimes." Gardenia nervously looked back over her shoulder at Kelly and Gen. "You know when things get a little scary. It's not the easiest thing to be neutral out here."

"Neutral," Deb sighed. "That's why I couldn't sense what you were, you're one of the Lost."

"Don't call me that!" Gardenia took a half step back. "I'm not lost!"

"I'm sorry," Deb relented. "I didn't mean to offend you."

"That's why I liked Marcus; he didn't judge me." Gardenia's eyes watered. "He listened, he understood. I mean what's so bad about not choosing between Heaven or Hell. This is not my fight and I want no part of it."

"Gardenia, I'm sorry and I want to talk to you, really I do," Deb paused trying to gauge how close the teen was from fleeing. "I need to find Marcus. Do you have anything that can help me do that?"

"He said he loved you." Gardenia's tone softened. "He said I could trust you and your family. He told me not to go to you unless something happened to him. You agree with me, you think he's missing too, don't you?"

"I do." Deb sighed. "I used to be able to find Marcus with little effort. I have been all over the place looking for him, not just me, but others have been helping me search as well. This place." Deb pointed back at the warehouse. "It was a risk, even for me and I have powers. I don't want you to come back here, understand?"

"Yeah." Gardenia nodded. "He gave me something to give you. I guess now's as good a time as any."

Gardenia pulled out a solid round object and handed it to Deb. It was about the size of a US half dollar, but heavier. The outer edges of the object were designed in a floral pattern. Deb guessed it was an old coin, the main part of which was decorated with ancient symbols on both sides. The etchings were raised. Deb ran her fingers over them, but she couldn't decipher any of the markings.

"I'm guessing he didn't tell you what it was?" Deb asked.

"No," Gardenia answered. "He said you'd figure it out. He had faith in you."

"We should get out of here," Gen yelled over to them.

"What is that Deb?" Kelly asked. "Feel like sharing?"

Deb nodded to Gardenia. "Thank you. Let's go rejoin my sisters."

Walking back toward her sisters Deb nodded toward Gen. "You're right, we should get out of here."

Deb handed the coin to Kelly. "You ever seen anything like this?"

Kelly took the coin and flipped it over a couple of times. "No, but the symbols are Aramaic. I recognize some, but not enough to tell you what it says." She handed the coin back to Deb who placed it in her pocket.

"Please take Gardenia home for me. Get her out of this rain," Deb pleaded.

"What?" Kelly asked. "No way, you're coming with us, you have no idea what's been going on Deb!"

"She's not safe here and I have to finish something," Deb remarked.

"Deb, you seriously have no idea what's been happening with Peter," Gen told her.

"Who's Peter?" Gardenia asked.

Ignoring Gardenia's question Gen continued. "We really need you to come with us Deb, so much has happened just since you left this morning."

"I don't care about Peter!" The now familiar well of anger swelled to the surface once more. "You are all focused on chasing another demon, that's fine. Marcus saved Kelly's life, that used to mean something to this family."

"Fine!" Kelly threw her arms in the air, clearly annoyed. "Whatever it is I will go with you and then we'll go back to the house and get this all sorted."

"No!" Deb announced. "You don't even believe in what I'm doing. Why should I accept help from someone who doesn't trust my instincts?" Deb paused. "You know what, don't answer that, it doesn't matter. I'm not going to stop until I find Marcus, and I'm starting to not care how I have to do it. I doubt you can say the same, Kell."

Deb teleported away, wrapping her shield around herself as a cloak. She knew that would keep them from seeing or sensing her, so she landed in front of the doorway across the street where she had originally been observing the warehouse.

"Are you kidding me?!" Kelly exclaimed. "Seriously, I am going to kick her butt once she stands still long enough!"

Despite the distance Deb could hear her sisters' exasperated plea.

"We need to go," Gen argued. "Deb's not stupid, she knows if we tell her what's been going on with Peter it might change her mind. Right now, she's not going to stop looking for Marcus and being oblivious to everything else is going to help her do that."

Gen turned and grabbed Gardenia's hand and teleported. Kelly looked around one last time as if committing the place to memory and then left as well.

"Thank you," Deb whispered. "Now that I have more information, I have confidence Marcus is truly missing."

CHAPTER TEN

*N*ow or never, Deb told herself. *I need to find Marcus, and this is the only place I can hire something from Hell with tracking abilities.*

She stepped out onto the street once again feeling confident that her sisters were truly gone. She crossed the street, reached the end of the alleyway, pushed the board aside, and yanked the door open. She entered the building, but before her eyes had a chance to adjust to the lack of light she was attacked. A large hulking figure grabbed her by the arm and yanked her through an open doorway. Thrust up against a wall she was lifted off the ground. Deb squinted as the beam of a flashlight illuminated her face.

"You're lucky I don't just slice you open right here," the male threatened. "Drink your precious blood and truly heal my wounds."

Garrick, Deb agonized.

A wave of panic washed over her, but she pushed through it. Deb kicked wildly and slammed both fists down upon the rubbery arm that held her tight. The male figure groaned and let go of the fistful of clothing he held knotted to keep her upright. Once she was back on solid ground, Deb pulled out her dagger and zeroed in on her attacker. With her vision adjusted, Deb took in his enormous size once more. He was more than six feet tall, with a thick neck, long hair, and bulging muscles. He had changed the shirt Deb had ripped open with her blade.

He took a threatening step forward and she used her shield to push him back.

"Again!" He yelled, "Using your powers in here is a violation!"

"What about attacking guests, where does that rate on the regulation scale?" Deb nearly spit her reply, angry that he had laid hands on her.

"Whatever," he snorted. "Where are your friends? I'd like to buy a drink for that sassy one with the knives."

"She's out of your league," Deb huffed. "Besides if you tried throwing her up against a wall, as you apparently do to all females, she'd kill you."

"Yeah." He grinned revealing shockingly white teeth. "I think I'd like to see her try."

"I'm looking for a Collector, or someone with the ability to track," Deb replied ignoring his crude commentary about Kelly.

"You're not going to find a Collector in here," he chuckled. "The only things inside are from Hell. Last Collector in here left a path of destruction management will never forget."

"Fine," Deb told him. "An entity from Hell with the ability to track it is."

"You know what, why don't you go on in. With your smart mouth you're bound to find trouble. If you're looking to hire help," he pointed left, "take the elevator down to the second floor and ask for Mac."

"There is a functioning elevator in this building?" Deb replied dryly.

"Ahh," Garrick chuckled. "You ain't never been here before, explains the rude entrance. Next time knock three times on the front door, and you won't get attacked upon entering."

Deb looked around, though her eyesight had adjusted to the lighting it was still very dark. "Where's the—"

As if on cue a light went off above a door and the chime of an elevator sounded. She walked toward it, sliding the dagger back inside her coat. When the door opened, she stepped inside and marveled at the gold railing, red carpet, and jewel-encrusted ceiling.

She tried to compose herself as she hit the button labeled L2.

"Have a lovely evening, Guardian," Garrick told her with a smirk. "I'm sure we'll meet again soon."

The vampire turned and headed toward the exit as the elevator doors closed. The thumping of bass reverberated through the floor. The elevator slowed to a smooth stop, dinged, and the doors opened.

Deb was shocked, and it took effort to keep her mouth from falling open in awe.

How is this possible? She wondered as she stepped out into a grand foyer made of marble. The ceiling seemed to stretch to the street level above. Perhaps it did.

Turning right, recessed lighting was everywhere. The walls were covered with tapestries and large gold-framed artwork of varying sizes. Tobacco and alcohol scents lingered in the air. There was a carpet runner in a rich chocolate brown that led up the wide hallway. Leather furniture and small glass side tables dotted the walkway.

There were several closed doors along the hallway, including the double doors at the end. Two beings, one male, one female, guarded the entrance. Both wore scowls with their near-matching suits. The male was Ray, the one who broke up the fight in the alleyway with Garrick. Flashing light flickered through the small opening under the doors, and thumping music grew louder as she approached.

Ray began walking in her direction.

Deb glanced from side to side as she strode confidently past the closed doors lining the hallway but sensed nothing coming from the interior.

The rooms could be cloaked, Deb thought unpleasantly. *That wouldn't be a good sign.*

Ray met her halfway. "Please remember the rules, Guardian. We don't tolerate fighting in the club."

"Yes, I remember. Thanks."

"Good," he said, with what she assumed was a fake smile. "Now, what's your business?"

"I'm looking for Mac," she told him.

He took a moment as if pondering how to respond, then he turned back toward the entrance and opened the doors for her.

"Mac's on bar tonight," the female snorted as Deb passed her. "Good luck."

Deb glanced at the female, and sensed danger. Demonic letters in cursive writing were tattooed along the female's neck, but Deb didn't know what they meant. The female guard had long brown hair on one side of her head while the other half was shaved close. She had piercing blue eyes that seemed to leer at Deb with plump lips she painted purple. Ray was harder to detect. He was clean-cut, but Deb couldn't read if he was from Heaven or Hell, or maybe he was neutral. It was possible, anything was in their world.

The bar was much darker than the hallway. The walls were gray with large wooden beams cutting across the ceiling. The lights were dimmed, and the oak dance floor was overcrowded with entities of all kinds. Sensations of danger bombarded Deb from every direction. Her stomach clenched and her head spun, but she pressed on.

The bar was rectangular in shape and made with a rich dark wood. The large shelving unit behind the bar was more than ten feet tall with a ladder attached to a rail at the top to allow the bartenders access to the top shelves. There were two openings with no shelves where mirrors ran the length of the unit. The barstools were made of thick cushioned black leather and every seat was taken.

Several bartenders worked behind the bar; almost all of them were female. Deb noticed each had easy access to a stash of weapons located on a lower shelf. There was everything one would need to defend against an attack from either Heaven or Hell: knives, makeshift clubs, and bottles of what she assumed was real Holy Water, not the symbolic water used in churches by humans. Jars of Hellfire venom swirled and glowed inside a glass jar—like a living organism, Hell's essence never stopped moving.

Taking in the clientele, Deb worked to calm her elevated heartrate. The place was crawling with Hellish figures. There were vampires, Roamer Demons, and Hollows everywhere. All appeared dressed for a formal evening out. Deb glanced down at her own attire feeling woefully underdressed—black jeans, a light pink blouse, beat-up boots, and a gray raincoat.

Someone tapped Deb on the shoulder. Startled Deb swung around quickly.

"May I assist you, Guardian?" The woman raised her voice over the music.

"Yes," Deb said loudly, trying to appear calm as if she'd done this a thousand times. "I'm looking for Mac."

The female was wearing red from head to toe. Her suit, her high heels, even her fingernails were painted red. Her short blonde hair was slicked back and tucked behind her ears. The woman's piercing blue eyes examined Deb. The female glanced toward Deb's old boots and then back up to her face.

"Mac is a little busy," the female replied. "As you can see, we have a full house. Perhaps I can help."

The statement was polished and polite, but underneath Deb could sense an uneasiness.

"I need a Tracker." Deb decided on bluntness; get in and get out.

The woman smiled thinly and then extended her arm out in front of her motioning for Deb to move away from the bar and back toward the entrance doors.

"Please," the woman pleaded. "Come with me, it will be easier for us to hear each other in the hallway. I don't think you understand the hiring protocols for this establishment."

"No?" Deb asked mockingly as she stayed rooted in

place. "Do I need to sign a non-disclosure agreement?"

"Look." The woman's voice was menacing. "I am trying to be polite, but you're not going to find anyone to assist you here."

"Why is that?" Deb yelled defensively. "No one is interested in a fair trade this evening. If I can't come to a neutral place to hire a Tracker, where can I go?"

The two guards that let her in swiveled their heads and began moving toward them.

"You're not exactly welcome here anymore," the woman in red told her. "I suggest you leave."

"Leave?" Deb bellowed mockingly. "I'm just getting started."

Using her shield as she did this morning, Deb pushed the two figures from the doorway back several feet. Then she thrust her hand toward the bar. She had no idea which item would fall, she hadn't mastered her newly discovered power, but anything by the bar would surely break easily with a little nudge. Releasing the power welling up inside her, bottles smashed as they fell off shelves and crashed onto the floor. The woman in red swore under her breath and began looking around for backup.

Deb's power knocked over glasses and broke one of the mirrors behind the bar. The female bartender closest to them squealed and sprinted away from the dust plume. Stunned customers halted their conversations and turned toward Deb. The music scratched and then stopped.

"I'm looking for a Tracker," Deb announced loudly when the room grew quiet.

Someone rushed to grab Deb from behind and

bounced off her shield. She sent the male demon flying backward. He landed with a hard thud, breaking a small side table along the way.

"Enough!" the woman in red yelled at Deb. "You are not welcome here Guardian, no one is going to help you. Your shield might work now, but it won't work forever."

Deb's time was up, she had to hope if a Tracker were in the room that he or she would follow her outside.

"Fine." Deb held up her hands in surrender.

Deb hastened her step toward the exit. As she reached the double doors a hand pierced her shield, grabbed her shoulder, and spun her back around.

Standing before her was a tall male with clear skin, dressed in a black suit and red tie. His eyes gave away his identity. A dark red ring encircled each of his irises. She knew there was only one entity in all of Heaven and Hell that had eyes like his. A restored vampire. He loomed over her with broad shoulders and a throbbing vein in his neck indicating he thirsted for her blood.

"Too late, Guardian." The vampire smirked. "I'm going to have you for din—"

"Stop!" the demand came from the far end of the bar, furthest from where Deb was standing.

The vampire grimaced and took a tentative half step away from Deb. The stillness that fell over the room was swift. The tension was thick, and the hair on the back of Deb's neck rose.

Who can stop cold a room full of demons? Deb pondered.

"You will do no such thing, General Kelce," the

female stated.

A General. Deb's breath caught in her throat. *There are no scars, his skin is perfect. That's not possible. Not unless he drank from something Heavenly and healed.*

Deb found the source commanding the room. The brunette female demon with stunning green eyes was making her way toward Deb. Her gate was so smooth it was as if she were gliding, not walking. The entities standing along the bar moved out of the demon's way as she sauntered forward.

Wearing a floor-length emerald-colored dress, with a gold belt in the shape of a snake, only her black stiletto heels made a sound as they clicked against the stone flooring in the bar area. She was beyond beautiful, like something ripped from the pages of a great piece of fiction. Her flawless sun-kissed skin shimmered in the hues of the up-lighting in the club. She looked like a Greek goddess and everything about her commanded *look at me.*

When she reached Deb, she simply said. "Let's have a chat outside, shall we?"

Deb nodded and exited the room with the female demon beside her. As they entered the foyer, the female demon turned back and stared at the two guards. Ray stepped forward and closed the double doors positioning himself and his partner on the other side, giving them privacy. Deb stood alone in the hallway with a demon powerful enough to silence a warehouse full of demons.

"My name's Jade." The female demon smiled. "Why don't you start over. Who's missing?"

CHAPTER ELEVEN

Kelly paced the small kitchen waiting for her brothers to catch up on what had happened with Deb in Beckinshire.

"Why was Deb there, do we know?" Dan asked from his seat at the kitchen island. His blue eyes watched Kelly as she paced, almost imploring her to sit down.

"I have no idea," Kelly blurted out getting more frustrated with each passing lap. "She wanted us to take Gardenia to our house, because of course she doesn't understand that we aren't staying there anymore with what happened with Jacob and Gerry."

When they returned to the cottage and called their brothers, Gerry took one look at Kelly and asked Gardenia if she wanted to take a walk on the beach. The two of them meandered along the shoreline hunting for sea glass, an item Gerry explained had become increasingly rare in the age of environmental awareness.

"Did Deb seem okay?" Frankie asked. "Was she hurt? Did she seem distracted?"

"She looked exhausted," Gen answered. "I don't

think she's really rested since this morning."

"That's not good," Greg commented as he sat comfortably with his feet up on the sofa, his wavy hair tucked under a red baseball cap. "Eventually, her body will give out. She'll end up shutting her eyes and zonking out somewhere."

"Yeah," Xavier added from his new favorite rocking chair in the corner of the living room. "It's better to have that happen on your terms, not your body's."

"What are we going to do?" Kelly asked. "Seriously, we have no way to reach her. When she puts her shield up and wants privacy, she can use it to cloak. It could be days before we're able to tell her what Peter has done."

"I don't think we can afford to worry about this right now," Tom stated. "I know it's difficult, but like you said there is nothing we have the power to do about it. We have to wait until Deb comes back to the house looking for Gardenia."

"Do you think Gardenia's up for a conversation right now?" Michael asked as he stoically stood in front of the window facing the ocean staring down at the two walking the beach.

"I don't know," Gen answered. "Gardenia has the power to teleport, if we pressure her or make her nervous, she can bolt. We can be pretty intimidating, especially when we're all together."

"Yeah," Kelly added. "and if she does take off, she'd be yet another person we would have no way of finding."

"Understood," Michael commented. "Tom and I will stay here with you two, the rest can continue the hunt for Peter."

"Seriously, Michael." Kelly smiled. "You think you're one of our least intimating siblings."

There was a brief pause before all snickered in agreement.

"Fine." Michael scowled at Kelly. "I'll take off then. Let's get going so you can get to work."

"I'll stay here with Tom," Xavier told him. "We got this."

The room filled with a mishmash of blue, green, and yellow light as their aura's collided and the rest of the brothers teleported away.

"I think you wanted to talk to Gerry more anyway Kell," Tom offered. "What if you went and talked with the two of them alone on the beach. Just stay open so we can hear and ask questions."

"That might be our best option," Gen told her.

"Okay," Kelly huffed. "You're right, but I'm starting to get hangry and there is literally no food left in this house."

"I'll go get food. You go get some information we can use." Xavier got up from the rocking chair and teleported from the house.

"Pizza and fries would be fabulous!" Kelly yelled after him.

Grabbing her sunglasses off the counter Kelly teleported down to the beach. The sun was still bright, and unlike England, it wasn't raining. In fact, the breeze was light and the sand warm. Seagulls squawked in the distance as they dove in and out of the ocean for small fish. Gerry and Gardenia were spaced out a bit, eyes downward searching the coastline. From her vantage point Kelly could see Gerry's contentment; even Gardenia was smiling.

I hate being the one to ruin their afternoon, Kelly groaned internally.

Kelly waded through the thick pebble-laden sand. Gardenia turned to meet her. Gerry stopped and waited for both to reach him since he was standing roughly in the middle.

"Hi," Kelly said, her voice lilting up more than normal. "Find anything?"

Gerry smiled. "Nothing for me."

"I found a few shells, but no sea glass." Gardenia held out her hand full of small white seashells ridged and chipped by the ocean.

"Nice," Kelly remarked. "I hate to interrupt, believe me I'd rather leave you alone to enjoy the rest of the day, but we really do need to talk."

Gardenia nodded. "Sure."

"Can you tell me how you know Marcus?" Kelly asked Gardenia.

"It's been a little more than a year since—" Gardenia trailed off not finishing her sentence.

Gerry's forehead creased with confusion. "Are you alright, Gardenia?"

"Yes," she answered. "I just realized that I've never actually said it out loud, you know?"

There was a moment of silence. *This is awkward,* Kelly told her siblings. *How do you go a year without talking about it?*

"Are you talking about your own death?" Gerry asked Gardenia. "Because I haven't been dead a day and I can't stop thinking about it. Honestly, this doesn't seem

119

real. I keep thinking I'll wake up and maybe this will all be a crazy dream."

"I know what you mean," Gardenia told him. "I died last fall, a car accident after a high school football game. It was a fun night, normal."

"What happened?" Gerry delicately asked the young teen.

"My friend Andrea drove us to the game. She was a grade ahead of me. I didn't have my license yet."

"Anyway," Gardenia resumed. "We were driving home when the car skidded around a corner. Andrea screamed as we went off the road and hit a tree. We were wearing seatbelts, but we didn't make it."

"Wait," Kelly interrupted. "Your friend died as well?"

"Yeah," Gardenia said quietly. "I died at the scene. It was crazy to suddenly be standing on the road looking back at our messed-up bodies. Andrea was slumped over the steering wheel, I couldn't see her face, but I saw all the blood. The car was wrecked."

"Did Andrea pass at the scene also?" Gerry asked.

"No, she died days later in the hospital," Gardenia told him. "She was in a drug-induced coma, but her body gave out."

"You left the scene and went to the hospital," Kelly stated.

"Yes. I needed to know she was alright."

"Was there anyone else at the scene, anything that only you could see?" Kelly asked.

"I don't know," Gardenia told them. "Once I realized I was dead, I never took my eyes off Andrea. I knew she was alive. I could feel her trying to reach me somehow, as if she knew, despite being unconscious, that I was dead."

"Wow." Gerry seemed to sing the word.

"Andrea wasn't just a friend, was she Gardenia?" Kelly tilted her head before continuing. "She was more than that."

Gardenia's eyes watered and tears trickled down her cheeks. "She was the best thing that ever happened to me."

"When Andrea died at the hospital, what happened?" Kelly asked.

"For a brief moment we were together." Gardenia smiled. "I thought we were going to be together forever. I know how stupid that sounds now."

"It's not stupid," Kelly assured her. "Most people hope for forever with their loved ones."

Gardenia looked up to the sky. "Then she left me. She said she saw a light; someone was calling to her. I saw nothing, heard nothing. She turned and walked away from me. I'll never forget calling out to her. It was like my words couldn't reach her, like she didn't know it was me anymore. I screamed for her. Don't leave me! I love you!"

Gardenia's voice quivered with the emotion of the moment, startling Gerry and moving him to tears.

"Then she was gone," Gardenia said solemnly.

Kelly stepped forward and grabbed Gardenia's free hand. "I can't imagine how hard that was. It sounds like Death came for Andrea. You couldn't see nor hear the Reaper because it wasn't meant for you."

Gardenia turned away from Kelly.

"It doesn't mean she didn't love you Gardenia," Kelly told her.

"I guess I'll never know, will I?" Gardenia's voice grew cold. "Heaven took her, didn't even let me say goodbye."

"How do you know what it was, that it was from Heaven?" Kelly asked her.

Gardenia crossed her arms in defense and Gerry gasped softly under his breath.

"If you couldn't see it, how do you know it was Heaven?" Kelly repeated. "Did you see a light or talk with someone at the scene of the accident? Did you ignore someone speaking to you that night, or run away from the light because you wouldn't leave Andrea behind?"

Gardenia's voice trembled. "I didn't understand what the light was. I was scared. I didn't know what was happening." Gardenia's face crumbled. She dropped the seashells and pulled her hand free from Kelly. Burying her face in her hands she wept. Gerry stepped forward, reached an arm around her, and comforted the young soul.

Gerry's so good at this, Kelly thought. *His fatherly instincts know how to ease Gardenia's grief.*

"I know it's hard to hear Gardenia," Kelly began again when the sobbing had quieted. "I don't know what happened that night, but you made a choice, and now you're here."

"Well, it doesn't matter now does it?" Gardenia snapped. "The light has never come for me. Here I am, just another member of the so called Lost, a group of what exactly? I don't even know what I am anymore. I have a body. I'm not a ghost. I eat. I sleep. I laugh. I cry. I can be hurt. I'm stuck here on Earth, living like a human, but unseen by every one of them. Do you know what it feels like to be invisible? Heaven doesn't care about me. All it cares about is this war with Hell. I don't want any part of a war between Heaven and Hell."

"Gardenia, Heaven will never ask you to go to war on its behalf," Kelly told her. "I promise you that. If your heart chooses Heaven, the light will come for you, but it will be on your timeline, your choice."

"You're wrong," Gardenia told Kelly. "I tried that. I sank to my knees and I prayed to God to take me too. I begged him to show me the light. All I wanted was to be with Andrea. I yelled that I would do anything for God, nothing happened. I got no answer and no light. No one in Heaven heard me that day."

Kelly was about to speak when she stopped. *What am I supposed to say to that?*

"If either of you tell me," Gardenia pulled away from Gerry crossing her arms across her chest once more, "that God works in mysterious ways," Gardenia sniffled. "I'm outta here and you'll never find me."

"I wouldn't presume to know how God works," Kelly told her. "And that's the truth."

Gardenia uncrossed her arms, Kelly's words dragging her back from the desire to flee.

"We need to find my sister Deb," Kelly told Gardenia. "Do you know what she was doing in that town, what she was doing at that warehouse?"

"I assume, like me, she was looking for Marcus," Gardenia told them. "Marcus has been helping me, mostly he just listens."

"Sometimes, that's all we need," Gerry told her reassuringly.

"He promised to train me," Gardenia admitted. "Marcus said he would show me some things so I could defend myself, but that was weeks ago. He hasn't come back. I know he's in trouble."

"I agree," Kelly told her plainly. "I'll make you a deal. You come inside and put up with all our incessant questions, of which there will be many, and I'll train you how to fight."

A barrage of concerns from her siblings telepathically came to Kelly but she ignored them.

Gardenia looked back and forth between Kelly and Gerry as if contemplating the offer.

"Have you seen her fight?" Gerry asked Gardenia. "I only saw a little. She's pretty badass."

Kelly smiled at Gerry. "Thank you, Gerry."

Gardenia's shoulders relaxed. "Okay, deal."

"Excellent!" Kelly announced. "Let's get back in the house and see what we can figure out, together."

Back inside, Gen was quiet. Before Kelly could ask her what was wrong, Xavier returned in a glow of light, and the smell of warm bread and fries filled the small space.

"Thank goodness," Kelly said emphatically. "I'm starving."

"I'm actually hungry too," Gardenia added.

"A girl after my own heart," Kelly told her. "I'll grab the plates."

Kelly had to open and close several cabinets until she found what she was looking for. Tom was behind her and spoke.

"I'm sorry about your friend Andrea," Tom told Gardenia. "That's not anything a person should have to experience."

Tom paused before continuing. "You entered the warehouse and were met with a vampire that tossed you out."

Gardenia nodded. "Yes, like I said I was looking for Marcus."

"What made you think he'd be there?" Tom asked.

"A few weeks ago he was supposed to meet me for dinner and a movie. Something we did once a month or so. He came by real late, apologized for missing it. I could tell something was wrong. That's when he told me if anything were to happen to him, to find Deb and give her the coin."

"What coin?" Xavier asked.

"She saw it tonight." Gardenia pointed at Kelly.

"Yes, we can chat about the coin later. Go ahead Gardenia, please finish," Kelly answered.

"Marcus asked me to follow him to that warehouse. He said it was some sort of club where Heaven and Hell could *cross the divide*." Gardenia made air quotes with her hands and rolled her eyes at the last part.

"Were those his exact words?" Tom interjected.

"Yeah, whatever that means. Marcus said I was forbidden to follow him inside. He made me promise that if he didn't come out of the club within an hour, I was to leave and find Deb. He handed me a note with her address on it."

Kelly held a plate out for Gardenia. "Help yourself."

"Thanks." Gardenia loaded up on fries and sat down next to Xavier at the kitchen counter.

"You knew about Deb?" Gen asked. "He talked to you about her?"

"Yes," Gardenia answered between bites, "many times. He told me about all the long walks they had. How he feels most like himself when he's around her. Marcus spoke of how beautiful and kind she was. He's definitely taken with her, maybe even in love with her."

"What happened the night you followed Marcus to the club?" Tom asked, handing her a napkin and a can of soda.

"He went inside, but I never saw him leave." Gardenia's voice cracked. "Maybe if I had known how to fight—"

"Don't do that to yourself," Gen said, as she came around the counter to stand opposite Gardenia. "Whatever happened to Marcus, it's not your fault."

Gardenia nodded. Kelly noticed the subtle stiffness in her shoulders and knew Gardenia didn't believe Gen completely.

"Is there another exit to the building?" Kelly asked. "Perhaps you just missed him leaving. Marcus is smart and being a Sentinel, he knows how to navigate all the planes."

"I know you're trying to help," Gardenia told them, "but I know he didn't come out."

"How long did you wait?" Tom asked.

"All night," Gardenia said quietly. "I know you doubt it, but Marcus never walked out of that building."

"What do you mean?" Xavier asked. "How can you be so sure?"

"The vampire," Gardenia told them. "The one from the warehouse. He told me where Marcus is."

The crack in Gardenia's voice reflected she believed whatever the vampire had told her. "Where is he?"

Gardenia wiped fresh tears from her face. "Marcus is in Hell."

CHAPTER TWELVE

The tension in the room rose as Gardenia's news settled across those present.

Marcus is in Hell. A lump formed in Gen's throat. *How are we going to break that to Deb? Or does she already know?*

"What in the world is she talking about?" Gerry had been so quiet Gen forgot he was standing behind them. "Hell, someone is in Hell? And vampires, those are real? This is crazy talk."

"Gerry," Kelly said, but he interrupted her.

"No!" He yelled. "You people are nuts. Vampires, that's the last straw. What's next, werewolves, witches, leprechauns?"

Kelly immediately pointed at Tom, but she couldn't get the words out.

"Don't even start Kell," Tom reacted. "You know leprechauns are not real."

"Oh yes they are," Kelly lobbed. "and I'm going to prove it to you one day."

Xavier laughed. "You've been obsessed with them

since Dan made you watch those scary movies."

"Guys!" Gen yelled silencing the room. "Can we focus here."

Why do I always have to be the adult in the room? Gen wondered.

"I'm sorry Gerry," Kelly told him. "Vampires are real, but nothing like what you've seen depicted in movies and books."

I thought Gerry was adjusting, Gen thought. *We need to start over.*

"Gerry, why don't you and Gardenia come sit at the table?" Gen waved her arm. "Kelly can give a brief history and we can try to answer your questions. That might help you both."

Slowly, Gerry made his way toward the table. He somehow seemed older to Gen than when they first met in the hospital months ago. The heart surgery he went through caused him to lose weight, the old gray T-shirt he wore was a bit swimmy. His unshaven face was a mix of black and white stubble. His brown skin had lost some of its luster and his eyes expressed concern. Gerry's shoulders pulled his whole body forward.

Weight of the world, Gen thought. *That's what it looks like.*

Gerry and Gardenia took seats next to one another at the dining table.

"It's true what you said before, Gardenia," Kelly began. "Heaven and Hell are locked in a war over the souls of all humanity. We're members of Heaven's Guard. We are on the front lines of that battle every day."

"No offense," Gerry muttered. "But, since I died

today at the hands of a crazy demon, seems to me you're losing."

"I can see how you would think that," Tom admitted as he walked to the other side of the island to stand next to Kelly.

"Your situation is unique, Gerry," Kelly told him. "You could see us before you died. That has never happened to any of us."

"Really?" Gardenia looked at Gerry. "Are you some sort of psychic or something?"

"If I was," Gerry responded. "I can tell you right now, I wasn't a very good one."

Gardenia smiled at him before turning back to Kelly. "What about me? Am I a unique case too?"

"I'm afraid we don't know much about you," Tom told her. "We are here to listen and help you as best we can, anything else would be speculation."

Gardenia sighed. "Yeah, I guess you're right. It's not like I could see the supernatural before I died."

"I'll be honest, there is still a lot about the Lost we don't understand," Kelly told her. "We know they are people who choose not to go with Death when they pass. We know they have physical bodies. Though they are unseen by humans, they require similar care as to when they were alive, such as eating and sleeping."

"You also eat and sleep, not to mention drink alcohol." Gerry pointed past Kelly to the bottle of booze left on the counter to her right.

"I don't know how I'd get through this war without whiskey," Kelly retorted.

Gerry laughed. "I understand. Let's say I'm with

you on everything you just said. Let's get to the hardest part." Gerry sighed and ran his hand down his unshaved face. "Tell me about the vampires."

"Well, where to begin," Kelly commented.

"I think you should tell them about the Accord," Gen told Kelly.

Kelly nodded. "Okay. Well, roughly one thousand years ago vampires roamed the Earth unimpeded. They targeted humans, slaughtering them and drinking their blood at will."

"With fangs?" Gerry asked. "Like Bela Lugosi in *Dracula*?"

"Bela who?" Gardenia asked.

Kelly smiled. "That's an old black-and-white movie."

"Before your time," Xavier added.

"To answer your question, Gerry," Kelly looked fondly at her charge. "No they don't have fangs. Vampires are not the folklore that humans have created. They are essentially soldiers who sustain life by drinking blood instead of eating food. That's pretty much where the similarities end."

"So," Gardenia pondered. "They can't be killed by sunlight or wooden stakes?"

"No," Tom told him.

"They aren't afraid of garlic, rosary beads, or the site of a crucifix?" Gerry added.

"No," Tom replied.

"That is somehow disappointing." Gardenia sighed.

"Don't misunderstand," Kelly warned. "They are

formidable, adept fighters who spend most of their waking time training."

"Training for what?" Gerry asked.

Kelly sighed. "Vampires are Hell's First Army."

"Army." Gerry let the word hang in the air before continuing. "So, there are like thousands of them?"

"The world was in chaos for a long time," Kelly tried to back up a bit. "long before my family was here. Heaven and Hell were locked in endless bloodshed, no side was winning, and humanity was caught in the middle. A deal was struck, we call it The Accord. It's more complicated but, it's essentially a set of rules both sides agreed to abide by to have some semblance of balance and peace. The Accord was ratified nearly a thousand years ago to make it so human blood could no longer sustain or nourish vampires. As we understand it, human blood is now toxic to them."

"How are they alive then?" Gardenia asked.

"They drink demonic blood," Gen told her. "They are able to heal, but because it's demonic blood they scar badly. They are earthbound, but they are not a threat to humanity."

"That's why the vampire had red and black patches all over his chest," Gardenia told them. "He had all these lumpy marks that were burnt looking."

"Yes," Kelly admitted. "When they would drink human blood, the skin would heal completely and restore them. It's thought that the essence of Heaven, which flows through every human, fortified the vampire's skin and left it free of imperfections—meaning no scars, no marks or deformities of any kind."

"That's part of the lore too," Gardenia said. "Vampires are always beautiful and sexy in movies and books."

"Well," Kelly nearly sang the word. "You met one, what did you think?"

"Definitely not hot," Gardenia deadpanned.

A palpable release overtook the room as Gerry chuckled.

I think Gerry's going to be okay, Gen told her siblings telepathically.

"I guess that's how you'll know if something changes, huh?" Gardenia added. "If suddenly all the vampires were hot again."

That is a petrifying thought. A pang of queasiness shot through Gen. *Now's not the time to tell them that a small amount of blood from a Heavenly being could heal and strengthen the vampire exponentially.*

***

Deb looked around the lavish suite in awe. Jade had ordered room service. She was insistent that Deb eat and had her come to her hotel suite on the top floor of the Savoy. The massive space had sweeping views of downtown London and many of its historic sites. The crisp white sectional sofa was larger than anything she and her sisters could fit in the house they shared.

The house we used to share I guess, Deb thought sadly.

Jade's heels clicked on the marble tile as she made her way back down the hallway to Deb.

"Bloody hell," Jade said to her. "You look

133

knackered, you're about to fall asleep standing up."

"I'm fine," Deb answered, though her fatigue betrayed her.

"The food won't take long," Jade told her. "They know not to make me wait. Please, grab a drink, the bar is fully stocked."

Deb really wanted to protest, to just get the information that would help her find Marcus and then head back to Gardenia, but a few minutes on the plush sofa sounded like Heaven.

"I think I will," Deb said, as she tossed her raincoat over the back of a desk chair and made her way over to the large inset bar. Everything was polished to a shine. The black and gold color scheme made it all glow in the recessed lighting. The floral wallpaper ran to the ceiling and doubled as a backsplash and a work of art.

"This place is beautiful," Deb commented as she poured herself a glass of white wine.

"I'll have a glass of that while you're pouring, darling," Jade told her.

Deb handed Jade the wine.

"Cheers," Jade said, as she tipped the glass up.

The smell of eucalyptus with a touch of lavender drifted through the air. Deb took a seat across from Jade and nearly sunk into the thick cushions.

"It smells like a spa in here," Deb commented.

"Yes, well I did treat myself to an in-room service earlier today," Jade confirmed. "the smell still lingers. It's brilliant."

"Yes, it is," Deb agreed. "I have to say, I've never met another entity quite like you."

Jade laughed, "You fancy me, Guardian."

It was the type of melodic laugh that men swooned over. "You can call me Deb."

"Of course," Jade replied. "Now, tell me more about this man of yours, Marcus."

Deb choked a little on her drink. "He's not mine, per se."

"Who, per se, does he belong to then?" Jade smiled.

"I'm not sure." Deb was flustered at the thought of Marcus belonging to her. "I heard there was an Angel once."

"Well, that's just downright scandalous." Jade leaned in close and leveled her eyes on Deb. "Do tell."

"I was in the club looking for a Collector," Deb told her. "Then found out the best I could hope for was a demon with tracking skills. Any chance you have the ability to track?"

"Mmm, sorry, no." Jade took a sip of her wine. "But, I do know an excellent Trader."

Deb's brain ached. "A Trader?"

"Yes," Jade reiterated. "One of the most reputable. You're sure to get a more accurate answer from him, and you won't have to wait for the results."

Deb sipped her wine as a way of delaying her response.

"Instant gratification." Jade snapped her fingers and smiled. "How does that sound?"

"That certainly would be beneficial," Deb answered. "Why would you help me? I mean not to sound ungrateful, but you're a demon, are you not?"

"I help those I choose to help." Jade's tone was

wary, and silence filled the space as she placed her wine glass down on a decorative coaster.

"When can I meet this Trader?" Deb asked as she placed her glass down as well.

Jade's face lit up. "I can give him a ring right now." Jade stood up. "I'm sure the food will be here soon after. You just relax. Here, let me put on some music."

Jade pressed some buttons on a remote and classical music hummed through speakers placed throughout the expansive space. Jade walked toward the bedroom, her long ballgown's numerous layers of chiffon billowing around her as she traipsed down the hall. Everything about Jade seemed alluring; her movements and demeanor were comfortable, yet seductive.

Captivating, Deb thought. *The kind of woman other women wish they were. What is she?*

The doorbell of the suite chimed and Jade answered it. A gentleman dressed in a formal tux with tails entered the room. He arranged all the food on a large dining table on the other side of the sofa. Deb was not in human view, so he was unaware of her presence. He left as quietly and swiftly as he had arrived. Jade was on the telephone at the other end of the hallway, but Deb couldn't hear any of the words.

Deb leaned back on the sofa and inhaled the sea salt and vinegar from the fish and chips.

That smells amazing, Deb thought. *If only I could manage to get myself off this ridiculously comfortable sofa.*

Deb gazed out the window at the giant lighted Ferris wheel known as the London Eye. The white lights seemed to dance across the sky as it rotated, almost lulling her to sleep.

Don't fall asleep, Deb told herself. *Not here, you don't know her.*

Deb's body sunk further into the warmth of the sofa. Closing her eyes for what was to be a brief moment Deb instead fell into a deep slumber.

CHAPTER THIRTEEN

The dizzying sensation of falling overcame Deb as she barreled downward into darkness. Spiraling she flailed wildly into the unknown. Spikes of cold air stabbed at her bare skin. Desperate, she tried to reach out to grasp onto something, anything to keep from continuing into the abyss. There was no light, nothing that resembled illumination. She was helpless.

Fear gripped Deb as her heart thumped loudly in her ears, deafening her to all other sounds. Something was burning but there was no flame. A scream bubbled up and she opened her mouth to release it, but no sound spilled out. She grew sore from fighting against the perilous journey. Tears flowed freely down her cheeks; she tasted the saltiness as the warm liquid streamed across her lips.

What's happening? Where am I? Deb tried to make sense of the absurdity of the moment. *No, no, no, please God no.*

Deb's body shivered and shook, the images and sensations fading away as her mind raced to the surface of waking and consciousness.

"Deborah," A deep male voice called to her.

"Remember who you are. Remember you're stronger than you realize."

Deb's body thrust upward to a sitting position. She was panting and nearly breathless from fright. Peering around the spacious room she looked for the source of the male voice but found no one. She let her body relax and fell back.

A nightmare, Deb realized in pure relief. *Just a stupid dream.*

The room's lights were dimmed, but unlike her dream, there was light. A soft lightweight comforter covered her body as she lay curled up on her side. Deb's head was cocooned into a large plush pillow. As her eyes adjusted and her heart slowed to a normal pace, she lifted her head and surveyed the large king size bed.

The hotel, Deb thought. *I'm still in Jade's suite.*

She knew it must be morning based on the sun burning through the small slit in the curtain. She slowly got to her feet and went to the window pulling the thick drapes apart. The morning sky was bright with the rain abated, at least momentarily.

The smell of coffee wafted into the room and Deb's stomach growled.

I need to eat. Deb placed a hand across her midsection. *This must be what it's like to be Kelly.* Deb smiled, the memory of her sister bringing joy and pain.

"I miss you guys," she whispered.

I need to find Marcus, but I wish I weren't alone. Deb brought her attention back to the predicament. *If Jade can't help me with all her obvious resources and curious interest in my story, I don't know what I'll do next.*

Deb found the bathroom lights and flipped the switch. Awash in white, the room had a large clawfoot tub on one side and a walk-in shower on the other. Two pedestal sinks anchored the tub, and the floor was covered with black-and-white marble tile. Cream colored walls with thick wooden doors and a panel of windows made the space luxurious and timelessly stylish.

Deb stood in awe. *So decadent, it reflects the demon who occupies the space.*

Deb washed her face and tore open the package that held a new toothbrush. It lay neatly next to a small tube of unopened toothpaste.

Either Jade thought of everything or this place really is over the top.

Deb was in no hurry as she made her way down the hall toward the living space. The gold-framed artwork adorning the walls was beautiful and, for a moment, Deb forgot she was in a hotel and not someone's home.

One bedroom, Deb thought as she neared the opening to the living space. She spied the cushy sofa she had fallen asleep on the night before. *Where did Jade sleep last night?*

The stunning demon sat at the dining table reading *The Guardian* and drinking coffee.

Wonder if she sees the irony in the name of her news medium? Deb mused.

"Morning," Deb announced. "I'm guessing it's morning anyway."

"Good morning my lovely." Jade put the paper down and looked at Deb taking in the site of her wrinkled clothing and ruffled hair.

The demon wore a bright green short sleeved

blouse. Small rhinestones outlined the scoop neckline. Though the top revealed nothing, it was paired with tight black pants that hugged all the right places. The demon's strappy peep-toe sandals revealed her dark brown painted toenails.

"You must be famished," Jade said to her. "Please, help yourself."

Jade gestured with her palm as she directed Deb's eyes to the other end of the spacious room. Sitting on top of an expansive buffet were silver warming trays with carafes of juice, milk, and coffee. Two individual silver teapots sat to the side.

"Thank you," Deb said, as she made her way toward the food. "Where did you sleep last night?" Deb asked. "I don't remember getting up and stealing your bed last night." Deb filled her plate with eggs, hash, and baked beans. Skipping the mushrooms, Deb poured a glass of juice and made her way back to the table.

"You were out, my dear," Jade told her. "I carried you to the bed. I couldn't leave you passed out on the sofa. You would have been miserably crooked this morning if I had."

Deb partially smiled. "I appreciate that, how thoughtful of you."

"Rubbish," Jade scolded. "If you wanted to know where I slept, all you had to do was rollover, darling."

"I see," Deb said between bites.

"You don't drink coffee?" Jade asked as she spied the glass of juice. "I thought everyone in The States did."

"I drink tea," Deb told her.

"Well, you're certainly in the right city for that,"

Jade said dryly.

"I have to ask." Deb took a sip of juice. "Why are you helping me?"

"You think me dodgy, don't you Deborah?"

"I think this is odd," Deb answered truthfully.

"Which part?" Jade asked. "and please help yourself to a cuppa, it is breakfast after all."

"All of it," Deb said, as she placed the napkin onto the table and made her way back to the buffet. "A demon staying in the penthouse—"

"The Royal Suite," Jade corrected abruptly.

There's the temper flaring again, Deb observed. *She snaps in and out of it with both ease and agility.*

"Ahh," Deb conceded. *That makes sense. That's how Jade acts, like royalty; maybe she is princess of the underworld?*

Steam billowed into the air from the small silver teapot. Deb prepared some English breakfast tea. The smell of warm toast and honey greeted her back at the table.

"Do you live here?" Deb asked.

"No, but I do love it and try to return often."

The doorbell to the suite chimed.

"Just in time," Jade declared and got up from her seat.

Deb finished a few more bites before Jade hollered a recommendation. "Don't forget the pastries, they're delish."

Why not? Deb thought as her eyes went back to the buffet.

Voices floated down the hall from the front foyer and the sound of Jade's small heel sandals preceded her.

"The stylist is ready whenever you finish," Jade told

142

Deb as she came back into the room.

"I'm sorry?" Deb asked in confusion, her eyebrows knitting together.

"Oh, don't be," Jade told her. "I don't know how long you were running around in that drab attire, but Veronica will spruce you right up."

Deb looked around, but no one else was in the room with them.

"I wasn't aware I needed sprucing." Deb looked down at her pale pink blouse creased with wrinkles.

"Don't get your knickers in a twist, darling." Jade sat down at the table.

"I don't know what to say." Deb stared at her blankly.

"You don't need to say anything," Jade told her. "Head on down to the bedroom and take a quick shower. Veronica will be waiting when you get out and she'll take care of you."

Deb thought about going for a second plate of food but was too curious. She nodded toward Jade and made her way to the bedroom where a petite blonde woman stood.

"Hello," Veronica greeted. "Lovely to meet you."

"Hi," Deb answered. "You're—" words seemed to fail her. Deb could feel herself blinking rapidly.

"I'm human, yes." Veronica smiled at Deb.

"How?" Deb started to question but stopped when Veronica held up her hands.

"I'm afraid that's a conversation you'll need to be having with Miss Jade," Veronica told her.

Deb walked into the bathroom and closed the door behind her. *What in the world is going on here?*

She turned the dial in the shower, noticing for the first time the virtual smorgasbord of high-end spa products dotting the shelf that ran the length of the stall.

After showering, Deb brushed her teeth and exited the bathroom. Veronica stood waiting by the king-size bed. The bed had been made and laying on top were fresh undergarments.

"I took a guess at your size," Veronica offered.

"You guessed correctly," Deb confirmed after reading the tags.

The sound of a zipper surprised Deb and she turned to find Veronica opening a black garment bag hanging on the outside of the closet door. Inside were dark brown leather pants and a leopard print blouse.

"I'm sorry, those must be for Jade," Deb told Veronica.

"Bloody hell, Guardian," Jade barked from the doorway. "Stop being a plonker and get dressed. At this rate we're going to be late."

Jade swiveled and left with Veronica following her out of the room and clicking the door shut behind her.

After getting dressed, Deb looked around the room for her boots but found a pair of wedge sandals instead. She examined herself in the full-length mirror, pirouetting in front of it.

In the living space a dining chair had been pulled to the middle of the room. Veronica stood in the center holding a blow dryer.

You've got to be kidding me, Deb thought.

Deciding that placating Jade was imperative to getting the help she needed, Deb sat down. Veronica styled

Deb's hair and applied a small amount of makeup. Thirty minutes later Veronica took an envelope left on the dining table and exited the room as swiftly and quietly as she had arrived. Deb stood in front of a mirror wondering who she was looking at.

I must be losing it, Deb thought. *I can't believe I'm here playing dress up with a demon. Marcus better appreciate this when I tell him.* Deb smiled. *One day we'll have a good laugh over this my friend.*

"You're thinking about your man, aren't you?" Jade said. "You're smiling, but it doesn't reach your eyes and your sagging shoulders carry worry."

"I am worried, about more than just Marcus," Deb answered.

"I can tell. You get a crease between those gorgeous blue eyes of yours. You should stop."

"Why? Concerned I'll get wrinkles?" Deb asked sarcastically.

"Cheeky lass, but no," Jade answered. "You look smashing, and the crease is ruining the look. Now let's hurry, your Trader awaits."

"What?" Deb asked in shock. "You connected with a Trader already? Where are we going?"

"I rang him last night. We would have met him then except I walked in to find you out cold on my sofa."

"I'm—" Deb stopped when Jade placed her hands on her hips readying for an argument. "I appreciate you setting up the meeting for today then."

"Well, aren't you a bright one," Jade replied. "I was ready to give up on you, thought for sure I was getting another bloody apology. Best be on our way. He's waiting in the atrium."

Jade grabbed a small black purse and made her way to the front door.

"Wait. I have more questions. How do you have a human working for you?"

"I found Veronica drunk one evening and saved her from a rather unpleasant encounter with a bloke. That's a story for later, perhaps over a cocktail and lunch at the bar."

"Who are we meeting?" Deb inquired.

"He's brilliant darling, absolutely the best in the business, the only one I trust to trade with," Jade answered.

Deb paused at the doorway and looked at Jade.

"Fine," Jade said with a sigh. "since you apparently need the Trader's CV, I will tell you all about him on our way downstairs."

She saved Veronica from an attack. Deb was mystified. *Who is Jade? What kind of demon saves humans and helps Guardians?*

"The name of the Trader we're meeting will do just fine," Deb mumbled as she entered the elevator and turned back toward the shiny metal doors already closing behind them.

"Torin," Jade said, tapping the button for the mezzanine.

Deb went rigid. Her heartbeat ticked up and her hands began to sweat.

Torin, Deb repeated silently. *I'm going to meet the Trader who bargained for Genevieve's soul.*

CHAPTER FOURTEEN

Deb inhaled slowly, attempting to bring her heart rate down. There is no coming back from this. If she made a deal with the demon that was looking to trade for her sister's soul her family may never forgive her.

"You'll need to be in human view, Deborah," Jade told her. "We can't very well expect to be served in a restaurant without being seen."

The elevator dinged and the doors opened, seeing no people on the other side of the door, Deb turned into human view as she crossed the threshold assuming anyone watching on video surveillance would disregard it as a glitch, or at least that was her hope.

The mezzanine was empty. They followed the signs for The Thames Foyer. Music and the sounds of conversation grew louder as they rounded the corner and stood inside the open double doors behind several other people waiting in line.

Deb peered through the glass doors looking for Torin. She had never met him, but she remembered Genevieve's description: tall, thin, older male demon with short graying hair and weathered skin.

Jade cleared her throat annoyed she had to wait. The male host stopped what he was reading and looked up. He smiled warmly and stepped around his podium motioning for Jade and Deb to step through the small crowd.

"Please madam," the host motioned to his right, "your guest is already seated at your favorite table."

"Thank you," Jade said, as she walked through the parting guests.

Everyone just acquiesces to her.

The room had an enormous circular glass cutout on the ceiling. Underneath it stood a floor-to-ceiling ornate atrium painted silver. Inside sat a mahogany-colored piano which no one way playing. Instead, music was piped through nearly invisible speakers spread throughout the room.

Heavy crown molding encircled the room. Oversized living room-style chairs, thick decorative carpet, and dark wooden tables of varying sizes dotted the room. Everything about it was extravagant. Windows and glass doors flooded the space with natural light. The beauty did nothing to abate Deb's growing anxiety as she spotted a tall male figure staring at her with beady black eyes that seemed to probe more than observe.

The demon stood from his seat to greet her and Jade. He was more than six feet tall and stood as if he were incapable of slouching. Wearing a dark gray suit and purple tie he looked the part of all the other businessmen in the room, one about to upsell a client.

The sight of him stirred up animus that rushed to

the surface. *How dare he trade for the soul of my sister, a Guardian no less?*

"Torin," Jade jubilantly greeted the demon. "How good of you to come on such short notice."

The two exchanged a kiss on both cheeks. Deb stood stoically trying to calm the warring factions raging within.

I should kill him where he stands, Deb fumed. *No, I need information and this demon makes reliable deals to get what I need. Think of the mission, as Michael would lecture. Get what you need and get out. The time for thinking is behind you.*

"This is the *who* I was telling you about, Torin." Jade turned and looked warmly at her. "Deborah is in need of your services."

Torin eyed Deb as if waiting to take his queues from her. "Yes, I am," Deb replied as she took a seat across from his chair.

"Very well then," Jade commented. "I have a quick errand and then I'll meet you in the lobby when you're done here Deborah."

Deb had to squash the appeal for Jade to stay that was dancing on the tip of her tongue. *She's not my ally,* Deb reminded herself.

Jade left without another word. A waiter appeared and took their order for tea and returned to the kitchen.

"How can I assist you?" Torin got right to business.

"I need information on the location of a," Deb paused remembering she could be heard by human ears. "police officer, who's suddenly gone MIA."

"I see," Torin replied. "May I inquire as to the nature of your relationship?"

"You haven't even asked me who it is?" Deb replied

coldly.

"I don't need to," Torin answered. "There's only one missing that I'm aware of. It's caused quite a stir amongst both sides of the political aisle. I have to ask," Torin paused while the waiter returned to drop off their order. "Is he friend or foe?"

"Oh," Deb stated dramatically, "I thought you were well versed in this arena. Police are neutral, and I didn't say it was a male, so we may in fact be speaking about the same individual."

"Touché', Miss O'Mara," Torin lobbed back at her.

Deb thought she had the upper hand when all along he knew who she was.

"Is the tone of this meeting normal for you?" Deb asked him but didn't wait for a reply. "Why don't you just give me the price? It will save us both time and energy."

"Fair enough," Torin replied. "I didn't mean to upset you, but you can imagine my surprise when you agreed to meet me."

"I didn't know it was you, until about thirty seconds before walking in," Deb confessed. "If you're wondering if it crossed my mind to call for back up and *end* this, and you, it did."

Torin leveled a stare that made Deb's skin crawl. "I'm a businessman, that's all. I trade in information and goods and I don't get involved beyond that. My reputation for completing my transactions with integrity and the utmost discretion is my currency. Neutrality is my existence. Can you really say the same for your police officer?"

Deb's body temperature rose, like her blood was

about to boil. Anger rolling like a wave elevated her heart rate and it thumped to its own unnatural rhythm. She bit back a reply. She didn't want to lose control, not here, not in human view with a demon sitting less than four feet away.

"Your eyes darken when they fill with hatred, did you know that?" Torin asked in reply to her silence.

"Do you have an offer or has this meeting been a complete waste of my time?" Deb pursed her lips.

"Of course," Torin responded. "I have the information you are looking for."

"You do?" Deb sat forward a bit. "You know where he is?"

Torin pulled an envelope out of the inside coat pocket of his suit. "I know where Marcus is and who took him."

"The cost?" Deb asked and then nearly held her breath as she waited.

"Five vials," Torin replied.

"Five vials of what?" Deb asked as her forehead creased with confusion.

"Your blood," Torin replied.

Deb's mind reeled. "What are you going to do with it?"

"I'm afraid that's not part of the deal, Miss O'Mara."

"Three and I'll consider it," Deb replied.

"Four and I'll hold the offer open while you ponder it overnight."

Torin pushed his seat back and placed the envelope down on the table.

"What's this?" she asked as he slid the envelope

forward.

"It's the offer, for you to take with you."

"Don't you need to amend it per our newly negotiated rate. You know five to four."

"No," Torin said simply. "Like I said, I'm a businessman. I will however offer you a piece of free advice."

"How generous," Deb sardonically sighed realizing she had been out played from the start.

"You should be careful who you align yourself with. I doubt you know anything about Jade, or what she is."

"I know she's the one entity who listened to me and offered to help," Deb replied dryly standing as she said it. "She got me to you, didn't she?"

"You realize that where Marcus is you may not be able to follow, Miss O'Mara."

"I'm touched by your concern." Deb held his gaze. "I think you should be more worried about those that took him."

Torin turned and walked away without another word. Deb walked in the opposite direction and re-entered the lobby to find Jade chatting animatedly on a cell phone.

Now what? Deb thought. *I need time to think, walk off the energy coursing through me. What's wrong with me? I have gone from the most patient person to a powder keg waiting to explode at every turn.*

"Did it all go to pot?" Jade asked. "You look like you could use a drink."

"It was fine," Deb told her. "Look, I know it's going to sound strange, but I am grateful for your hospitality last night and for arranging this meeting."

"But," Jade added. "there's a but coming."

"I need time to think," Deb answered.

"Well of course you do," Jade replied confidently. "No one accepts Torin's offer on the spot. Come on, let's go."

"Where?" Deb asked.

"Shopping," Jade replied. "I have several things to buy, and I could use the company. Trust me, walking is good therapy."

Deb didn't have a chance to reply. Jade hooked her arm around Deb's and dragged her off toward a grand staircase that led down to the main lobby.

"How long did he give you to decide?" Jade asked.

"Overnight," Deb replied.

"Oh, bugger off," Jade declared. "If you need more than that, let me know. I'll call and straighten him out."

Deb smiled. She couldn't help it. *This demon is the strangest being I have ever come across.*

Deb knew the walking would help, but she also knew in the end, she couldn't make a final decision without talking to her sisters. Despite their recent arguments, this was way too big a deal not to discuss with them.

Maybe, they will help me now that I have entities in both Heaven and Hell believing he's missing. Maybe they'll help me form a plan and we'll rescue Marcus together, as it should be.

***

Genevieve was grateful to have Gerry's help cleaning up after breakfast.

The rest of the evening had been quiet after Xavier and Tom left. The beach house wasn't large enough for all of them with only three bedrooms. Kelly and Gen took the room with bunkbeds providing Gerry and Gardenia with some privacy.

"They're still down on the beach Gerry, you want to go join them?"

"Sure, I never turn down walks on the beach," he said with a smile. "This place is amazing, little bit of Heaven right here on Earth."

Gen smiled. "Yeah, it is beautiful. I can see why the ocean is one of my sister Deb's favorite places."

"Where is your other sister, if you don't mind me asking?"

"She's out chasing leads. Someone she cares about is missing," Gen told him.

"I'm sorry to hear that," Gerry replied as Gen led the way out the back door and down the steps to the small beach.

Gardenia jogged up to Gerry. "I found some. I found a few pieces of sea glass!"

The teen held out her hand to show Gerry her treasure, which consisted of three small pieces of glass in varying shades of green.

"Well now," Gerry said, as he took the time to pick them up and examine them. "It does appear you have found sea—"

Gerry didn't finish his sentence. It took Gen a moment to realize something was wrong as Kelly arrived behind them.

"Hey," Kelly greeted them. "What's going on?"

"Are you okay, Gerry," Gardenia asked.

"Something's wrong, I think." Gerry's face grew pale, and he took a small step backward.

"What is it?" Kelly's voice was laced with concern as she stepped closer to Gerry.

"I feel a pull, like something is tugging at me. I see a house, as if it's right in front of me." Gerry reached out as if trying to touch the image he was seeing in his mind.

"What does it look like?" Gen asked.

"It's two story, dark brown shingles," Gerry told them. "There are window boxes in front, but the flowers are wilted and dying."

"What else are you feeling Gerry?" Kelly asked him.

"This is crazy," Gerry told them. "I'm inside the house now. There's a living room on the left, a staircase in front of me, and an empty office to my right. A long hallway leads down to a large kitchen with a fireplace."

"Oh my," Kelly gasped.

"How did you get so far away?" Gerry asked them.

"We're right here Gerry," Gardenia told him as she placed a hand on his arm.

Gen was shocked as Gerry and Gardenia were enveloped in a haze of light and disappeared.

"No!" Kelly yelled. "Gerry, fight it!"

"I can't believe we just witnessed that," Gen told Kelly.

"The house Gen, did you hear the description of the house."

"Yeah," Gen replied. "Gerry either teleported or was just pulled to our house."

"I'm going to assume he teleported," Kelly said

firmly. "My mark isn't going off so it can't be demonic. Is our house on some sort of supernatural billboard? I hate to say it Gen, but I don't see how we can ever go back to living there."

"Let's just go get the two of them and bring them back. Then we can worry about why so many people are suddenly visiting our house."

CHAPTER FIFTEEN

Kelly arrived in the kitchen. She looked around. She saw nothing. All was silent.

Great, Kelly announced telepathically to Gen, *I don't see nor hear them.*

Gen arrived on the second floor. *I'm just going to check upstairs.*

Downstairs Kelly quickly walked the first floor, peaking into the living room and office. Back in the kitchen she opened the back door and stepped out onto the screened-in porch to check the yard.

"Come on Gerry, where did you go?" Kelly mumbled.

Gen descended the stairs and walked out to meet her.

"I see them," yelled Gen. "They're outside, standing across the street."

"Thank goodness," Kelly said relieved. She reached the front door and peaked through the glass to find them.

"So strange," Kelly remarked. "They aren't just across the street they're sort of diagonal."

Gen came up beside her and was about to open the front door when Deb arrived in the kitchen behind them.

Spinning around Kelly stood frozen as she caught sight of her sister standing tall in gorgeous wedge sandals, brown leather pants, and a leopard print blouse. Her hair was styled, and you could see a soft touch of makeup as well.

"Wow!" Kelly said dumbfounded. She stared lost in thought. Gen elbowed her to snap her out of her stupor.

"What are you wearing?" Kelly asked.

"Deb, where have you been?" Gen asked, replacing Kelly's question with one of her own. "I thought you were running a quick errand."

Deb stood in the kitchen as the two of them made their way toward her.

"I can explain later," Deb told them as she glanced quickly down at her attire. "I need to talk to you both."

"You keep telling us you'll explain later," Gen lamented. "When will that be exactly?"

"Look!" Deb snapped. "I didn't come here to fight. Is Gardenia safe, where is she?"

"We're fine," Gen said sarcastically. "Thanks for asking."

"Actually, we aren't fine," Kelly interrupted. "We tried telling you that when we found you with a vampire of all things. And in England of all places. But you took off, again!"

Deb sighed. "I know you're mad at me. I get that you don't understand why I'm searching so hard for Marcus, but it would have been nice to be supported."

"Supported!" Gen hollered. "You've got be kidding

me."

"Deb," Kelly started. "Peter came back, after you left with Leo and Lucas."

"What?!" Deb's voice sharpened.

Well, at least she didn't know, Kelly was relieved. *It's better that she wasn't willingly ignoring deaths at the hands of Hell.*

"What happened?" Deb asked, her pretty blue eyes blinking with concern.

"You want us to share, but you don't feel the need to," Gen told her. "That seems fair."

"Gen," Kelly tried to calm the temperature in the room. "This isn't helping."

"Fine," Gen said as she waved her hands in front of her before folding them across her chest. "Go ahead and tell her everything, it's probably not going to make a difference."

"What's that supposed to mean?" Deb glared at Gen.

"Look at you," Gen told her. "Whose clothes are those? We left you in a bad section of some town outside London wearing jeans and an old raincoat, now you look like you just walked off a runway."

"She's right," Kelly added. "You do look amazing."

"That's hardly the point Kelly," Gen argued.

"None of this is the point," Kelly answered. "Peter returning and murdering my charge and an Arch Angel is the only point."

"Oh no . . ." Deb's voice trailed off. "I can't believe it."

"Well, believe it!" Gen said sharply.

The front door creaked as it was pushed open, and all turned to face Gerry and Gardenia.

"Oh my goodness," Deb said in a hushed tone. "It's Gerry's soul."

"Deb, you're back," called Gardenia as she made her way quickly down the hallway. "Did you find Marcus?"

Deb's face fell. "No, not yet. I have a lead though."

Gerry walked into the kitchen behind Gardenia. "Hello."

"I'm so sorry, Gerry," Deb said to him. "That a demon would do this to a human is tragic and unacceptable."

"Thank you," Gerry responded looking uncomfortable.

"Deb, it's not safe here," Kelly told them. "We really should get back to the beach house."

"Back to the beach house," Deb repeated. "You've been at the beach house?"

"Something you'd know if you bothered to communicate." Gen let the accusation hang in the air.

"Would you mind sitting in the living room?" Gen asked Gardenia and Gerry as she escorted them out of the kitchen. "We need a few moments of privacy with our sister."

"I know for sure Marcus is missing," Deb told them when Gen returned and closed the kitchen door. "I have confirmation."

"From who?" Kelly asked. "Friend or foe?"

Deb's shoulders sank and Kelly knew it was the latter. "Deb, who did you talk to about this? Was it someone in that bordered up warehouse you went to?"

"Yes," Deb told them. "I met a demon who has been helping me."

"Oh, a demon." Kelly tried to remain calm using sarcasm to hide her concern. "That's insane."

"When you say the demon has been helping you," Gen added, "do you mean with your style choices or with looking for Marcus?"

"I know what I'm doing, I'm getting the information I need," Deb huffed. "I get that working with a demon is no one's first choice, but she got me in touch with a Trader. He made me an offer. One I need to talk to you about."

"What's the offer?" Kelly asked feeling a tightening in her chest.

"No!" Gen interrupted, her voice cracking slightly. "That's not the right question. Which Trader made you the offer?"

"Four vials," Deb said quickly, as if spitting out the words. "That will buy me Marcus' location and the identity of the entity that took him."

Gen and Kelly froze. Deb kept talking, using their shock to get the rest of it out.

"This demon, her name is Jade," Deb continued. "She put me in touch with him and he made me the offer this morning. I only have until tomorrow and I need to know you're with me. I mean I know you're upset that I've been gone and that I wasn't here for you after what happened with Gerry, but you must understand, I need to do this. I have to do this."

The tension was palpable. Gen looked like she was going to cry.

"Are you out of your mind?!" Kelly squealed.

"Deb," Gen sighed. "Why would you agree to a deal like that?"

"I'm trying to explain."

"You cannot make that deal," Kelly told her.

"This is the only way to get real answers."

"Why are you risking everything for him?" Kelly asked. "You aren't even sure how you feel about Marcus. Before you say I'm wrong, remember that I know you."

"You two are missing the point," Deb scolded. "It's not about Marcus."

"Then who is it about?" Kelly deadpanned. "It certainly isn't about us, or our charges, or any human."

"Deb, I think you need to come with us." Gen approached her, but Deb recoiled.

"Why are you looking at me like that?" Deb asked Gen. "I'm not crazy. The deal is real."

"I'm quite certain the deal is real too," Kelly mocked. "Do you have any idea what Hell could do with that? Can you hear yourself right now?"

"Deb, I'm sorry I snapped at you earlier," Gen pleaded. "Please don't leave right now, stay and we'll talk it out, like we always do."

Gen's voice had a noticeable tremor.

Something's changed. Kelly's head was swimming. *Gen changed her tone, she's pleading with Deb now, no longer argumentative. Gen's afraid, and so am I. What has Deb gotten herself into?*

Seconds ticked by and then a look of hardness crossed Deb's face. Her shoulders squared and she seemed to stand taller.

"No," Deb told them. "I can see now that coming here was a mistake. I thought you most of all would understand Gen. I never questioned why you had to look for Gabriel and I always helped you when you asked."

Gen was holding her hands up in the air as if in surrender. "I know, now let us help you."

"You never were a good liar Genevieve. You don't want to help me." Deb's line stung Gen, who let out a small groan. "You just want to call Michael to stop me."

"No." Gen shook her head. "No, that's not true."

"I can see the fear in your eyes," Deb told her. "I'm not you, I know what I'm doing. I'm not suffering in silence and waiting any more. I'm going to find Marcus, with or without you."

"You have to at least tell us why?" Kelly demanded. "Why are you so willing to put yourself, this family, and all of humanity, in danger?"

"Humanity is already in danger," Deb scoffed. "Every day we fight off the negative influence and interference from Hell. They lie and they cheat. We're the only one's following the rules!"

"You're frustrated, Deb," Gen sympathized. "I understand."

"No," Deb answered. "It's more than frustrated, I'm on a mission. I'm here to let Hell know they cannot just take a neutral or Heavenly being into Hell and not suffer the consequences."

"But at what cost?" Gen asked. "Do you think Marcus would be okay with what you are doing?"

"It's not about Marcus," Deb seethed. "I would be doing this for any of you, for Harry, for Antonio, for anyone they targeted. If we don't stand up and make this right, who will? What are we doing down here if we don't fight back against aggression like this? They already murdered a Watcher, Lacey said she told those in charge about Sebastian and nothing happened! Now, they've killed a human and an Arch Angel you said? What next, one of us? I'm not waiting around for someone to give us the green light to do the right thing here."

The room fell into an eerie silence. Kelly was searching her brain for a response. *She's not exactly wrong,* Kelly thought. *There has to be a way for us to get Deb to see we understand, to see what we see.*

A reddish-brown glow formed around Deb.

"Deb, wait!" Kelly yelled.

Deb teleported out of the house and the streaks of light faded away.

Gen turned and looked at Kelly. "Did you see the color of her aura?"

Kelly nodded. "It's darkening."

"Is everything alright with your sister?" Gerry's voice startled them.

"No," Gen answered. "I'm afraid it isn't."

"We need to go." Kelly tried to free herself from the fog her mind was drowning in. "It's not safe here. We need to head back to the beach house. Gerry how are you feeling?"

Gerry seemed to contemplate the answer before he gave it. "I feel like this is where I'm supposed to be."

"What does that mean?" Kelly asked.

"When I arrived outside, across the street, all the weird sensations I'd been experiencing went away. It was a relief."

"That's interesting," Gen told him, "especially since you described the house but then didn't arrive inside it."

"Wait," Kelly yelled. "You didn't arrive inside, you arrived outside."

"That's what I literally just said." Gen cocked her head to the side and stared at Kelly confused.

"We need to get out of here!" Kelly waved a hand at Gen to come closer. "Let's get them back and I'll explain what I think is going on."

Kelly grabbed Gerry. "I have him." Kelly looked at Gen. "I know Gardenia can teleport, but she might not be able to find a cloaked house easily. Perhaps you should take her."

"Got it," Gen said, without further questioning. Clasping Gardenia's shoulders, Gen's face filled with horror as they were unable to teleport from the house.

"Crap!" Kelly exclaimed. "It's too late, whatever is coming, is coming now."

"The house is cloaked?" Gen said. "How did Deb just leave then?"

"We can worry about that later," Kelly told them. "We need to focus."

"How are we getting them out of here?" Gen asked.

"The old-fashioned way," Kelly announced. The back door was the fastest option. "Is the yard still clear?"

Gen stepped toward the double doors. "Yes."

Kelly looked at Gerry and Gardenia. "I know our urgency is scary, but we need you to run out the back door."

Kelly motioned to the door in front of Gen. "Go

through the yard to the gate in the back. It leads to an alleyway that will take you out to the street perpendicular to the one we're on. That will bring you away from the house. Gardenia hold Gerry's hand, as soon as you are able, teleport away from here. Get to the beach house as quickly as possible and tell our brothers what happened."

"Are you sure I can get there?" Gardenia's voice trembled. "You just said you weren't sure I could find it."

"We have faith in you Gardenia," Gen said softly.

"Whatever is coming," Kelly added. "Is not coming for you."

"She's right," Gen added. "It's coming for us. We will keep them here while you get away."

"Go!" Kelly yelled.

Gen pulled the back door open. "Run, and don't look back!"

Kelly stood paralyzed waiting for Gen to give her the all-clear. "They made it through the gate."

Kelly ran toward the stairs at the front of the house. There was movement outside coming toward the house.

"They're here, Gen!"

The back door slammed shut and Gen yelled. "I have no weapons!"

"I have the ones Dan left me. I moved them upstairs!" Kelly grabbed the railing to help anchor her as she made the tight turn. Taking the stairs two at a time, she made it just high enough to avoid being hit with the front door as it came crashing into the house.

Risking a glimpse over her shoulder she immediately recognized the vampire who barreled into the house and locked eyes with her. He wore dark gray camouflaged pants and black army boots. The standard red and black medieval jacket that completed his uniform hung open, exposing his bare chest. The long leather toggle buttons flapped when he walked.

He smiled at Kelly. "Running away so soon, Guardian."

Kelly's breath caught in her throat. She turned back continuing to leap up the stairs as fast as she could. Garrick's hair was pulled back and instead of looking like a sweaty drunken mess as he did that night at the warehouse, he was stunningly handsome. There were no blemishes, no patchwork of black and red scars anywhere on his chest, neck, or face. His eyes had a dark red ring around the iris.

His skin is perfect and those eyes! Kelly agonized. *They've been healed! I need to warn Gen.*

"Hot!" Kelly yelled. "They're hot!"

CHAPTER SIXTEEN

Deb stood in the lobby of the Savoy Hotel. It's black-and-white checkerboard tile already feeling familiar.

I should wait, Deb chided herself. *Calm down a little more, all this will pass, right? Gen seemed like she was trying to reach me.*

Deb was not in human view, but she was in the lobby because she wasn't all that sure about the plan to return to Jade.

Everything's upside down. Jade is helping me, while Gen and Kelly think I'm reckless. I could see it in Gen's eyes, she was desperate to stop me. But if we don't stop Hell now, who will they target next? Will it be one of us? Will it be another human, or have they already killed more? I don't know how else to explain this isn't about Marcus. This is about stopping Hell from thinking they can do anything they want. If Guardians don't protect against this, then why are we even here? Why am I here? Torin's deal will give me the answers I need, it's the only way.

Deb let out a breath she didn't know she was holding.

I can't let this lead go. If I don't take this deal, who knows if I'll find another Trader to meet with me.

Deb teleported to the door outside Jade's suite, pausing only a moment before pressing the doorbell.

Jade's heels clacked as she neared the entrance. The door swung open. In the few hours since Deb had seen her, the demon had changed into a dark green suit. The skirt was short, the heels tall, and the cream-colored V-neck blouse underneath revealing.

"Deborah!" Jade declared. "You look absolutely gutted. We must get a drink, immediately."

Jade pulled the door open wide, inviting Deb to come inside.

"You know where the bar is darling, Jade called as she walked into the bedroom across from the front door. "I'll call down for a starter."

Deb's shoulders relaxed walking into the living space. She went to the bar and poured two glasses of white wine. When Jade returned, she handed her one.

"Tell me," Jade said as she made her way to sit down. "Let's hear it."

"I went home to talk to my sisters," Deb told her. "It didn't go well."

"Mmm." Jade made the sound as she was finishing her first sip. "I see. I have to ask, were you expecting it to go well?"

Deb was taken aback. "Of course."

"Really?" Jade looked quizzically at Deb.

"Yes," Deb affirmed. "We've always been close. This isn't our first disagreement or anything, but it's never been like this. I never felt like they weren't there for me, but—"

"Ahh," Jade said, as if she finally understood. "I think that was your first mistake."

Deb sat on the sofa across from Jade. "What was?"

"Reliance on siblings," Jade told her. "They will always let you down."

"You have siblings?" Deb asked. "Are you close?"

"Yes, I have many siblings," Jade told her. "Let's just say that when we get together wars have a tendency to break out."

Jade crossed her legs at the ankles and stared over at Deb, the green suit picking up all the brightness of her eyes.

"Do you wear anything other than green?" Deb asked.

"With how well it matches my eyes?" Jade asked playfully. "Rarely."

"I want to take the deal Torin offered me," Deb said solemnly.

"Ahhh," Jade responded. "Now I understand the childish sad face you wore when I opened the door."

"I know you've already done a lot for me," Deb began, "especially considering we're on opposite sides of the aisle."

"Nonsense!" Jade declared. "If you see aisles, it's because you made them. We make our choices, we live with the consequences of them all the same, just like you."

"Will you reach out to Torin and arrange a meeting?" Deb asked.

"Already done, darling." Jade's smile was thin. "I did it when you walked in. I'm not daft, as much as you enjoy my company, and of course you do. I didn't think this was a social call."

Deb shook her head realizing Jade must have informed Torin when she said she was calling for food. "Thank you."

"You're welcome." Jade nodded. "Although, being fond of you, I must ask, are you sure you want to go through with this?"

"I'm as sure as I'm going to be. This is my only option for finding Marcus."

"It's no small thing to make a deal with a Trader," Jade told her. "There is no backing out, once you sign the paper, it must be adhered to."

Is she trying to talk me out of it? That can't be good if a demon doesn't think I should take the deal. If I don't take it, how else can I find him?

Before Deb could follow up with a question, the doorbell rang.

"Well, seems Torin doesn't believe that haste makes waste," Jade announced as she stood. "He must be eager to make the deal with you."

Jade walked toward the door, but then turned back to Deb. "Are you certain, darling? I can easily make him go away."

Deb's head hurt. She closed her eyes to chase the clamoring thoughts away and calmed her breathing. The last thing she wanted was for Torin to see fear.

"I'm sure," Deb answered without looking back at her.

I'm coming for you. I won't leave you to rot wherever you are Marcus.

The door swung open and Torin entered wearing the same suit from earlier. He carried a dark red leather briefcase and set it down on the coffee table in the living room.

"I'll give you two some privacy," Jade told them as she walked out of the room.

The only sound in the room was the minifridge humming. Torin sat down next to her, rather than across from her. With his stature and flawless posture, it was as if he towered over her. Deb caught a whiff of aftershave and leather. The case was shiny, as if it had just been polished.

Torin removed papers with dried blood on them. He lifted a divider of some kind and Deb spotted several vials laying underneath. Many of them were full, four lay empty.

Deb swallowed, her palms beginning to sweat. Without realizing it, her knee was bouncing. She slid her hand down her thigh and over her knee to steady herself.

Heaven forgive me, Deb pleaded. *I pray this works.*

"I'm going to use a needle," Torin told her as he pulled out a small case and some plastic tubing. "Jade is rather insistent this be civilized."

Deb didn't say anything, so he continued.

"Seems Jade has grown quite fond of you, Miss O'Mara."

"Let's get this over with," Deb said, through gritted teeth.

"Of course," he told her. "Do you have the paperwork I left with you?"

Deb got up and went to her raincoat retrieving the unopened envelope, she handed it to him.

He looked at it and then back to her as if he were contemplating scolding her for not reading it. Saying nothing he tore it open, unfolded the document and directed her.

"You'll need to sign or mark your name here, prick your finger, and smudge it here." He handed a pen to Deb. "It's a pen on one side and a sharp edge on the other."

Deb signed her name, flipped the pen, and pricked the tip of her finger. With a droplet of blood, she smeared it underneath her name, leaving crude proof that it was she who had made the deal.

"It's done," he said simply. "It's easier to get blood from the main vein in your arm."

She rolled up the sleeve of her blouse and he injected her arm with the needle. He was proficient, filling the vials quickly and placing them back inside the case for safe keeping. He pulled the needle out and before she could stop him, he healed her.

"You didn't need to do that!" yanking her arm back away from his cold grasp.

He scarred me. Deb looked down in horror at the bumpy red mark still burning on her arm.

"It was part of the deal," Torin told her. "Something you would have known had you bothered to read it."

He packed everything away in the leather satchel and stood.

"Wait, where's the information I paid for." Panic ran through Deb escaping through cracks in her voice.

"I'm simply getting a drink Miss O'Mara." He walked to the bar and poured himself a whiskey. "It's customary to share a drink once the trade is complete. It's where humans got the idea to toast in celebration after closing a deal."

He came back toward her and held up his glass. *"Sláinte."*

She picked the wine up from the coffee table and tipped it toward him before taking a sip.

He smiled thinly. "There's no reason we can't be civilized."

"I can think of a lot of reasons not to be civilized with you," Deb retorted.

"That's a tad hypocritical of you, don't you think?"

Deb angrily placed the glass back down on the table, nearly shattering it in the process.

"I don't like delivering bad news," Torin told her as he swigged the rest of his whiskey, emptying the glass. "I'm afraid where Marcus is, you cannot follow."

"Just spit it out, Torin," Deb scolded. "Where is Marcus and who took him?"

"Marcus is in Hell," Torin said plainly.

Deb's stomach flipped and her headache kicked into high gear.

"How do you know that?" Deb questioned. "Did you see him?"

"Personally?" Torin asked but didn't wait for the answer. "No, but I confirmed it the with entity that took him."

"And who was that?" Deb could feel her body shaking, anger coursing through her like it was a pinball just shot out of a cannon.

"Wrath," Torin answered, then turned to leave.

"Who?" Deb asked.

"If you want to know more about who he is," Torin told her, "I suggest you start by asking Jade."

Torin was finished. He took his case and left the room, as the click of the door echoed down the hall, Deb practically fell onto the sofa.

What have I done? she lamented. *What is Jade? If she knows Wrath, did she know where Marcus was all along?*

"What the bloody hell did he tell you?" Jade asked when she returned to the room. "Did he tell you where Marcus is?"

Deb nodded. "He's in Hell."

"I'm sorry, luv." Jade's tone was soft, affectionate almost.

"Did you know?" Deb asked.

"No," Jade answered coolly. "Why would I?"

"Torin told me to ask you about the demon who took him."

"Ask away, dear." Jade opened her arms in mock invitation. "I know a lot of demons."

"Wrath," Deb stated. "Who is Wrath?"

"Bollocks!" Jade declared. "Torin's lying!"

Jade made a beeline for the bar, pouring herself a shot of clear liquid that Deb assumed was vodka. She tossed the drink back in one swallow.

"You told me Torin was trustworthy, the only Trader you'd do business with." Deb stood, gazing at Jade through the mirror behind the bar. "He's not lying, is he Jade?"

Jade turned to face Deb, her eyes brimming with tears. "Torin is a lot of things, but a liar is not one of them."

Sniffing, Jade straightened and seemed to pull

175

herself together.

"Who is Wrath?" Deb insisted. "What's his real name? I'm assuming Wrath is a nickname. What is he?"

"He's a bloody bastard is what he is." Jade nearly spit the reply.

"I need to get to Hell," Deb said calmly. "I need to go get Marcus."

Jade laughed. "Are you insane?"

"I'm beginning to think so," Deb said sardonically. "It's the second time someone's asked me that today."

"Even if I could get you to Hell," Jade began. "If Wrath has Marcus, you aren't getting him back."

"Well, I appreciate the vote of confidence," Deb retorted.

"It has nothing to do with you," Jade scoffed. "You don't know what you're dealing with."

"Then tell me!" Deb yelled. "Who is Wrath?!"

Jade's eyebrows arched in surprise at Deb's tone. The demon's cheeks flushed a rosy shade of pink. "He's immortal, as are all the Deadly Sins."

The room fell quiet.

"Deadly sins," Deb repeated. "you're saying they're actual demons?"

"That's right, Guardian," Jade told her as she picked up the wine glass she had temporarily traded for a shot of alcohol. "Let it sink in, although I'm surprised you didn't already know of the Deadly Sins, guess I expected more of someone your age."

"How do you know Wrath?" Deb sensed the answer coming but needed to hear her say it.

"He's my brother, darling," Jade said plainly. "And he's not someone I would cross if I were you."

CHAPTER SEVENTEEN

Kelly reached the top of the stairs and turned right. The vampire stomped up after her.

Good, Kelly thought. *He's taunting me. That will buy me a few extra seconds.*

Pushing through her bedroom door, she slammed it shut behind her. Grabbing the navy-blue field bag in the closet, she tore it open sending weapons scattering to the floor. At the bottom of the bag was a leg holster, she wrapped it around her thigh. She slipped a few knives, throwing stars, and a dagger into the open slots. Sitting against the back wall of her closet she picked up a morning star. Kelly knew the club-like weapon with a spiked metal ball bolted to the end of it was intended for maximum damage. She hid the morning star behind a bookcase on the other side of the room. Unsheathing her scabbard, she went back to the wall near the entry and mentally readied herself for a fight.

Kelly put herself tightly against the wall leading to her closet. She would be just out of view until Garrick fully entered. If he kicked the door in, she would also be clear from its path.

"Come out, come out, wherever you are," the vampire serenaded as he opened and shut the bathroom door.

Kelly inhaled deeply holding her breath for four to five seconds before deliberately emptying her lungs, slowing her heart rate. Vampires had excellent hearing—a thumping heartbeat, blood pulsating through your veins—those might as well be alarm bells.

Kelly wiped her hands on her jeans to dry them. She tightened her grip on the scabbard as the footfalls got closer. The vampire didn't make a grand entrance with a kick through the door. He simply turned the knob and pushed the door inward while remaining in the hall.

Kelly closed her eyes to focus on the sound of his steps. She had to time her attack perfectly. If she turned and swung too soon, he would have the doorframe as a shield. If she waited too long, he would see her upon entry. She listened as he entered the room, *one, two,* then the floor creaked, *swing* she thought as her eyes flew open and she pivoted to her left.

As the blade neared Garrick's chest, he moved his forearm up and blocked it with a black Falchion, weapon of choice for Hell's First Army. The two weapons clanged against one another, the fierce collision sending tiny orange sparks into the air. She swung up as he pulled back to swing again. While in mid-swing, Kelly sliced him across the chest, but it left no mark. She shoved him backward.

Wasting no time, she punched him in the face and sent him several more steps back into the hallway. He jumped up, grabbed the molding around the door with one hand and swung his body forward kicking Kelly hard in the chest. She tumbled backward over the bed to the other side of the room.

Kelly grabbed a throwing star with her left hand on her way to a standing position. He was on her quickly. Garrick swung his blade down again. Kelly released the throwing star, aiming for his bare chest while dodging his blade. The sharp metal object scraped the skin, leaving a large red mark, but no real damage.

Confirmed, he is fully restored. His skin will be tough to break.

She spun out of the way of another strike and he adeptly pulled his Falchion back. Kelly angled herself so her back was to the bed, when his blade whipped toward her, she kicked him in the stomach and slid to her left. Garrick bowled over and lurched forward. He fell onto the bed, his weight sending the bed careening toward the corner of the room where her remaining weapons were on the floor. The scratching of wood on wood ended with a thunderous crash. The top part of the bedpost smashed through the wall and disappeared. Artwork fell to the floor as the house seemed to rumble.

What was that? Was that the bed, or Gen?

As the vampire pushed off the bed to spin around, Kelly grabbed the stashed morning star and was already in full swing. He put his arm up to fend off the blow. Garrick was faster than she anticipated, only the wooden handle made contact. He grabbed for her weapon, but she pulled it back just in time.

He got to his feet and thrust his open hand square into Kelly's chest. The weapon fell from her grasp as she flew backward smashing into windows on the far side of the room. They were showered in glass as the windows broke inward thanks to the cloaking mechanism surrounding the house. Kelly winced as small shards of broken glass pierced her back. Covered in an itchy coating of dust that burned and scraped her skin, Kelly's chest ached like someone was standing on top of her. She coughed and heaved as she lifted her head to spot where he was, but she had no time to recover; he was on top of her again.

Garrick's giant hand reached for her. Kelly grabbed the fallen nightstand and smashed the vampire on the side of the head. The cherry wood furniture splintered like it was a piece of deadwood. The impact knocked him to one knee. Laboring to her feet, she grabbed the toppled lamp, wrapped the cord around Garrick's neck and dragged him across the floor toward the door.

Snapping the cord, Garrick got to his feet and shoved Kelly from behind. She sailed through the air crashing through Deb's partially opened door and rolled to a stop in the middle of her sister's bedroom.

The vampire loomed in the doorway, shadows casting in all directions. "I knew I was going to like tussling with you, sweetheart."

Kelly noted he was in incredible shape: every muscle toned, each movement deliberate and impactful.

"Who sent you, creep?" Kelly asked with loathing as she got back to her feet knowing he probably wouldn't answer.

"Remember me, sweetheart? The name's Garrick," he smiled. "I figure we should know each other a little better if we're going to dance like this all day. What's your name, Guardian?"

"I'm an O'Mara." Kelly pulled a knife from her leg holster. "You need to leave or be thrown out."

"Come on," he toyed. "I just got here."

Garrick lunged and surprised Kelly with a football style tackle. Even though she quickly side-stepped to her right, it wasn't fast enough to avoid someone of his size.

Her knife clanged against the hardwood floor and spun away. His weight landed on her left side. She fisted her hands together and slammed them down on his back. Garrick groaned and tried to pull his knees up to pin and straddle her. As he was moving, Kelly grabbed the ponytail he fashioned at the nape of his neck and yanked hard to her left as she thrust up. She managed to move their bodies enough to squirm free from underneath him.

She stretched for the knife, fingers grazing the handle and spinning it toward her. She picked it up and swung back around swiping at Garrick's chest. She connected and managed to scrape the surface of the skin, leaving a mark, but still no blood.

One more, Kelly believed. *Another blow and I think it will break through his armor-like skin.*

Before Garrick could regain his footing, Kelly jumped on top of him. Using the butt end of the weapon she punched him several times in the face and head. He moved his arms up around his head to stave off the attack and knocked the knife from her hand. She changed focus and jabbed at his ribcage. The vampire yelped after several bruising shots. Garrick punched Kelly hard in the shoulder sending her tumbling off and away from him. As she got to her feet, she threw another star at his chest, this time a thin red line of blood bubbled to the surface.

"Gen!" Kelly screamed.

Waiting the few seconds for her sister to reply was like an eternity.

"I'm here!" Gen's strained yell told her everything.

"You need to keep going after the same target!"

The sound of glass breaking reverberated back to Kelly.

"Got it!" Gen hollered.

Kelly and Garrick faced off again, like a heavyweight bout they sized each other up from several feet apart. Garrick was the aggressor. He stepped forward and swung at her head, but Kelly blocked it. As she swung toward him, he jabbed at her stomach, folding her over. He grabbed her by the hair and threw her against Deb's closet door. The double folding doors clanged together forcefully, one side falling off its hinges. Kelly was slow to stand. She glanced up and Garrick stared down at her.

"I could do this all day, O'Mara." He smiled. "Damn Accord has kept me from having a proper fight, but I've been preparing for this day for nearly a thousand years."

The metal end of a baseball bat just inside Deb's closet caught Kelly's attention and she grabbed for it. As Garrick leaned down to grab her, she spun away from him. Kelly lifted the bat in the air and struck a blow to his lower back. The vampire went down to one knee, but Kelly didn't stop. She connected again. On the third swing, Garrick turned toward her and managed to grab the bat and yank it free from her hands. He angrily hurled the bat behind him, sending it nearly through the wall to the exterior of the house. Kelly grabbed a vase, the only thing left on a nearby shelf. She broke it against the wall, giving her a crude jagged knife. With her other hand, she picked up a small table and threw it at Garrick. He easily deflected it, but the movement exposed his chest. She sliced across his body several times attempting to open a second wound. She had never fought a renewed vampire, but texts she'd read told her swiping in the same area was the best way to cut the skin. Unfortunately, his skin held firm. He angrily batted the makeshift shiv out of her hand.

Out of weapons, Kelly backed toward the door. Garrick took two large steps and reached her position easily. The frantic boxing match continued. Kelly was blocking some of his punches but not all. Her muscles were screaming under the strain, her ribs sore, the pain increasing with every punch he landed. In the frenzy of their fight, they blew through what was left of the door tearing it from its hinges. The frame and molding crumpled to the floor behind them as they forcibly left Deb's bedroom.

Kelly punched him several more times in the chest, forcing him to fall backward taking down a plant stand that held an antique oil lamp and a potted ivy. Soil from the plant spewed through the air as the lamp shattered against the hard pine floors.

Garrick got to his feet and lunged toward Kelly. This time she was ready for him, as his arms wrapped around her, she grabbed hold of him. Kelly pulled as he pushed, and their combined force sent them hurtling through the air. The two collided with the second-floor railing and broke through it. Garrick slammed against the staircase wall and brutally landed on the steps below. Kelly landed partially on top of him.

Grunting, Kelly crawled over Garrick, trying to get past him to slide down the steps to the first floor below. The shards of glass split her skin as they had embedded further into her back. She tasted blood on her lip. The pain shooting through her left shoulder told Kelly it had popped out of its socket.

I need to get downstairs to Gen, Kelly agonized. *I was so close to making it, I need to try again. Gen and I will be stronger together.*

As she cleared Garrick's body, the vampire grabbed her hair and violently thrust her toward the ceiling. Cool air rushed over her as she was catapulted toward the second-floor landing. Kelly crashed through what was left of the side railing and into the wall. The force was so strong Kelly got temporarily stuck in the hallway wall between her room and the bathroom. Wiggling free, she gingerly stood leaving a giant hole behind. Gray dust mixed with her own blood and clung to her clothing.

Well, that hurt like hell, but I think it popped my shoulder back into place.

There was a painting that hung on the wall just outside the bathroom, the brown-wooden frame was broken, the painting ripped and torn to shreds.

Gone, Kelly thought wistfully, *just like this house.*

"Ain't nothing better than a good old fashioned bar fight, huh O'Mara?" Garrick smirked as he slowly stalked toward her.

"You don't know how to have a good time,

Garrick," Kelly told him. Through gritted teeth and labored breathing, each of them stood sweating and panting.

The vampire swung with his right hand and she blocked it with her left forearm. He didn't land the intended shot at her ribs, but deflecting it still hurt. Using her right hand, palm out, Kelly jabbed Garrick several times in the nose, snapping his head back each time. She drew a trickle of blood.

Nice! Kelly exulted inside. *I broke through again.*

Garrick groaned in pain. Stumbling, he thrashed for control and nearly fell through the broken part of the railing. Garrick recovered and the two of them traded a whirlwind of punches. The vampire was on the offensive. Kelly was forced to back into the small bathroom. She yanked the medicine cabinet off the wall and struck it across the vampire's face. The mirror shattered into what seemed like a million small shards of silver. Garrick returned the favor by smashing her face into the small, frosted window on the far wall. The glass broke slicing her across the forehead with a large piece puncturing her cheek. Blood colored her vision, everything awash in red.

Kelly yanked the glass free and wielded it like a knife. Swinging haphazardly, she targeted Garrick's chest in the same area she had been focused on earlier. He shrieked when his skin broke. This time she got more than a trickle of blood.

Garrick's shoulders squared and his eyes darkened.

Perhaps he's done playing, Kelly thought in horror. *If he's been holding back this entire time, I'm in real trouble.*

Kelly held his glare with one of her own, though everything was still tinged with red from her own bloody vision. The only sound came from their labored breathing. Swirls of dust and debris floated in the air around them. Kelly's body ached, her skin burned from bruised muscles and widening wounds.

I really need to get to Gen. I've worn down Garrick, so his cloaking could be weakened. If Gen and I connect, maybe we can break the cloaking. If not, one of us will have to make a run for the perimeter.

The house shook and the two of them nearly lost their footing. Bouncing off the shower door the top of the wall behind the sink cracked and split down the middle, exposing the insulation inside.

Gen, Kelly exhaled in relief. *That had to be her power rattling the house.*

Garrick swung his arm toward Kelly's head, but she blocked it and braced for the next blow. Instead, Garrick charged at her and the two of them crashed through the weakened wall and back into her bedroom.

Failing to withstand the assault of their momentum, shards of wood tore at her clothes, some of her hair catching on the framing and yanking free from her scalp. Garrick took out some pipes causing water to spring from the floor. The back of Kelly's head slammed against the floor with Garrick landing on top of her. The violence of the collision, coupled with the weight of his body, forced the air from her lungs. With the wind knocked out of her, she lay still, her body momentarily shocked into stasis.

Kelly slowly turned her head to the left. Garrick rolled off her and was on his side facing away. Kelly crawled in the opposite direction until she could stand. She stumbled through the wreckage, wading back through the bathroom heading for what used to be the door. It was the fastest route to the staircase. She could see the top of the steps from her position. Garrick was coming up behind her, but Kelly's head was rattled, probably concussed, so she was slow to react. He slammed into her from behind and the two of them exploded through the bathroom linen closet and into Gen's bathroom on the other side.

"I'm not through with you yet, Guardian." Garrick coughed as he tried to sit up.

"I hope . . . you're bleeding out . . . inside." Kelly's words strained through her own gasping.

Kelly pulled herself up using the makeup table in the bathroom. She glanced over her shoulder. Garrick was struggling to his feet as well. She picked up the glass top table and smashed it over his back.

He yelled and reached for her leg. Kelly was tired, her strength now coming in short bursts. She could not swat him away. He hauled her up across his back, then burst through the bathroom door and into Gen's bedroom. Kelly punched Garrick hard in the lower back, collapsing him to his knees. She yanked free as another wave of energy rocked the house, this time splitting the wooden floor below her. Garrick stumbled forward and onto Gen's bed, while Kelly fell to the floor and rolled to the window seat.

Garrick managed to partially sit up and swing his legs over the side. "You aren't easy to get into bed, O'Mara."

"I'd rather die . . . than sleep with you," Kelly rebuffed as she pulled herself up again.

He pulled a knife from a holster around his waist and stepped toward her.

"Guess this is it, O'Mara," he said, as he wiped blood from under his nose. "It was even better than I imagined."

"Gen!" Kelly yelled. "We're above you . . . I could use a little help!"

Garrick smiled. "I don't think anyone's coming to your rescue, certainly not your friend downstairs."

The shiny blade glistened as he raised it above her. Michael's advice when dealing with a new enemy ran through her mind. *If you don't know how to strike the final blow, don't forget, if it has ears, strike them. They're an opening and they can affect balance.*

Kelly instinctively thrusted her left arm up to block Garrick from stabbing her in the chest. Simultaneously, she leaned back and grabbed a book off the window seat swinging it hard against the left side of his head. It rattled him enough that he missed stabbing her. Kelly fisted her hands and swung them as hard as she could striking both of Garrick's ears simultaneously. She then grabbed the last knife in her holster and stabbed him in the ear as he started to falter toward the floor. Garrick wailed and recoiled as blood spurted from the wound. The vampire pulled at the knife as Kelly pushed past him toward the hole Gen's power made in the floor. Garrick yelled in a language Kelly didn't understand. It sounded like Gaelic mixed with intermittent whale cries. The noise was nearly deafening, and Kelly had to put her hands over her ears to dim the pain.

Kelly peered through the widening crack in the floor and spotted a sliver of the kitchen island below them. Garrick stopped yelling once he removed the knife from his ear. He was in a rage.

When he was half a step away, Kelly yelled. "Now Gen!"

The house rumbled and shook causing Garrick to lose his grip on the knife. Kelly lunged forward. Wrapping her arms around the vampire, she used all the strength she could muster to tackle him. The momentum of their violent collision drove their bodies through the damaged pine floor hurtling toward the kitchen island below.

CHAPTER EIGHTEEN

Gen had smashed just about every dish she owned over the female vampire's head. The two had thrown each other around the room so much that most of the chairs were broken. The smell of fresh cut wood floated in the air with splinters of mahogany blanketing everything. The vampire's falchion had punctured the wall, embedded up to its hilt. Gen was punching at the female's head but receiving counter punches to her ribs in return. Each of them was winded and Gen wasn't sure how she was going to tear at the skin with the vampire wearing a thick jacket buttoned all the way to her neck. The male vampire that went after Kelly had his jacket open, exposing his bare chest, the female was obviously smarter.

This vampire was taller than Gen and thin but strong. She had long brown hair twisted into a tight bun at the base of her neck. With violet eyes and young glowing skin, Gen knew if she were human, she'd probably be on the covers of magazines.

This house is in shambles. Gen's mind raced in random directions. She found it hard to concentrate on the fight when this precious space she had once shared with Gabriel was being destroyed. *Death by a billion fragments of glass.*

Gen grabbed a pair of scissors from the office drawer half broken on the floor. She swung toward the vampire's thigh, taking several quick jabs toward the same spot. Gen managed to slice the pants open, scrape and bruise the leg, but drew no blood. Kelly had just told her she'd need to hit the same spot several times before the skin would break. That was going to be difficult if she didn't have a target like the male vampire's chest to aim for.

The female swung a baton and Gen blocked it with her forearm, using the opportunity to punch the female in the face several times. With a howl the vampire's head snapped back, and blood spilled from her nose.

Blood. A glimmer of hope soared within Gen. *That's a good sign.*

The vampire lunged. They crashed into the large hutch, the only piece of furniture still upright. The glass in the decorative front doors was already shattered, the cause of the slice in Gen's forehead, and the bottom cabinet had a hole in it from one of their kicks. The one hundred and fifty-year old floral-patterned china littered the floor. Their stomping feet turned the artisan plates into a fine powder that hung like a fog in the air.

She heard loud thuds, toppling furniture, and glass breaking upstairs and knew Kelly was most likely near her own bedroom toward the front of the house.

The female vampire roared back, grabbed Gen's arm, and tossed her across the room. Gen landed hard and rolled to a stop near the double doors to the screened-in porch. The vampire was on Gen quickly. The female reached down to pick Gen up by the throat, but Gen kicked the same leg she had stabbed earlier with the scissors and the vampire collapsed to one knee. Gen kicked again landing a blow to the vampire's side, pushing her into a sitting position.

Gen got to her feet and grabbed the thick material around the collar of the vampire's jacket, throwing her toward the kitchen door. As she scrambled to her feet, she braced herself on the refrigerator for support. Gen came around the island and pummeled the side of the vampire's head with the freezer door several times. The vampire slumped to the floor and Gen attempted to race past her to the staircase to help Kelly.

The vampire grabbed Gen's leg and tripped her, slamming her onto the pine floor. Her hands barely broke her fall, but they were enough to keep her head from banging against the unforgiving surface. The female climbed on Gen's back and started beating on her. Each punch akin to a stab to her already bruised ribcage. Gen twisted against the onslaught but couldn't shake the vampire loose. More of her skin ripped open. The wound on her forehead worsened and blood trickled down her face.

The female leaned down close to Gen's face, sniffed the air, and then snickered.

"Smells delicious," the female whispered.

I can't let her taste my blood. Panic gripped Gen's chest. *She'll be healed and I'll be starting from scratch. That's game over.*

Gen bucked like a bull and jerked forward. The

weight of the vampire shifted. Gen kicked her way free and crawled further away from the blood thirsty creature. There was a side table in the hallway that Gen smashed. She grabbed one of the legs to use as a bat. Backing up toward the front entrance, the vampire locked eyes with Gen and smiled.

"You will never get to your friend." They were the first taunting words the vampire spoke since the ambush. "Like you, she'll be dead soon, but not before me and Lieutenant Garrick drink the blood from both your broken bodies and feel it restore and nourish us." The vampire almost hissed the words. A loud bang erupted from above and Kelly screamed.

"Worried about your friend, Guardian?" the female mocked with an exaggerated pout.

Gen swung at the female's head but missed. The vampire was quick to use Gen's own momentum against her by pulling Gen's arm and throwing her violently through the air. Gen's body banged off the kitchen doorway and crashed against the top row of cabinets to the right of the sink. As she bounced off the counter below, something snapped. She rolled to the ground and a sharp pain roared in her side. One of the cabinet doors broke off and fell on top of her as she labored to breathe. Gen struggled to stand. The vampire stood in the kitchen doorway and leered.

The plant Gen carried with her through decades of moving from house to house drew her attention. The vampire followed Gen's gaze and snatched the plant ripping it from the hook. The plant was torn from its roots and scattered in small pieces to the floor. Welled-up tears mixed with the blood spilling from the wound on her forehead.

The vampire laughed. Gen knew her own face must have expressed her heartache.

The ground shook, and the vampire dropped the planter as she steadied herself. Every remaining window still intact shattered inwardly. Gen stood taller biting the inside of her mouth through the pain. She could feel energy racing through her body, like a pinball it seemed to be bouncing around at warp speed. Cracks ripped up the sides of the walls sending spiraling crevices across the ceiling, a spider web of destruction.

When she inhaled deeply to calm herself the house stilled. A loud crashing noise came from the second floor. Gen glanced at the ceiling, she could hear hissing from the pipes inside the walls, then came the sound of rushing water.

Gen pushed the pain aside. The vampire had regained her balance, pressed forward, and took aim at her head once more. Gen parried the shots and counterpunched with jabs of her own. The two slammed around the island once more. The female dragged Gen toward the back wall of the kitchen. Once again Gen was further from the stairs, no closer to getting to her sister.

A thunderous boom came from the second floor causing both women to look up. Then Kelly screamed for help.

The vampire locked eyes with Gen. "I tried to warn you, seems she'll be going before you Guardian. Such a shame, I really wanted to get the first kill."

Gen noticed the wrought iron frying pan on the

floor. She waited for the vampire to attack. Gen knew it was going to hurt, having to lunge for something while her side was this battered, but she had to try. There was no teleporting away and with the severity of her injuries there was no way she could run.

The female was about to pounce once more, but then stopped at the sound of shrieking. Gen's heart nearly stopped but then it became obvious it wasn't Kelly's voice. The male vampire was yelling in a language Gen didn't understand. The guttural nature of the howl meant Kelly had hurt him.

"It's a mistake to count the victory before it's won, vampire."

The female snapped her attention back to Gen. The vampire swung her right arm toward the side Gen was favoring. Bracing for impact Gen rolled to her right when it came, using the punch to mask what she was aiming for. As Gen forced herself to her feet, she had the handle firmly within her grasp. The heavy pan slammed into the side of the vampire's skull. The vibration reverberated up Gen's arm. The female was knocked violently to the ground with one hit. No screeching, just the sound of her limp body rolling to the base of the hutch. The female lay in a small pool of her own blood now flowing freely from a broken nose.

Gen pulled what remained of the hutch down on top of the vampire who lay motionless on the floor. The familiar sensation of Gen's power swirled inside her and with it the ground shook and opened beneath the female's body. Then Kelly pleaded from above. Squeezing her eyes closed Gen tried to aim for the ceiling, but the entire house rattled once more.

The ceiling crack widened and with a thunderous roar Kelly and Lieutenant Garrick burst like a wrecking ball through the opening, spectacularly destroying the island on impact. Her sister was on top, using Garrick to cushion the blow. Kelly groaned and rolled off the immobile vampire who was encased in marble, wood, and plaster dust.

Kelly was covered in a reddish-brown sludge, her clothes were torn, and her normal wise cracks were conspicuously absent. Gen limped over to Kelly now noticing her own left leg had been speared with a small knife. When Gen reached her sister, she quickly evaluated the extent of Kelly's injuries and cringed.

Kelly coughed and blood gurgled out as she sat up. Gen grabbed hold of Kelly's hand and pulled her sister to a standing position.

Kelly placed her palm on Gen's bleeding forehead. Gen could feel her sister trying to heal her, but it was weak.

"Let me heal you first." Gen pulled Kelly's hand down from her forehead.

"Good idea," Kelly said, as blood escaped her lips.

Gen healed Kelly as quickly as possible but was weak herself. They would only get so far without Deb to help them.

"Getting to each other didn't break the cloaking," Gen whispered.

"I know," Kelly agreed. "We just need enough for one of us to get out the door and away from the house."

That's it, Gen thought. *I'll heal Kelly enough to get her out. She can bring everyone once she makes it past the cloaking.*

Kelly's surface wounds were healing, and she was standing straighter now.

Gen surveyed the wreckage of the kitchen. The microwave was collapsed in on itself, sparks still bursting from its core. The cabinets were a mishmash of broken doors, missing panels, and dangling pieces of wood left swaying in the aftermath. The air was heavy with glass powder dusting everything in the room. The acrid smell of burning electrical wires hung heavy in the air. Lights flickered on and off. The refrigerator whined its disapproval at having its door ripped off. The faucet in the sink was broken with water sprouting upward like a waterfall of malevolent design.

Garrick moved and rolled off the remnants of the island while the female stirred from underneath the cabinet.

Before Gen could tell Kelly the plan the female vampire started yelling.

"No! No, no, no!" the female cried. "Get me out! Let me out! Not buried, I can't be buried!"

"What the—" Kelly muttered.

"Her lower half is trapped in the subfloor that opened when the house shook," Gen told her.

"Lieutenant, get me out!" the vampire protested. "You have to get me out!"

Garrick was holding his side as he limped toward the hutch.

"I'm coming Keeva," Garrick told his distraught partner.

Gen pulled Kelly into the hallway away from the kitchen.

"I know you hate running." Gen tugged her sister over the shattered remains of the front door. "I need you to run until you can hear our brothers."

Keeva wailed again. "Let me out! Don't leave me buried!"

"No," Kelly resisted. "Come with me, I have an idea."

The sound of the hutch toppling rang out and Gen knew Garrick was rescuing Keeva.

Kelly supported Gen's weight as they stepped down the front steps and out onto the street.

"She fears being buried," Kelly said to Gen from the middle of the street.

"Yeah, I got that," Gen answered as Kelly healed her. "What's your plan, that we both run and hope they don't catch us? I think that will take too long."

Gen's heart skipped, being outside made her feel close to escape, yet she knew the vampires were fast and unrelenting pursuers.

"No," Kelly answered. "You're going to bury them both."

"What?" Gen asked in bewilderment.

"Don't think about it, Gen," Kelly ordered. "Bring the house down. It's still cloaked, it will implode inward."

"I don't know if I can," Gen faltered.

"Do it!" Kelly snapped. "Now, before he frees her or gives up trying and comes after us."

Screams emanated from within the house. A few precious moments later Garrick labored toward the front door with Keeva draped against his side.

Kelly took hold of Gen's shoulder. "You can do this.

I will go and get our brothers."

Gen closed her eyes and the power inside her awakened. The ground rumbled beneath her feet. When she opened her eyes, Kelly was moving in the opposite direction, flopping from one vehicle to the next.

She's going to make it. Gen breathed a sigh of relief.

Turning her attention back to the house, Garrick and Keeva were struggling to maintain their balance. Gen limped closer toward the house; her hands balled into fists. The closer Gen got, the more the house rattled. With the sound of an avalanche the roof caved first. Everything creaked and cracked as wind whipped up all around her. Then the right side of the façade was pulled into the center. The house seemingly folded in on itself burying both vampires in the rubble. A large dust plume floated up toward the sky and then it was still, the death of the house serenaded by the blaring of car alarms ringing in Gen's ears.

Gen couldn't take her eyes off the pile of debris that was once her cherished home. A teardrop streaked through the blood and dirt caked on her face.

It's gone, Gabe. Gen succumbed to the heartache and openly wept.

CHAPTER NINETEEN

Deb paced the small park on the south side of the city of Boston. The ocean beyond the old forte churned. The steady morning wind formed small white peaks of seafoam across the surface and the cool air nipped at her exposed neck. She had changed into her own clothes and left Jade's ensemble behind when she raced from the hotel room the night before.

The discovery of who Jade truly was unnerved Deb. Even in Jade's large hotel suite, the space closed in around her like she was claustrophobic. She couldn't trust what would happen next. The swirling emotions inside her practically made her nauseous. She was filled with disappointment, anger, even a little betrayal.

Why? Deb wondered. *How could I have expected honesty from Jade? I knew she was a demon. Why did I trust her?*

Jade tried to stop Deb from leaving. She told Deb not to 'go off half-cocked and to stop acting like a petulant child,' when it was obvious Deb was upset. As the argument raged between the two of them Deb knew she made the mistake of all but telling Jade she was hurt by the demon's lack of truthfulness.

Deb wasn't sure why she was feeling so hurt. She clearly wasn't over her family's lack of support in finding Marcus, so was her disappointment deflected onto Jade?

What was I expecting from a demon? Deb scolded herself silently. *It's not like we could ever be friends.*

Deb's eyes watered, tears straining to escape. Swallowing hard she inhaled sharply and buried the pain and anxiety welling up.

Remarkably, Jade seemed to soften. She told Deb she had planned to explain it all to her in good time. The demon even argued that with the truth out there, she and Deb should have drinks and chat about whatever Deb wanted.

Yeah right, Deb thought. *If ever there were code words for "I was never going to tell you," pleading your case about a grand future conversation of transparency was it.*

Jade raced after Deb into the bedroom. Deb removed her borrowed clothes, tossing them aside. She tore open the plastic dry-cleaning bag that held her freshly laundered jeans, blouse, and raincoat. Jade had even purchased a new pair of ankle boots. Deb nearly left barefoot but decided to take the footwear.

Jade was speaking hurriedly, trying to tell Deb she was safe, that she had nothing to fear from her, that there was no need for Deb to rush off.

Jade is a Deadly Sin, Deb agonized. *How did I not see it? Could she have been any more obvious? Her name alone should have been a clue. Jade's beauty, commanding nature, people falling all over themselves to please her.*

Deb could see it clearly now. *Even humans, the way*

people seemed to stare when Jade walked by, as if they longed to be around her, to be in her presence.

Deb thought through the last couple of days. *Jade's piercing green eyes always seemed to do more than gaze, they penetrated, they read your heart, your wants and needs. Jade was the physical embodiment of Envy.*

How did I not know each Deadly Sin was an actual demon? Does my family know about The Deadly Sins? Kelly and Tom must know, but I don't remember hearing any stories about them. How can that be?

Even Jade questioned how someone, such as Deb, who had roamed Earth for hundreds of years could not know of their presence.

Maybe it's one more thing I've forgotten. One more thing I can't trust my mind to recall. Are the lost memories of Dmitri just the tip of the iceberg?

Normally, the small park by the ocean would calm Deb. Since the revelation, Deb's mind raced in all directions with no end in sight. Deb reached into her pocket. Her fingers traced the edges of the gold band and ancient coin that Marcus asked Gardenia to give her.

With each passing hour, finding Marcus seemed further and further away. She was terrified she may never see him again, may never have the chance at a normal conversation. Will she ever know the truth about their relationship and the ring?

Will I learn if the ring binds? And what about this coin? What am I supposed to do with it?

She breathed in deep and allowed the calmness of Heaven to surround her.

"Deborah, thank you for reaching out," Lucas

stated. "Have you found Marcus?"

Deb turned to face the twin Angels and nearly cried at the sight of them. Leo looked like he hadn't slept in weeks, appearing to age in the short couple of days since she had seen him last.

"I'm sorry," Deb began. "I have news and it's not good."

Lucas nodded. "Tell us."

Leo bit his lip. "We need to know."

"I know," Deb told them. "I have it on good authority that it's what we suspected. Marcus has been taken."

"Where?!" Leo blurted.

Deb had been searching her mind all night for the gentlest way to tell them, but there wasn't one. "Hell," Leo gasped in response. "Marcus is being kept in Hell by demonic force."

"No." The word fell from Lucas' mouth, barely audible.

"What do we do?!" Leo demanded. "Who do we tell?"

"I might have a way of getting to him," Deb began.

The puzzled looks might as well have been glaring yellow warning lights.

"What do you mean?" Lucas asked. "How would you *get* to him?"

"You would do that?" Leo interrupted. "You would go to Hell to save Marcus?"

"What?!" Lucas said startled. "No, Deb you cannot go to Hell. You know that already. You know going to Hell breaks the Accord. Opens the gates. Starts a war!"

"How do you know?" Leo scoffed. "Maybe, it doesn't do any of those things."

"Please," Deb held her hands up trying to calm the two Angels. "I have made a," She paused searching for the right word to describe Jade. "Acquaintance. Someone I think can get me in and out of Hell."

"That sentence screams of secrecy," Leo retorted. "What wildly dangerous idea have you come up with?"

"Stop," Lucas announced. "I mean it, stop right now! I don't know what you're planning, and I don't want to know." Lucas wagged his finger between he and his brother. "We don't want to know."

"I do," Leo insisted.

"No, you don't, brother," Lucas said calmly. "Anything we know, Heaven will know."

"Ooohh." Leo nearly sang the word in understanding. "He's right, the hierarchy, they can read our minds when they want to, and we cannot resist."

"What do you mean?" Deb asked Leo. "Who can do that? Why would they do something like that? That's not right."

A tinge of anxiety within Deb began creeping toward impatience.

"I agree!" Leo said emphatically.

"It doesn't matter," Lucas said. "Whatever you are going to do to help Marcus, please keep us out of it. Not just for our sake, but for your safety too, Deb. You don't want the hierarchy hunting you down."

"Okay," Deb said, recognizing the forlorn look in Lucas' eyes.

"You have to trust me," Deb assured them. "I am

going to find him, but the news about where he is, I wanted you to hear it from me."

"We appreciate that," Lucas told her with a tear in his eye. "We know you'll do everything you can. Please, just be careful. We know our uncle wouldn't want you to put yourself in danger to help him. I'm sure he would be mad we weren't doing more to talk you out of it."

Leo came forward and enveloped Deb in a giant bear hug. "Thank you for not giving up," he whispered.

"We will let you go." Lucas grabbed Leo by the elbow and pulled him away from Deb. "We're sorry to hear about the house. We've never heard of a Guardian's place of residence being compromised that way."

"Yeah," Leo added. "That's too bad, we didn't know it was your sister's original home with her husband. Their love story is rather epic. This just adds to the legend."

"Thank you," Deb said. "How did you find out about the house?"

"Everyone knows, it's big news," Leo said, as if he were talking about some celebrity TV show.

"We should go," Lucas told her. "Please, stay safe Deborah."

The white light enveloped the pair and they vanished from the boardwalk. The chill in the air returned as if it had been waiting for her, a coldness that bore through to her bones.

The house, Deb thought. *Seems odd that they were nearly distraught over Peter's intrusion into the house. Maybe I should go check on Gen and Kelly. Maybe Leo and Lucas know something I don't.*

Deb didn't move. She looked at the ocean and knew

where she had to go next.

I can't go back home now, Deb sighed. *I've come too far. I can't abandon Marcus, he's like a charge now, and I fight for my charges. Deserting would be easy. The right course of action is often the most arduous and the loneliest.*

The wind picked up and it carried the sound of laughter. A few children were playing on the small grassy area just outside the snack hut by the main entrance. In the summertime, the park would already be bustling with activity at this morning hour. It was fall though, and there would be no crowds till much later.

Deb had spent the night checking on charges, walking the circular trail around the park, and even spent an hour or so at St. Ann's. She wasn't in human view, but the early morning quiet hour of the church always cleared her mind. She had come to terms with all she had learned. Deb was as prepared for what needed to happen next as she was going to be. She would return to Jade's hotel room. It would be early afternoon in London now. She must convince Jade to share what she knew about her brother's plans. It was a long shot after their tense encounter, but she had to try.

I'm going to Hell. The truth gave Deb a start. *I need Jade to get me there. I will not let Marcus pay with his life for helping me and my family. Their violent outbursts stop now.*

***

Gen stared over at the still smokey remains of the house she had brought down in a hail of angry terror.

Vampires, Hell's First Army. They're restored and on the

attack once more.

After nearly eighteen hours the smell of burning debris still permeated the air. Despite the early morning hour some people were out on the street watching her home's demise. The fire inspector had just returned, with the street blocked off she could park in the middle of the road.

A gas line broke when Gen toppled the house yesterday, and a fire erupted. Gen assumed it was from the many sparks that were going off on the first floor, but it didn't really matter. The response to the fire was quick; the flames were contained within a short time. Gen never saw the fire; she and Kelly were helped back to the beach house to heal and stumble into bed. A few of their brothers stayed behind to see if they spotted any sign of Garrick or Keeva, but there was nothing.

Michael will be waiting when I return to the beach house this morning, Gen thought. *He was patient yesterday, satisfied with Kelly's abbreviated explanation of what happened and who attacked.*

When Xavier had arrived last night, he took one look at the house and wrapped his arms around Gen. He cradled her in a warm hug, whispering she was safe, that she could rebuild when Gabriel returned. Xavier teleported her back to the beach house where she was near catatonic as Frankie and Kelly healed her. She didn't speak. After working with her brother to heal Kelly, Gen simply went to bed and cried herself to sleep.

The normal rhythm of cars driving nearby brought her back to the present. She couldn't draw her eyes away from the ruins. She stood before the house preparing to pick through debris, but first she had to reconcile it hadn't been a nightmare.

I wish I had dreamt it all. I just want the house to myself, time to walk through and salvage anything that might be left.

She knew having the house to herself was unrealistic. Though she wasn't in human view there would be only so much she could move around or pick up if people were there to witness it. She was resentful over the first responders trampling through her property. There were police cruisers at each end of the street, parked behind sagging yellow tape, keeping local television crews at bay.

The cruiser's lights weren't flashing but their radios crackled from time to time. On the corner stood one of her neighbors chatting with Father Donovan, the Pastor from St. Ann's church.

Gen didn't know how Dan was going to handle this situation. There would be an inquiry for sure. Just because there were no bodies found inside, didn't mean the O'Maras wouldn't have to come forward and make statements. They would have to explain their whereabouts, probably deal with insurance paperwork.

Before Gen could muster the confidence to step forward, she noticed the light blue aura indicating her brother's arrival.

"Digging through wreckage isn't easy. Are you ready for this?" Xavier asked.

"I was just summoning the courage," Gen told him. "You didn't have to come back here this morning."

"Would you do it for me?" he asked simply.

Gen turned to face him. Xavier wore a light blue sweatshirt, gray pants, and black combat boots. His hair was longer than it had been in recent years. The ends were peeking out from underneath the baseball cap he had crushed down on his head. His eyes always seemed to twinkle with mischief.

"Yes," Gen answered. "You know I would."

"Let's go then." Xavier grabbed her hand and pulled her delicately toward the house.

"I don't know why I'm bothering," Gen commented. "There isn't much left to sift through, probably not even enough to fill the front pocket of your sweatshirt."

The fire inspector's phone rang, and the woman walked into the street to answer it. The two firefighters poking through the rubble followed her, one saying something about coffee. Gen and Xavier were suddenly alone.

"What is that all about?" Gen wondered. "That was convenient."

Xavier laughed. "Not so much. Kelly and Dan are behind us influencing for our privacy. Even though we aren't in human view, we certainly don't want anyone seeing boards moving or objects sailing through the air."

Gen fought back tears so full of gratitude. "That's amazing, thank you."

"You know you don't have to thank us," Xavier said, as he released her hand and walked toward what had been the kitchen. "Now, let's see what we can find. We won't have much time."

They searched for about fifteen minutes, more time than Gen thought she would have. It was enough to uncover a few items, but not so much that would cause human suspicion. When the firefighter's voices signaled their return, Gen knew she was out of time. Sadness crept back in, but somehow it wasn't as pervasive as it had been just the day before.

'It will get better in time,' Harry used to tell her on those difficult days living with the loss of Gabriel. *At least this is not as bad as that.*

Gen had one throwing star and a dagger, both Kelly's. She slid them into a holster she wore along with her Haladie double-curved knife. She didn't know the Haladie was still in the house. She hadn't seen it in some time, but now here it was buried in the remnants of her burned down house. It was better the weapons were not left at the scene. It was bad enough that any inspector worth their paycheck would know a near disaster happened inside the house before the fire. The last thing the O'Maras needed was to leave all these weapons lying around for the police to discover.

"Guess it was a good idea that Michael took Kelly's weapons stash," Xavier said from behind her. "This is going to be tough enough to explain."

"Yeah." Gen spotted a piece of thin wood in Xavier's hand. "What's that?"

Xavier handed it to her. "It's from the hallway. I figured you spent all that time stripping and restoring it, you probably want to take it with you. Sorry, there was only that small piece intact and unburned. The rest crumbled when I picked it up."

Gen flipped the piece of chair rail over in her hand. The detailed decorative ivy could still be seen. Gen gingerly rolled her fingertips over the ivy. It wasn't more than four inches long, but it was in perfect condition. Gen held it to her chest. She could no longer push back the tears and began to openly cry.

"Thank you, Xav." Gen shook her head. "You have no idea—"

"I think he might." Harry's voice came softly from behind her.

"I'll see you both back at the beach house," Xavier said, as he walked toward the street to meet up with Kelly and Dan.

"I appreciate you coming, Harry," Gen told him.

"Where else would I be?" Harry grasped her shoulder. "I'm here to support you. It can't be easy coming back here, not after everything you've been through."

"I needed to come," Gen told him. "I had to see it one last time."

"Saying goodbye," Harry offered. "It's never painless, but it is healthy, allows one to move forward."

"Yeah," Gen said. "I've spent enough time holding on to the past."

"Best to get back now," Harry said, as he turned to walk down toward the street.

"We'll build a new one, Gabe," Gen whispered. "We'll build one with a screened-in porch large enough for our family and friends. One with a bigger garden and a yard that disappears into a forest of old trees, just like we always wanted."

CHAPTER TWENTY

Deb arrived outside Jade's suite and listened for any movement inside before entering. It was the second time she'd come here and not landed where Jade was. No matter how firmly Deb's convictions were about what she was doing here, it seemed her subconscious mind sabotaged her efforts to achieve it.

It's probably trying to stop me, Deb thought. *Finding Marcus is no longer an option, it's a mission. I won't fail.*

There was a light thud on the other side of the wall and the cloaking mechanism of Deb's shield burst outward defensively.

Seems Jade has company, Deb thought. *Doesn't mean it's friendly.*

Deb pulled the card key from her coat pocket, something she assumed Jade had slipped inside her jacket when Deb wasn't looking. The demon was inviting Deb to return. Jade's confidence was alarmingly accurate, but at this point, getting the demon to help her was her only recourse.

Family is always an option, but not now, Deb thought

sadly. *I must accept their position as they should mine. I started this journey with Jade and I'm going to see it through.*

Deb had dropped her shield several different times in the last day or so to preserve energy and no one arrived to speak to her. As siblings they were always able to shut off the telepathy when they desired, but now it was like radio silence, a severed connection.

Deb slid the keycard into the brass box below the handle and the door lock clicked open. Pushing lightly on the decorative thick wood she stopped short when she heard raised voices and breaking glass.

More than unfriendly, a confrontation. Who would have the nerve to cross Jade?

Slipping quietly inside, Deb held onto the handle to keep it from slamming shut behind her. With a steady hand Deb eased the door back to a closed position and then carefully peeked around the wall of the round entryway toward the living room.

A large male figure stood in front of the bar. Jade was on her knees, her hands bound behind her back. The male was knocking the crystal stemware off the bar and onto the floor next to Jade. The stemware smashed into tiny fragments bouncing off the marble tile floor, splattering on and around Jade.

Even though she could only see the side of Jade's face, Deb could see tears flowing freely down the demon's flushed cheeks. Jade's mascara was running in dark rivers.

A female voice boomed through the air. "Stop! Throwing her wine glasses on the floor isn't going to get her to confess where the Guardian is."

Deb's heart skipped. *They're looking for me.*

"Garrick and Keeva got the better assignment," the male complained. "We have to bring this one and the Guardian back alive."

The male grabbed Jade by the hair and threw her across the room toward the wall of windows, no longer in Deb's line of sight.

"What are we still doing here?" The female asked. "She's obviously not going to tell us, and even if we wanted to, we can't kill her."

"No," the male huffed. "It doesn't mean we can't take our time with her. I mean I'm hungry, I don't know about you, but when have you last fed on someone?"

"We can't feed on her either, dumbass," the female barked. "I would classify cutting her open to taste her blood as the very definition of harmful."

Taste her blood. Vampires.

A moment later Deb ducked as a chair came sailing through the air, slamming off the far wall and shattering into several large pieces of wood.

"I don't care what you think!" The male yelled. "If we have to sit here all night waiting for something from Heaven to just materialize then I'm going to do whatever I want with her!"

Jade screamed and Deb heard grunting noises from the other side of the room.

I have to do something, Deb pushed herself off the wall and darted down the hall.

Peering around the exterior bedroom wall into the living room Deb spotted the female sitting in a chair staring out the window. She had a drink in one hand, her Falchion in the other. Despite her warnings, the female vampire didn't seem to care what her male counterpart was doing. It was obvious she was not going to protect Jade from her partner's planned assault.

The male had used his Falchion to cut Jade's right shoulder deeply. She was drenched in her own blood. Jade's clothing was torn, her hair disheveled. The vampire had thrown her against the table and was pressed up against Jade's back. He sniffed the air and then using his forefinger he swiped through the steady stream of warm red liquid escaping her wound.

Deb stared at the scene playing out in front of her in horror. Jade's mouth had a gag around it, and she was struggling to catch her breath. Her body quivered under her assailant's pressure. Her arms were covered in bruises already turning black and blue. If Deb didn't know better, she'd say Jade was powerless, certainly not the demon those she encountered had come to fear.

The cloak from Deb's shield was working. The vampires didn't seem to sense her presence, but she wasn't sure what they were using to cloak the hotel suite. Then Deb noticed the vampire's skin; it was too perfect. She glimpsed the male's eyes. The extra line encircling the outside of the iris was dark red. He was restored. Deb had to assume the female was as well.

She needed a distraction, something that would give her time to get to Jade and try teleporting them out. Turning back toward the bedroom, Deb raced to the door of the hotel room, pulled it open, and let it go.

After the door slammed shut the female vampire rounded the corner first. Deb had squeezed herself behind the open bathroom door in the hallway. Even though they couldn't see her she didn't want to take any chances of being sensed. When the male walked past a few seconds later, Deb ran into the living room aiming for Jade. She enveloped Jade and attempted to teleport but couldn't. The cloaking was preventing her from leaving the room.

I should have realized sooner that they were cloaking the entire space, Deb thought. *Plan B. Hide and hope they believe we escaped.*

Deb stopped cloaking momentarily, just long enough for Jade to see her face. Though Jade was gagged, her eyes closed in acknowledged relief.

Not wanting to leave a trail of blood for the vampires to follow Deb healed Jade's open wound. The sound of banging furniture and the closet door in the bedroom slamming told Deb they had run out of time. The short search of the bedroom was complete.

Dragging Jade across the room away from the table Deb tucked the two of them into the corner between the buffet and a large end table. Deb knew her shield would hide them from view, but she didn't want to inadvertently be trampled when the vampires came bounding back into the room.

The male entered first, "What the—" He yelled to his partner. "Jade's gone."

"You idiot," the female scolded. "All you had to do was watch her while I went to check out the noise."

Deb was crouched on the floor with Jade's rigid body leaning against her. She was staring at the vampire's feet under the dining table. Their combat boots traipsed back and forth crunching as they walked over broken glass scattered across the floor.

"I'm outta here," the female announced. "You explain your stupidity for losing her right out from underneath you, literally."

"What are you talking about?" The male yelled. "You're the one who wanted to wait here to see if the Guardian showed up again. You were all acting like a Sentinel when you could only find one keycard in Jade's stupid bag."

"Whatever," the female retorted. "I'm not sticking around, do whatever you want."

The female stomped out of the room toward the bedroom once more. The male followed quickly on her heels as he continued to argue with her. The hotel room door banged shut and the room fell still. Only Jade's labored breathing could be heard. Deb carefully undid the gag and removed it from Jade's mouth. She inhaled sharply but then spit and coughed.

"Deborah." Jade's voice was unrecognizably raspy. "Thank you."

Deb stood up and helped Jade to her feet. Taking a knife from the buffet, Deb used it to cut the binding off the demon's hands.

Sneaking a quick look down the hall to be sure they had gone, Deb dropped her cloak and looked at Jade. "They were here for me."

"Yes." Jade nodded. "They were supposed to bring us to Wrath. It sounds like he suspects you want to rescue Marcus and that I'm helping you."

"How could he know that?" Deb asked. "Did you call him?"

"Are you mad?" Jade made her way to the table and

poured whiskey into one of the few remaining glasses left on the bar top. "I wouldn't call Wrath to save my life, or yours for that matter."

"Torin?" Deb questioned.

"I don't know," Jade snapped. "But we should bloody hell get out of here and fast before they return with friends."

"How did you know I would come back here?" Deb asked plainly.

"You went home, didn't you?" Jade asked without waiting for reply. "Last time that didn't go so well. I wanted you to know you had a place to come after that."

Deb didn't know what to say.

"What place do you have in mind?" Deb asked.

"My sister, Desire," Jade answered. "I want to ask her if she knows what Wrath is up to."

"Thought you didn't talk to your siblings," Deb asked cautiously.

"I don't," Jade snapped. "but I know where to go to get in touch."

"Where?" Deb asked.

"The Last Refuge," Jade said, slamming down the glass as she finished her drink.

"You want us to go back to the club?" Deb raised her eyebrows. "Those vampires were restored, not a mark on them. The second ring around their iris was red. There is no way you are making it past all of them to get into that club tonight."

"I don't need to," Jade said, as she walked toward the entryway.

Deb followed Jade down the hall and stood in the

bedroom doorway. Jade pulled clothes from hangers in the closest and tossed them on the bed. Jade quickly changed into jeans, a brown sweater, and a soft black leather jacket. She threw on black socks and ankle high boots.

"That's not really your style," Deb commented. "Where's the green?"

"I don't wear pants," Jade said dryly.

"What?" Deb asked dumbfounded. "Are you exaggerating?"

"My dear, when you get everything you want," Jade spanned her hands out around the room, "is there really ever a need to inflate? These were not meant for me. They were meant for you. Given that we have to weed our way through to the back entrance of the club, they will have to do."

Jade grabbed Deb's arm, "Let's go."

***

The club looked as inconspicuous as it had previously. Deb followed Jade along the exterior wall facing the empty field beside and behind the building. They were winding their way through the heavy overbrush, stepping around broken bottles and small piles of trash.

Better than the storefront I was holed up in a few nights back. The air smells stale rather than pee soaked.

When Jade reached the back of the building, she turned left. Approaching one of the boarded-up windows, Jade pushed the splintered wood out of the way and cautiously slipped inside. Turning back, Jade grabbed Deb's hand and pulled her through also. A few steps later a metal door creaked open and in the hallway beyond were dim lights with concrete steps and metal handrails.

"Not as glamorous, I know," Jade whispered.

Deb descended the stairs behind Jade. The hallway smelled of stale antiseptic. There was little airflow and everything about the enclosed space seemed sterile and hospital like. They passed level two, continuing down to level three. When Jade opened the door to the space, it was empty. The floor was made of hardwood and the light came from candle-filled sconces hung neatly along the wall. It was too dark to see the artwork on the wall, but at the end of the hallway a door was partially open.

Deb was tempted to use her cloak. She grabbed Jade's arm to spin her around. Jade lifted her finger to her lips to quiet Deb, then turned back and softly walked toward the open door. As they neared it, hushed whispers and moaning came from within. There was an opening in the hallway to the left of the door. Deb didn't notice it until Jade was dragging her inside and pushing her up against the wall.

From that position Deb could see inside the room. A man sat on a sofa with a blond naked woman straddling him. The two were obviously having sex.

What now? Deb thought. *Was this her sister? If so, why would her sister, Desire, need to come to the club to have sex?*

Deb was frustrated and knew she rolled her eyes at the site of the engaged couple. Jade must have sensed her irritation and grabbed the sleeve of Deb's jacket.

"They're nearly done, dear," Jade whispered. "Be patient."

That's new. I'm not usually the impatient one.

A few excruciating moments later the groaning and breathless gasps subsided.

Footsteps neared the doorway. "Tell Desire I'm no longer satisfied with the scraps of meat she sends me."

A loud clang rang out as something was thrown across the room. "Screw you!" The female yelled.

"Don't be annoying or I'll end you right here vixen," the male scolded. "Explain to Desire that you saw I was healed, not a scar to be found anywhere."

Exiting the door, the male glanced over his right shoulder back inside the room and Deb saw his face. It was the vampire she had confronted in the club a few nights back.

General Kelce. Deb stiffened. *She didn't just bring me back to the club where all the vampires were, she brought me to their leader.*

CHAPTER TWENTY-ONE

Gen sat with her legs curled-up underneath her, a beach blanket with printed seashells and sand dollars draped over her lap. She held a cup of tea in one hand and the piece of the recovered chair rail in the other. Xavier sat in a rocking chair moving gently beside her. They were staring out at the panoramic view of the bay nestled quietly behind Harry's house. Gen's comfy chair was on a swivel and she was able to look at both the kitchen and the ocean with just one glance.

Kelly and Harry were down on the beach talking with Gardenia and Gerry. The rest of Gen's brothers hadn't returned. Kelly insisted Frankie and Dan go shopping for more food. She warned them not to return unless they had cake.

Greg and Tom were hunting down which Trader may have offered Deb a deal for her blood. Michael went to get Lacey. Gen hadn't seen the Historian in several weeks, but Kelly said she needed her help.

Xavier had opened a few windows. Gen could hear seagulls cawing as they fed along the salt rocks. The wind occasionally whipped through the open space. It was cool and Gen was glad she had the blanket.

"Has Kelly explained anything more about Gerry?" Xavier asked.

"No," Gen answered. "The last couple of days have been one giant blur."

"I bet," Xavier told her. "Do you think Deb went through with it, traded her blood for information on Marcus?"

Gen didn't answer so Xavier continued. "I had no idea she felt that way about Marcus. I mean to give her blood, to risk the consequences of that, it's big. Now some of Hell's First Army are restored. I don't have to tell you what that looks like."

"Yeah, I know what it looks like," Gen said. "Even if she made the deal, the two that came to the house were already restored, so that couldn't have been from Deb's blood."

"What about Jacob's blood?" Xavier asked. "Peter did take the Arch Angel's hand.

"Maybe, but we have no way of knowing," Gen told him. "I knew there was something going on between Deb and Marcus, something she was struggling with. I wouldn't have said they were in love, but maybe I was wrong."

"I doubt it," Xavier told her. "The three of you are so close, you'd know if Deb was in love."

"I used to think she was in love with Dmitri," Gen commented. "I used to think a lot of things."

"Like what?" Xavier asked.

"I used to think nothing could tear this family apart." Her eyes fell to her lap and the remnants of the chair rail her sisters once helped her restore.

"You worry Deb's not coming back?" he asked.

"No, you don't think that do you, Gen?"

"I don't know what to think anymore," Gen confessed. "She was so casual about the news. Telling us she met and was working with a demon, like it was nothing."

"She'll come home, Gen."

"She was pretty upset. I think my approach may have pushed her away. I just couldn't wrap my mind around why Marcus meant more than finding Peter. It seemed so disproportionate, but now with what Leo and Lucas said."

Xavier nodded but didn't say anything, and Gen let the words hang in the air.

"I can't stop blaming myself." Gen's voice cracked. "Maybe if I'd have done more or was more approachable."

"Don't do that, Gen."

"How can I not? Looking back, I realize how out of character all this is for Deb. I should have seen the signs. I should have helped her. I know better, I know what can happen. What if I drove Deb toward the demon?"

"No matter what happened between you two, Deb knows better than to make a deal with a Trader or to trust a demon. Whatever her reasons, maybe what she needs is for us to have faith in her, to trust her."

Gen sighed. "I hope you're right Xav. We can't lose her."

"We won't." Xavier leaned over and placed his hand gently on Gen's arm. "This family has been through it all, we'll get through this too. Together."

Gen gave a smile she didn't feel. She grasped Xavier's hand and gave it a little squeeze before he let it fall back to his lap.

"How do you think it's going down there?" He nodded toward the beach.

"About as well as can be expected. Kelly's getting better at counseling. She's grown quite found of Gardenia and Gerry. She'll find the words, plus she has Harry."

***

"Okay," Kelly began, "I have no idea how to tell you this Gerry, so I'm just going to spill it."

Harry coughed mildly as if he wanted her to rethink that option, but she knew speaking plainly was all she had.

"What is it?" Gerry asked.

Kelly took a sharp intake of air. "I think you're a Watcher."

Gerry's right eyebrow shot up. "A Watcher, and what are they?"

"Do you mean a Historian?" Gardenia's nose scrunched in confusion.

"Yes," Kelly continued. "We call them Watchers because they don't engage in the battles between Heaven and Hell. They take notes, so to speak."

"Huh?" Gerry asked perplexed.

How do I tell him he's meant to be in this world? All he probably wants to do is get away from it, from us.

The sound of birds in some sort of feeding frenzy distracted her. Ever since Kelly encountered the gargoyles in the park between night and day a few months back she had been uncomfortable around birds. Especially birds diving in and out of water like these were doing. Harry's voice brought her back to the present

"That's actually not what they do," Harry reassured them.

"Well, I mean it's kind of what they do," Kelly insisted.

"Let me clarify," Harry began again. "Historians are supernatural Earth-bound entities that bear witness to the major confrontations between Heaven and Hell. They record what they witness as the fair arbiters of fact in our world. They are the truthtellers of what really happens here."

"Why do you need that?" Gerry asked.

"We don't," Kelly lobbed.

"We absolutely do!" Harry contended.

Kelly shook her head.

"Kelly O'Mara," Harry scolded. "You stop that right now!"

Kelly shrugged and made an exaggerated face as if she were in trouble. Both Gardenia and Gerry laughed.

Kelly grinned. Even Harry cracked a small smile. *We'll connect him with Lacey and then they'll be safe.*

"Let's assume I believe you," Gerry told her. "What does that mean for me, for Gardenia?"

Before Kelly could answer Michael appeared on the beach with Lacey. The doe-eyed Historian seemed to be trembling slightly.

"Hi Lacey!" Kelly announced.

"What's going on?" Lacey asked as she pulled at the bottom of her blue cotton shirt. Swiping her hand through her long shiny black hair she appeared to be trying to pull herself together.

"Did you not explain where you were taking her?" Kelly glared at Michael.

"You made it sound urgent," Michael retorted.

Harry groaned and rolled his eyes. "I'm sorry Lacey, we are in need of your expertise."

"You just showed up and kidnapped her?" Kelly asked her older brother. "What goes through you mind in those moments? You're like a Neanderthal sometimes."

"You said go and get Lacey," Michael said flatly. "So that's what I did."

"I didn't say rip her from her home without explanation," Kelly retorted.

"Well, I had no explanation," Michael shot back. "You haven't told any of us what's going on!"

Kelly waved her hands in the air shooing at Michael. "Never mind. Thank you for escorting her here. Why don't you head back inside? We'll join you in a few."

Michael mumbled something incoherent, turned, and headed to the house.

"Lacey," Kelly began again. "This is Gerry, my former charge. And this is Gardenia, a friend of the Sentinel Marcus."

"Marcus?" Lacey repeated. "The Sentinel presumed missing?"

"One and the same," Kelly told her. "You don't happen to know where Marcus is, do you?"

"I've heard rumors," Lacey replied coolly. "I wouldn't want to speculate."

"Well," Kelly retorted. "Sometimes speculation is

all we have. Anyway, I asked Michael to bring you here because I believe Gerry is a Watcher. I don't suppose you know of any voodoo magic way of telling if that's true, do you?"

Lacey smirked. "Very funny. We are Historians, not witches for goodness sake."

Lacey stepped forward and held her hand out, palm up, in front of Gerry.

"Place your hand out, palm down, and hover it just above mine, please," Lacey asked Gerry.

Gerry looked around at the group before complying. With his hand mere inches from Lacey's, a small round ball of light formed between the two. Lacey closed her eyes, while Gerry gasped. Harry took a few steps forward and placed a hand on each one's shoulder. Harry said a few short prayers in Latin and then stepped back next to Kelly.

Lacey broke the connection when she let her hand fall back to her side. The light disappeared and Gerry stood, mouth agape, clearly shocked at the encounter.

"I have no idea what just happened," Gerry faltered. "But I think I understand those words you just spoke, Harry."

"Yes," Lacey answered. "We connected, some of my knowledge is now your knowledge and I speak several languages. How did you come to be with the Guardians?"

"You know," Kelly started with an awkward chuckle, "it's not really important. I think you should come inside, say hello to the family. Maybe have a drink before you head off to Watcher school."

Lacey crossed her arms. "Watcher school? Are you

229

trying to offend me?"

"I think Kelly saved me when she wasn't supposed to," Gerry announced.

"I don't think we know any such thing!" Kelly scoffed.

"He's out of time?" Lacey unfolded her arms and looked at Gerry, then over to Gardenia. "And who are you again?"

"I'm one of the Lost," Gardenia replied. "Gerry, do you think I could stay with you, while you're in Watcher school."

Harry cleared his throat. "I'm afraid there is no school for Historians. Gerry will live with the Historian he has connected with, in this case Lacey. He will have to learn in the field. It's not an easy road."

"What if I don't want that?" Gerry replied. "No offense Lacey, but what if I go and stay with Gardenia?"

"I live in an abandoned school on the outskirts of a washed-up town," Gardenia answered. "There is room, if you don't mind sleeping on a mattress out in the open with everyone else who happens to be staying there that night."

"Oh my," Gerry said, as he looked at the young girl. "I had no idea, I'm sorry."

"It's okay," Gardenia said. "I don't have invisibility powers like Guardians do. The Lost, we blend right in with the homeless. Most humans just ignore us. I wonder how they'd react if they knew the truth." Gardenia shrugged but looked away appearing uncomfortable with the attention.

"I thought you said Marcus would go by for movie night?" Kelly asked confused.

"He does," Gardenia told her. "We use an old

whiteboard we found in the building. One of the kids that lives there is good with electronics. He was able to hook up the old electrical panel to a stolen generator, so we have power. Once we had power, we were able to hook up a DVD projector. We'd watch whatever movie Marcus would bring with him. Last time, it was an old movie about demonic possession. She was young and her head spun around in a circle. She vomited green soup everywhere, it was gross, but it was a little scary."

"The Exorcist?!" Kelly asked enthralled.

"It has to be," Gerry said. "I don't know any other movie with that scene."

"Marcus would bring snacks too," Gardenia said, with a tear in her eye. "He knew sometimes it would be days since any of us ate anything."

"I think we're getting a little off topic," Harry said softly. "Let's head back inside and regroup with everyone, shall we?"

Everyone turned and began walking toward the steps. Harry grabbed Kelly's elbow and when she looked up at him, he whispered. "We need to get them out of here."

"What's wrong?" Kelly muttered.

"That connection Gerry and Lacey just made," Harry told her. "It would have sent a signal. If Lacey doesn't report to her superiors within an hour, they're going to come looking for her and the newly found Historian she just met."

"We don't want that, right?" Kelly said, in huffed exasperation. "I mean we should sort out what we're going to do about Deb before the Watchers sound the alarm about the vampires. That could send any number of Heavenly beings down here to start investigating."

"You're assuming they don't already know about the vampires," Harry replied. "They might, Lacey knew about a missing Sentinel."

"Yeah," Kelly huffed. "I guess my instinct was just to protect Deb. You're right though, we should ask Lacey to expedite a check-in with her superiors, find out what they know. Maybe, if we agree to keep her updated personally, that will buy us some time. She's been a good ally."

CHAPTER TWENTY-TWO

The elevator door chimed, and in the silence of the cold hallway the doors swung shut and the elevator motor hummed. General Kelce didn't sense Deb or Jade, he walked right past the opening to the offshoot hallway to the back stairwell.

Jade pushed off the wall and walked toward the open doorway. Deb cautiously followed, her eyes darting around trying to see if anyone else was present, but there was no one.

They approached the door. The woman inside was rummaging through something. Jade pushed the door open wide and sauntered inside.

"Eloise, it's below you to run such errands for Dee."

The blonde snapped her head around, and after one look at Jade she grabbed her clothes off the floor and began getting dressed.

"What do you want Envy?" Eloise barked.

The woman was about five foot six, thin but with curves. She had long thick blonde hair that fell in waves just beyond her shoulder. Only partially dressed, Eloise wore a navy blue silk blouse that had long strips in the front to form some sort of bow that was undone. Her red underwear was bikini style that showed off all the natural contours of her body. When she pulled on her gray trousers, she grabbed her black high heels and briskly walked to the bookcase on the far side of the wall.

"I'm afraid you won't find what you're looking for in here, my dear," Jade commented as she entered the room further and walked to a nearby bar to pour a drink. "Would you care for a drink?"

Eloise turned and pointed at Deb. "Who's this?"

Deb jumped in not allowing Jade to answer for her. "I'm not here to make friends."

"I see," Eloise said, as she turned her attention back to scouring the bookcase. "defensive from the start, fair enough."

The room was a massive library, with built in floor-to-ceiling shelves on two of the four walls. It looked like something out of a Hollywood movie set. The wood was dark in color and the lighting was dim. There was a stone fireplace on the wall to Deb's right, just beyond the sofa with an enormous painting of some battle hanging above it.

An old wooden desk and a credenza ran the length of the wall leading to the door opening. The large pieces of furniture were dotted with a slew of marble sculptures of varying shapes and sizes. Some were of people, but others appeared to be animal-like.

The furniture in the room was made of soft leather. The sofa was cream-colored, while the accompanying chairs were of a deep woodsy green. There was a long dark brown rectangular shaped coffee table between them.

This is Jade's room, Deb thought. *Shades of green were everywhere, but it was all so put together and sophisticated you had to really look to notice her stamp of color.*

Deb took a few steps over the dark green oriental rug under her feet. The plush carpet had colors of beige, gray, and dark brown running through it. She was compelled to look more closely at the artwork hanging above the fireplace; it seemed to almost have a presence about it.

The painting was as large as the flat screen TV her brothers had in their living room. It was roughly five feet across and four feet tall. It was framed in decorative brass inlaid with some sort of black flower-like etching. The whole thing was encased in museum glass to keep it protected from pollution and corrosive light.

Not that Jade had to worry about light in this dim windowless room, Deb mused.

The painting depicted a chaotic scene with burning half-collapsed stone buildings, falling bodies, and fire raging in the background. There was a bright red orange glow in the top left corner of the image with shooting flames coming out of it. It was a stark contrast to the rest of the painting's darkness. There were bodies falling from above, over the cliffside and into a ravine. In the background more bodies floated along in what Deb could only assume was misery. Small fires dotted the landscape. Most of the images were of men and in the lower right corner there were male figures wielding swords.

Torturers. Deb realized. *The painting is one of many depictions of Hell. Why would this be in here? It looks like an original, but it can't be, can it?*

The bodies were piled on top of one another in a macabre scene at the bottom. Winged and horned creatures feasted on the dead. The medieval period spawned many nightmarish depictions of what humans thought of Hell. Most showed levels of Hell but in another world, something not of this Earth. This one stood out depicting Hell on Earth. Deb shivered.

"Deborah, would you care to join us?" Jade's voice snapped Deb's head around. She didn't know how long she has been staring at the painting, but long enough for the two females to be sitting down now.

Eloise was fully dressed. She even tied the two pieces of silk into a bow on her blouse. The keyhole it left had the intended effect of accentuating her generous cleavage. She sat on the sofa while Jade sat across from her. Each had a glass of wine in their hands.

The coffee table between them had a centerpiece made of blown glass. Nearby candlelight bounced off the varying shades of red color within the glass. The shimmer gave the illusion the object was moving, as if it were a living organism.

Sinister, Deb thought, *just like the vibe of this room.*

Deb spotted a third glass of wine in front of the empty chair next to Jade and took a seat.

At least she didn't ask me to sit on the newly soiled sofa, Deb thought in disgust.

"Do you like the painting, my dear?" Jade asked Deb.

"It's horrific," Eloise scoffed. "Who would like that? Plus, you can barely see it in this dungeon of an office."

"It's actually impressive how the overlay of brush strokes gives it a three-dimensional feel," Deb answered ignoring Eloise's remarks.

"Agreed," Jade told her. "Brueghel was a master at painting the scenes of Hell. Maybe one day I'll tell you how he came to be in possession of such knowledge, Deborah."

"Brueghel?" Deb questioned. "He wouldn't have painted anything that large, not in the sixteenth century."

"Well, like everyone else, he took commissions." Jade smiled. "The smaller ones floating around in private collections are replicas of mine."

"You're saying this is not a replica or stolen or missing from a museum?" The words tumbled from Deb lips.

"Are you calling me a thief, Deborah?" Jade asked in genuine offense.

"Envy has many skills," Eloise commented dryly. "I don't think stealing is one of them."

"This painting is not missing," Jade told Deb. "It's right where it belongs, with me, it's owner. And for the record, I have no need to steal."

"Okay." Deb left the wine glass untouched.

"Now, let's get to business, shall we," Jade began. "Eloise, I need you to deliver a message to my sister."

Eloise took a long slow sip from her wine before answering. "Why don't you tell her yourself, Envy," Eloise said the name with disdain.

"I normally enjoy your cheekiness, Eloise," Jade told her. "Such a fighting spirit for a low-level follower, but today I'm in a rush. I frankly don't have time for your childish nature."

Eloise sat forward and leaned over the coffee table. "I wouldn't help you if you were enveloped in Holy Fire."

Holy Fire, Deb thought. *Can that hurt a Deadly Sin?*

Jade stiffened and the candlelight seemed to flicker in the windless room. The smell of Jade's perfume mixed with sweat as the demon's neck and face reddened.

"Tell Dee to meet me at the cottage," Jade said, as she stood staring down at Eloise. Jade placed the wine glass down and stepped toward the door but then stopped next to Eloise. The blonde sat back into the cushions of the sofa and sneered up at Jade.

"Don't dawdle, Eloise. I wouldn't want to have to explain to General Kelce that he has been having sex with the same vixen for nearly a decade."

Eloise's crude smile was wiped from her face. "How did you know?" the blonde said through gritted teeth.

"Like you said, my dear." Jade smiled down at Eloise. "I have many skills."

"You wouldn't dare tell him." Eloise seemed to spit the words.

"You have no idea what I would and wouldn't do." Jade's voice grew deep with malevolence. "I get what I want, when I bloody well want it. Understand how this works now, minion? Now go give my sister the message. And, if I see you anywhere near my office again, the General will be the least of your worries."

Jade walked to the office door and held it fully open inviting Eloise to leave. The blonde clinked her glass against the table and stormed out in a huff. Jade slammed the door shut behind her.

"Well," Jade said in irritation, "that was most

unpleasant."

"Uh huh," Deb grumbled. "Is she going to deliver the message?"

"Yes," Jade said. "Otherwise, General Kelce will hunt her down and destroy her for deceiving him all these years. She's not just a member of Desire's court, she's a chameleon. Eloise can change her look, her coloring, her accent, everything really, and appear as someone else. She's been doing that on behalf of my sister with General Kelce for a long time."

"Interesting, and strange." Deb said sarcastically.

"She's not compensated enough if you ask me," Jade told her. "General Kelce is a savage. How she's put up with him for nearly a decade I have no idea."

"What was she looking for?" Deb asked. "You told her she wouldn't find it in here, what was it?"

"You're too perceptive, Guardian." Jade smiled.

"You don't want to tell," Deb replied. "just say that."

"Don't be so grouchy, Deborah," Jade mocked.

"Eloise is sent here to see General Kelce?" Deb asked.

"The General has been obsessed with my sister for many decades. He's foolish enough to think Desire stays away from him because of his scars. His newly found fountain of youth will be trouble for Dee, but it may be our good fortune."

"How so? I can't see any upside to fully restored vampires."

"It should make Desire more open to assisting us."

"I hope Eloise doesn't meet us pretending to be

your sister. She didn't exactly seem like a fan of yours. I take it your real name is Envy."

"No," Jade snapped. "My name is Jade. As for Eloise and me, we have history. It's a tad complicated."

"Is there anything in your life that isn't complicated?" Deb asked.

"All in good time, my dear," Jade quipped. "Now, we should probably get going. I want to arrive at the cottage before Dee does."

***

Kelly sat at the kitchen island eating an enormous bagel smeared with raspberry cream cheese. She had already eaten a blueberry muffin and two glazed donuts. Gen was finishing retelling her story of what happened during her battle with Keeva. Fortunately, Gerry and Gardenia agreed to go with Lacey back to her house. Harry went with them to smooth the way.

Was there any gentle way to deal with this? Kelly sulked. *I wasn't supposed to save him. Gerry was supposed to die that day and meet Death. He would have been escorted to the Watchers. They would have eased him into this world, appropriately and over time. Now's he's out of sync with everything. The transition will be much harder for him and he'll be vulnerable until he has fully acclimated into his role. Until then, if he encounters Hell, they will sense weakness and target him.*

"Kelly?" Dan asked. "Are you in a carb coma?"

"No," she remarked, "but not for lack of trying."

"What do you think of Tom's idea?" Dan asked.

"Sorry," Kelly replied. "I'm a little distracted. What's your idea, Tom?"

"We ask Antonio to help find Deb," Tom replied. "He can drop cloaking mechanisms. I think we all agree we need to know if Deb made that deal with a Trader."

"Okay," Kelly answered. "I still don't know where we start. It's not like Antonio can drop cloaks worldwide. We'd have to give him a general idea of Deb's location."

"She's dropped her shield a few times," Frankie confessed. "I briefly felt her. It was intermittent, but I assume she has no choice but to take breaks from time to time. Keeping her shield up, with the cloak, it must be draining."

"Unless she's learned to truly harness that power," Michael answered. "It might take less and less energy as she lets it become part of her, instead of fighting it."

That's a frightening thought, Kelly bristled. *What if that means we'll never find her?*

"Don't worry," Dan said to Kelly. "We'll reach her, she'll be back."

"We're all caught up, right?" Kelly asked as she got up from the table. "Deb is hunting down leads. Befriending demons. Making deals with Traders using her blood as currency. She's never going to stop until she finds Marcus."

"We, on the other hand," Gen added. "have witnessed the murder of a charge and an Arch Angel. Fought and nearly lost to fully restored vampires and are no closer to finding out who Peter is and what he wants."

"That about sums it up," Kelly huffed. "Seems very familiar, lately we always seem to be a step or two behind what Hell is doing."

"There is one other thing," Xavier told them. "Greg and I heard some rumors about the Trader Deb dealt with. They were just rumors, but—"

"But what?" Gen asked.

"We heard the same name from more than one entity we interrogated," Greg answered.

"What did you hear?" Michael asked.

There was a pause in the room as Xavier and Greg exchanged a look.

"No." Gen's voice cracked. "You don't want to tell me because it's him, isn't it?"

Gen had been standing in the open space between the living room and kitchen. Her forehead creased and her face crumpled as realization fell across the room.

"She made a deal with Torin?" Gen's voice was quiet. "How could she do that?"

"We don't know anything," Tom interrupted. "We shouldn't jump to conclusions."

"I asked her who the Trader was at the house," Gen said, as she backed up and slid into one of the chairs in the living room. "She didn't answer. Now I know why."

Gen met Kelly's eyes. The memory flashed in her mind. "Gen's right, she asked the question and Deb didn't answer it, even though there was time for her to do so."

A glow formed beside Gen. Harry was arriving. "I'm afraid I have bad news."

"I don't know if it can get much worse," Gen told him. "Deb talked with Torin, the Trader that bartered for my soul at the gates."

"No," Harry said in barely a whisper. "I'm afraid that's not the only thing she's done."

"What do you mean by that?" Kelly asked.

"Heaven is sending someone to Earth to search for Deborah," Harry said with sad eyes.

"What?" Kelly was struggling to process what Harry was telling them.

Before anyone could respond a strong wind blew in from the ocean, the curtain billowed up and knocked Gen's empty teacup to the ground. The sky seemed to crack open with a thunderous rage and lightning streaked across the landscape.

The O'Mara family walked to the windows at the far end of the house and looked down at the beach. A large male figure stood alone at the water's edge. He had his back to them as he faced the ocean. As quickly as the storm blew in, it began to clear. The sun beamed down once more against the sandy shoreline.

"No. No, no, no," Gen repeated in a rush. "He shouldn't be here!"

Kelly was in shock as the figure turned and looked up at the beach house.

"We have to do something!" Gen yelled.

"He won't hurt her," Kelly said to Gen. "Dmitri would never hurt Deb."

"I won't let him take her." Gen rushed to the door and threw it open charging down to the beach to confront Heaven's most prolific Collector.

CHAPTER TWENTY-THREE

Deb stood in the foyer of Jade's so-called cottage. It was a large two-story unpainted house made of light-colored stone. There were English gardens along the side that extended across the back as well. The circular driveway and double wooden front doors made for a grand entrance. Jade had teleported them arriving in the driveway entrance where Deb had the full view of the massive structure.

This is a far cry from a cottage, Deb thought. *I don't think Jade understands the meaning of the word* minimal.

Jade pushed open the doors and entered. The house was decorated in varying shades of cream, gray, and yellow with pops of red.

This is a change, Deb thought. *Not a speck of green to be found.*

In the main living room, there was a fireplace with wrought iron grates. Wooden beams ran across the high ceiling drawing the eye up. The cottage-style windows flooded the room in natural light. The room was wide enough to have two sofas set across from one another. The smell of apples wafted from the lit candle sitting on the mantlepiece.

In contrast to Jade's office, the furniture was made of fabric with numerous yellow and blue throw pillows adding pops of color to the space. Draped along the backs of the couches were yellow and gray striped blankets. On the oblong oak coffee table rested a hardcover book, still spread open, as if someone were just in the middle of reading it.

"Is this Desire's house?" Deb asked.

"How can you tell?" Jade remarked. "The shabby furniture and awful red color throughout?"

"I think it's kind of cozy," Deb remarked.

"That's one word for it," Jade replied.

The backdoor opened and shut. A moment later a petite brunette woman appeared in the doorway carrying several logs of wood. She looked between them before speaking.

"What are you doing here Jade?" The woman asked as she walked between them heading for the fireplace.

"I assume you've been in touch with Eloise," Jade replied.

"Yes." The woman turned back and faced the two of them. "That still doesn't explain what you're doing here and why you're running around with a Guardian."

The woman wore dark jeans with a black angora sweater. Her hair was braided and folded under, with a pin holding it in place at the nape of her long neck. Her bright blue eyes seemed to sparkle. Everything about her came across as understated. She wore no makeup, she was stunningly beautiful in the most natural way, not exactly what Deb was expecting.

She looks more like the girl next door, Deb mused. *Not the epitome of desire.*

"I need a favor, Dee," Jade began.

"No. I don't want to know what this is about."

"Fine," Jade insisted. "I won't tell you a thing. Now, I need to know what our brother W is up to."

"Oh," Dee mocked. "Is that all?"

"No," Jade continued. "I need you to take Deborah here to Hell."

Dee laughed. "You must be joking."

"When have you ever seen me joke, darling," Jade refuted.

"You realize her family is looking for her, right?" Dee responded. "Not only that, but I heard W took her boyfriend. If she thinks she can just waltz into Hell and rescue him, she's as insane as you are."

"Disagreeable as ever," Jade huffed.

"Now," Dee announced. "I am obviously off the clock. If you want help to double-cross our brother, you're going to need to seek out another ally."

"Desire," Jade scolded, "what I am asking of you is quite simple. What do you know about W's plans? That's all."

"Don't talk to me like that, Jade. I'm not your servant," Dee snapped. "If you want to help get this Guardian past the gates, break the Accord, and bring about the next war between Heaven and Hell on Earth, then why don't you just take her yourself? Oh wait, it's because you aren't welcome there anymore are you, sister?"

Jade's eyes darkened. "I would hate for General

Kelce to learn of this place, it's such a treasure of yours."

Dee smirked. "I can handle General Kelce."

"Can you?" Jade said insincerely. "Well, I just figured with him being fully restored and all you might not be able to get away from him this time."

Dee looked between Jade and Deb as if she were trying to gage the veracity of the statement.

"That's right," Jade continued. "Eloise didn't give you all the information, did she? General Kelce is healed, not a mark on him. Seems the war you fear might have already begun."

"You're lying." Desire's shaky voice betrayed her. Deb could see fear ripple across her face.

"She's not lying." Deb spoke for the first time since arriving. "He is healed, he has been for several days. We heard him tell Eloise to give you a message. He said he was 'tired of the scraps of meat you keep sending him'."

"How?" Desire asked. "I have heard nothing about this. Is it just him that is restored or is it his army as well?"

"More than General Kelce," Deb answered. "Two showed up at Jade's house under orders to deliver us to someone. Jade thinks it was to Wrath."

"Don't you say that name in this house, Guardian!" Desire's hands clenched. "I haven't seen W in decades. The last time was not a pleasant encounter."

"Are they ever?" Jade quipped.

"I can't help you." Desire was shaking her head. "You need to go, if you want someone to help you against W you know who you should go visit, Jade."

"Bollocks!" Jade's voice shook with impatience. "Desire, you know we're stronger together. The two of us outmatch most of our siblings combined."

"No," Desire interjected. "I am not doing this with you. If you are helping a Guardian, I want no part of this. Whatever you're up to, you are on your own this time. Don't come back here, ever."

Desire walked out of the room, opened the backdoor, and left the house. A few moments later Deb could see her through the window carrying a red canister she must have retrieved from a small shed in the yard. Desire walked along the side of the house pouring the contents all over the foundation.

"What is she doing?" Deb asked.

"She means to burn the place down," Jade answered. "We need to leave before she does something stupid like call our brother and warn him about what we're planning."

Deb and Jade walked out the same way they entered. The sound of fire catching crackled through the air. Billowing black smoke rose toward the sky. The house appeared to be out in the middle of nowhere. Deb doubted anyone would reach the fire before it consumed everything inside.

"I can't believe she just did that," Deb said. "Why?"

"Vampires have heightened senses," Jade told her. "They can track an entity for thousands of miles, even throughout their teleportation paths."

"Fire destroys the ability for them to do that?" Deb asked.

"No," Jade answered. "It will dampen it though, slow them down. It might give her time to get away."

"You're assuming they know to come here," Deb

stated.

"They do," Jade answered. "Why do you think I told Eloise the location. She's in love with General Kelce. That ungrateful wench wouldn't pass up the opportunity to take out her competition."

"So, when you say General Kelce is obsessed with Desire," Deb commented. "You mean literally, in an unhealthy way, like a stalker?"

"You are clever, Deborah," Jade said coyly.

"You're all immortal," Deb stated. "She's not just running from General Kelce, is she? She's running from her own brother."

***

Gen rushed through the back door and over the deck to the stairwell. She raced down the stairs, panic propelling her to the bottom and driving her legs across the thick sand. She could have teleported, but she was trying to put her thoughts in order, trying to find the right words to tell Dmitri not to look for Deb.

Please, Gen agonized, *don't take her from us.*

Gen didn't know how to process the news that Heaven sent a Collector. In their world if Heavenly beings were falling, they sent an expert tracker to hunt them down and convince them to change their ways. If the Collector couldn't sway the entity to correct course, they were reaped, taken from earth, and delivered back to Heaven. If Dmitri took Deb, none of them would ever see her again.

Gen's heart raced at the thought of losing a sibling. She already lived through losing her husband for forty

Earth years. She wasn't going to lose her sister. She would talk to Deb. Gen more than anyone understand the pain of loss, she could get through to Deb, bring her home. All Gen needed was time, but Dmitri's presence meant she had run out of that.

Dmitri turned toward her as she approached. He seemed to tower in the short distance between them. Her five-foot-four frame was dwarfed. His broad shoulders and bulging muscles seemed to strain against the fitted red T-shirt he wore. He had a holster around his shoulders, his sabre was sheathed in the middle of his back, the silver hilt glistening in the afternoon sun. His gray cargo pants and black combat boots were a stark contrast to the beachy scene around him.

His normal shoulder length hair was buzzed to a crew cut. His short black hair couldn't hide the scars that marred his scalp. His dark brown eyes fell upon her and she stopped short nearly breathless at the realty of his presence.

Xavier appeared in front of her partially blocking Dmitri from view. "Calm down, Gen. Going off on him isn't going to get us anywhere."

Gen nodded and moved around her brother continuing toward Dmitri. The Collector's shoulders were relaxed with his hands comfortably nestled in his pants pockets like he was enjoying the moment. He had turned his attention back to the sea. The water was choppy, the wind threw the sounds in odd directions, while the sun colored the ocean a green-gray hue.

"You don't seem happy to see me, Genevieve." His voice was deep, and the simplicity of the words made her throat constrict.

"Please, Dmitri," Gen began. "I need more time to get to her."

"Then I'll give it to you," he said simply.

"You'll leave." Gen was stunned. "Just like that?"

"No," he told her, "if you're looking for more time to talk Deb out of her plan, then I can give it to you."

"You know where she is?" Xavier had wandered over to stand next to Gen.

"I can find Deb," Dmitri told them. "What are you all doing here?"

"You remember this place?" Gen asked him.

"Of course," Dmitri answered. "I assume Deb told you that. Did she pick it?"

"I think you should come inside Dmitri." Xavier reached out and patted him on the arm. "We should probably share what we know."

"I don't think your sister shares that sentiment," Dmitri answered. "I have to be honest; your angry face wasn't the welcome I was expecting."

Shame washed over Gen. "I'm sorry. It's just, I've taken a lot of losses recently."

"I don't plan on adding to that list," he told them. "If you want to get to Deb before she does something she can't come back from, then you're going to need my help."

"As long as that's what this is, Dmitri," Gen answered stiffly.

"I love your sister. You would have to know that, so why such caution?" Dmitri asked.

Love. Gen's mind reeled. *He just said he loved her. Why would Deb keep that from us? Why does she claim to not remember being romantic with him, even though she has a memory core proving otherwise?*

"Everyone's inside," Xavier told Dmitri. "Including Harry, let's go in and catch up old friend."

Dmitri maneuvered around Gen and walked alongside Xavier toward the stairs. Kelly appeared in front of Gen.

"Well," Kelly asked. "What did he say, is he here to Collect Deb?"

"He just said he loved her," Gen could hear the confusion in her own voice. "That he would never hurt her."

"You're kidding?!" Kelly said emphatically. "He said that?"

"Yeah," Gen confirmed. "He flat out said he loved her. So, either he's lying, or she is."

"Or neither are." Kelly's eyes drifted up toward the house. "She said she couldn't remember, what if she can't?"

"You think he did something to her memory?" Gen asked.

"I don't know," Kelly replied. "but Deb didn't appear to be lying when she told us she had no recollection of being on this beach with Dmitri, even after she saw the images from the memory core."

"We need to go ask him what he remembers then," Gen answered. "If Deb can't remember Dmitri, we need to find out why."

CHAPTER TWENTY-FOUR

Despite the cordial reception Dmitri received from her brothers, there remained an undercurrent of tension. Dmitri was a long-time friend to Jared and Gabe. Though he was a Collector, he interacted with Guardians on a regular basis and even fought alongside them on occasion. He was a looming presence on the battlefield, an excellent tactician. Gen always feared his kind and she knew she wasn't the only one. Dmitri had the power to remove Heavenly entities from Earth. She shivered at the thought he was here for one of them.

The air filled with the scent of coffee as Kelly made a fresh pot. She had her back to everyone, but Gen knew she would be listening intently.

"How are you even here, Dmitri?" Tom asked. "We were under the impression you were in the Pit."

"I was," Dmitri answered as he took a steaming cup of black coffee from Kelly. He inhaled it deeply. "I haven't had coffee in years, how did you make it without boiling water?"

Kelly smirked. "It's a little machine that allows for

quick individual servings."

"Miraculous," Dmitri mumbled.

"You left the Pit?" Michael asked. "Like Gabe and Jared did?"

"No," Dmitri answered after taking a short slurp from his cup. "This taste nothing like the brown burnt sludge of old." He blew into the cup to cool it down before taking another small sip. "I was pulled out of the Pit. Heaven told me a Guardian was falling. I was to do my best to immediately rectify that situation. I didn't know it was Deb until I arrived on Earth."

Kelly made herself a cup of coffee and slid into one of the stools at the kitchen island. The room paused.

"Why would they pull you out of the Pit for that Dmitri?" Kelly asked through the steam swirling above the mug she grasped with both hands. "You were one of the best Collectors, but you aren't the only one. Were they assuming your connection to Deb would give you an advantage?"

"I assume so, yes," Dmitri answered. "I'm hoping they're right. Anyone feel like talking? Want to fill me in on what's been going on?"

"Why should we help you?" Frankie grew defensive. "You show up here after all this time and expect us to believe you have Deb's best interest at heart. How do we know you're not going to take her as soon as you find her?"

"We should remain calm and be grateful they sent someone who knows us, who will work with us to help Deborah," Harry interjected.

"There is no need to view me as anything other than

a friend, Frankie," Dmitri replied.

"What happens if you cannot get through to her?" Frankie filled the kitchen entrance. He stood taller and took a step toward Dmitri. Her brother's near six-foot trim frame was overshadowed by Dmitri's enormous presence. The Collector's sizable muscles and broad shoulders made him seem larger than life at times.

Dmitri seemed to ponder the question. "I'm not going to lie to you, nor will I sugar coat this situation."

Gen's breath caught in her throat. She didn't want to hear this, but she knew what was coming. She must have made a noise because Dmitri glanced her way.

Please don't say it. Gen's heartbeat skipped a beat. *Don't say you'll have to take her back to Heaven if you cannot stop the Fall.*

"You know what happens to Heavenly beings who cannot or will not change course."

"You will not take Deb," Frankie told him.

Harry held up his hands. "Hold on. Let's focus on what we can do to help Deborah."

"Why did Deb trade her blood with Torin?" Dmitri asked plainly.

Oh no. Gen's heart broke. *I can't believe she really did it. How could she? Not only did she give her blood she made that deal with Torin. Even though she knew he was the one who bartered for my soul.*

Tears welled in Gen's eyes. Gen glanced over at Kelly. The glistening sheen of her sister's big brown eyes reflected the same heartache was hitting Kelly.

"She really gave her blood to Torin?" Frankie asked the question, but it was more like a statement. The truth of

Dmitri's words crushed the room.

"We understand that a demon has kidnapped a Sentinel and is keeping him in Hell," Michael told Dmitri. "We believe Deb is doing what she can to free him."

Dmitri snapped his head back around toward Michael. His jaw tightened and a small vein pulsed across his forehead.

Doesn't seem Heaven has told him everything, Gen pondered. *That's curious.*

"Why would she do that?" Dmitri asked.

"That's a really good question," Kelly remarked. "I'm sure there are many possible answers, the obvious one being love."

Michael's eyes darted between Dmitri and Kelly.

"What are you talking about?" Dmitri asked.

"Well, isn't it obvious?" Kelly said dramatically. "Who would you go to Hell for?"

"Enough," Harry scolded. "Deborah needs us right now. We should not be bickering amongst ourselves. Dmitri, to answer your question, we do not know why she was willing to trade her blood for information about Marcus' location. What we do know, from a reliable source, is the two were in love and before Marcus disappeared; he had given Deborah a ring. So—"

Dmitri squeezed his coffee mug so hard that it shattered. The ceramic pieces scattered across the table and onto the floor. No one moved. The coffee streamed toward the edge of the table and off the end. Dripping liquid falling on tile was the only sound in the room.

Tom grabbed a roll of paper towels and tossed them at Dmitri. "You want to tell us why you're so angry."

"You know why! You saw the memory core." Dmitri caught the roll in one hand, ripped a few sheets off, and did a haphazard job at cleaning the mess he made. He stormed to the waste basket and tossed the brown stained towels inside. As he wiped his hands on his pants, he strode toward the back door. He walked out onto the deck slamming the door shut behind him.

"What just happened?" Harry asked obviously confused.

"I think you just broke his heart," Xavier stated. "The guy looks devastated."

"Yeah," Frankie echoed. "That seemed to really hurt."

"Dmitri and Deb were a couple?" Harry asked befuddled by the news.

"We don't know anything for sure," Kelly answered. "Between the memory core we saw and Dmitri's reaction just now, I would say something romantic was going on between them. He told us he built this cottage for Deb. I was under the impression this was your cottage, Harry."

"No, it's a safe house that the Arch Angels let me use. I had no idea who built it. Amazing that it was Dmitri."

"Strange coincidence," Kelly answered.

"It doesn't matter who built the house," Gen told them. "I'm heading out to talk with him. I don't want him to take off looking for Deb without one of us."

"Good thinking," Kelly told Gen.

Gen walked down to the beach. When she reached his position, he didn't turn to face her.

"I know where she is," he stated.

"Right now?" Gen asked. "You can already feel her?"

"Yes," he answered simply. "It's part of my powers, the ability to find those who are falling."

"Look," Gen's tone softened. "I'm sorry you had to find out about Marcus and the ring like that. Me and Kelly always thought there was something between the two of you. It's been a long time, but I remember how Deb would smile at you. How her cheeks would blush at the mere mention of your name."

Dmitri turned to face Gen, the tension across his forehead softened. "Things between us evolved over time," Dmitri told her. "Just before the Pit we were spending nearly every day together, our individual missions becoming joint ones purely by the fact we were rarely apart. You probably wouldn't have noticed. Deb was living with Kelly back then while you and Gabe were in that house in the city."

Gen closed her eyes as the memory of the destroyed house stabbed her chest. *He's right. I wasn't around my sisters as much back then.*

"I'm sorry for my reaction when you arrived. So much has happened while you've been gone."

"Yeah." Dmitri shook his head. "Gabriel and Jared told me about some of the new technology. Surveillance cameras everywhere, people who carry portable telephones, and cars that drive themselves. Then there's something called the internet. I mean, what is that?"

Gen laughed. "If we had more time, I would show you. I can't imagine the shock."

"No, you can't." Dmitri's voice lowered to a near

whisper. "It's impossible to measure what me, Jared, and Gabe lost while in the Pit for forty years; it's devastating."

"Yes, it is," Gen said simply.

"Why are you all here?" Dmitri asked.

"You mean at this house specifically?" Gen asked but didn't wait for an answer. "We thought it was Harry's cottage. He has some cloak on it, although I have no idea how. I haven't gotten around to asking him."

"It's not Harry's house," Dmitri told her. "It's mine, I built it for her. Deb loves the ocean, I hoped it would be better than a ring."

Oh my. Gen's eyes spun across the scenery once more. *He built this house for Deb. It's cloaked because Collector's have that power.*

"I need to go talk to her," Dmitri abruptly announced. "I'll be back."

"No!" Gen yelled. "Please, Dmitri, take me with you."

He contemplated her plea, before grasping her shoulder and taking her as the two left the beach.

***

Deb looked on in horror at Desire's burning house. The female demon had broken several windows when she threw three Molotov cocktails inside the house. The double wooden doors in the front were mere remnants of an entrance at this point. The stone frame held a blazing inferno inside; everything would be lost.

"How could she just leave and let it burn?" Deb said out loud, not really expecting an answer.

"I told you, they're just material possessions, Deborah," Jade answered as the two stood side by side as the fire flickered and thrashed throughout the first floor.

"None of it meant anything?" Deb asked. "There were pictures and artwork on the walls and what appeared to be homemade blankets on each sofa."

"Just things, darling," Jade sighed. "All will be replaced, don't worry your little heavenly heart over it. My sister has more money than she can count. We all do."

"Real homes aren't about money."

"Don't be so daft. We're demons, remember. We don't have emotional connections to things."

"If it's that easy, why build a cozy home to begin with?"

Jade groaned, but before she could argue further a light appeared to the left of the house.

"I take it these are friends of yours," Jade commented.

Through the billowing smoke she recognized Gen, but it wasn't her sister who caught her attention, it was the large figure with her. The male companion stepped forward and stopped when their eyes met.

Everything about him seemed ripped from a dream. His crewcut and piercing dark eyes seemed to bore right through her. The red T-shirt strained against his broad chest and bulging muscles. Deb's heart immediately jumped. He looked like he had been through the horrors of war. Maybe that was just Deb projecting, for she knew he had been in the Pit with Jared and Gabe these last forty years.

"Dmitri." Deb let the name fall from her lips, and

heat rushed up her neck and across her face. She was fortunate to have the fire to mask her reaction.

Dmitri always had a handheld weapon but based on the chest holster he wore, she assumed he was battle hardened now. Yet his eyes looked at her with the same gentle expression she suddenly remembered.

"Deb," Dmitri's voice betrayed a pleading nature as he stepped toward her. "We need to talk."

Deb's chest tightened a wave of emotion crashed into her so strongly she nearly burst into tears as he moved closer. She had an overwhelming desire to run into his arms. It so alarmed her that she took a tentative step back as he grew closer.

"Stop," she managed to say to him, and he did.

"Well, isn't he the definition of a scrumptious bad boy," Jade commented. "Where have you been hiding him, darling?" Jade looked at Deb. "I take it you fancy him, Deborah."

Deb looked away from Dmitri and over to Gen who hadn't said anything since arriving.

"Deb, can we talk?" Gen asked, her eyes focused on Jade. "Alone, please."

"What is he doing here?" Deb asked, hearing the confusion in her own voice.

"I came for you, Deb," Dmitri answered.

"I'm gobsmacked," Jade droned. "How could you want to go to Hell when you have this piece of lush right here!"

"What?!" Gen exclaimed.

"Sorry." Jade shrugged her shoulders with exaggeration, as if she were sorry to have broken the news about Deb's goal to her sister.

"Deb," Dmitri asked, "will you come back with us, to the beach house?"

"The beach house," Deb repeated. "Why?"

"We'll explain everything once we get there," Dmitri told her.

"Did something happen to the house in Boston?" Deb looked at Gen.

Gen simply nodded. "Yes, Peter sent vampires. It's gone, collapsed and burnt to the ground, much like this house will be soon enough."

"Oh my goodness, no." Deb once again had to choke back tears.

I should have gone back to the house. Deb remembered her conversation with Leo and Lucas. *They were basically telling me something bad happened.*

"I'm so sorry," Deb told Gen.

"I know," Gen replied. "We can talk all about it when we get back to the beach house."

"I can't," Deb defiantly told her sister.

"Why not?" Dmitri asked.

"I have to keep going," Deb replied. "Marcus, he's trapped in Hell."

"What do you think you're going to do about that?" Dmitri asked.

"I'm going into Hell to get him out," Deb answered.

A troubled look crossed Dmitri's face. *Hurt,* she thought. *He's distressed by my words, but why?*

"Deb," Gen interrupted her rambling thoughts. "You know what going into Hell means. At a minimum you'll break the Accord. More importantly to me, you'll be in mortal danger."

The words hung heavy in the air, even Jade stayed quiet.

"We know Marcus gave you a ring, I have to ask," Gen said. "Did it bind?"

"That's irrelevant," Deb snapped. She was not going to tell them she hadn't yet put it on. She was waiting until she was with Marcus. "This is about more than a mere ring. Marcus put himself in harm's way for our family. He did that because I asked him to. Now he's trapped in Hell and our family is doing nothing about it. That's not right!"

Deb was shaking and her voice cracked under the strain of trying to hold it all together. The house fire was moaning in the background, the stress of the heat testing the home's fortitude to remain standing. The smoke turned charcoal in color, thicker now that the entire house was consumed. Everything about the moment was surreal, like a warped waking dream Deb couldn't shake free of.

"If we don't stand up for someone who risked everything to help us," Deb stammered. "if we don't make this right, stop Hell from the usual lying and cheating, then what are we doing here? Why are we even on Earth, if it isn't for making things like what happened to Marcus, right?!"

The weight of her words truly hung on Deb for the first time since she started down this path. *There's no turning back*, Deb thought.

"Marcus would come for me," Deb told them. "I don't know what will happen when I put on that ring. But, if Heaven is okay with allowing someone like him to die alone, trapped in Hell, that is not okay with me. And it shouldn't be okay with this family."

Deb suddenly sensed they were not alone. She stared across the field. Genevieve and Dmitri noticed, but before they could respond Deb spoke.

"We aren't alone anymore."

Jade looked around and two figures appeared around the side of the burning building.

"Those are the two vampires from my penthouse," Jade told them. "My brother sent them to get Deborah and me. We should leave now. Those vampires are fully restored."

Deb grabbed Jade, but it was too late to teleport. The vampires were close enough to cloak the area.

CHAPTER TWENTY-FIVE

"Who is your brother, demon? Is it Peter?" Gen asked. "Deb, how can you be allying yourself with the sister of the demon that's hunting us?"

"I don't know who Peter is," Jade answered. "Don't presume to know who I am, Guardian."

"Gen, her brother is Wrath," Deb paused. "Jade is a Deadly Sin."

"I'm more than my bloody title, Deborah," Jade snapped.

"What?!" Gen exclaimed. "Is Peter working for Wrath then? Or do we have two demons after us? Why is Wrath after you two?"

"I don't know," Deb answered. "Until the other day, I didn't even know the Deadly Sins were actual demons."

"We need to get out of here," Gen said urgently. "One of us should run. If the perimeter the vampires set up is small, like in Boston, we should get past the cloaking in fewer than a hundred yards. Then we can call for reinforcements."

"If you want to run, then do so," Dmitri told them

unfazed. "The Pit has taught me there is nowhere to run. You hold your ground, or you die."

Dmitri unsheathed his sabre and stepped forward. Luca smiled confidently.

"Look Sky!" the male vampire pronounced with his arms stretched wide as if he were happy to see Dmitri. "It's a soldier."

Sky rolled her eyes and removed a jar of Hellfire from her front pocket. "We don't have time for this, Luca." She threw the bottle at Dmitri, but he made no move to get out of the way.

Deb's shield burst outward and enveloped Dmitri. He glanced over his shoulder at Deb knowing she was protecting him. The contents of the Hellfire exploded off her shield and fell upon the ground, burning through the cement driveway around Dmitri's feet.

"Looks like they have a shield, Sky," Luca commented practically with joy. "No one is coming willingly. If they are putting up a defense, then we must fight."

Dmitri turned back to the rapidly approaching vampires. His stance was more defiant than defensive; he was ready to engage. Gen seemed frozen in place. Deb moved toward her sister. Deb grabbed Gen pulling her out of her trance.

"We have to help him," Gen told Deb. "You don't know what restored vampires are like, they'll kill him. Two nearly killed me and Kelly at the house."

"I know first-hand what these two are capable of," Jade snapped. "And so does Deborah. No need to speak to her like a child, Guardian."

"Deb, please," Gen said to her sister, ignoring the demon's barb. "You must see how crazy this all is now. Protecting this demon, running from vampires, making a deal with Torin. With Torin, Deb! You know how badly that hurt to hear? When we get through this, just come home, we'll work it out."

"Bloody hell," Jade mocked. "From where I'm standing it looks like I'm the only one listening to Deborah."

"Deb, I'm begging you," Gen cried. "don't make the same mistakes I made, you're better than that. Just talk to us, come home, without that demon."

Gen's voice was shaking, but she pulled her Haladie from inside her jacket pocket and turned toward the confrontation.

"Run, Deb," Gen ordered. "Don't stop until you can teleport. Send the rest of our siblings."

What do I do? Deb's mind raced. *I can't leave them. At some point, I have to stop running.* A moment of clarity hit her like a freight train, and she made her decision.

"No." Deb pulled out a dagger she'd taken from Jade's office. She walked to Dmitri's right, as Gen stood off to his left. "Jade, stay behind us."

Luca smirked and as he approached, he looked elated for the confrontation.

Sky kept her eyes on Jade. "No point in running Envy!" the female vampire yelled. "We have your scent now. We'll find you no matter where you run off to."

Anger rose in Deb. The thought of the vampires taking Jade, just as they probably took Marcus, enraged Deb.

You have no right. Deb's mind raced in discontent. *They'll take no one from this field.*

The burning energy was intensifying inside of Deb, needing a release. As Michael had instructed her at the beach house, just a few days prior, Deb breathed through the sensation. Frankie wasn't with her to help augment her focus and direct the energy. The power was stronger now than it had been at the house, yet she could tell she wielded more control of it. She was both astonished and confident she didn't need help from her brother. She knew now that her power was just that, hers. She could do this herself.

The air in front of Deb thinned, she pictured a battering ram and the air seemed to form into the image her mind conjured. Deb yelled as she thrust her power toward a charging Luca. The impact on the male vampire was crushing. It pushed him into the air tumbling end over end to the ground, rolling more than thirty feet away. The shock caused Luca to lose his grip on the falchion and the weapon flew deep into the overgrown grass by the tree line.

"Well done, Deborah!" Cheered Jade from behind her.

The violent collision distracted Sky as she looked behind her at her fallen comrade. Taking advantage of the situation Dmitri took two steps forward and punched Sky squarely in the chest. The force sent the female vampire backward where she collapsed to the ground clutching her chest.

Last time Deb had used her power like this, it had exhausted her, not this time. In fact, Deb was ready to use the energy once more.

Sky recovered and was back on her feet. Deb called

to Dmitri, "Move out of the way and give me some space." Heeding Deb's orders both Dmitri and Gen stepped aside.

Deb pushed her shield outward once more, this time directing it lower to the ground so that it would pick Sky up. Deb pictured her energy enveloping Sky as if Deb were holding the vampire in the palm of her hand and raised her toward the clouds. Deb jerked her hand and sent the vampire barreling through the air.

Sky sailed like a missile over the burning home's gardens. She smashed into a thick tree with a sickening crack. Her body dropped limply into the thick brush below and out of view.

The intensity of the heat from the fire grew with fiery embers cascading down on them. The smoke thickened and the acrid smell of burning debris stung her nose and eyes.

"That was bloody fantastic, Deborah!" Jade exclaimed.

Luca found his Falchion and ran straight for Dmitri. Deb's confidence waned and her body shook under the terror of the vampire's aggression. He was large and seemed to be salivating for a worthy opponent to fight. His unmarred skin and youthful glow seemed more enhanced in anger.

How many have been restored? Deb thought in horror. *Please God let me find Marcus and force Heaven to take action for what Hell has done. Whatever has come of my blood I will atone for. Hell has broken the Accord on countless occasions, and I'm pushing back, no matter the cost.*

As Luca reached Dmitri, their blades clashed. They traded aggressive strikes moving toward and away from one another. The clanging of metal echoed through the air, Desire's engulfed house with burning gardens a chaotic backdrop.

"Deb," Gen yelled. "when Kelly and I encountered the vampires at the house, they were afraid of being buried alive. When the female recovers, can you get her closer to the house? Maybe I can collapse part of it on top of her."

"I can try," Deb answered. "She hasn't come back out yet, maybe I hurt her."

"I don't think we can count on that," Gen told her. "Not after what Kelly and I endured. One on one they are ferocious fighters. Dmitri has this one, let's look for the female."

Deb looked back at Dmitri as he blocked another swing from the vampire. He must have studied Luca's moves while they fought. Luca had demonstrated just about everything in his repertoire: he was good with a sword, obviously highly trained.

Dmitri was better. Parrying the next swing, Dmitri disarmed Luca. Keeping his eyes on the vampire, Dmitri kicked the fallen sword toward Deb and Gen. Fear crept into Luca's eyes.

Dmitri did not advance, instead he sheathed his blade behind his back and motioned with his hand for the vampire to advance. Luca thrust back his shoulders and appeared to regain confidence.

What is he doing? Deb thought in aguish. *Why didn't he just finish him off with the sabre?*

Luca rushed. Dmitri remained straight. When the vampire reached Dmitri, he swung up. Dmitri avoided the uppercut and maneuvered his arm around Luca's throat pulling the vampire into a headlock. Dmitri squeezed and the vampire gasped and thrashed to get free. Luca's feet slipped out from underneath him as Dmitri pulled him off the ground.

Luca elbowed Dmitri in the ribs repeatedly finally landing one that allowed him to break free. Before Luca could regain his composure, Dmitri continued his offensive. He jumped up and slammed down a vicious right directly into Luca's face. The punch carried the full force of Dmitri's mass. A crushing blow that broke the vampire's nose. Blood sprayed through the air and stained the vampire's blue jacket.

As Dmitri pulled back, he left an opening. Luca ignored his bloody face, jumped up, and kicked the Collector hard in the chest. Dmitri stumbled back a few steps but stayed on his feet. It would take more than that to bring the Heavenly warrior down.

"You're a sturdy fella, aren't ya," Luca mumbled in respect.

They continued to throw haymakers at each other, the majority of which were blocked. Dmitri focused on Luca's face as that was now the weakest part of the vampire's body.

Luca connected with an uppercut into Dmitri's abs. He coughed blood through his wheezing lungs. Changing tactics Dmitri surprised Luca by grabbing hold of him and tossing him through the air toward the fire now leaping from the house.

Dmitri was quick to pull a vial of Holy Oil from his belt and chuck it at the vampire already getting back to his feet. The glass amulet shattered against Luca's chest soaking the vampire's jacket.

An explosion rocked the house, the force of which knocked both Luca and Dmitri to the ground. Fire rained down around them. They were nearly encircled in flames, which had leapt from the house, raged along the tree-lined yard on both sides of the structure, and now sounded like a freight train. Only the small patch of grass between the driveway and the street was intact.

Dmitri got to his feet first. He grabbed a piece of wood and used it like a torch to light Luca's jacket on fire. As the garment was consumed in flame the vampire yelled and flailed attempting to squelch the fire. It was no use. Luca was enveloped in Holy Fire. Luca would need to shed the protective garment to keep the flame from penetrating his armor-like skin. The vampire jumped to his feet and jerked himself free from his jacket, but not without harm. His chest was swollen and streaked with burn marks.

"Sky!" Luca spit blood on the ground, a small trail left hanging from his bottom lip. "Where the hell are you?"

As if on cue the female stumbled from the garden path. Her hair was tousled, her blue jacket tattered, and blood ran down her face from an open gash on her head.

"Gen!" Deb yelled. "I'll ram her, you target that wound."

"Do it!" Gen replied.

Channeling her energy, Deb focused on Sky and knocked her off her feet. The female grunted as she landed in a heap. Gen lunged and used her weapon to slice at the open skin on the top of her head. Blood exploded from her scalp and Sky shrieked in agony.

"I don't care what our orders are!" Luca yelled. "I'm

going to kill the bitch!" The vampire pointed at Deb. "Then I'll kill you!" He taunted as he looked at Jade who was now in the road trying to escape the heat and flames of the fire.

Dmitri raised both arms up and wide, then he swung down hard with closed fists on either side of Luca's head. The impact sent the vampire down to one knee.

Dmitri looked at Deb, not seeing Luca pull a blade from his boot.

"No!" Deb screamed. "Don't hurt him! Dmitri, look out!"

Luca stabbed Dmitri's left thigh deeply and then pulled the blade down. Dmitri yelped in anguish and once again used his fists to clobber both of Luca's ears simultaneously.

Deb grabbed Luca with her shield. She knew what she wanted to do but didn't know if it would work. She stood with her arms outstretched above her head. She could feel the effort causing sweat to form on her forehead and along the back of her neck.

Deb remembered what Michael told her. 'The strain is because you're fighting against your own power. When you feel it come, direct it and let go.'

Deb inhaled deeply, held it for a beat, and when the power reached the tips of her fingers, she let it go. Luca flew through the air, smashing through what used to be the front doors, soaring through the flames and into the middle of the burning structure.

"Bloody hell, Guardian," Jade said from behind her. "How did you do that?"

Gen didn't waste the moment. She shook the ground underneath the house and the remaining walls of the blazing structure came down on top of the vampire. Luca's screaming pleas reverberated back to them.

"Sky! I'm trapped!" Luca screamed. "Get me out! Sky, don't leave me buried in here!"

Sky looked at the three of them in horror. "How?" the vampire shook her head. "This isn't over!" She ran into the flames to save her trapped brethren.

The fire raged on, consuming everything in its path. It lapped up the sides of nearby trees and the flames grew stronger as they fed on dying leaves. Deb took in the breath of the inferno's reach in awe. The smoke blew all around them and acted like a thick blanket of fog that made part of the backyard no longer visible.

"The cloaking is weakening, they've left," Dmitri told them.

"Are you alright?" Deb asked Dmitri as she stepped toward him. "How bad is it?"

"It's nothing." He looked down at his bloodied leg and then back to her. "Just a gash, it'll heal."

Deb used her powers to heal his open wound. His chest heaved up and down.

He moved a piece of hair away from her face. "Deb, please come with me." He spoke in her ear. "I want to know everything you're going through. I want to help you."

Deb's heart thumped faster, and her hand shook a bit as she placed it across his chest. He covered her hand with his own giving it a light squeeze.

"Have I been in your arms before?" Deb's head swirled as she struggled to grasp onto a memory hovering just below the surface.

"Many times," Dmitri said in reply.

To her very core, Deb knew the truth of his statement. "Why don't I remember?" Tears spilled from her eyes and his face crumbled in confusion.

"What do you mean you don't remember?" Dmitri asked. "What don't you remember?"

"I don't remember us." Deb looked up into Dmitri's dark brown eyes.

He placed both hands on her face and used his thumbs to wipe away her tears. "I don't know what happened after I left. I can help you, Deb. Let me help you."

"I don't know what to believe anymore." Deb stepped back from him. "How could I forget you? If we were together, how could I forget that?"

"I don't know," Dmitri said, crestfallen. "Truly, I don't, but we can work through it."

"No," Deb said. "This isn't what's important right now. Hell started this when they killed Lacey's mentor, Sebastian. And they've continued their aggression with kidnapping a Sentinel. I'm not letting Marcus be collateral damage."

"Deb, listen to me." Dmitri took her hand in his.

Deb snatched her hand back. "I don't trust you, I can't. If my mind erased you, there must be a reason."

Deb turned and walked to Jade.

"Are you sure, Guardian?" Jade asked. "He seems sincere."

"I know," Deb answered. "He's a Collector, empathy is his secret weapon."

"No!" Dmitri insisted. "This is not a trick, Deb!"

"Deb!" Gen yelled. "I love you, we both do." Gen's eyes sprang fresh tears at Deb's turned back.

"What of her?" Jade added. "She's family."

"I know." Deb grabbed Jade's hand and looked into the demon's emerald green eyes. "I'm trusting myself for once. Now get the two of us out of here."

Jade stared at Deb for a moment. Then she smiled, different from any other time Deb had seen her smile.

"Whatever you wish my darling friend."

Then they were gone.

CHAPTER TWENTY-SIX

Kelly owed Gerry an apology. Though she didn't know how she was going to give it, she knew it had to be done in person. She arrived about a quarter mile from Lacey's home. It was typical of Watchers to live in more rural isolated places. Even though they often lived with or collaborated with others of their kind, the places they rested were often referred to as 'off the grid.'

A Historian's role is to lay witness to the combat between Heaven and Hell on Earth. This means they are often on the front lines of violent and grisly confrontations. The solitude allows a Historian to reflect and meditate, useful tools to recover from such abhorrent events.

The idea of living a more remote life sounded peaceful. As Kelly surveyed the acres and acres of tree-lined woods and hilly landscape, she doubted her own ability to be happy outside the hustle of city life.

She walked across the patches of brown grass and fallen yellow leaves. It was peaceful, the only sounds that of nature stirring. The occasional caw announced her presence, but as she got close the birds and insects scattered at her intrusion. The air smelled fresh and crisp on this autumn afternoon.

The large white farmhouse stood before her, nothing but open space between them. The house sat majestically on a small hillside showcasing its wooden shingles and large windows. The sprawling front porch wrapped around on the left side, and the front door was ajar. Gerry and Gardenia sat on the front porch. The young girl had her head in a book while Gerry sipped from a mug. Gerry was in a red rocking chair and Gardenia sat with her legs stretched out on a porch swing, a plaid blanket covering her lower body.

Kelly knew the house would be cloaked. It was a small amount of protection, but it was something. She only found it with Harry's help. He pointed to a spot on the map and gave Kelly an approximate place to focus. Now that she was here and could physically see the house, she could teleport the last four hundred yards or so to the front yard, but she didn't move. Instead, she took in the scene of Gerry and Gardenia sitting outside.

They look content, like they've been sitting on that porch for years. Like it's home already.

Kelly walked on for a bit until Gerry cusped a hand over his eyes indicating he had spotted her and was trying to get a better look at the approaching figure. Gardenia put her book down and yelled something, a light gust of wind carried the sound away from Kelly. Lacey pushed through the screen door and onto the porch. Her hands on her hips indicated she was unhappy with the idea of a visitor.

Kelly forged ahead trying to gather her thoughts. In years past she would have moved on, glossed over her actions, but witnessing what happened to Gerry changed her. She knew she needed to take responsibility for what happened to him. She knew what she should say, her mind kept rehashing it. She wasn't sure going over it in her head this many times was helping, but she couldn't seem to quiet her inner monologue.

How does one say sorry to a man you saved that you shouldn't have? Hey, so about that aspirin, apparently it saved you from a heart attack and messed up Death, who knew? Kelly sighed. *Sarcasm will get you nowhere in this situation.*

Harry tried to help by telling her to just let it come from the heart, but it's not like she's had a lot of those conversations in the last several decades.

I wish Jared were here. He used to help me focus. He was always so calm it was easy being around him. I miss him.

When she had cut the distance between them in half, she smiled and waved. Lacey dropped her arms back down to her side and Gardenia threw off the blanket and got up. She gave an enthusiastic wave in return and then started down the front steps jogging toward her.

Poor kid. Lost had a double meaning with this teen, she really didn't fit in this supernatural world. After meeting her, Kelly understood why Marcus was trying to help her. Gardenia was smart and funny. She had an infectious laugh and was quick with a smile. This world had taught her to be cautious, suspicious even, but once she let her guard down, she was trusting and had a big heart.

"Hey," Gardenia said to Kelly. "Is it over, did Deb find Marcus? I really need to know he's okay."

"No," Kelly answered. "I'm afraid not."

"Oh." Gardenia's shoulders fell and her eyes

dampened.

"We aren't giving up," Kelly told her as Gardenia turned toward the house.

"I know," Gardenia responded. "It's just tough, the waiting around for news on his rescue. I would rather be doing something about it, but I have no idea what."

"Well," Kelly pointed up at the porch, "at least you have a nice place and good company to do the waiting with."

"Yeah." Gardenia smiled and the two made their way onto the porch.

"Hi," Kelly said to Gerry and Lacey who were now waiting for her to reach them. "I was hoping for a few minutes alone with Gerry."

Lacey nodded and walked through the front door holding it open for Gardenia. "We'll just be in the kitchen if you need anything."

Kelly nodded and took a seat in the empty rocking chair next to Gerry. He sat back down but turned his chair slightly toward Kelly.

"Sorry to bother you guys," Kelly began. "I didn't mean to get Gardenia's hopes up. I wasn't thinking about that when I came here. I feel bad. How's she doing?"

"She's doing alright," Gerry answered. "She shared some more stories about her time with Marcus, seems like he might have been a father figure to her."

"Yeah, with how vested she is in his return, that adds up. How are you?"

"I'm just fine," Gerry answered.

"Fine is better than going insane, not to mention stir crazy way out here in ruralville USA," Kelly remarked.

"You do that a lot," Gerry commented. "You use humor to mask things."

"I absolutely do," Kelly answered. "I'm not used to apologizing, taking responsibility, helping after the fact. It's all new to me."

"Is that what this is?" Gerry mocked. "I didn't realize you did anything wrong."

"Now who's being the funny one?" Kelly joked.

Gerry grinned, the mischief reaching his deep brown eyes. He turned his face back toward the yard. "It's amazing out here."

"Yes," Kelly agreed. "It is very pretty and incredibly quiet."

"Best night's sleep I've had in a long time," Gerry remarked. "Who knew I'd need sleep after I died."

Kelly's heart broke a little. "I came here to try and explain everything."

"Everything, huh," Gerry repeated. "Could be a long conversation."

"Well, now that I'm here, it seems pointless," Kelly replied.

"Why is that?" Gerry asked.

"It changes nothing," Kelly told him. "I messed up. I saw you in distress, figured it was a heart attack. I went looking for aspirin and when I couldn't find any, I left and got some."

"Seems perfectly reasonable to me," Gerry told her.

"That's just it," Kelly added. "It wasn't normal. We aren't allowed to interfere like that. We can influence and we do, but we aren't supposed to insert ourselves into the situation like that. I don't know, I guess I just wanted to help you."

"Well, it's kind of hard to be mad at you for that." Gerry smiled.

The two sat in silence looking out over the hilly landscape. There was a small orchid of apple trees off to her right. In the distance she could see neighboring farmers working the land, the buzzing of their giant tractors nothing but a low hum.

To her left were dozens of eastern hemlock and sugar maple trees. A scattering of wild goldenrod and St. John's wort littered the ground between the house and the tree line. On either side of the front porch were large rhododendron bushes, the purple flower was all but gone, but the hearty leaves were still green in the sun.

"I don't know why I did it," Kelly told him. "I wish I had a better explanation. It feels like I should, considering the cost."

"The cost?" Gerry asked.

"You're out of sync with your ending," Kelly told him. "Death would have come for you if I hadn't intervened. You would have been brought to the Historians and eased into this new life. You may even have had the opportunity to see your late wife.

"You mean I could be at peace, in Heaven, with my beloved wife."

"I'm really not sure," Kelly answered, hearing the crack in her voice. "This is your destiny, to be a Historian, but the transition should have been easier. I don't know enough about the process. I'm sure Lacey can help with details when you're ready. I know saving you made me feel better, but it wasn't the right thing for me to do and I need to own that. You have witnessed many things since being stuck here on Earth with me and my family. The things you've seen, those would have all come in due time, I guess with us you're getting the crash course so to speak."

"I saw you that day," Gerry told her. "You looked like an angel. You were glowing, a light was all around you."

"That was my mark," Kelly replied as she grabbed her left arm. "It lights up when a charge is in need. We get pulled to where they are. We never know exactly what they need. It's not always clear when, and if, Hell is the cause."

"Sounds like a tough gig," Gerry told her.

Kelly chuckled. "It can be. At least I'm not alone, I have my family."

"Yeah," Gerry remarked. "That is something to be grateful for."

"I see that you're okay, that you have handled this amazingly well and I wonder." Kelly paused. "Maybe we were meant to meet, that I had something to learn from you."

"Well," Gerry sighed, "that would be something."

A quietness hung in the air between them.

Finally Gerry broke the silence. "Who is Harry to you?"

"He's like an advisor, a mentor," Kelly told him. "Sometimes I think he's there to keep me sane."

"Your family doesn't keep you sane?" Gerry asked.

"They try." Kelly smiled over at Gerry. "Most days they have trouble keeping me from starting a war down here."

Gerry laughed. "I bet."

"I'm sorry, Gerry," Kelly told him. "Truly I am. Please know if there is anything I can do to make things easier during your transition, I will."

"I think I'm right where I'm supposed to be, Kelly," Gerry told her.

He's so gracious, Kelly thought. *Maybe one day he can help me achieve that mindset.*

"Everything happens for a reason," Gerry interrupted her racing mind. "That's what my Georgina used to say."

"What was she like?" Kelly asked. "I saw pictures of the two of you in the house, you both looked so happy."

"We were," Gerry smiled. "Thirty-years and two kids, it doesn't get much better than that. When the cancer came, Georgina told me we were lucky. That at least we had a chance to say goodbye. She was always looking on the bright side, you know?"

"And you?" Kelly asked him. "How did you feel about the cancer?"

"Oh, I was angry," Gerry admitted. "One time when she was overnight in the hospital, I left and went to the boatyard. I drove way out, past the bay and into deep waters. I stopped in an area where there were no other boats on the radar, dropped anchor and screamed up at the sky. I must have cried a thousand tears. Were you there? Were you on that boat with me?"

"Sorry, no," Kelly admitted.

"I was never much of a believer, you know," Gerry confessed. "Georgina had great faith. She used to talk about how she would meet me at the gates. I used to joke that I didn't need to go to church, that she had enough faith for both of us."

Kelly sighed. "It reminds me of how I used to feel about my sister, Deb. She has such a big heart, a strong belief in what we're doing here, in the mission."

"You think she's lost that?" Gerry asked.

"I think she's on her own boat yelling up at the sky," Kelly answered, a tear trickling down her cheek.

"Yeah." Gerry reached over and placed his hand on Kelly's arm. "If Georgina were here, she would tell you the one thing of value in this world is love. She would remind you that love comes in many forms, not just the romantic kind."

Kelly looked at Gerry. "You don't think Deb's in love with Marcus? Why?"

"I don't know anything about your sister," Gerry told her. "It's you who doesn't think she's in love with Marcus, that's why you're struggling with her choices."

"You are very wise for a rookie," Kelly told him.

Gerry laughed. "A rookie? I haven't been a rookie at anything in many years."

"Any advice on how I fix this crazy situation with my sister?" Kelly asked.

"Not all things are meant to be fixed." Gerry sighed and got up from the rocking chair. "Come inside, let's have some iced tea and talk some more."

Kelly followed Gerry into the house. The hardwood floors were shiny, and the walls were painted a creamy antique white. The ceiling vaulted with wooden trusses that made the large space feel homey. There was a plush sofa and oversized chair facing a stone fireplace in the living room.

In the kitchen, pots hung from hooks connected to the ceiling above a small island. The cabinets were royal blue with black handles and there were stainless steel appliances, all the conveniences of modern living.

Beyond the kitchen through wide open French doors sat a rectangular table and chairs in an enclosed screened-in porch.

The smell of cinnamon and brown sugar wafted through the air. Kelly looked around but Lacey and Gardenia were nowhere to be found. On the stove a mixture of what appeared to be the contents for apple pie were nearly boiled away. Another few minutes and it would be completely burnt on the bottom.

Dough lined a pie plate on the marble countertop. The sink was filled with dirty bowls and dishes. Ingredients such as sugar, butter, and spices still littered the counter. Gerry looked around and then began calling for the women as he walked off to search for Lacey and Gardenia.

Kelly made her way to the stove and shut off the gas, removing the pot from the hot grate to a cool one.

Gerry re-entered the kitchen and stared at Kelly. "I don't know where they went."

Before Kelly could answer her mark went off. Burning white hot light glowed through her anchor beneath her long-sleeved shirt.

"Something's wrong." Kelly turned and began pulling open drawers. "Has anyone else been here besides me?"

"Yeah," Gerry answered. "This morning some woman came by. Her and Lacey went outside to talk, but it quickly turned into an argument."

"About what?" Kelly asked frantically looking through drawers. "Who did Lacey say she was?"

"She didn't," Gerry answered. "What are you looking for?"

"Knives, weapons, anything to defend ourselves. Remember while in transition you are vulnerable to attack. You don't have mastery over your powers yet and Hell knows it," Kelly told him.

"There are no weapons here," Gerry answered. "Lacey said she doesn't believe in them. There is a butcher block on the counter, right there."

Kelly looked in the direction of Gerry's outstretched finger pointing at the block full of knives. She grabbed the largest one. Looking around Kelly spotted the fireplace poker and grabbed that too.

"Stay close, Gerry," Kelly warned. "I don't know what's coming, but my siblings aren't answering. I'm not sure if that's the cloaking Lacey put in or whatever is coming."

"I've been practicing teleporting, but I do not have that down yet," Gerry told her. "Do you think someone has taken them?"

"I don't know," Kelly told him. "Any chance Lacey believes in cell phones?"

"No," Gerry told her. "She says she's old fashioned. She said she doesn't even use a computer."

"Of course not," Kelly muttered. "Not that I blame her. Okay, we're going to make our way outside and away from the house to the valley below. Once we are far enough away, we'll call my siblings."

"Kelly," Gerry whispered.

287

She snapped her head around at the sound of fear in Gerry's voice. His eyes displayed disbelief and his mouth hung open. Gerry slowly pointed at the window above the sink. The yard was empty, but a potted plant was floating through the air as if being carried by a ghost.

"Son of a—" Kelly grabbed flour off the counter and ran through the open French doors to the back door and exited the house. She could hear Gerry running behind her. She sliced the flour open and threw it in the air around the floating plant.

The flour covered three figures, two of which were tied up and gagged. The third, a male, coughed and tried to wipe the flour away from his eyes. Kelly punched the male in the back of the head. He yelped and dropped the metal chain he carried in his hands. Before he could recover Kelly swung hard with the fireplace poker and landed a blow to his lower back. He screeched and dropped to the ground on both knees.

"Stop!" The male yelled.

Kelly grabbed the male by his hair. "Drop the cloaking shield, demon."

"Okay, okay," he said, as he put both arms shakily in the air in surrender.

He dropped the cloaking and both Gardenia and Lacey became visible. Gardenia was crying, Lacey looked shell shocked. Blood dripped from both their wrists where they were bound with pieces of the Chain of Chaos. Gerry ran to them and pulled the gags from their mouths.

"Don't touch the chain, Gerry," Kelly yelled. "Lacey, drop the shield you have around the house."

Lacey closed her eyes and a moment later Dan was

standing in front of her. "What the heck happened?"

"Who is he?" Tom asked from Kelly's right.

Kelly pulled the demon up from the ground. Spinning him around to face her, Kelly was startled. "I recognize you. You're a soul catcher." The male had wavy brown hair, dark brown eyes, and a fresh scar across his left cheek. He wore jeans and an oversized plaid jersey.

"A what?" Gerry blurted from her left.

"Miles," Kelly said, ignoring Gerry's question. "That's your name, isn't it?"

"I didn't think there were any soul catchers left," Tom commented.

"Me neither," Dan added. "Didn't Heaven annihilate them during the Arch Angel–vampire war?"

"They didn't get all of them," Kelly told them.

Dan freed the two women from the Chain of Chaos. He let the demonic weapon drop to the ground in a clanging heap. He sprinkled Holy Water on top of it and it burned into the ground.

"Where did you get the demonic weapon?" Dan asked the demon.

"I don't answer to you," Miles sneered.

"You're going to answer to us," Kelly huffed, "or your face won't be the only thing scarred."

"All I want is what's mine," Miles told them.

Lacey was hugging Gardenia as she quietly sobbed.

"What is it you're looking for?" Tom asked.

"A coin," Miles remarked.

Kelly's ears perked up, but she turned and made her way to Gardenia and Lacey. She used her powers to heal them from where the demonic weapon had ripped open the skin.

"What makes you think it's here?" Dan asked.

"The girl has it," Miles pointed at Gardenia.

"Well, looks like you're out of luck then." Kelly glared at him. "Possession, you know it's nine-tenths of the law."

"I was just going to ask the ladies some questions," Miles told them. "Maybe bargain for it back."

"You were taking them away from the nearby Guardian," Tom said dryly.

"Or you were taking something else in lieu of the coin," Dan added.

Gardenia, Kelly thought in horror. *He was going to take her soul, maybe trade it for something of value. Lacey was just in the way.*

"Who took your coin?" Tom asked Miles.

"The sentinel took my coin," Miles answered. "You know, the one that's missing. I asked around, seems he was quite found of this one." He motioned back at Gardenia.

"How did you know they were here?" Kelly asked.

"Once I get a scent, I'm as good as any at tracking," Miles answered.

"The house is cloaked, protected!" Lacey yelled. "How did you find us?"

"Heaven," Miles laughed. "Heaven broke it this morning, all I had to do was wait for the right time."

Heaven? Tom spoke to Kelly and Dan telepathically. *Do you know what he's talking about, Kelly?*

No, Kelly answered. *I only just heard about a female being here earlier today from Gerry, just before the confrontation. Gerry said he didn't know who it was, but that there was an argument between she and Lacey.*

"And you thought the time to act was when a Guardian showed up?" Dan asked Miles sardonically.

"No one said he was smart," Kelly uttered. "They were though, one of them swiped a plant off the deck railing and made sure we saw it floating in the air through the kitchen window."

"What's the coin used for?" Tom asked.

"None of your business." Miles smirked through a bloodied fat lip.

"You just made it our business," Dan told him. "Did you give him the fat lip, Kell?"

"No," Kelly answered. "I punched him in the back of the head."

"Seems like you have lots of enemies," Dan remarked. "Who gave you the scar?"

"Someone who's already paid your sisters a visit," Miles told him.

"Peter?" Tom asked.

"Peter and one other," Miles told them. "You're behind once again, Guardians. You'll never stop what's coming."

Miles disappeared from the yard, there was a palpable sigh of relief from Gardenia and Lacey.

"Who has the coin?" Tom asked.

Gardenia looked up through teary eyes. "I gave it to Deb."

CHAPTER TWENTY-SEVEN

Jade pushed the doorbell and took a half step backward toward Deb standing just behind her. The row of terraced dark gray stone houses on the street looked like they were ripped from a travel magazine. The gutter that lined the cobblestone street was immaculate and each cottage-like house was adorned with a generous number of windows.

When the door opened a fair skinned blonde looked up in bewilderment. Deb recognized the petite female right away, it was Veronica, the seamstress that came to the hotel with clothes for Deb to change into ahead of her meeting with Torin.

"Miss Jade," Veronica said, her voiced laced with concern. "What's happened?"

"Veronica, my lovely," Jade said. "May we come in?"

Veronica nodded and opened the door wider. Deb followed Jade inside the home.

"The remodel turned out beautifully," Jade gushed.

Deb looked up at the freshly painted ceilings, the

height of which made the home feel bigger than it really was. There was wainscoting and stencil work on several walls. The deep brown of the hardwood floors warmed up the space. Area rugs added small splashes of color. The faint smell of industrial fumes was masked by a tall vase full of white lilies.

"Yes," Veronica replied with a smile. "The laborers you sent over just banged on and it was done in a jiff."

"They outdid themselves," Jade replied. "I can't wait to see the rest of it."

"Of course," Veronica answered as she closed and locked the front door behind them. "Please, let's go to the kitchen. I'll find us some bits n bobs."

"Thank you," Jade said, as she followed Veronica to their left through a small dining room and then into an open kitchen in the back of the house. The large marble island with four seats gave a grand view of the rest of the high-end kitchen. Light gray cabinets and stainless steel covered the space. There was a large ornamental hood vent above the oversized gas stove and brightly colored mosaic tile adorned the small wall space above the jets.

Jade made an exaggerated gasp. "Smashing, it's absolutely brilliant!"

"Yes, I'm so pleased with it," Veronica answered.

"Deborah," Jade invoked. "Do you fancy it?"

"It's very nice," Deb answered. "with the soot on our clothes I'm actually afraid to sit down anywhere."

"Nonsense!" Veronica waved Deb off. "Sit down, I'll make us a cuppa and find some biscuits."

Veronica filled a large kettle with water and moved it to the stove. She then opened the cabinet for a canister of tea. She filled the tea strainer inside a ceramic tea kettle and busied herself with pulling teacups together. She returned to the island with cups, spoons, and small plates. I have a few biscuits, but if you're okay with waiting I can reheat some stew."

"Biscuits are fine with me," Deb answered.

"She's got a sweet tooth this one." Jade smiled.

Veronica laughed. "You wouldn't know it by looking at her. She's a fit bird isn't she then?"

"That she is," Jade remarked and sat down at the island.

Veronica went about preparing the tea. She poured each of them a cup and placed a larger plate with custard cream biscuits in between her and Jade.

"Veronica darling," Jade's voice was light and nearly playful. "We could use a rest, a clean-up, and some new clothes. Could you be a dear and help us?"

"Of course." Veronica nodded. "I'll make my way down to Vernon on the Square and pick up a few things. You two enjoy your tea. It's a bit late for me to have it now anyway. Then you can make your way up to rest."

Veronica opened a few drawers, found her keys, and grabbed her purse off a nearby chair. Jade winked at Deb. "I'll be back in a moment luv. I'm just going to see Veronica off."

Jade followed Veronica to the front door. Deb could feel the weight of the past few days pressing down on her. The two women spoke in hushed whispers, then the front door opened and clicked closed once again.

Jade made her way back to the kitchen. "Deborah, you look run-down."

"Thanks," Deb replied dryly.

"Go on upstairs, the back bedroom overlooking the quaint little garden is the spare. Get some rest, when you wake Veronica will be back with clothing for you to shower and change into."

"What about you?" Deb asked. "You're not tired?"

"I'm going to take my cuppa and nestle in front of the fireplace and wait for Veronica. I might shut my eyes for a moment or two."

Deb couldn't find a reasonable argument against Jade's suggestion.

We're obviously safe here or Jade wouldn't have risked coming. I have so many questions, but right now I can barely think. I'm not sure I could even drink a cup of tea, never mind sit in a stranger's house and make small talk with my demon friend. Deb let the last word linger in the fog of disarrayed thoughts. *Friend.*

"Go on then," Jade told Deb, motioning with her hands as if to shoo Deb away.

Deb was more than tired. Her mind was circling but not finishing a complete thought. She simply nodded in agreement and got up from her seat at the island making her way back toward the front door to the staircase. Jade was moving about in the kitchen. The sound of dishes clanging followed her as she ascended the steps to the second floor.

When Deb reached the second-floor landing, she made her way down the lush, carpeted hallway toward the back of the house. Artwork lined the walls, but very few were framed photographs. Everything about the house seemed a bit cold, certainly not Deb's taste.

With Jade's help, Deb sighed. *Not only was she friendly with this woman but financially assisting her with a home renovation.* She was an enigma. Deb assumed Jade would enjoy being thought of that way.

Deb opened the door to the bedroom and her eyes widened in pleasant surprise. She expected a nice simple guest room: a bed, side table, and closet.

Well, this is a surprise, Deb thought as she walked in to take a look around.

The bedroom was large, with tall ceilings, similar to the first floor and with matching windows. The walls were painted a rich cream color, and the large canopy bed was draped in white chintz. The rich brown color of the king size bedframe matched the twin nightstands. Floor-to-ceiling built-in shelving on her left brimmed with novels, candles, and baskets filled with dried flowers.

The bed was pushed against the wall to her right with a door on either side. Straight in front was a wall of windows with a large window seat. A wine-colored blanket lay across the plush cushions. The first door to her right was an oversized closet filled with handbags, belts, and matching shoes that filled the numerous cubbies. There were tons of clothes hanging, most of which still had the price tag affixed to them.

Closing the closet door, she made her way around the bed to the door on the other side of the room. As she walked by the windows, she spotted a small yard in the back with a quaint little garden. For the time of year, it was mostly green, with little patches of brown indicating there had been a slightly dry summer. If you looked hard enough you could see a late blooming rose or clematis.

Inside the second door was a large bathroom with a claw foot tub, walk-in shower, and double sinks. The room had everything a guest would need. Although Deb would have loved to relax in a hot bath in the luxurious tub, she opted to wash up instead. Taking a washcloth and towel from the linen cabinet she walked to the sink. Deb picked up a new toothbrush, opened the package, and discarded the wrapper. Before turning on the faucet, she looked up and was stunned at her reflection.

Deb's eyes had dark circles under them, and her ribcage stuck out a little more than normal; clearly, she had lost weight. In various spots she had bruises, most of which she could not remember getting. The blemishes were in varying degrees of healing. The small yellow one on her neck added to the gauntness of her overall appearance.

I look as awful as I feel.

After cleaning up, she made her way back into the guest room, pulled the blackout curtains closed, and practically fell into the gloriously decadent bed. As she pulled the covers up to her chest, her heavy eyelids closed. She thought it would take a bit to fall asleep in yet another strange place, but she was wrong. Like the undertow of a raging sea, slumber dragged her toward unconscious.

***

"How many donuts can you eat before you throw up?" Dmitri asked Kelly.

"Throwing up is a waste of good food." Kelly drank the last of the milk she had poured.

"I don't remember your appetite being this large or

this unhealthy," Dmitri commented.

"Well, I don't remember ever eating with you."

"Maybe all the sugar has adversely affected your brain."

"If you want a donut, just ask. Making rude remarks will get you nowhere with me big man."

"The sarcasm I remember." Dmitri chuckled. "The stuffing your face every moment, not so much."

"I think we have more important things to discuss," Gen commented from behind them.

Gen and Dmitri had explained to her family and Harry about the fire and what happened when they found Deb.

Kelly, who had returned from Lacey's house with the Historian, Gerry, and Gardenia, told all of them about encountering a Soul Catcher.

These few moments were a respite while they processed the information dump.

Dmitri poured himself another cup of steaming coffee. "I know where Deb is. From what I can feel, she's sleeping."

"Well then, I guess we aren't in any rush," Kelly offered. "There's no need to save Deb from the Sandman." Kelly hesitated. "Wait, is the Sandman real?"

Dmitri chortled and shook his head while Tom rolled his eyes.

"What?" Kelly mumbled through her next mouthful of donut.

Dmitri sat down next to Tom who returned to skimming pages of an old text.

"What are you looking for?" Dmitri asked.

"Information about restored vampires," Tom answered, but never looked up. "Their numbers dwindled during the great war, but no restored vampire has been seen on Earth since."

"Harac has led what are now considered legendary rebellions in Hell," Kelly told them. "The first one was still his most successful. He drove the Hellions in a wave through the Pit and onto Earth. Angels and Guardians suffered great losses during those battles. Hell's first Army, the vampires, pounced on the opportunity to slaughter Heavenly beings and push Hell toward victory. This became what is now known as the Great War between the Arch Angels and vampires. The result was an amendment to the Accord that removed a vampire's bloodlust for humans. From that day forward vampires could only feed on other demons for survival and their wounds would scar."

"Harrowing," Lacey stated. "In the old Historian archives the battles are much more descriptive and they have some accompanying artwork that adds to the gruesomeness."

"That's right!" Kelly bellowed. "You guys have a massive library hidden somewhere. Where is it?"

"Well telling you would sort of defeat the purpose of keeping it hidden." Lacey's eyebrows arched as she smirked.

"This still doesn't explain why Deb doesn't seem to remember me," Dmitri snapped.

"We have a bigger problem," Michael barked. "We have never encountered restored vampires in large numbers and now Gen and Kelly have come up against four in just a few days."

"That's what I'm combing through the text for," Tom told them. "Once Kelly finishes eating, she can help me."

"I can help too," Lacey told them. "I can read in most of the old languages."

"Really?" Kelly asked. "That is awesome and will definitely speed things up."

"What should I be looking for exactly?" Lacey asked.

"Ways to defeat them," Tom said bluntly.

"We know about Holy Fire," Dan told them. "Though you obviously have to manufacture that by engulfing Holy Oil in available fire."

"Well, there's also Holy Water," Lacey told them.

"Yes, but that's not readily available in large quantities," Kelly remarked.

"What do you mean?" Gerry asked. "It's in every church across the globe."

"Well," Kelly began, "that's not really Holy Water."

"Am I supposed to understand that?" Gerry asked.

"Um . . ." Kelly hesitated.

"What's in the churches is made by humans," Xavier answered. "It's symbolic."

"I see," Gerry said, but it was obvious he didn't really understand.

"Holy Water comes from Heaven only," Xavier explained.

"Right." Gerry nodded.

"The church gets Holy Water from the Vatican," Kelly added. "it's water blessed by the Pope which is a symbolic gesture."

"The vampires also fear being buried," Gen told them. "That was certainly not well known."

"It's the opposite of vampire lore," Gardenia spoke for the first time since arriving. "In books and movies, the un-dead sleep in coffins, in the dark, or underground."

"Look, you guys have fun reading history books," Dmitri said, as he got up from the table and walked through the living room toward the back door. "I'm going for a walk on the beach. This brainstorming is giving me a headache. I don't know how you get anything done this way."

"Wait!" Gen shot out of her chair. "Please promise you won't go after her alone."

Dmitri stopped and turned back. "Don't worry, Gen. I'm just going for a walk on the beach. But I'm not promising anything when it comes to Deb."

The screen door slapped shut behind him, like a physical assault on Gen. *He won't promise. That means he'll take her when he decides he can no longer stop her from Falling. And only he knows when that will be.*

CHAPTER TWENTY-EIGHT

Deb woke to the sound of the ocean washing across the shoreline. The plastic straps of the chair stuck to the bare parts of her body. She looked down. She was wearing a simple black bikini, the same one she wore during her memory core. The seashell coverup lay crumpled at the bottom of the lounge chair under her ankles.

She cupped her hand over her eyes and peered around the beach. She was alone.

I must be dreaming. Deb's mind was still steeped in the fog of sleep. *The same dream as before, I'm back at the beach house.*

The lilting of voices rising and falling floated down to her. She looked up at the familiar cottage Harry had invited her and her sisters to just a week ago. The back door was open, but no one was in sight.

She slowly pulled her back away from the chair, the plastic straps straining to hold suction and remain glued to her skin. The smell of the salt air mixed with suntan lotion. As she stood a breeze tossed the beach coverup through the air where it rolled over the sand several feet away.

The vision should pop up any minute now, Deb thought as she got up and walked toward the thin cotton garment. *Every time I fall asleep, even for a moment, this dream haunts me.* Deb heard something behind her and spun around quickly.

The screen door to the back deck slammed shut, but no one was there.

Sufficiently creepy, Deb groaned. *It's new though. At least I can definitively say I am not in a twisted version of the movie* Groundhog Day.

She turned back toward the chair and it was gone, nothing was there, not her beach coverup, not the lounge chair, nothing.

"Great," Deb grumbled. "Now what?"

The seagulls and small black birds that had been airborne all settled on the salt rocks, covering nearly every available space. Their normal incessant chatter quieted to a near murmur.

Reminiscent of the movie The Birds. *Not a movie I want to experience, even if it is just a dream.*

No one else was on the beach, just her and the birds. The wind swirled and threw the sand around her bare feet, but overall, the weather was pleasant.

Why isn't the vision starting? It normally starts right away.

Not that she understood how to deal with her missing memories. She assumed her mind was trying to tell her something, but it would be easier if she could just remember or talk with someone who does.

"Deb?"

The male voice startled her. Despite the fact she was

waiting for the vision, there had never been any words heard clearly before, just the sounds of laughter and whispering voices. Certainly not her name being spoken aloud.

Deb turned. Dmitri was standing on the beach. He wore a dark gray sweatshirt over the same red T-shirt she had just seen him in at Desire's house.

"Dmitri?"

"What are you doing here?" he asked.

"I'm dreaming," Deb answered.

"I don't think so," Dmitri responded.

"What do you mean?" Deb asked.

"You're here with me on the beach, your siblings are inside." He nodded his head in the direction of the house.

Deb pushed her shield and cloak out around her.

Did I sleep teleport? she thought in confusion. *I guess that could be a thing.*

"I can still see you Deb," Dmitri told her. "Why don't you drop the cloak? It must take a lot of energy to project that continuously especially on top of your shield."

"You can see through my cloak?" Deb asked.

"Yes," Dmitri stated, taking a few tentative steps toward her. "I've always been able to."

"I don't remember that." Deb's words were barely above a whisper.

"That's okay, I don't remember you being able to project your shield around others," he replied. "I sensed it around me at that fire. I didn't have a chance to say thank you."

Dmitri had managed to get within a few feet of her. "Don't come any closer," Deb demanded.

"I haven't moved," Dmitri told her. "You did."

"What?" Deb asked him. "What do you mean I moved?"

"Deb, you seem confused," Dmitri told her. "Can you tell me what you're feeling, why you came here?"

"I'm not sure," Deb paused. "I'm still groggy, I guess. I fell asleep and woke up on a lounge chair here and I thought I was dreaming. The vision from my memory core, it plays in every dream I have now and it's from what looks like this beach. I must be dreaming because the chair I woke up in is now gone."

"A memory core," Dmitri asked. "You saw one of your own memory cores?"

"Well, Greg helped me to see it," Deb told him. "He made it stop looping. It somehow got stuck and was really painful."

"Yeah, I can imagine that would be painful," he answered. "Do you know why I'm here, Deb?"

"No," Deb said simply.

"No idea?" He added.

"Look, I've seen the memory core," Deb told him. "So, I guess at some point we kissed."

"I see the memory core too," he answered. "It's playing just behind you."

Deb swung her head back around toward the salt rocks. The vision was there, just as before. Her and Dmitri laughing, kissing, and holding hands.

"I don't remember this moment," Deb said, her eyes filling once again. "It seems sc —"

"Perfect," he finished.

"Intimate is more the word I was searching for,"

Deb confessed.

"Yes," Dmitri answered. "We were all that and more."

"It's not that I just lost the memory, Dmitri," Deb told him. "The feeling that one would have in a moment like that, it's also gone."

"What are you saying, Deb?"

"I have no romantic feelings for you, Dmitri," Deb said, as she looked into his brown eyes and saw sorrow.

"Do you have feelings for this Sentinel you're trying to save?" he asked, his voice trembling with a hint of anger.

"I care about Marcus, yes," Deb answered.

"Care?" Dmitri repeated. "I think I would have to do more than care if I were attempting to go to Hell to rescue someone."

"It's a long story," Deb told him. "I don't have time to explain it to you."

"Make the time," Dmitri demanded. "Why would you risk everything for him if you aren't even sure how you feel about him?"

"He risked everything to save Kelly," Deb told him. "He did that for me."

"So, this is guilt?" Dmitri asked. "You feel you owe him something? Deb, you don't owe him anything."

"You don't know anything about it," Deb snapped. "What we went through, how close we came to losing Harry, Michael, and Kelly. You weren't there."

"I know," Dmitri said in a huff using his foot to kick some random sand. "I'm sorry, I know how hard that must have been. But what you're doing now Deb. Giving away your own blood. Befriending a Deadly Sin. Talking about going to Hell! You must know what that sounds like."

"What are you trying to say, Dmitri?"

"Deb, what you want to do to rescue him. You know it would break the Accord."

"I don't care," Deb replied. "Hell has probably broken the Accord a thousand times with little to no consequence. It's not right. Hell is constantly cheating, doing whatever they want down here, and no one does anything about it. Marcus shouldn't have to die alone in Hell because we're too afraid to push back. I'm done being afraid. I'm done letting Hell get away with things like this. They kidnapped a Sentinel off the face of the Earth, never to be seen or heard from again. What if next time it's me, or any one of us? If a Guardian doesn't rescue Marcus from this injustice, then why are we here?"

"Deb, Heaven believes you're Falling," Dmitri told her. "Do you understand why they might feel that way?"

"What?" Deb scoffed. "That's ridiculous, of course I'm not."

There was silence between them. There was a bit of fear in his eyes and she knew Dmitri was afraid for her.

"Look, saving Kelly should have been enough for this family to help Marcus," Deb argued. "But it wasn't, and all because they made judgements about me and him being together."

"Are you together?" Dmitri asked.

"Not exactly," Deb confessed. "It's complicated."

"It's actually not complicated," Dmitri said sharply. "You know that already. Guardians are heart bound to only one other entity for all their existence."

"I told you it's—" Deb paused not knowing what to

say.

He's right, and he knows I know that. Is that why I'm dreaming of this, is my mind trying to get me to face the truth? Dreaming, I am still dreaming, right? I'm not actually on this beach having a conversation with Dmitri, while we watch my memory core together. He and I, watching he and I.

"Deb, you would know if Marcus were meant for you."

"My family should have helped me." Deb ignored the comment. "I would have helped them."

Dmitri pointed past her. "Deb, that vision you keep seeing."

Deb turned back toward the salt rocks. Dmitri came up close behind her. "It happened—on this very beach—the day after we made love for the first time."

Deb spun around and pushed Dmitri back away from her. "No!"

"Look me in the eyes, Deb," Dmitri pleaded. He grabbed her hand and placed it across his chest. "Better yet, sense if I'm telling you the truth. Your power, it identifies authenticity. Am I lying to you?"

Deb's heart raced and her breath caught in her throat. She trembled as she stood there feeling the weight of his words wash through her. Her skin prickled with goosebumps and the sand beneath her feet suddenly quite cold.

He's not lying.

"I'm dreaming." Deb's head started to spin. "This has to be a dream."

"Look down, Deb," Dmitri told her. "You're not dreaming."

Dmitri took his sweatshirt off and draped it around her. "Please, come with me. I'll take you anywhere you want to go. We can just talk. We can work through this, together."

Deb glanced down at her toes in the pebbly sand, his black boots inches away. The warmth of his body heat was still trapped in the sweatshirt as he wrapped it around her. Though the aroma of the fire lingered, the edges of the fabric held Dmitri's scent.

How would I know what he smelled like? Deb's mind reeled.

She stood there trying to wrap her mind around what he had just told her. After several moments, she made a choice to face it head on.

"You're telling me that we were in love." Deb looked up into his eyes.

"Yes."

"Prove it," Deb told him defiantly.

He placed his hands on either side of her face and she trembled. "Let me." Dmitri paused before bending down to kiss her.

Dmitri's mouth engulfed hers as she parted her lips. She fell into his chest. His arms dropped and wrapped around her. Everything about the kiss was familiar. The softness of his lips, the strain of her neck as she craned upward toward his face. The taste of him was intoxicating. The way he moved his hand up behind her head and gently held her in place made her feel comforted and safe. He kissed her with hunger, and she responded in kind as if they had kissed a thousand times. His hand grasped the side of her hip and she nearly moaned aloud.

Deb's mind found a moment of clarity to hold onto and she pulled back from Dmitri breathless. She had been completely lost in his arms.

Wake up, Deb demanded silently as her heart hammered on.

"Deb."

"No," she interrupted him. "Don't say another word, this is all in my head. I just need to wake up."

"I told you," Dmitri's forehead creased with concern. "You aren't dreaming, look down. Look at what you're wearing."

"Yeah, I know I don't normally wear a bik—" Deb stopped as she spotted her bra and underwear underneath the unzipped sweatshirt.

"Come inside," Dmitri told her. "I'm sure Kelly and Gen have clothes you can borrow."

Deb spun back around to find the memory core vision gone. She was fully awake and very cold.

"Don't come for me Dmitri." She took a few steps backward. "If you want to help me, let me do this. I need to do this!"

"I can't," Dmitri told her. "I can't let you go to Hell, Deb. I can't risk losing you."

"No, no," Deb mumbled as she picked up her pace backing away from him. "I've come too far. I will find Marcus. He will not die in Hell."

Deb closed her eyes and shook her head willing herself off that beach.

Deb's eyes were scrunched tight, the blanket wrapped around her ankles. The soft cotton of the sheets twisted as she tossed around the king size bed. She thrust upward, eyes flying open, panting, her brow covered with sweat, but somehow chilled to the bone.

She threw the thick blanket off and got out of bed. The clock on the nightstand registered nine o'clock. She had been asleep for three hours. She fumbled in the dark and made her way to the bathroom. Once inside she brushed her teeth and turned on the water in the shower. What she needed was time under Veronica's rainfall shower head and some food, then she'd deal with her mind.

As she waited for the water to warm up, she stripped off the last of her clothing. Something was between her toes and Deb bent over to run her finger between them. She came away with a large clump of sand.

"Oh no," Deb gasped. "That was no dream."

CHAPTER TWENTY-NINE

Deb sat in a cushioned chair with a view overlooking the Pacific Ocean. The water rolled in unimpeded, a glorious spectacle that normally relaxed her body and fed her soul. Now, the stunning scenery made her long for answers. Her heart ached for closure, for understanding. There would be no going back to the way things used to be, even if she were able to get Marcus out of Hell.

I told Dmitri I didn't feel anything romantic toward him, but that wasn't exactly true. Deb's scattered thoughts were adrift in the warm breeze. *All those times I was with Marcus, especially when we kissed, I felt a flood of feelings. I would push away from Marcus when those emotions assaulted me. Not because they weren't real; they were very real. I questioned those desires for Marcus because I felt there was something off about them. Dmitri presented a plausible reason why they were off.* Deb tried to make sense of the last week and all that had transpired.

She and Jade had decided to shower, dress, and quietly slip out of Veronica's house while the seamstress slept. Veronica was kind enough to find them new clothes to wear. Thankfully, the seamstress must not have had strict orders from Jade on what to buy Deb. At this moment, Deb was quite comfortable in dark wash jeans, black ankle boots, and a short sleeve gray blouse with a thin cotton jacket. Jade wore a wine-colored pencil skirt, strappy black sandals, and a black sweater. Not a stitch of green, but the outfit was polished and fit like a glove showing off her perfect shape.

They left the rain-soaked suburbs of London for the sunshine of the West Coast of the US. She was on an outdoor deck of a restaurant, in human form taking in the smell of fresh ocean water mixed with the aroma of garlic and oil.

Jade convinced Deb to come to the restaurant, something Deb was grateful for given the scenic view. Jade lingered at the front desk taking her time chatting with the host. Deb contemplated that she really had teleported to the beach house and encountered Dmitri.

A waiter delivered two glasses of white wine, placing them on the wooden table in front of her. She thanked him and spotted Jade making her way over.

"Your brothers live here?" Deb asked. "I take it they're not expecting you. Is that the reason we're at a nearby restaurant instead of their house?"

"No," Jade commented. "We're here because you needed it after whatever happened to you during your early evening kip."

"I don't know if I'm ready to deal with that," Deb mumbled.

"Bollocks, Deborah," Jade admonished. "Now, what happened?"

"Well," Deb began, "I apparently slept walked, if you know what I mean, to the house where my siblings are. Did you know doing that in your sleep was a thing? I certainly didn't."

Deb was doing her best to be discreet with what she was saying. There were too many human ears around them. Although it was later in the afternoon, the bar was still full after the lunch rush.

"I've never heard of that happening while you were asleep," Jade answered with a puzzled look. "Are you sure you weren't dreaming? You were out cold when I checked on you about an hour in."

"I was convinced it was a dream," Deb answered. "Then I found sand between my toes when I got back."

"Sand?" Jade asked. "What about clothes?"

"Hey!" Deb remarked feeling the warmth of embarrassment flush her face.

"Was that a no?" Jade asked.

Deb sighed. "I was in my bra and panties."

"With whom were you in your bra and panties?" Jade's eyes sparked.

She lives for this, Deb thought.

"Does it matter?" Deb asked knowing the answer.

"Bloody hell, Guardian," Jade huffed. "It's the only thing that matters. It was that hunk from the fire, wasn't it?"

Deb picked up her glass and took a big swig. "Yes."

"I knew it!" Jade exclaimed. "We're going to have a good old chinwag, that's why we're here."

Deb laughed. She couldn't help it. Somehow Jade made her feel like her worries were not something to actually worry about.

"Honestly, it wasn't long," Deb told her. "I got some sense of clarity and left. I came fully awake in Veronica's guest room."

"No skimping, Guardian," Jade teased. "I want every salacious detail."

"Well," Deb smiled over her wine glass. "there was a kiss."

"Blimey!" Jade exclaimed. "Look at you, being all cheeky. Don't even pretend it wasn't devastatingly good. I can tell by the look on your face you're still feeling it."

What am I doing? Deb thought as she looked at Jade and then to the ocean. *Marcus is in Hell. My family thinks I'm crazy. Heaven thinks I'm Falling. And I'm sitting here drinking wine with an immortal demon who spreads envy like an angel spreads their wings. Maybe I am losing it a little.*

A waiter appeared with several plates of food.

"What's all this?" Deb asked. "I thought we were just stopping for a glass of wine while you contacted your brothers.?"

"You need food," Jade commented. "When you go too long without it your mind wanders far away."

The artichoke appetizer looked amazing. Deb scooped some onto her side plate.

"I am hungry," Deb admitted. "Thank you for ordering appetizers."

"I'm famished," Jade told her. "We'll eat quickly and make our way over. My brothers are only a few minutes away."

"On the beach?" Deb asked.

"It's more like an estate that has a path to the beach.

Not sure which of them owns it. I don't know the financial arrangement between the two, only that they have always lived together."

"Care to share which of your siblings we're going to chat with?"

"You'll see soon enough," Jade sighed between bites. "I know things have gotten a bit pear-shaped of late, but let's take a moment to get back to more important matters, shall we?"

Deb pondered how much to share.

Jade picked up her wine glass. "Cheers."

"Cheers. I love the ocean, this is amazing."

"Who wouldn't love this view?" Jade said firmly.

"True," Deb spoke softly.

"Now," Jade began, "about Mr. Tall Dark and Handsome, spill."

"I wish I could," Deb said, after taking a sip from her wineglass. "But I can't, and I mean that literally."

"You are duty bound to keep your relationship with him secret from me?" Jade asked confused. "You just told me he kissed you."

"No," Deb answered. "I can't tell you, because I don't remember anything about us, not romantically anyway."

"Yet," Jade cocked her head to the side. "You swept off to him in the middle of dreamland and shared a kiss."

"During the conversation he insinuated we were in a relationship," Deb told her. "But, if we were, I don't remember it. So, I asked him to prove it."

"Really?" Jade said exaggeratedly. "Did he, prove it that is?"

"Well if a really incredible kiss is proof," Deb answered, "then I guess he did."

"You don't sound convinced, darling," Jade commented.

"I'm having trouble trusting what I don't remember," Deb answered.

"Totally reasonable," Jade agreed. "Simply telling you a story isn't enough, you need to remember it. He should have known you can't go on blind faith. That no one would."

Faith. A pain ached in Deb's heart. *She just described someone having a crisis of faith.*

"I'm gobsmacked," Jade told her. "You basically dared him to kiss you, and he did. You said it was amazing, yet you came back to Veronica's, why?"

"I guess I was hoping whatever he did or said would jog my memory." Deb sighed and put down her empty plate. "But it didn't. I ran from the moment, which feels juvenile but wasn't intentional. Honestly, it must have been a subconscious reaction. When I woke, I really thought it was a dream."

"Well, maybe a visit with my brothers will take your worries away for a bit."

***

After Jade paid the bill, the two of them made their way down the steps to the beach. Slipping off their shoes they waded through the soft white sand.

Jade insisted on being in human form for the visit to her brothers. She said her brothers rarely, if ever, left

317

human form. Deb stopped about ten feet from steps that led up to a gate. There was a guard posted in front of it.

"Sway the guard so we can enter," Jade told her. "This is the beach access for all the people who live on the water. The path to their house is just beyond it."

"What?!" Deb blanched. "No, we don't use our powers on humans for selfish reasons."

"Bloody hell, Guardian." Jade tilted her head toward Deb. "I think we're a bit past all this, are we not?"

Could I be falling? What if Gen and Kelly's worst fears are coming true? I really am in trouble when I don't have a legitimate reason not to do something like this.

Jade shooed Deb toward the guard.

Deb dug her heels into the sand kicking back small slumps as she went. The young man standing behind the gate greeted her with a warm smile.

"Can I help you ma'am?"

"Yes," Deb replied smiling broadly at the attendant. "My friend and I are here to visit the people who live at 1095, can you check your list to see if we have been added?"

"Your name?" The attendant asked as he looked town at a tablet.

When Deb reached his position, she placed a hand on his upper arm. "It's the first one on the list."

Without looking up he said. "Yes, here you are Mrs. Rothstein, please come in." He pulled the gate open wide and welcomed the two of them inside.

Jade smiled at him. "Lovely, thank you."

Deb rolled her eyes.

"Now," Jade told her, "that wasn't so awful, was it?"

It actually was. This better work. I don't know if I can keep arguing I know what I'm doing and I'm not actually falling if I keep bending rules to suit my own purposes.

"Come along, Deborah," Jade said, as she made her way past the first two lawns. Their house is the cheery yellow one up there with the giant outdoor patio."

Deb followed Jade up the path mesmerized by the enormous houses along this stretch of beach. Each one was a little different, but all had giant windows taking advantage of the view with outdoor living spaces that included fireplaces, kitchens, and pools.

When they reached the top of path, the space looked more like a hotel entrance than one found in any normal house. A fire was going in the outdoor fireplace, but no one was there to enjoy it. The seven-seat outdoor bar was empty. A large TV above the bar was turned to a music station. Jade walked to the door and knocked loudly, but then turned the knob and proceeded inside.

Expansive views of the ocean flooded nearly every vantage point in the house. Large pieces of beachy artwork hung on the painted white walls. Floor-to-ceiling windows were encased in black steel. Hardwood floors ran throughout the space with a vaulted ceiling crowning the room.

"Gentlemen!" Jade announced. "Your favorite sister is here."

"Greenie!" a male voice exalted from another room.

Jade glanced over at her. Deb did her best not to snicker at what she knew Jade would consider an insulting reference to her name. A moment later a tall man stood in front of them. He wore linen pants and a white unbuttoned cotton shirt that billowed when he walked. His flip flops slapped against the floor as he took a few steps closer then stopped. Gold necklaces were draped across his neck and hung loosely around his wrists. He wore large jewel-encrusted rings on several fingers of each hand. He held a cocktail glass in one hand and tilted his head as he took in the sight of them.

"Why are you not wearing green?!" he asked in clear astonishment. "What the devil happened to you, sister?"

Jade walked to her brother and they kissed each other's cheeks in a feint warm greeting.

"Why are you with a Guardian?" He whispered as if Deb were unable to hear him. "Is the world ending?"

"Hello, Decadence." Jade took the glass from his hand and took a sip. "Please, get Deborah one while you are pouring a new one for yourself, darling."

"Of course," Decadence answered and proceeded outside toward the bar setup. As he passed a large chair on his left, he yelled to a male wearing his headphones. "Languor, our sister is here for a visit, don't be anti-social."

The male glanced over but made no attempt to get up or say anything. Instead, he moved his head in Jade's direction and slowly raised his hand in an awkward wave. The tips of his fingers were tinged with an orange powder from the open bags of chips in his lap.

"There's no need for that Languor," Jade replied. "We won't be here long enough to make it worth your while to stand up."

Jade followed Decadence outside and sat down on one of the black leather stools with views of the landscape below.

"I hate to intrude like this, my darling," Jade said softly. "I'm afraid I need a favor."

Decadence scooted behind the bar and went to work making drinks. There was a generous pour of alcohol, shaking, and the sounds of ice cubes clinking against glass. Deb made her way into the living space and noticed Languor was surrounded with everything one would need if they were never to move from their current position. He was surrounded with food, bottles of energy drinks, several remotes to what Deb assumed were all the devices connected to the television. A large bong sat on the table in front of Languor and there was the hint of skunk as she passed him.

"Go," Languor whispered over his shoulder at Deb. "Leave us."

"What on earth could you need from us?" Decadence asked.

"Deborah, come and sit down," Jade commanded. "I want to formerly introduce you to Decadence."

Decadence. Deb didn't need the name to identify which of the two siblings these were. *Gluttony and Sloth here don't seem the type to visit Hell under any circumstance.*

"Jade, it is so wonderful to see you," Decadence told her. "I wish you had told me you were coming. I would have arranged a fabulous party. You know how much I like parties!"

"It was truly last minute, brother," Jade answered.

Deb made her way to the bar but didn't sit down.

"I'm glad you came," Decadence told her. "Languor hasn't gotten off that chair all day."

"Does he normally get up off the chair?" Deb asked.

Decadence ignored the swipe. "We had the most delicious meal last night. I hired a chef to come by and cook a meal for just the two of us. It was amazing."

"Yummy," Jade said in an exaggerated tone. "Do go on."

Deb grew tired of the charade. "I just met Desire yesterday." She stood off to the side of the bar where she had a view of all their faces.

Decadence stopped what he was doing and stared at her. "I see. Well, how is she?"

"Fine," Jade began.

"Sure," Deb interrupted. "She seemed totally at ease with lighting her cottage on fire with a gas can from her shed."

Languor dropped a remote onto the floor and made something of a grunt. Everyone grew still.

Jade put her glass down and gave Deb a cold look. "Deborah, please. Can't you see I am trying to catch up with Dec here."

"I can see it just fine," Deb deadpanned.

Jade huffed and took another sip of her drink before getting to the point of the visit. "Do you happen to know what W is up to?"

"What?" Decadence's nose scrunched as if he smelled something bad.

"You haven't heard anything, at all?"

"Go," Languor told them. "Leave us."

"What have you brought to our doorstep, sister?" Decadence asked in obvious fear. "Why are you really here?"

Jade stood up. "I need to know if you'd be willing to take Deborah here to Hell. If not, I need to know the last time you saw W."

"You want me to willingly go into Hell?" Decadence laughed nervously. "I would prefer death, dear sister. You know that. You've seen it yourself."

"What about W," Jade continued without missing a beat. "Have you heard anything?"

Decadence came around the bar, took Jade by the elbow, and pulled her toward the door. "You need to go. I can't believe you just drug in this mess. After everything we did for you after the—"

Jade snapped her arm away from Decadence causing her brother to stop in mid-sentence. "We have always known it could come to this."

"Go." Languor seemed to moan the statement. "Leave us."

Deb just looked at the demon seemingly stuck in some sort of slow loop from his encampment on the sofa.

"If you want to help her get to Hell so bad, then why don't you just ask your husb—"

"Decadence!" Jade shrilled. "Don't you dare."

"Fine," Decadence responded. "We will not be going to Hell. We like it here just fine, thank you very much. You have no idea how powerful we are at this point. The two of us, I mean seriously, have you seen how fat and over the top the humans have become? No, we won't be risking it all getting between you and W."

Jade lifted her chin defiantly. "You should be careful then; we've seen vampires. Seems our brother has new ambitions. He might be looking for me, but I might not

323

be the only one this time."

"Go," Languor stated once more. "Lea—"

"We get it!" Deb snapped. "You want us to leave, you're not helping, understood. I'm out of here, this was useless, I don't know why you thought they would be of any help."

Deb stormed through the house toward the front door. Before pulling it open, she changed out of human view. Jade was quickly following Deb, her heels clacking loudly.

"Deborah!" Jade yelled. "Bloody hell, Guardian."

Deb turned back slowly. "What? Where should we head off to now? I hear there's a sleeper cell of nuns just down the road that might help us get to Hell."

"That's not funny, Deborah," Jade remarked. "You get deep wrinkles on your forehead when you're angry, it's not attractive. Now, I have other siblings, I just hoped these two would be more helpful."

"I see no evidence for why you would have thought that." Deb pointed back toward the house.

Before Deb could respond Decadence appeared beside them out of human form. "Look, I'm sorry Jade. I want to help you, but Languor and I avoid W like the plague. Why do you think we're always in human form?"

Jade huffed. "I understand, but have you heard anything? Anything at all?"

"A few days ago," Decadence began, "Avarice came by, that in and of itself is not unusual. We see him from time to time, especially if he knows we're throwing one of our large parties."

"And." Deb snapped having about run out of

patience.

"He got drunk," Decadence answered. "Avarice told us that he heard General Kelce was looking for Dee."

"That's not really a newsflash brother," Jade quipped. "General Kelce has been pursuing our sister for decades."

"That wasn't the news," Decadence replied. "Avarice said General Kelce was restored. He said there wasn't a mark on him. The vampire was bragging about how he made a deal in exchange for Desire."

"Well," Jade huffed. "That's not good news for Desire."

A deal? Deb thought. *Who the heck do you make a deal with to give you power over a Deadly Sin?*

"We need to go," Jade told her brother before hugging him. "Please be careful, stay alert. I don't know what's going on, but I have a feeling W is behind it and he's not afraid to put his siblings in the crossfire."

Decadence simply nodded then made his way back inside the house where they could hear him yelling playfully at Languor to get off the couch and have drinks with him.

"Where to now?" Deb asked. "Greed's house?"

"No," Jade stated. "I'm taking us to my second strongest sibling, Glory."

"Are you going to share who your husband is?" Deb asked.

"What?" Jade tried to laugh off the comment.

"I get it," Deb told her. "It's only me that has to spill all the salacious details. You get to keep secrets."

"Bloody hell, Guardian," Jade huffed. "I'll tell you about him over our next glass of wine, but fair warning, it might be a while. If Glory is willing to send you, she might give you no warning and just shove you off to Hell right on the spot. I hope you're ready."

CHAPTER THIRTY

Kelly walked past Xavier and Greg playing a video game in the living room. They were yelling at the TV as brightly colored avatars ran up and down a soccer field. Xavier stood more than he sat, but from a passing glance Kelly could see the two of them were beating whichever imaginary opponent they were facing.

"Is he still outside?" Kelly asked Dan who stood behind the sofa stealing casual glances to the beach in between important plays of the game.

"Yeah," Dan answered. "He's worn a path in the sand with all the pacing."

"He must have heard me talking about him," Kelly responded as she neared the glass. Dmitri turned and looked up at the house. "He appears to be making his way back in here and he doesn't look happy."

"I could have guessed that," Dan commented. "I don't know anyone who paces when they're happy."

"I don't know why he got so mad over us talking through things," Kelly responded.

"Something tells me that's not what he's upset

about," Dan added.

Michael arrived back at the house with Tom. The two of them had left to gather a stockpile of Holy Oil.

"That was harder than we thought," Tom commented.

"No one wanted to share their stash of Holy Oil with you?" Kelly asked.

"The Guardians we went to wanted to know what was going on," Michael added. "We couldn't just ask for it and leave."

"I don't blame them," Kelly answered. "I would want to know too."

"Most of them had heard rumors," Michael told her. "The O'Mara sisters facing off against restored vampires, was it true? Were you okay? What does this mean, etc."

"Who knew we were so famous." Kelly smirked.

"Frankie back yet?" Tom asked.

"No," Dan replied. "He did get Gardenia to Leo and Lucas. They've agreed to watch over her and keep her safe while we deal with this, but I'm sure he's having to answer his own questions. He should be back soon."

"Hey," Lacey hollered from the kitchen. "I might have found something."

The sound on the TV paused and the back door opened as Dmitri made his way back inside.

"We need to talk," Dmitri announced.

Gen came down from the second floor looking between them all. "What's going on?"

"I was about to tell them something I found in this old literature," Lacey answered. "Then he barged in."

Lacey nodded over at Dmitri who had command of

the room. Before he could speak Frankie arrived back at the house with Gerry.

"Everything okay?" Gerry asked obviously feeling the tension in the room.

"Something's wrong," Dmitri told them.

"I'm afraid you'll have to be a bit more specific," Kelly quipped.

"I mean it," Dmitri snapped. "Do any of you know why Deb doesn't remember me?" Dmitri asked. "Save the jokes for later Kell."

Kelly cocked her head. "I don't remember you ever calling me that."

"See." Dmitri raised his arm and pointed at Kelly. "That's what I mean. You don't remember that, why?"

"Dmitri, what's going on?" Michael asked calmly. "You haven't been here for forty Earth years. You would have to know how long it's been from Gabriel and Jared."

"Gen didn't forget referring to Gabriel as Gabe, did she?" Dmitri argued.

"Are you seriously trying to equate you and I to Gen and Gabe," Kelly commented.

"No." Dmitri shook his head "I'm trying to equate Deb and I to the two of them. Deb doesn't remember me. None of you seem to remember me."

"We remember you, I mean," Kelly stopped mid-sentence.

"Why don't you tell us Dmitri?" Gen suggested.

"We were in love," Dmitri stated. "It wasn't that new either. I used to stay at Deb and Kelly's house all the time. I can't tell you how many meals we shared together, too many to count. Today," Dmitri paused as he looked at

Kelly. "Today, you told me you couldn't remember eating with me. Was that true or were you being sarcastic?"

Kelly opened her mouth to speak but stopped. Her mind drifted back some forty something years to when she and Deb lived together. They had a two-bedroom bungalow in California. In a sleepy little college town where most of the neighbors thought she and Deb were out-of-state students. The widower across the street used to say he was jealous because she and Deb kept 'young people's hours' coming and going at all hours of the day and night.

"Well?" Dmitri demanded of Kelly. "Do you remember?"

"I remember the house." Kelly pushed away a faint headache as she tried to grab hold of more memories. "I remember the mountain trails nearby me and Jared used to hike. The local college right by our house gave us a convenient cover. I remember Frankie coming by to grill for us on Friday nights."

"Nothing about me?" Dmitri asked.

"I remember you at the house," Frankie interrupted. You were close with both Jared and Gabriel. You'd come by most weekends, take Deb to the lake if I remember correctly."

"I don't remember that," Kelly told them. "Like, at all."

"Neither does Deb," Dmitri told them. "Someone's messed with memories about me and Deb."

"What?" Gen asked. "How? Who?"

"I think I know who," Dmitri said calmly. "Michael, can you go get Harry?"

"Why?" Michael asked. "He can't pull memories free, but Greg can."

"I need to speak with Antonio, now!"

"Antonio?" Kelly asked. "Why do you want to speak with him? Now is not the best time given what just happened to Jacob."

"What happened to Jacob?" Dmitri asked.

"Antonio didn't tell you?" Michael asked but didn't wait for the answer. "The Arch Angel was murdered along with Gerry by the demon Peter we've been hunting. It's why Gerry is here under our protection."

Dmitri inhaled deeply as he ran his hands through his short hair. The pause in the conversation was like a bubble about to burst.

"Before I was pulled off Earth." Dmitri stared at Kelly. "I came to the house you shared with Deb. I was carrying your unconscious bruised and battered body. I placed you on your bed. I told Deb you'd be fine after a good night's sleep. Deb followed me into the bedroom and pulled your comforter over you. I remember asking Deb why you had a little girl's comforter set. It had pink strawberries all over it. It was an odd thing to think of as I lay your near broken body down to heal."

Kelly's heart began to race, her mind was circling trying to search for a memory like that but there was nothing there.

What happened that I was unconscious? Kelly's mind reeled. *I don't remember encountering anything alongside Dmitri that would cause such harm.*

"Strawberry shortcake." Kelly remembered. "How could you know that?"

"I was there," Dmitri told her. "Deb wouldn't let me leave without telling her what happened. I told myself I should stay quiet, I was ordered to keep it confidential, told it was 'need to know.' But one look at Deb's horrified stare and worried eyes and I couldn't leave without telling her what happened. I told her everything."

"Dimitri," Gen said. "You aren't making sense."

"I left here to take a walk on the beach thirty minutes ago," Dmitri told them. "I ran into Deb."

"You what?" Frankie scowled as he made his way over to the window to look outside as if Deb would still be there.

"She told me she didn't remember me," Dmitri stated. "That she had no memory of us together as a couple. That she had no romantic feelings for me."

"Dmitri." Tom walked over and put his hand on the Collector's shoulder. "Maybe you should sit down, you don't look well."

"You don't understand," Dmitri told him. "Deb and I were in love. I built this house for her. This is my beach house. A gift, something I hoped would be better than a ring."

"We know," Kelly told him. "Gen told us. We had no idea. We thought this was Harry's cottage. Although, he never really specified whose house it was."

"That's because you don't remember, just like Deb," Dmitri scoffed. "I want to know why all of you have forgotten me and Deb. I want Antonio here, now!"

***

Deb and Jade stood at the end of a treelined private roadway. The street was wide, with only six large houses on it. At the far end stood the tallest home. A modern house made of glass.

"It's the ugly monstrosity at the end," Jade commented.

"I take it you don't like modern homes," Deb asked dryly.

"I bloody well don't!" Jade snapped. "This one does have a gorgeous back deck with stunning views of the mountains and waterways below it."

"All your siblings seem to live in beautiful houses with envious views," Deb told her. "I'm afraid to ask where Greed lives."

Jade laughed. "Like I told you already, Avarice lives in Europe. If we're lucky, Glory will be our last stop."

"I'm not sure luck will have anything to do with it," Deb noted.

"Are you nervous, Guardian?" Jade asked. "I mean in the next few minutes you could be bloody Hellbound."

Deb shook off the desire to shiver in response. *Hellbound.* The word rattled around in her brain.

"We don't have to go," Jade told her. "You can turn around right now and head back to the safety of your family."

Safety. There is nothing safe about my situation. Dmitri accused me of Falling, my family is chasing after yet another demon who attacked us, and Marcus is trapped in Hell. There is no going back. If Deb wanted safety, she would have to create it for herself.

"Let's go," Deb told her as she began to walk

toward Glory's house.

"Wait," Jade said from behind her. "I never use the front door. I always enter from the back deck. It's where Glory normally is anyway, follow me."

The two of them made their way to the driveway and cut through the yard along the side of the house. As they passed the midway point, Deb stopped and looked around.

Deb's heart began to race, and she sensed something was coming. Jade had kept walking and was too far away to grab hold of. Deb didn't want to yell in case something was already there with them. She closed her eyes and let her shield and cloak rush out in front of her and stretched it to wrap around Jade.

Deb took a tentative step forward then froze. Someone was there, to her right. She turned her head slowly. In the large window peering down at her was General Kelce. The restored vampire's reflection a nightmarish silhouette in the afternoon sun. The sight of him nearly made her yelp, until she realized he seemed to be looking through her and not at her. He turned his head away from the glass and then walked away.

He didn't see me. Deb sighed in discernable relief. *That was close, too close.*

Jade stared back at her from the deck. She signaled with a nod of her head for Deb to join her.

Good, Deb thought reassured. *Jade seems to know we aren't alone and since I have us cloaked it means we cannot speak to one another aloud.*

Deb made her way as swiftly and quietly as possible to Jade's position. She followed closely behind as Jade made her way around the backside of the house. The modern home was equipped with an accordion style wall of windows that was partially open. As Deb and Jade stepped past the last of the wooden frame, the inside of the house came into full view. The two of them were the furthest thing from alone.

Inside General Kelce stood next to Desire who was turned away from him and staring out the glass toward the mountain view. Her puffy cheeks and bloodshot eyes a stark contrast to when Deb first met her last night.

Deb continued to follow Jade who walked past Desire to see the rest of the living room. There was a woman on her knees, her hands bound behind her with a piece of the Chain of Chaos. A tall male figured with blonde hair and a long trench coat loomed over her. It was Peter. Deb threw her hand up over her mouth to keep a gasp from escaping.

Deb had surmised Peter was working with Wrath, but now seeing him again made her skin crawl. Peter grabbed the woman in front of him by her ponytail and pulled it so the woman was forced to look up at his face. Peter sneered down at her and placed his other hand on her forehead and began chanting in a language Deb did not understand.

Deb forced herself to look away. Michael's lessons rang in her head. *Make sure you are aware of your surroundings at all times. Don't get focused on one aspect of an event, you may miss vital clues you'll need later, and you may miss other forces that could do you harm.*

Deb breathed in and out slowly driving down the escalating rhythm of her heart.

Deb looked down and to her left. A foot was sticking out from behind some furniture. She touched Jade softly motioning for her to follow what Deb's eyes were seeing. Jade walked further to her left standing in the center of the open doors. Yet, no one appeared to see the two of them on the back deck.

My cloak is holding. Deb sighed softly. *I'm not sure for how long though, there is a lot of demonic force here.*

The woman on her knees started panting, tears rolled down her face. As Peter's words became more rushed and his tone grew loud the woman moaned in response.

Is this some sort of ritual? Deb wished she could ask Jade who had walked to the other side of the deck.

Jade crouched down and peered through the glass. Her small gasp muffled by her hand rushing up to cover her own mouth. Deb walked up beside her and understood the cause of her reaction. The male on the floor was unconscious in a pool of his own blood.

Who's that? Deb wondered. *Another sibling?* Before Deb could mouth any words to Jade a scream rang out from inside. Both she and Jade rushed back to see the woman on the floor now shaking, blood pouring from her eyes while some sort of gray black smoke filled the air in front of Peter.

Is he killing her? Deb's mind raced. *He's definitely hurting her, but assuming she's Pride, is Peter capable of murdering a Deadly Sin?*

Deb reached for Jade, but then stopped. Jade was shaking. Her eyes were wide in terror as she stared inside the house at the scene unfolding in front of them.

We need to get out of here, Deb thought. *It's obvious*

we've both seen enough. We need to leave before we're inadvertently discovered.

Before Deb had a chance to move, Luca and Sky arrived inside with Languor and Decadence bound and gagged.

"Hey, we brought two more to the party!" Luca yelled as he kicked Decadence behind the knee sending him spiraling to the floor next to who Deb assumed was Glory.

The screams continued. Sky pushed Sloth and he fell to the floor next to the unconscious male figure's feet.

Peter stopped and let go of Glory's ponytail. She slumped to the floor falling partially on top of Decadence.

"It's done," Peter answered. "Did you find them?"

"We're working on it," Luca retorted.

"That's not good enough!" Peter screamed.

"We tracked Jade back to London," Sky added. "Her and the Guardian were staying with a human after the fire."

Oh no, Deb thought in horror, *Veronica, they tracked us to her house.*

Peter grabbed Decadence who started wailing a muffled cry of resistance. Peter grabbed him by the head and began chanting once more.

Decadence thrashed about until the cotton gag came loose enough for his yelling to be heard. "You'll never get away with this, brother!"

The yelling and screaming got louder. Desire stepped closer to the glass where Jade now stood in front of.

"Wrath!" General Kelce bellowed. "Is this really necessary? I would prefer you get your kicks in after we

337

leave."

Wrath. Deb froze.

Desire breathed hot air onto the glass causing it to fog.

Peter is Wrath. Deb's mind tried to make sense of it, but she was mesmerized by Desire who was now writing something in the vapored glass.

RUN!

CHAPTER THIRTY-ONE

Deb and Jade arrived in Veronica's kitchen. The house was eerily quiet, the only sounds were of running water and the two of them breathing heavily. They had run back through Glory's yard, down the private street, and onto a nearby walking trail for a quick chat about where to go next. They were in perfect agreement about coming to Veronica's to check on her, but Deb was unprepared for what they might find.

I hope she's okay. Deb's eyes scanned the room, there were a few things out of place.

The water from the faucet was running, the tea kettle was in the sink and the gas stove was still lit. On the counter was a box of chamomile tea and an empty mug. Veronica was interrupted as she prepared tea. Deb reached over the sink and shut the water off. As she turned back to speak with Jade, something on the floor drew her attention. It was a stain between the kitchen and dining room. Deb nodded toward it and walked around the giant marble island and Jade followed. A large pool of reddish-brown liquid soaked through the edge of the area rug beneath the dining table. The fluid had trailed off and spilled around the corner into the foyer.

Blood.

She quickened her steps and rounded the corner into the front entryway nearly slipping on the blood.

"Where is she?" Jade whispered.

Deb turned left toward the steps to the second floor and stopped short. Veronica's limp body was lying face down across the bottom three steps. Deb spun back quickly and tried to stop Jade from looking.

"Jade, stop." Deb grabbed her hands and tried to spin her back around.

"No, Deborah." Jade gasped. "Let me go, I need to see her!"

Jade pushed passed Deb and moaned as she took in the sight of Veronica. The demon ran to the stairs, grabbed Veronica's lifeless body, and cradled her gently as she wept.

"Those bastards had no bloody right, Deborah." Jade's voice croaked in pain as she spoke. "She didn't have anything to do with this! She would have been completely unaware of what we were doing or where we had gone."

"Jade," Deb said, looking at her rocking her friend back and forth. "We need to leave. I'm sorry but you know we can't stay here."

"I bloody well know that Deborah!" Jade spewed. "I can't just leave her here like this."

"When we leave, we can notify the police with an anonymous call," Deb implored. "Please, we need to go. Now."

"Where the bloody hell are we to go now?!" Jade

snapped. "I have nowhere left to go! Veronica was the closest thing to family I had. They killed her, she's dead because of me."

"No," Deb said firmly. "She's dead because of Wrath. This is not your fault, it's his. He's planning something and we need to figure out what it is."

"I need to bury Veronica," Jade told her. "She doesn't deserve to be forgotten."

"We will do all that, but right now we need to go," Deb announced.

"No," Jade told her. "You go Deborah, go back to your family. I'll deal with mine."

Deb walked to the stairs and crouched down so Jade could see her eyes. "We went to your family. I trusted you with that, I need you to trust me now."

"I do," Jade said. "But you cannot defeat Wrath."

"Not alone I can't," Deb countered.

"Even with your family, it's not enough," Jade said through fresh tears.

"Let me worry about that," Deb told her as she gently took Veronica from Jade's arms and carried her to the sofa in the living room.

Jade grabbed a blanket and draped it over Veronica's body. "Goodbye my friend," she whispered. "You may not have gotten justice in this world, but vengeance is mine."

Deb turned to walk out of the room and spotted her and Jade's belongings piled up neatly against the wall. Somehow Veronica had time to launder their clothes in the short time they were gone. Jade and Deb picked up the bags on their way out.

"Where are we going?" Jade asked.

"East Coast of the United States, on the beach," Deb replied.

"I look gutted I'm sure," Jade huffed and swiped at her tear-stained cheeks.

"This cottage will not be up to your penthouse standards," Deb told her, "but it has a bathroom with a working shower if you need it."

Jade paused before speaking. "Why are you doing this?" The demon's voice cracked and with it escaped a vulnerability that Deb hadn't seen before.

Deb sighed and took Jade's hands. "Because Veronica isn't your only friend."

"Are we friends now, Guardian?" Jade asked, her eyes blinking rapidly. Before Deb could answer Jade pulled her hands back. "You might want to keep that to yourself, Deborah. Your family is already worried about you."

"My family will accept it," Deb told her, praying that statement was true.

"Will they?" Jade grasped Deb's arm with her hand. "No matter what comes, I want to thank you, Deborah."

"Thank me when it's over," Deb answered. "We'll have that glass of wine where we discuss the fact you have a husband. Don't think I forgot about that little tidbit."

"You're a cheeky one, Guardian." Jade smiled broadly.

"Wait until you meet my sister, Kelly," Deb said, as she placed her hand over Jade's. "Let's get out of here, and whatever happens, try and be patient."

***

Gen's head was pounding. The swell of information coupled with fatigue and stress about Deb weighed on her. The smell of coffee filled the air, another round of caffeine for their weary minds. Gen turned in her seat at the kitchen table and opened the window next to her. The air was crisp, early autumn rode in on the ocean breeze. Gen got chills and zipped her sweatshirt near to the top, but she left the window open. The fresh air calmed the sickening sensation rolling through her stomach.

Things are coming to a boil, Gen thought. *I always feel like this right before my world erupts in some way. The eye of any storm is just an illusion.*

Michael had brought Harry back to the cottage. Dmitri was insisting on speaking with Antonio and only Harry could make that happen. It took several minutes to bring the sharp-witted Angel up to speed, but Harry had questions of his own now.

"You think Antonio had something to do with Deb's memory loss?" Harry asked Dmitri.

"That's ridiculous," Kelly told them. "This is Antonio we're talking about. He wouldn't do something like that."

"There are so few who knew anything about what happened to us." Dmitri shook his head. "He either knows or he's responsible."

"That's quite the accusation," Harry sighed.

"We need more information Dmitri," Michael interjected. "You're not making a whole lot of sense."

"That's because you don't know what happened," Dmitri snapped. "You don't know what we did to land in

The Pit, but he does."

"Antonio knew you were in The Pit!" Kelly exclaimed. "He knew where the three of you were this entire time!"

"Harry," Gen began then stopped when Harry raised his hands in the air to stem the onslaught.

"I think there must be a reasonable explanation," Harry began. "Let's give Antonio the benefit of the doubt and ask him to explain, alright?"

"I can't believe we are even suggesting this!" Kelly bellowed. "He has been such a good friend to me over the years. We have fought alongside one another in battle. He would not betray me or this family."

No one spoke, and Gen's chest tightened. *What if Dmitri's right? What if Heaven has been keeping this from me, from all of us?*

Harry closed his eyes for a moment and then opened them. "It's done, he should be here momentarily."

The light outside grew stronger and brightness pierced the dusk skyline. With a flapping sound of wings, Antonio arrived on the deck. Dmitri stomped toward the back door, but Michael stepped in front of him.

"There'll be no private conversations," Michael told him. "Antonio comes inside and tells us all what happened."

Dmitri seemed to ponder the demand, but then nodded and waited for Antonio to fold his wings and enter the cottage.

Antonio wore gray cargo pants and a white T-shirt. His chiseled jaw clenched slightly when he entered the house and encountered their demanding stares.

"What is it?" Antonio asked the crowd.

"What happened to Deb's memories?" Dmitri asked through gritted teeth.

"You found her?" Antonio asked in return as he scanned the room. "Where is she?"

"You didn't answer," Michael stated. "Dmitri claims he and Deb were romantic."

"It's not a claim," Dmitri snapped.

Michael continued. He stared at Antonio watching his every move. "Deb has no memory of that. Do you know why that would be?"

Antonio stiffened. "I just buried my brother and you call me down here with these ridiculous inquiries. Do you not have enough to do with finding your sister and keeping her from Falling?"

"Maybe Gerry and I should leave." Lacey's eyes turned downward, clearly uncomfortable with this conversation. "This seems like a family matter."

"No, don't," Kelly told her. "There's nowhere safer than with us."

"Just answer the question." Dmitri seemed to growl the words at Antonio.

"I'll answer all the questions when you find Deborah."

"No!" Dmitri yelled. "You tell me what you did! Tell me what she did!"

"You think Deb did something to her own memories?" Gen was confused.

"Not Deb," Dmitri answered without turning to face Gen. "The Magistrate, it was either Antonio or the Magistrate."

"You're on thin ice Dmitri," Antonio warned. "Be careful where you step."

"Let's take it down a notch," Kelly suggested. "Antonio, why don't you just tell him you had nothing to do with this crazy notion of messing with Deb's memories, as if you could do that." Kelly stopped short and tilted her head slightly. "Wait, can you do that?"

"What a fine idea!" Dmitri mocked. "Antonio, just tell me what happened!"

Gen shivered at the anger in Dmitri's tone. Tension and silence encircled the room.

Why won't he answer? Gen thought in agony. *Just tell us, Antonio.*

Gen sensed Deb before the dull haze rippled around her.

Kelly! Gen said to her sister telepathically. *Deb's not alone!*

When the glow faded, Deb stood before them next to Jade. The two of them were covered in what looked like dried blood.

"What happened, Deb?" Kelly asked making her way across the room toward her sister who was now standing next to Antonio.

"Whose blood is that?" Frankie asked. "Are you alright?"

"I'm okay," Deb answered. "It's human blood, a woman, a friend of Jade's was killed by vampires."

"Are you sure?" Tom asked.

"Why is she here?" Kelly interrupted. "It's not smart to bring a demon to a safe house. Sort of defeats the purpose."

"I assume this one is Kelly," Jade commented.

"Yes, that's Kelly," Deb answered. "And yes, I am sure vampires killed a human. That's not why we're here though."

"Okay, I'll bite," Kelly told her. "Why are you here?"

"We need to protect Jade," Deb answered.

"Are you kidding me?" Kelly squealed. "We don't have time and why should we help a demon?"

"Because," Deb responded dryly, "Peter is after her. He's already gotten to her other siblings."

"This has gone far enough," Antonio exclaimed. "Deb, you're helping wretched demons now!"

"Deb," Dmitri ignored Antonio and stepped toward her. "I'm sorry but Antonio's right. This is too much, and you can't even see it. This pains me so much, but I can help you, please just come with me."

Dmitri shook his head and stalked off across the room toward her sister.

Michael stepped in front of him for the second time today. This time, Dmitri stepped aside as if to go around him. Her brother would have none of it. Michael punched Dmitri hard in the chest sending him crashing against the far wall to the right of Gen.

"You won't be taking her anywhere, Dmitri," Michael said emphatically.

Dmitri was stunned but recovered quickly. As he stood up to face off against Michael, Frankie stepped forward and stood to Michael's left. Kelly slid in on Michael's right. Xavier and Greg who were silently taking in all the activity lined up behind Frankie and Kelly.

They were sending a message: Michael wasn't alone, the family was united in protecting one of their own.

"I think you should stand down, Dmitri," Tom commented.

"You are severely outnumbered here," Dan added.

"Well, seems you were correct, Deborah," Jade whispered. "They certainly appear to have your back."

"There's no need for this," Harry told them. "We all want what's best for Deborah, but I think we owe it to her to hear her out, don't you?"

"Thanks, Harry," Deb said.

"Agreed," Michael added. "Tell us what happened Deb."

"I just witnessed Peter take powers from several of the Deadly Sins," Deb answered.

"Peter's strong enough to take down the Deadly Sins?" Michael asked. "How?"

"Because he is a Deadly Sin," Deb answered. "Peter is Wrath."

There it is, Gen thought in horror. *The explosion that will rocket us into war.*

CHAPTER THIRTY-TWO

Deb's words were a metaphysical blow on those in the room. Some of them hadn't said a word since she arrived. She looked across the crowded room, it was filled with exhausted faces.

Why are Lacey and Gerry here? Deb asked her sisters telepathically.

Seconds passed with no response. For a moment Deb doubted if they'd heard her. *Did I lose my ability to talk with them?*

Gerry's a Historian, Kelly responded. *We asked Lacey to help us.*

Talk to us, Deb, Gen insisted. *Please tell us what's going on? Why did you bring her here? How do you know Peter is Wrath, did she tell you that?*

You have to trust me, Deb told them. *I know Peter is Wrath and Jade is in danger, we must protect her.*

"Deb," Harry's words pulled her attention away from Gen and Kelly. "Start from the beginning. How do you know Peter is Wrath?"

"We just saw the bloody bastard torturing Decadence," Jade said with irritation.

"Why would he do that?" Tom asked the demon.

"I can't be sure," Jade huffed. "He was enjoying every torturous moment as he drained them."

"Can he do that?" Frankie asked Jade. "I mean, is he capable of stealing powers, is that one of his abilities?"

"No," Jade said plainly. "But I shouldn't be the only one answering questions."

"You're not exactly in a position to preach about fairness," Kelly mocked.

"What happened to Deborah's memories?" Jade asked. "We heard you arguing about it while we were inbound. It seems this Arch Angel still hasn't answered the question."

Antonio looked at Jade. "How dare you, demon? You are the scourge of the Earth, the bringer of self-loathing, the spreader of lies, envy, and mistrust."

"Well, well." Jade sneered back at Antonio. "If I know anything, it's what guilt and shame sound like."

"Enough!" Dmitri demanded. "Tell them."

"No," Antonio responded. "Absolutely not!"

"They won't let me help Deb," Dmitri told him. "They don't trust me; she doesn't trust me."

"That's not true." Deb stepped between Xavier and Michael to face Dmitri.

"Be careful, Deb," Frankie whispered.

"I do trust you Dmitri," Deb told him. "I have no memory of us romantically, but I can feel something when I'm around you, something warm, something loving. I trust my instincts, and I don't believe you would hurt me."

"I would never," Dmitri admitted.

"I know," Deb answered now within feet of the

Collector. "I can't go with you. I'm going to finish what I started."

"What does that mean?" Frankie asked.

"I'm going to find a way to Hell," Deb told them. "I'm going to free Marcus."

The heaviness in Deb's chest matched the tension that now filled the room.

I owed them the truth, Deb thought. *Now, we'll see what they do with it.*

"That is madness." Antonio's voice trailed off making the last word sound like a hiss.

"Tell them what happened that night," Dmitri insisted. "If you don't, I will."

"You know how this works, Dmitri," Antonio answered. "If you tell them you add more time to all the sentences. If I tell them I may be sentencing myself to The Pit."

"Are you sure, Dmitri?" Gen interrupted. "Gabe offered to tell me, I said no. I didn't want him or any of you to get more time added on."

Dmitri stared over at Antonio. "I told Deb everything that night. I only saw two beings before I was sent away, you and the Magistrate. Now I get summoned back here to find out Deb doesn't remember me. She doesn't feel anything for me. You tell me how that happened, Antonio!"

Antonio sighed. He ran both hands over his face. "Fine, the spoken word will fall on the wind and with it our fate."

"No." Tom stepped out of the kitchen entryway and into the crowded living space. "If it is a violation to speak of such things, you will not tell."

"There's no other way, Tom." Dmitri looked confused. "You need to know what happened forty years ago. Deb needs to know why she cannot go to Hell."

"There is another way," Tom answered. "We can see it for ourselves."

It took a moment for Deb to understand what Tom was proposing. Greg and Frankie then stepped forward.

They were going to pull out Dmitri's memories.

The room became a flutter of movement.

Jade looked at Deb in confusion. "What the bloody hell is going on?"

"Greg is going to pull memories forward," Deb told her. "Frankie can augment his powers and project the image for all of us to see."

"That's tragic," Jade answered. "I hope you're ready for that. Secrets are generally secret for a reason."

The couch was turned away from the TV and Dmitri and Antonio sat down next to one another. Everyone else moved to the other side of the room. Greg sat in a chair between them, but at an angle where he wouldn't interfere with the image Frankie would project.

The kitchen table was pulled into the living area. Most of them, including Lacey and Gerry, joined them on or around the table. Xavier took turns between rocking and pacing, the method he used to deal with the constant energy coursing through his body.

The lights above the sofa were shut off. Greg closed his eyes and his breathing slowed as if he were sleeping in a sitting position. He was trancelike.

"He's ready." Frankie looked at Dmitri and

Antonio. "When Greg goes in, don't fight him. It's useless and painful if you try."

Antonio nodded. "How does this work?"

"Think back to that day," Frankie told them. "Bring the memories forward, anything fuzzy or difficult, Greg will focus on and clarify."

"How does this work with two people's memories?" Antonio asked. "We don't have the same memories."

"Greg will align them," Frankie told them. "He can see the bigger picture of things and where they overlap. He'll project as one continuous moment."

"This is going to be knees up, Deborah," Jade said with true glee in her voice. "I had no idea your siblings were so gifted. I can't wait to see what the devil that Arch Angel got himself into."

Deb rolled her eyes at Jade and looked around the cramped space. Her siblings looked tired. Gen had bags under her red-rimmed eyes. Kelly looked like she lost weight, a near impossibility with what she normally consumed for food on any given day. The room was chilly, one of the windows in the kitchen was open. The smell of the ocean swept through the first floor, but it did nothing to calm Deb's nerves. Whatever they were about to see, Deb knew it would change everything.

No matter what they show us, Deb thought, *it changes nothing. Marcus does not deserve what happened to him and it's about time Hell got a taste of their own medicine.*

***

The sensation of electricity danced across Kelly's arms. The cold air blowing in from the window Gen opened was not the cause. The energy and mixed emotions of the last several days was manifesting itself in new ways.

When this is over, Kelly thought, *when the three of us find a new place to live and get back to the normal grind, Michael will have to help me with what's happening. I feel as if I'm burning from the inside out.*

Someone turned more lights down and the image came into view. Two people walking the beach, one was obviously Dmitri, his height and wide shoulders a dead giveaway. It took Kelly a moment to recognize herself from so long ago. Her face looked the same, but the dress caught her attention. She wore a pastel rainbow-colored swing dress with a sweetheart neckline. She was carrying white wedge sandals and her hair was a lighter brown color and fell well past her shoulders in thick waves.

Kelly was one of only a few of the family standing. She was too afraid if she sat her leg would bounce up and down and irritate whoever was next to her. The hardest thing about this process was staying quiet while Greg did his thing and let the memories play out before you. Her own voice alongside Dmitri's voice then caught up to the image being projected. Kelly tried to send her mind back forty years to find what he was showing them, but it was blank.

***

"Why do I need a ring?" Dmitri asked Kelly. "I just built her a dream house on the ocean."

"Hello," Kelly sang the response. "This is amazing, but you can't use a house to exchange wedding vows or speak telepathically to one another."

"Deb doesn't really wear jewelry," Dmitri lobbed.

"Um, that's an excuse and a bad one at that," Kelly snorted.

"You are not helping," Dmitri shot back.

"Actually, I am," Kelly told him. "You need to go buy a ring, plan a romantic dinner here, and propose right here on the beach."

Dmitri looked away and Kelly grabbed him by the arm and swung him toward her. "Why are you really avoiding the ring? You have nothing to be afraid of, Deb is in love with you. And I am in love with what you've done here."

Dmitri laughed. "You are insane."

"Yet you still brought me here and told me all about this."

"Yes," Dmitri agreed. "I'm pretty sure if I didn't tell you first you would have kicked my butt."

"True, but that's what sisters do, so you better get used to it," Kelly admitted. "Now, where do you want to shop?"

Dmitri coughed and grabbed his chest, suddenly laboring to breathe.

"What is it?" Kelly asked.

"An Arch Angel—" Dmitri sputtered as he bent over and closed his eyes to calm his breathing. "I have to go. An Arch Angel is Falling."

"Right now?!" Kelly exclaimed.

"Yes." Dmitri's brow beaded with sweat.

"I'm coming with you," Kelly told him and grabbed onto his arm. "Don't give me any grief, you are in no shape to argue anyway."

"I'll be fine in a few moments." Dmitri grabbed her hand and pulled it off his arm. "Sometimes the signal is much stronger than others. The wild sensation is already passing, but I need to go."

"You are absolutely not going alone," Kelly scolded. "If it really is an Arch Angel Falling, you need all the help you can get to stop it."

Dmitri shook his head. "I don't know why I'm trying to talk you out of it, there is no talking you out of anything."

"So true, now let's go," Kelly demanded.

The image jumbled and then clarified. The Dmitri and Kelly from forty years ago were no longer on the beach. They were now on a dirt path in a wooded area. Raised voices were rising and falling over the landscape. There was obviously an argument, but the images of who was fighting took a few moments to catch up with the sound.

Antonio and another male were on a hiking trail above where Kelly and Dmitri arrived in the woods. Kelly's rainbow sundress mixed into the greenery of the background.

Antonio and the male were arguing with a female Arch Angel. Her wings were spread wide, and she was crying.

"Come with me!" She yelled to Antonio. "I love you! We can be together anywhere in this world or another, just take my hand."

The female stretched her hand out to Antonio who

looked like he was in shock.

"Azza," Antonio began, "I cannot go with you. Aside from God, Christian is the only true love I have ever felt. He is all that matters to me, you know this. I have told you all this."

"This is ridiculous," Christian snapped. "We're going in circles. She refuses to hear what you are saying Antonio."

"Just give us a moment longer," Antonio pleaded with Christian. "Please."

"No," Christian scoffed. "She knows we are in love and she is still pleading. We should go and let her have some space to deal with this."

"Don't go!" Azza screamed. "Leave him Antonio, he's no good for you! He is not like us, he is not your soulmate, I am."

"Stop!" Antonio warned. "This is not helping."

"Hello," Christian stared down in the direction of Kelly and Dmitri. "Who's there?"

"This is why I come to these things alone," Dmitri whispered. "I can usually make a more graceful entrance."

"Hi Christian!" Kelly yelled up toward the three of them. "It's Kelly O'Mara."

"What are you doing here?" Christian asked. "Who are you—" Christian gasped when he recognized Dmitri.

"What is it?" Antonio asked Christian,

"It's a Collector," Christian told him. "This is more serious than I thought."

"What?" Antonio stepped forward leaning over the edge of the path down at Dmitri and Kelly as they began making their way up the trail toward their position.

"No," Azza said breathlessly. "What are you doing here, Collector? Leave, this has nothing to do with either of you."

"I'm afraid I was pulled here," Dmitri told the frightened Arch Angel. "I'm here to help you Azza."

"This is your fault." Azza pointed a dagger at Christian. "You called your Guardian friends here."

"No," Kelly stated, as she and Dmitri walked to within feet of the three Heavenly beings. "I asked Dmitri to bring me with him. I didn't know Christian was here."

"Liar!" Azza screeched, fresh tears falling down her face. "You're here to take Antonio from me, but I won't let you do that."

Everyone paused. Azza was clearly unstable.

"No one has to get hurt here today, Azza," Dmitri began. "No one is taking anyone away. I just want to hear your story, that's all."

"Antonio and I are partners," Azza babbled. "We've gotten close these last few months. He won't admit it. Why won't you admit it Antonio? We're in love!"

"Azza." Antonio lifted his hands in the air as if in surrender. "We are partners, friends, soldiers. We are not lovers. I never kept Christian a secret from you, you know that."

"You called your great love, *Chris*," Azza said, her tone turning accusatory. "I thought it was another female Arch Angel. I tried to find her, to tell her we had fallen in love. To apologize to her and explain how it all just happened. Then I find you here with him."

"Azza." Dmitri moved closer. He was maneuvering to step between the distraught Arch Angel and Antonio.

"Why don't you start over. I'm afraid Kelly and I do not understand what has happened here today. Can you tell me your story from the beginning?"

Azza's eyes were wild, bloodshot, and wet with tears. She shook her head in response. "No, stay away."

"Can you tell me what's happened here today?" Dmitri pressed her to talk as he slowly pushed forward. He just needed to get between them, close enough to grab her, disarm her, while keeping Antonio safe.

"Azza, please." Antonio stepped forward. "Stop this madness, put the weapon down. Show this Collector you are not Falling."

"It's too late," Azza said, as her arm shook in the air in front of Christian. "He's ruining things, messing with your head. He doesn't love you. He can't, he doesn't know you like I do!"

"He does know me, Azza," Antonio told her as he stepped even closer. "I'm sorry that you misunderstood, but you don't want to hurt Christian."

"You're right," Azza told him. "I don't want to hurt him. I just wanted you. But, if I can't have you, then no one will." Azza's face crumpled, her eyebrows knit together, and her face turned as red as her wings.

There was a brief moment where the image of the forest seemed to still and time slowed to a virtual crawl. Kelly guessed Antonio was fighting the memory, struggling to keep the images from displaying, but Greg was stronger. With Frankie augmenting Greg's power, he was able to reach the deepest recesses of Antonio's mind and retrieve the memory.

The image roared to life once more as Christian

jumped in front of Antonio as Azza's dagger came down and pierced the Guardian's body. In the image, the Kelly from forty years ago screamed and leapt forward, but it was too late. Christian's limp body fell to the ground in a heap, blood pooling all around him.

The projection played on in horror. Dmitri pulled Kelly back as a portal opened behind Azza. A torrent of wind pushed out from the portal. Kelly, Dmitri, and Antonio were pushed away from Azza. The swirling vortex wrapped around Azza's feet, knocking her face first to the ground. The Arch Angel's wings blackened as she screamed in terror. The Fallen Angel was being pulled toward the darkness. She dug her hands into the ground but couldn't stop. In a desperate attempt to save herself she kicked and dug her hands and feet into the ground hard enough to make her fingers bleed. She neared Christian's body and pulled the weapon from his chest, slamming it into the ground to anchor herself.

A moan escaped the portal and more wind enveloped Azza. The swirling was so fierce that dirt and debris nearly blinded her from view. Azza grabbed hold of Christian's body and the two of them flew backward through the air and toward the opening of the portal.

Kelly ripped free from Dmitri and charged after Azza and Christian. She threw her body forward and landed on top of Christian's legs. Instead of keeping Christian from being pulled into the portal, Kelly was sucked toward the vast darkness with them.

Dmitri and Antonio fought their way forward, but they couldn't get to them in time. The portal closed taking Azza, Christian, and Kelly into its frenzied depths. Dmitri yelled up into the sky. Antonio fell to one knee, his face in his hands as he wept.

Dmitri labored to his feet. "We need to go get them."

"No," Antonio tearfully answered. "It's too late, we can't reach them in time."

"What do you mean?" Dmitri asked. "They just left. You can track them still."

Antonio got to his feet his face streaked with sorrow. "They're in Hell. There is no recovering them, not without breaking the Accord and starting a war."

"She's family!" Dmitri yelled. "We can't leave her there. You know what they'll do to a living Guardian in Hell!"

"I can't, we can't," Antonio said breathlessly. "I'm sorry, no."

"Then I will find brothers who will," Dmitri said, anger trailing through his voice.

"We cannot break the Accord," Antonio warned.

Dmitri closed his eyes and when he opened them Jared and Gabriel were standing on the trail.

"What's happened?" Gabriel asked.

"Kelly just got sucked through a portal," Dmitri said.

"A portal," Jared repeated. "What kind of portal, to where?"

"To Hell," Dmitri answered.

CHAPTER THIRTY-THREE

Kelly's entire body shook as the image faded. Before the projection stopped another female Arch Angel showed up. She was blonde, with fair skin. Her white wings sticking out against the backdrop of the greenery. Dmitri shot up and off the sofa.

"What happened next?" Kelly asked. "You can't stop sharing with us now! What happened? Why do I not remember ever meeting Christian?"

"Jared and Gabe went after you," Dmitri told her. "I helped them get in and get out."

"You know how to get to Hell?" Deb asked Dmitri. "All this time and you could have helped me."

"I will not help you go to Hell, Deb!" Dmitri exclaimed. "You must have figured out the cost by now."

"Who was the blonde woman, the one at the very end?" Lacey interjected. "She was the woman who came to the safe house yesterday. She wanted to know where you were all staying. She wanted to know about this safe house."

Antonio stood and rubbed his hand across his

forehead. "She's the Magistrate."

"Why would your commanding officer go to Lacey's?" Michael asked. "And why would she want to know where we were all staying?"

"This can all wait!" Kelly yelled. "What happened to me?"

The room fell silent, Gen stood and made her way over to Kelly as she faced off against Antonio.

"You owe her an explanation," Gen told Antonio. "You owe all of us an explanation of what happened and why none of us remember this."

"Neither of us know what happened to Kelly while she was there," Dmitri told them. "Gabe and Jared never talked about it, but—"

"But?" Kelly pressed.

"When they got you out, three days later," Dmitri told her, "your mind, it was broken."

"What does that mean?" Kelly's eyes sprang fresh tears as Gen grasped her shoulder.

"Time down there is not the same as on Earth," Antonio told her. "You were tortured, then healed, and tortured again."

"By who?" Kelly asked. "Who did that to me?"

"Azza," Dmitri told her. "Jared told me he fought her, but she was strong from being infected with Hell Fighter venom. He said he couldn't kill her, but he managed to cut off her wings."

"What happened when I got back to Earth?" Kelly asked him, her voice cracking under the emotional toll of the news.

"When Jared got to you, he said you were

screaming." Dmitri paused. "You couldn't stop. They couldn't calm you down. Jared couldn't get through to you."

"The torture must have been tremendous," Antonio added. "The only way to make it stop was to put you in a coma-like state and—"

"And, what?!" Kelly yelled. "Just spit it out."

Genevieve was crying before the words even came out. She looked at Deb who was doing the same.

"Your mind, it couldn't process what happened, it wasn't meant to," Antonio told her. "We had to bury the memories of your time there. We think, we don't know, but we think it's why you're immune to Hell Fire venom."

"You didn't just bury those memories, did you?" Kelly's voice tinted with rage. "You took the memories leading up to them, you took the memories of Dmitri too."

"I'm sorry Kelly," Antonio told her.

"You lied to me," Kelly spit the words at Antonio. "This whole time you lied to me. You aren't my friend. You betrayed me. You betrayed this entire family. How could you do that?"

"I am your friend, Kelly O'Mara." Antonio stepped toward her, but she pulled back.

"No!" Kelly screamed at him. "Stay away from me!"

Kelly's aura burst out and she wrapped it around herself leaving the house. The O'Maras were stunned.

"I should go after her," Gen told them.

"I got this." Dan walked to Gen. "I know where she's apt to go when she's this angry."

Before anyone could argue Dan left the house in a glow of yellow.

***

The room erupted into a cacophony of heated discussion. The noise was dulled by a throbbing in Deb's head.

How could Heaven do that to us? Deb's mind raged.

"Are you alright, Deborah?" Jade asked as she sat down at the table next to her.

"Honestly," Deb responded. "No, I'm definitely not."

"Stop!" Jade yelled and the voices quieted.

Just like in the club, Deb thought. *She can still command a room.*

"I assume there is more to this twisted tale." Jade looked at Antonio. "How many of their memories did you bury?"

"More importantly, why?" Deb added. "Why did you take my memories of Dmitri?"

"There's more," Dmitri confessed. "When I got Jared and Gabriel out, The Magistrate was waiting. She must have known what we'd done. She ordered Jared and Gabe to The Pit. She told me I would be following if I didn't help her clean up the mess. That if we weren't careful, the Accord would be found to be broken and war would break out between Heaven and Hell, all because of our selfishness."

Dmitri paused and looked at Deb. "When I took Kelly back to the house you shared with her in California, I told you everything. I told you we needed to stay with Kelly, keep an eye on her. I didn't know how long it would take for her to heal."

"I don't remember that," Deb told him.

"We watched over her for a week. On the last day Xavier called. He told you Gen had stopped sleeping as she was hunting down every possible lead to find Gabriel. He lost her along the way and hadn't seen her in days. He needed you and Kelly to help find her."

Deb looked at Gen who was staring at him in confusion. "I do remember that."

"I do too," Xavier added.

"The ring," Dmitri told her. "It's not supposed to connect across realms, but it did. Gen, you were somehow feeling everything that was happening to Gabe in The Pit."

"I thought I was going crazy," Gen told him. "I couldn't think clearly. I couldn't sleep, my mind wouldn't shut off. I was being constantly pummeled both physically and emotionally."

"I tracked you down." Dmitri's eyes filled with sadness. "I told Deb to watch over Kelly and I would take care of it. I found you collapsed in the middle of a field from exhaustion. You were barely conscious. I didn't know what to do, so I called Antonio."

"I remember now," Gen told them. "The images were always fuzzy and in disarray, but now I see them. The two of you hovering over me, talking, but I don't remember the words."

"I'm so sorry," Dmitri told her. "I was planning on explaining everything, but I never got the chance."

"You somehow got my ring off," Gen said to Antonio. "How?"

Antonio's face flushed. "I planted a false memory."

"His death," Gen said in barely a whisper. "From time to time I still have nightmares about Gabe dying."

"Dmitri," Michael said from behind them. "You brought Gen to me, told me she would heal in a few days, and that you would explain everything then."

Dmitri nodded.

"We never saw you after that," Michael added. "What happened?"

"I left Gen with you," Dmitri told Michael. "When I got back to California, the Magistrate was waiting for me outside Deb and Kelly's house. She told me Antonio was inside, checking on Kelly. But that wasn't what you were doing, was it, Antonio?"

Nausea filled Deb. She knew why she didn't remember Dmitri. She didn't need the Arch Angel to say it.

"We went there looking for you, Dmitri. You knew the deal," Antonio looked at the Collector whose eyes were locked on Deb. "The Magistrate gave you a week to watch over Kelly and make sure no one came for the family. You were not to speak about what happened, but you did! Deb was all over me about what happened and why her family was not informed. You weren't supposed to say anything!"

"I had to," Dmitri argued. "They deserved the truth."

"I went in the house," Antonio continued. "when I saw you weren't home, I told Deb I was going to check on Kelly. I went outside and told the Magistrate instead. She commanded me to remove the memories of your conversation with Deb, then she went further."

"She had you remove all my memories of Dmitri," Deb said. "But why?"

Tell me you can put them back, Deb pleaded silently.

"She said she didn't want you looking for him, the way Gen was hunting down Gabe," Antonio told them. "The Magistrate ordered me to remove the romantic memories between Dmitri and Deb from all three O'Mara women. Gen knew the least since she wasn't as close back then living and patrolling different coasts. Kelly was already passed out. I wasn't even sure she'd make it out of her ordeal, messing with memories was the least of my worries for her. Deb was the hardest, I think you knew before I did it, I think you knew it was about to happen."

"What makes you say that?" Deb asked the Arch Angel.

"When I came back from checking on Kelly," Antonio told her. "I came into the room and I couldn't look at you. You must have been afraid. You asked me why the house was cloaked, why Frankie couldn't hear you calling for him."

"You traitorous bastard!" Jade's voice boomed across the table. "You sit there all high and mighty lecturing me on being devious, look at what you've done!"

"Put them back." Deb's voice was barely a whisper. "Tell me you can put the memories back."

"I'm sorry, Deb," Antonio told her. "I don't think I can."

"Get out," Deb yelled at Antonio. "You should be ashamed of yourself for what you've done."

"You probably should leave, Antonio," Frankie added.

"This is bad, bro," Xavier told him. "What you've done, orders or no, it's just wrong."

"Very," Tom seconded. "This family has put their very existence on the line for Heaven and this is how we were treated. You should go back to The Magistrate and tell her we want a conversation."

"Agreed," Harry spoke firmly. "This is unacceptable. I have been around a good long time and I have never heard of anything like this happening."

Antonio nodded. "I was wrong, I should have pushed back against her."

"Michael!" Deb stood. All eyes fell on her. "Somethings coming, and it's strong."

Michael and the others shot into action. Michael opened the box of Holy Oil and ordered everyone to take some.

Tom grabbed several large black bags out of a nearby closet and hoisted them onto a table. He unzipped them and began pulling out weapons.

Gen went to Deb. "Are you alright?"

Deb shook her head.

"What are you feeling?" Jade asked as she got up from the table. "Is it Wrath? If so, we should all leave. If he is with The First Army you will not defeat him."

The cawing of birds outside stopped Deb from answering Jade.

Her siblings were strapping on weapons and readying for battle. *It's upon us, what have I brought to our doorstep?*

Frankie handed Deb a dagger and slid two jars of Holy Oil across the table. She caught them and put them in the pockets of her jacket.

"Can you fight, Jade?" Dmitri loomed across the

table.

"Not exactly," Jade answered. "If they just want me, then I will go with them willingly. There should be no reason for more bloodshed."

"No!" Deb ordered. "You will not do that. Peter or Wrath or whatever his name, is not taking anyone else from me."

The room fell quiet as everyone was now armed and ready for attack. The sound of screeching filled the room. Michael opened the back door and the high-pitched noise echoed off the water and into the small cottage.

"Whatever is coming is almost here," Lacey announced. "I can feel it arriving."

"I can too," Gerry added. "It's like sensing something about to physically hit me."

The sun was long gone, but the moon was high above the water and illuminated the small stretch of beach to the salt rocks.

The birds that made their home along the rocks were under assault. Swirling in and around the rocks picking off the birds one at a time were two large gargoyles.

"Gargoyles on Earth," Harry muttered. "Never thought I would see the day."

"There!" Frankie yelled from the far-right corner of the deck. "There, coming at us under the cover of the trees."

"Ready yourselves," Michael ordered. "That's one squad, be on the lookout for at least one more."

Deb turned to Jade. "Stay inside or close to one of us at all times, do you understand?"

Jade shook her head. "Be careful my dear Deborah."

"I will," Deb told her.

The O'Maras lined up on the deck. Greg and Xavier passed out large tree branches with oil-soaked cloth on the end of each.

"Take a lighter," Frankie told Deb. "We'll wait until they get closer before we light them."

Deb caught the vampires as they lined the beach at the bottom of the stairs.

"We have the advantage of the higher ground," Michael told them. "Let's try not to lose it."

"Where's my sister?" Wrath yelled up from the beach. "The spoiled brat made this difficult by friending Deborah."

"You should leave Wrath," Michael yelled. "Everyone knows who you are and what you've done. The killing of an Arch Angel, the attack against my family, this will not go unnoticed, nor unpunished."

"No?" Wrath mocked. "Well, if they're passing out punishment, let me know, I'm happy to share. Your sister probably deserves a bit. After all, without her vials of Heavenly blood I wouldn't have been able to restore General Kelce's squad of elite soldiers. Hell's First Army has been itching for a good fight."

"Sergeant Garrick!" General Kelce bellowed from the beach where he stood next to Wrath. "Attack!"

CHAPTER THIRTY-FOUR

The first wave of vampires got pushed back from the house by Deb's brothers wielding torches of Holy Oil. The army kept coming, eventually different parts of the area ignited and fire tore through the scenic property. Gen was on the beach engaged with one of the vampires. She got the better of him, now straddling him and stabbing both ears with the knives she wielded in each hand. The vampire screeched in pain, sending the gargoyles up into the sky in a thrashing frenzy.

The sound of battle reverberated back to Deb as she stood alone on the deck. Any remaining animals in the woods were fleeing, trampling through the underbrush of pine needles and some early falling leaves.

Dmitri had already taken out a vampire. He managed to get behind the soldier and ripped its head from its neck. The sand absorbed the blood, each fiery drop created an odd-shaped piece of glass from the extreme heat of the Damned.

The smell of burning wood seeped through Deb's nostrils, a familiar scent as this would be her second battle surrounded by fire in as many days. Michael yelled for Deb to stay on the deck and make sure no one got inside the house. The first gasps of fear escaped Gerry's lips as he looked out at the battle from the relative safety of the living room. Harry was inside with Jade, Lacey, and Gerry. Harry was equipped with several weapons, but she hoped the Angel wouldn't have to fight.

"Just stay inside Gerry," Deb told him. "It'll be alright."

Frankie had fastened tiki torches along the front railing, all of them were ablaze in Holy Fire. A good deterrent but not a guarantee of safety. Someone landed with a thud on the far end of the deck, around the side above the outdoor shower, just out of view from Deb.

Sky turned the corner of the deck and sauntered toward Deb. "You O'Maras are always brawling. Wouldn't it just be easier to hand her over?"

Deb counted the planks as Sky approached until she was lined up more closely with the torches.

"You're not taking anyone from this house tonight," Deb told her.

"Aww," Sky taunted. "Are you two like a thing now?"

Deb refused to get pulled into the game. She pulled her powers through her body and used her mind to direct them. Sky's body crashed into the railing, her armor catching fire quickly. Deb threw a dagger at the vampire, but Sky batted it away. The vampire recovered pulling off her armor and dropping it onto the grass. It was a more even fight now; the armor would have made it nearly impossible to aim for the skin.

"I don't think you're going to like having that pretty little face of yours burst wide open and bleeding."

Burst wide open, the words echoed around Deb's mind. *I wonder if my powers could open her skin.*

Deb thought of everything that had happened. Marcus being taken. Finding out Antonio had messed with her and her sisters' memories. Heaven keeping secrets, deciding which wrong they would make right.

The anger boiled in her stomach. "You don't scare me, vampire."

"No?" Sky mocked. "You don't look too good, Guardian. Little pale if you ask me."

The vampire kept taunting, but Deb focused on controlling her breathing. She slowed her heart and waited for the familiar vibration of her power to stir. Deb listened for the low buzzing she knew to be power, her chi as some would call it. She told it what to do, and it reacted.

Deb had gone so far inward she could no longer hear the voices around her. She was completely cocooned within herself. She breathed in and out, feeling the rhythm of her power coalesce and respond to her will. She pushed her shield outward. Slowly the voices picked up in intensity. Jade yelled for her to be careful.

Deb opened her eyes and Sky was within a few feet of her position. Normally, she'd be startled, but after this past week of learning to deal with deadly situations, she was calm, collected, confident even.

"You're not getting in this house," Deb told her.

"You going to stop me?" Sky smirked. "Your little tricks from Desire's house only held us at bay, we'll come back. We won't stop until we get what we want."

"And what is that?" Deb asked.

"Hell on Earth of course." Sky laughed.

Deb looked into Sky's eyes and telepathically threw her powers straight at her face.

The vampire's nose exploded, and Sky yelled out in pain as she staggered back away from Deb.

"Now look whose face is burst wide open," Deb retorted.

Sky bounced along the exterior of the house and Deb walked toward her. Dmitri yelled out to Deb and began to run toward the steps. Deb knew Wrath and the vampires would be strategic in their attack and cloak the house and surrounding area. Doing that negated the advantage of telepathic communication. It also kept them from calling for reinforcements, they were on their own.

Deb didn't need to turn, she knew another vampire was behind her on the deck, she could sense it. Her whole body tingled and the hairs on the back of her neck stood on end. For the first time she noticed where her shield flowed to a particular spot. It burst out above her, not behind or to the side. That meant somehow her power could sense the position of the threat, even before her mind could process it visually.

Your power is talking to you, Michael used to tell her. *You need to learn to listen when it speaks.*

Her power was a language finally beginning to make sense to Deb. Michael was right, it had been speaking, now she was listening and directing it in return.

Amazing, Deb thought. *I know exactly where the vampire is. I can practically hear the rhythm of his breathing.*

Sky had recovered and wiped the blood from her

face. She pushed off the wall of natural shingles and faced Deb once more. Sky lunged and the vampire above Deb dropped down. Without looking up she suspended the vampire above in mid-air. Sky reached Deb but bounced off her shield, rolling to a stop a few feet away.

Dmitri reached the top step and looked at Luca squirming in suspended animation above the door. Deb moved her arm out in front of her and raised Sky in the air as well. She focused her eyes on the ocean and used her powers to throw both Sky and Luca hovering above her as far out into the ocean as she could. Sky screamed as she went barreling through the air. The vampires on the beach along with Wrath looked up in the sky as their comrades sailed overhead bound for the water.

"How in the world—" Dmitri didn't finish the sentence.

"You've been gone awhile," Deb told him. "Things have changed. I've changed."

"I can see that," Dmitri answered. "I would apologize Deb, but I'm not even sure where to start."

"Don't," Deb told him. "You, Jared, and Gabriel risked everything to save Kelly. I would have done the same. You couldn't have known what The Magistrate would tell Antonio to do or that Antonio would actually follow through with her orders."

Another vampire jumped the railing and lunged toward them. Deb pushed her shield out and around Dmitri. The vampire bounced off Deb's shield and rolled down the stairs to the beach where he was met by Xavier and Greg.

"That's the second time you've used your shield to

protect me," Dmitri told her. "Thank you."

"I wasn't telling the whole truth when I told you I had no romantic feelings for you, Dmitri."

"No?" Dmitri asked her.

"I used to feel all these romantic things around Marcus." She saw the pain cross Dmitri's face and quickly continued. "But if he got close enough, I knew those feelings were not for him. I sensed they were misplaced. Marcus kissed me once, and I saw a fuzzy image of you in the background. I convinced myself the image was too unclear to recognize, but now I know it was you. That my mind was trying to tell me those feelings belonged to someone else, not to Marcus."

"Why are you trying so hard to get to Hell for him?" Dmitri asked.

"Aren't you tired of paying a price that Hell never pays?" Deb asked. "What if my memories weren't gone? What if I were like Gen, fully aware of what I've lost? How many transgressions are we going to allow Hell to make before we make a stand against it?"

"I know how you feel," Dmitri told her. "My memories weren't affected and every day I wondered, were you okay? Were you out there looking for me? Would I ever make it back to you?"

"Oh, bloody hell you two," Jade squawked from inside. "Just kiss and make up already, there's an all-out war going on!"

Deb sighed, her mind realizing their intimate conversation was on display for all those inside.

"Stay safe, Deb," Dmitri told her. "I'm going to help the others."

"Wait!" Deb demanded as he turned to go back to the beach.

Dmitri turned back and Deb leapt into his arms. "Kiss me one last time like you mean it."

"You remember?" Dmitri began. "You used to say that to me before—"

Deb kissed Dmitri hard, her lips smashing down upon his. Desire shot through her body as he pulled her close to his chest.

When she pulled away, she said simply. "Stay alive."

"For you, I would do anything." Dmitri stomped down the stairs to the beach and Jade pushed through the door.

"Still want to go to Hell to rescue an old flame, love," Jade asked.

Deb looked into the house. Harry and Gerry had walked away obviously wanting to give her privacy. Lacey smiled broadly at her.

Deb grabbed Jade by the arm and escorted her away from the window and Lacey's view. "Yes, I do want to go get Marcus. Do you suddenly have a way to get me there?"

"No," Jade sighed. "But I'm quite certain my husband bloody well does."

Jade looked down at her left hand. She wore two rings, one of them was a large emerald, the other a clear band outlined in black onyx. Jade pulled the latter ring off and jammed it onto her ring finger. The ring cut her finger and blood poured into the clear section of it turning the band red.

Fear coursed through Deb's body. "What did you

just do Jade?"

"I called my husband." She sighed heavily.

"That's not going to work," Deb told her. "They have the area cloaked."

Deb could feel something change. Whatever Jade had done worked. Something was coming. It was something stronger than anything on the field, darker, more ominous in nature, but somehow familiar.

She looked down at her siblings, hoping whatever was coming did not put them in more danger.

I will see you again. Deb's thought was more prayer than fact.

The gargoyles circling the sky flew up and away from the scene. Whatever was coming they wanted nothing to do with. The vampires stopped fighting and momentarily looked up at the deck then over at Deb and Jade.

Deb's siblings turned quickly in her direction. A red aura then encircled the deck. It looked like streaks of a beautiful sunset but the heaviness in the air made her stomach tighten.

Behind Jade a dark outline formed in the brightness. When the glow faded a large male figure, easily over seven feet tall, wearing a maroon suit with dark brown shoes stared over at her. His bright green eyes practically bore a hole right through her chest.

"Jade my lovely." The male's gravelly voice sent a chill straight up Deb's spine.

"Vermillion," Jade answered. "I need a favor."

Vermillion, Deb silently agonized. *Jade is married to one of the Four Horsemen.*

"Sonoran told me my own wife wasn't even willing to look for me while I was missing. And now you want a favor?"

"We can fight about that later." Jade waved her hands dismissing Vermillion's claim. "I need you to send Deborah to Hell. She needs to find a Sentinel who's been kidnapped by my brother."

Vermillion looked down at the beach. "I see Wrath is up to his old tricks again."

"I just need you to send her to Marcus," Jade told him.

"It doesn't work like that," Vermillion answered. "But I know this family. I will send her, but that wipes my debt to them clean."

The field erupted once more in battle. Gen was yelling up at Deb and fighting to get back to the stairs and up to her sister.

"Fine," Deb told Vermillion. "But you need to take Jade out of here."

"Deborah, don't interfere," Jade scolded.

"That's part of the deal," Deb retorted. "You can't stay here, if Wrath gets to you, he'll steal your powers too."

"Stealing powers," Vermillion repeated. "What is she going on about?"

"I will explain later." Jade brushed Vermillion off once again. "Send her, I know you can."

"I can't send you to the Sentinel's exact position," Vermillion told her. "I can get you relatively close, but it won't be pleasant. In fact, it will be quite painful. You are not meant to go there Guardian. It's against the natural order of things."

"What does that mean?" Deb asked.

"It will be like shoving a square peg in a round hole." Vermillion snickered. "Also, you can't take anything with you."

"I have to take at least these two things with me," Deb told Vermillion as she pulled out the ring and coin Marcus had intended for her.

"Fine," Vermillion spat. "Here, he pulled a piece of what looked like aluminum foil out of his pocket. Wrap it in this and hold it in your hand. If you let it go during your journey it will be lost forever, understand?"

"Yes."

"You be careful, Guardian," Jade demanded. "Get in and get out, Marcus should know the way home."

Deb nodded her agreement. "How does this work?"

Vermillion pushed Deb's forehead and the world dropped out from beneath her. Deb screamed as she went spinning out of control downward into the abyss.

***

Gen reached the stairs and was about halfway up when Deb disappeared. Harry had run outside but it was too late, Deb was gone. The giant of a demon with glowing green eyes took Jade from the deck. He was powerful enough to make it past the cloaking the vampires had setup. Gen didn't need to hear his name. She knew who it was. It was one of the Horsemen, she could never forget their eyes.

She reached the top of the stairs and Harry's face was racked in horror. "She did it. Deb got someone to send her to Hell."

"I know." Gen was panting as she looked down at the beach below. Her knees went weak as she thought about her sister in Hell. Gen could see Wrath's face as he smiled up at the two of them. He mouthed the words *thank you*.

That's not good, Gen thought. He hasn't won the battle, yet he seems confident and pleased. *What's coming now?*

"I have to get back down there Harry," Gen told him. "The gargoyles are returning. Antonio will continue to do everything he can to keep them at bay. and away from us, but this is going to be a long battle."

"I'm afraid so," Harry told her. "I'm going to take Gerry and make our way out the front. I've been watching and I don't think any of them are patrolling that side, if one of us can get out, we can let others know to come help."

"It's a risk Harry," Gen told him. "At least with Gerry you wouldn't be alone."

"I know it's a risk," Harry answered. "But so is staying here doing nothing."

Gen nodded. "Good luck, stay safe."

"You too Genevieve," Harry told her. "God bless."

Gen grabbed the railing and began to run back down the stairs towards the battle. As she neared the bottom a portal opened behind Wrath.

"Your family is getting predictable," Wrath taunted Gen. "I needed one of you to break the Accord, something to allow my compatriot to escape Hell unimpeded."

From the darkened portal out stepped the female from Antonio's memory. She took two rings Wrath handed her and slipped them onto her hand.

From the sky Antonio's voice boomed. "Azza!"

The Arch Angel landed hard on the sand shaking the ground below him. Before he could step toward her, thunder cracked in the sky and the gargoyles shrieked in response. Azza yelled out as if she were in pain but then her wings sprung from her back and unfolded. They were blackened, but completely healed. She leapt toward Antonio and grabbed him by the throat.

"You have one last chance my dearest Antonio," she implored. "With the power of The Deadly Sins released through an Arch Angel's ring, I am completely restored. Come with me. We can still rule this world, the way we were meant to, together at last."

"I will never be with you." Antonio used his wings to push her backward.

Xavier was closest to Azza and he took his sword and sliced at her wings. She pulled her wings inward to avoid impact. Xavier was too quick, his blade caught a piece of her wing and tore it, which made the Fallen Arch Angel screech.

Gen's breath caught as Azza turned toward Xavier. Her brother had lifted his sword in the air again to strike, but the Fallen angel turned and deftly used her wings to slash him deep across the chest. Xavier dropped his sword and fell face first onto the sand.

"No!" Gen screamed from the bottom of the stairs.

"You will all die by my hands, but not tonight," Azza threatened. "First, you'll live with the consequences of what you've done. This world will run red with the blood of humanity at the hands of Hell's First Army."

The vampires began to disappear one by one from the field. Wrath left as the gargoyles flew off over the sea disappearing in the distance. The sky above grew bright, and Gen could feel Heavenly Warriors coming down from above.

Harry made it. Gen realized. *Please God, let Xavier be okay.*

She reached her brother and collapsed into the sand next to him.

Rolling him over she took in the site of him and screamed. Xavier was gone, his body nearly sliced in two. His vacant eyes lay open, crusted with sand. Gen howled and cradled his limp body.

"No, no, no," she wailed. Her chest heaved and tightened. "She killed him. She killed Xavier!"

Her brothers knelt beside her. Greg wrapped his arms around Gen, but she wouldn't let go of Xavier's body. Gen's heartache broke through the surface and rattled the ground below them.

The Arch Angels landed on the beach and surrounded them as Gen fell into a fit of sorrow. She wailed, the pain of loss stabbing through her repeatedly.

How could this have happened? Her mind reeled. *Kelly is gone, Deb is in Hell, and Xavier is dead.*

CHAPTER THIRTY-FIVE

Deb's body flailed uncontrollably. Her arms and legs banged and scraped off the sides of something sharp, but she couldn't make out what it was. Heat rose from below to envelope her. Flames burst across her chest with sparks igniting in mid-air. She realized in horror her clothes were on fire. The acrid scent of her own hair burning assaulted her nostrils.

Landing at such high speed caused something to crack, and pain coursed through her. For a moment Deb couldn't catch her breath. Air was forced out of her lungs. Groaning she rolled over, something thick and sludge-like caked her body. The fire that had consumed her was extinguished with her movements.

She dug her hands into the dirt and pushed herself to her knees but couldn't see. The entrance was so violent and hot that it burned her hair off and left her wounded and naked. The place was pitch black and it took several moments before her eyes adjusted. She stood and turned in a circle. Behind her was a small glow. She began limping her way toward the tiny flicker of light in the distance. Her brain was rattled from the spiraling fall. It wasn't until she was three or four steps along before she was aware that several spots on her body radiated heat. She looked down but could barely assess the damage. She lightly touched her skin near the warmest spots, it was like a sunburn magnified by a hundred. Certain wounds were already raised and bumpy, while others were damp with blood and puss.

Deb grazed the top of her head feeling nothing but scalp. Her other hand was still fisted into a ball protecting the items Marcus had left for her. She slowly uncurled her fingers. The metal coin and the small circular shape of the wedding band survived the violence of the fall. The material protecting them must have disintegrated. She slipped the ring on her middle finger and held onto the coin as she continued forward.

After a few tentative steps, she was mugged by a hideous odor, a horrible mix of blood and rot. She recoiled at the stench and abruptly stopped. The stillness that followed was broken by something breathing. She wasn't alone.

The pungent air grew stronger until it enveloped her. Metal scraped against itself and clanging chains slinked ever closer.

The outline of a figure came into view. It dragged a large piece of the Chain of Chaos through the muddy ground. Something smashed against the far wall and Deb shook with the sound. Her heart raced and her mouth went dry.

The wall began to glow, some sort of liquid caught fire, and suddenly the figure in front of her became clear.

His feet were bare, the Chain of Chaos had burrowed into his left leg, and the open wound leaked a brownish-red fluid. His pants were torn at the bottom while his tattered shirt hung loosely around his chest. His beady black eyes bore through her.

"What took you so long?" The male voice raked every nerve in her body.

Deb's chest pounded in her ears. Only one word escaped her scorched lips.

"Schlosser."

ABOUT THE AUTHOR

JL Rothstein lives in western Massachusetts with her husband and their two cats Brady and Mr. Thumbs. Jennifer is a business professional pursuing her MFA in Creative Writing. Hellbound is book two in the Heaven Sent Series.

Visit her online at www.JLRothstein.com or via social media Facebook.com/authorjlrothstein. Follow her on Twitter & Instagram @jlrothstein1